A SPEED CITY SISTERS
IN CRIME ANTHOLOGY

Scenic *and* SINISTER

FEATURING
INDIANA LANDMARKS

EDITED BY MB DABNEY & JANET E. WILLIAMS

Published by Speed City Press

Edited by MB Dabney and Janet E. Williams

Front cover design by Teri Barnett/Indie Book Designer (http://www.indiebookdesign er.com/)

Ebook ISBN: 978-1-7375257-2-1

Paperback ISBN: 978-1-7375257-1-4

First printing edition 2026

www.speedcitysistersincrime.org

We dedicate this book to Hawthorn Fire Mineart for their invaluable help and commitment to our Speed City Sisters in Crime Chapter.

They will be greatly missed.

CONTENTS

FOREWORD

When I lived in the San Francisco Bay area, I rode a cable car to work every day. I sat on the outside, assuring myself of the best view of familiar sites from the Golden Gate Bridge to Chinatown. The car rumbled up and down hills until it reached Lombard Street, known as the "crookedest street in the world," where riders had a panoramic view of the San Francisco Bay. It was breathtaking. There wasn't one moment that I didn't appreciate those morning rides and my proximity to the landmarks, so readily identified with California.

When I decided to move back to my home state of Indiana, my friends in California bombarded me with endless questions. Where was Indiana? Wasn't that the state located in the middle of corn-fields? What was I going to do there?

I didn't know whether to be amused or insulted, but when I identified Indiana as the home of the Indianapolis 500, there was instant recognition. It was that landmark that helped make the connection.

In California, I viewed the historic landmarks I saw with awe. In Indianapolis, having grown up there, the landmarks were so famil-iar, I took them for granted. Thank goodness, the writers who penned the sixteen stories in the latest Speed City Sisters in Crime anthology, Scenic and Sinister, didn't do the same. Each story in this book brings Indiana's historic landmarks to life, and with the most tantalizing twists.

The Madame Walker Theatre is the setting for murder in the story by John F. Allen, while in her contribution, Carol Hall reveals secrets discovered within the confines of the Indiana War Memorial. Crown Hill Cemetery proves to be the perfect place to find an unburied body in the story by B.K. Hart, while the baseball stadium in Indianapolis, once called Victory Field, and later renamed Bush Stadium, is just right for murder in two different stories, one by Lillie Evans and the other by MB Dabney. Janet Williams spins the tale of a reporter who uncovers intrigue in Indiana's State House.

Elizabeth A. San Miguel takes us north to the Indiana Dunes, located on the shore of Lake Michigan, where she introduces us to a quirky family that readers will find hard to forget. Mary Bischoff takes us to southern Indiana, transporting us back to the year 1927, when the Rose Island Amusement Park was a place where anything could happen, and does.

Scenic and Sinister is an eclectic collection of stories that introduces readers to the state of Indiana, both present and past, where readers will find there's more to the Hoosier state than cornfields. I invite you to grab a snack, get cozy in your favorite relaxing spot, and prepare to take a unique journey. Enjoy the read!

Crystal V. Rhodes

Co-author of the Grandmothers, Incorporated cozy mystery series

Author of the *Sin* and the *Stillwaters* romantic suspense series

SECRETS OF A DYING CLOWN
BY LILLIE EVANS

"I hate the bastard."

Eddie Evans roused from his nap. "Peanut," he called weakly. Pushing himself up, he shouted, "Damn it! You got a hole in that glove?" Then he fell back into a fitful sleep. I was becoming used to these delirious outbursts. At first, I thought it was the morphine talking.

I pulled the bedcovers close to his neck. Eddie was dying, and his death wasn't going quickly. An aggressive cancer was claiming the ninety-year-old man, and the only thing that could be done was to make him as comfortable as possible.

When my patient finally settled, I wandered into the living room. Eddie lived in a small ranch-type house in the Douglass Park neighborhood on the east side of town. The view from his window didn't provide much to see, but I enjoyed watching the kids playing in the playground across the street.

About a month ago, I was hired by Evans' family to sit with him in the afternoon. It was his wish that he die at home. There wasn't much to the job lately. His worsening condition caused him to sleep more, especially after his medication. That was fine with me. After our conversations last week, I felt I knew more about Eddie "Lightening" Evans than I cared to know.

I ambled back into the bedroom, and stood watching Mr. Evans' chest rise and fall and listened to his labored breathing. I reflected on my decision to become a home healthcare nurse. I had planned to teach, but by my third year in the classroom, I decided to change professions. Children's lives depended on it.

Life went along smoothly for a while. I'd cared for many wonderful and not-so-wonderful people, but my assignments had gravitated toward hospice care—those who didn't have long on this earth, and I enjoyed giving them what comfort I could.

Eddie Evans had extended family, but their personal lives did not accommodate taking 24-hour care of a bitter old man. When I took on the job three weeks prior, I knew little about him beyond his medical history. I know a great deal more about him now, and I wish I had never met him. Evans was anything but talkative when I first started to work. He divided time into reading sports magazines, watching sports on television, or staring thoughtfully at nothing at all. When he did speak, the tone was sharp and the words spat at you like bullets. I went about fixing meals, checking his medications, and cautiously trying to engage him.

"You know anything about baseball?" he asked one day. He was sitting in his recliner with a clear view of the outside world, but he seldom showed interest in looking.

"I used to love it as a kid," I said, "but as an adult I don't follow it that much."

"Ever been to a game?" He sat hunched over, rheumy eyes studying me as if waiting to catch me in a lie.

I gave him a curious look. I was surprised and pleased that he was so engaged. "As a matter of fact, my Godmother took me to Chicago a couple of times in the summer and we'd see a game. Our weekend get-away-trips to Chicago museums, fine dining places and nice hotels disguised the fact that she really went there to go to River Downs racetrack."

The thought of me going to a racetrack as a child solicited a hoarse cough that passed as a laugh. He hunched over even more, his shoulders nearly touching his ears.

"What about the Indianapolis Clowns? Ever hear of them?" His tone dared me to say otherwise.

Images of oversized bats, a midget—the little person, I guess you say now—and players catching balls behind their backs burst into my mind. "Of course. I'd nearly forgotten about them. That was great entertainment back then."

"Fools," he shouted. "A rat's nest of deceitful liars!"

"Why would you think that?"

Trembling hands wiped the spittle that covered his lips from his outburst. It appeared he had expended his last bit of energy as he settled back in his chair. "I want to lay down."

Out next conversation—a lengthy one for him—was a couple of days later. That day, my shift started later than usual, and as I walked in, I caught the smells from breakfast still lingering.

"Mr. Evans, you're up! It looks like you had a good breakfast. Must be feeling better?"

"Yeah. Feel pretty good for a dying man."

I didn't want to start on that note, so I said, "I've been thinking about what you said about the Clowns being a bunch of deceitful liars. What did you mean by that?"

"Been thinking," he said. "I believe I can trust you. You've got an honest face, missy." Coming from him, I took the comment as a ringing endorsement.

As I moved around the room preparing his medications, I could feel his eyes following me, watching intensely. I fixed lunch for the both of us and because he seemed to be feeling so much better, we sat down at his worn dinette set to eat. He had not felt like eating the day before, much less sitting up, so I warmed up the previous day's vegetable soup. The patient even enjoyed a thick slice of French bread with a pat of butter. Occasionally, Evans would look up from his bowl, studying me.

Once lunch was done, Evans shuffled to the window and settled in his favorite chair. The window was slightly ajar, and sounds of children shouting and playing drifted into the room. He seemed content, so I cleared the dishes and then sat thumbing through a magazine.

"You know I played baseball?"

I lifted my head in surprise that he was again in a talkative mood. "Really? When was that? When you were growing up?"

Evans turned his head to give me a contemptuous stare. "I played *professional* ball in the American League."

My mind quickly shifted through the few baseball teams and names I knew, which weren't many: the Yankees, Dodgers, and Oakland, but I couldn't connect his name with one. "With what team?" I named the teams I remembered.

"The Clowns. The American Negro League." Evans stiffened and gripped his chair, defying me to contradict him.

"The Indianapolis Clowns? That's great. My godmother took me to see them when I was a little girl. I still remember when one of the players ran out with this big bat. They were funny."

Evans grew quiet, rose from his chair, shuffled over to the sofa, plopped down with a "Humph," and mumbled. "Send in the Clowns...we weren't a circus act, that was some serious ball."

Several minutes passed before he spoke again. "I had an uncle. Name was James. Evans. Played for the Kansas City Monarchs for a while."

My raised eyebrows must have given the clue that I didn't know what he was talking about.

"The Monarchs, one of the Negro League teams! Don't you know shit about nothin'?"

"Don't get excited. I knew there was a Negro League, I just didn't know the names of the teams nor did I know about an American Negro League."

"Thought you said you knew about the Clowns. We was in the American Negro League. Except my uncle left the Monarchs and signed with them when they was the Ethiopian Clowns. They changed the name when the team moved here from Cincinnati. Bush Stadium was our home base."

I dug through my mind for a recollection of going to Bush Stadium. "I vaguely remember going to Bush Stadium. I think they renamed it Victory Field at one point."

"Truth was we really didn't have a stadium, the white team owners let us use their stadiums when we was barnstorming across the country."

For a while, Evans was doing fine. Then he started to ramble.

"Satchel Paige didn't have a ounce of table manners. Uncle James brought him and a bunch of guys over one time for dinner."

"*The* Satchel Paige?" I couldn't keep the skepticism out of my voice.

"Hell yeah, woman. *The*...Satchel...Paige! Right here to *this* house. You don't believe? Where else you think Negroes gonna eat and sleep. Try going to a hotel and ask for a room. All you get was a 'nigger, please' and a boot out the door." Again, there was that laugh/cough as his comment amused him.

The coughing spell subsided. "Of course, they didn't even try in those sundown towns. Get out of town by sundown meant exactly that. Try to ignore it, might as well put a noose around they own neck."

"I thought you said you played for the Clowns, too."

He ignored the statement. "Mama wasn't pleased that I spent more time playing ball than studying. I didn't have time for that. I wanted to play ball. She should'a knowed it too. It was in my blood."

Evans went quiet for a moment, then he pointed a shaky finger toward a square table on the side of the sofa. I finally deciphered the action. He wanted me to open the table drawer. I pulled out a worn scrapbook that smelled of dust and stale cigarettes. Another finger gesture indicated I should look through the book. The first page revealed a tattered Kodak picture of a smiling young man, leg high in the air, arm cocked back, ready to throw a pitch.

"That's me," Evans acknowledged. "I played ball anywhere and everywhere I could, little league, bush league. Didn't matter. By the time I was seventeen, I could pitch a ball so fast it whistled by before the batter knew a pitch had come. That's how I got the nickname 'Lightening'.

"My Daddy took us to Bush Stadium to see Uncle James play one summer. That man was a force to be reckoned with. The Clowns played against the Philadelphia Stars. Uncle James played center field. It was the bottom of the ninth, and the batter hits a fly ball to deep center field. I still see Uncle James on a dead run while watching the ball. He made the catch at the wall. The batter's out. I knew I was going to play for the Clowns one day—and with my uncle."

I was mesmerized by the story and how animated he was in the telling. The slow, angry speech gave way to a coherent narrative. Until.

"I hated that bastard." Evans's eyes were bugged, and the veins in his neck were thick and throbbing. I followed his eyes to what seemed to upset him.

The photo album had tumbled off my lap, and I hurried to retrieve the pictures. "You keep saying that. Who are you talking about?" I picked up a picture that had escaped under the coffee table.

"That low-life S-O-B right there. Hosea Richards."

I looked down at a photograph of a tall, dark-brown-skinned man. His hair was parted in the middle and conked so it lay smoothly on either side of the part. A thick but well-trimmed mustache adorned a snide smile. I waited for him to say more, and when he didn't, I prompted. "So, who is this guy?"

"He was the relief pitcher. But he was a straight-up snake in the grass. He was always jealous of my uncle. For the longest time, I didn't know why." The words hung in the air. Then he muttered, "I found out, though, and I..."

Evans's malevolent grin reminded me of a cat who swallowed

the canary, and enjoyed every crunch. The air seemed to have left the room. "Mr. Evans, maybe it's time..."

The evil smile that had crept across his face slowly disappeared. "I'm ain't lucinatin' and I ain't crazy. And before you think I'm some kind of homicidal maniac, I had a good reason to hate the man.

"I was around seventeen when I started going to Bush Stadium whenever the team was allowed to practice. Uncle James would let me sneak in a practice with the team—or at least Coach Willie didn't mind. He was a pretty good guy."

Eddie gazed off into the distance, perhaps visualizing himself on the field all those years ago. "When Coach asked me if I wanted to bat round with the team, I nearly shit my pants with excitement. Maybe they would sign me if I showed what I could do! I grabbed a bat and jogged over to the batter's box. Good god! My heart went to beatin' like a jackhammer! Preacher Henry was on the mound!"

I frowned. That was a tall tale too far. "There was a preacher playing for the Clowns?" The look on the old man's face expressed his contempt for my ignorance louder than any words could have. I wanted to grab the words and stuff them back in my mouth.

He lost the story's momentum as he returned to spitting sharp bullets for words. "His real name was Leo. No one called him that. He was the starting pitcher for the Clowns, and a dammed good one."

"When the East-West Game was played in 1941, he was voted to play, and he got the third most votes behind Satchel Paige and Hilton Smith. I know it was before your time, so before you ask, let's just say it was like voting for a player to be in an all-star game." Satisfied that I was not going to interrupt, he continued.

"Anyway, Preacher threw a meatball right down the middle. Needless to say, I knocked it out of the park. Well, I yelled, 'What the hell was that? I ain't no Punch and Judy hitter. Give me a real pitch.' The next one was low and outside. On the third pitch, I could see the stitches as the ball came at me. I whacked it deep into center field."

The storytelling abruptly stopped as thunderclouds gathered on his face. "My uncle was out in center field that day. He dropped the catch. That's when that rat bastard, Hosea Richards, ran out on the field shouting at James, calling him a hack and a cheat. We were playing a practice game and he carried on like it was the world series. Yelling that Uncle James was never going to get a shot, and I wasn't neither. 'Your sawed-off nephew' is what he called me."

Admittedly, I'm a nurse who doesn't know much about baseball, but that Richards guy's response sounded harsh, and I said so.

"Richards was more than that. Long after the game was over, I sat in the dugout fuming over what had happened. I should have been pleased that I got to play, but I felt partially responsible for the scrape between my uncle and Richards. If I hadn't hit the ball to center field, Richards wouldn't a got a shot at my uncle like that. Whatever the reason was that he hated Uncle James, I couldn't figure out. I figured I got the shaft just because he was my uncle. Richards always looked at me like I done killed his best friend."

It was getting late, but I was so intrigued by Evan's story I figured that hanging around a little longer couldn't hurt. I wouldn't claim the extra time. I asked, "Did you ever figure out what the problem was?"

Evans' laugh was sardonic. "Yep. Thanks to Jackie Robinson. He signed in the major leagues in '47, you know. Most of the guys figured he would, and they were pretty upset about it."

I frowned in confusion, wondering why anyone, especially Black ball players, would be upset. I glanced out the window. Judging from the shadows cast on the lawn, it was about time for me to give Evans his final medications and take my leave from my day shift. But why were the players upset, and what did Jackie Robinson have to do with the Clowns or the feud between James Evans and Hosea Richards? Why did Eddie Evans hate Richards so much? Reluctantly, I turned down Mr. Evans' bed and prepared him for the night. It was still relatively early, but the poor man had exhausted himself. My questions would have to wait another day.

Eddie Evans was subdued the next day. He took his medications, but after a half-hearted stab at lunch, he lay in bed watching with the sound turned low. I sat in a chair by the bed. After an hour of silence between us, Evans turned to me.

"Did you know I used to play baseball?"

"Yes, we talked about it for quite a while yesterday. Remember?" I watched his rapid eye movement as he sifted through his memory. "You were talking about your uncle, a man named Hosea Richards and Jackie Robinson."

The words activated his mind, and his voice gained strength. "Oh yeah. Jackie Robinson. I told you my uncle played for the Kansas City Monarchs before he played for the Clowns. Well, he was playing for the Monarchs in '45 when they wrote to Robinson offering him a contract. Robinson wasn't satisfied with how the team was structured, the schedule, nothing. So, he wrangled a tryout with the Boston Red Sox but that was just a joke to shut up some bigwig hollering for Black folk to play in the Majors. But the Brooklyn Dodgers was seriously looking. Jackie Robinson *and* my Uncle James got the call. He was on their radar. It was a race to see who would get to break that color line." Evans eagerly searched her face. "Betcha didn't know that, did ya?"

My head was spinning as I tried to discern how much of what Eddie was saying was real and what was the product of an active imagination. I didn't have long to speculate.

"Do you know how many players was better than Robinson? Damn, some of those bush-league boys could hit a ball into the next county. And run! Who-o-o, we-e-e! They coulda beat Robinson in a foot race while they were dead drunk!"

"Then why...."

"Because he was the white man's dream. Educated, served his country. One of the 'good' ones. The point is it coulda been my uncle if not for Richards."

He began to gag, and a harsh coughing spell broke into his narrative. After a few minutes of deep breathing and slow sips of water, he calmed down. I fluffed his pillows and eased him back down. I stood there until a wrinkled hand motioned me back to my chair. Satisfied that he was comfortable and no longer in distress, I settled down and listened, fascinated by the story that was unfolding.

"It happened in southern Indiana," he started, "before I got on the team. The Clowns were barnstorming some team in a town just outside Evansville. Bout the middle of the fourth inning, the umpire stops the game. Someone had accused a Clown player of using a corked bat."

I had to interrupt. "What's that? Is it a problem?" My question was met with a dramatic sigh and rolling eyes.

"That's when rubber or some other type material is put into the barrel—the base of a bat. Makes it easier to swing and it's as illegal as hell. Anyway, there was a big to-do and Uncle James was accused of having the bat. Somehow, he was able to prove he didn't use it, but he told me he always suspect it was Hosea that told the lie it was him."

I got up, stretched, and rubbed my neck. I realized I had been tensely straining forward this whole time. "If they proved it wasn't him, case closed. Right?"

A deep sadness clouded his eyes. He shook his head. "It's taint, Marie. Uncle's reputation was tainted. Proof or no proof, it can follow you around for the rest of your career."

Evening shadows were creeping across the room. As I prepared to end my shift, I made sure Mr. Evans was tucked in, and I laid my hand atop his shriveled ones. "Try to rest."

"You coming back tomorrow?"

Startled by the desperation in his voice, I turned. "Of course, I am." And I left, wondering about his concern.

THE NEXT DAY WAS UGLY. There was no other way to describe it. Ominous clouds hung in the eastern sky, and the air was still like the earth was holding its breath. There was surprisingly little traffic as I drove across town. The streets were eerily still. Usually, the old man had little strength and rarely attempted to move about on his own, so I was pleased to see him sitting up in his recliner.

"Good morning. Did you rest well?"

"Morning," was his only reply.

I bustled about getting medication ready. Before fixing breakfast, I asked my typically lethargic patient if he wanted anything in particular.

"Two eggs, three bacon, toast, grapefruit and black coffee."

His response stopped me. I turned to face him, thinking maybe the answer was facetious, but he was wearing his usual dour expression. Not only was his meal request more than what he usually ate, but he was never so specific.

After I made breakfast, we sat in silence and ate. I watched him sop up the remainder of his sunny-side-up eggs with his toast and slurp the last of his coffee.

"Should I read you something," I asked, "or would you like to watch television?"

"I want to talk," he said. "Ever hear of a man named Jeremiah Johnson?"

I tried to ignore the foreboding timbre of his voice.

"Johnson, or J.J. as they called him, played ball for the Atlanta Black Sox when he was seventeen. He was so good that the Major Leagues got wind of him after a while. Mind you, this was back in the '30s. It was rumored that several MLB teams were interested in breaking the color barrier, and J.J. was their top pick."

"That was quite a while before Jackie Robinson," I noted.

Evans nodded. "Well, his coach, 'Harry' Thompson, had different plans. Harry was bitter and jealous. The coach had dreams of playing Major League Baseball that didn't pan out, and he couldn't stand the thought of a younger Black man achieving what he could not. So, Harry began to sabotage J.J.'s chances. At first, it was piddly stuff like benching J.J. during key games, spreading rumors about his bad temperament, and getting in his head to eat away his confidence. But it didn't matter. The scouts was still interested."

I moved to halt the conversation because Evans' breathing was becoming more labored, and the slight tremor I had noticed earlier was getting more pronounced. He was so determined to tell his tale that I decided not to interrupt him again. "Go on," I said.

"Fine." The old man's glare told me he believed a victory had been won, so he continued. "The next time Harry benched him J.J. confronted him in the locker room. You can imagine how heated that became. Then Harry gloated. 'You'll never play in the Majors, boy. They don't want your kind.' Well, that was all she wrote. J.J. grabbed a bat and swung like it was the ninth inning in a series game. He let all that rage shut the old bastard up for good." The demented smile on the old man's lips was chilling.

"That boy ran for all the good it did him. By the time they caught up with him, Harry Thompson was dead and Johnson was tried for murder."

My head was throbbing, and I went to the bathroom partly to grab an aspirin but also to momentarily get away from Evans. I returned with questions I knew I didn't want answers to.

"Why did you tell me that story, and what does it have to do with your uncle or Hosea Richards?" My hands trembled as I sat down, afraid of the answers I might get.

"I told you that I trusted you, and before I go, I had to tell someone—not that there's much anyone can do about it now."

"Do about what?"

"The same crap that Hosea pulled on my uncle, he tried to pull on me. One night I confronted him in the stadium tunnel, and he admitted it! Richards admitted what he had done to my Uncle James. Sabotaged him every chance he got. How he had given the corked bat to Uncle James. What he had tried to do to my baseball career. It was all out of spite and jealousy. That's all. The man didn't have the talent to make it to the majors and couldn't stand anyone else getting the chance. I felt the rage that J.J. Johnson must have felt. I felt the disappointment my Uncle James felt. I felt that pain of every player—no, every person that was just trying to do their best and hateful people come along and try to ruin their lives." Evans' breathing was getting progressively worse.

I tried to slow my own breathing. "What are you saying Mr. Evans?"

His laugh bordered on hysteria. "I-I swung my bat and hit a home run! H-h-his head split like a over-ripe melon. But I wasn't no fool like Johnson. I wasn't going to jail for ridding the world of a dream killer." His next laugh was weaker. "Heh, heh, heh. That sucker wanted to be a star, torpedo people's dreams, so I torpedoed him."

"What did you do with the body, Eddie?" I studied him as he grinned.

"He's at the stadium. All over Bush Stadium."

"Bush Stadium on 16th Street? Bush Stadium isn't there anymore. Apartments are there now. The Stadium Apartments. If there was a body or parts of a body it would have been found."

Evans sighed. "Then I guess it didn't give up all its secrets." He was smiling as the last rush of breath left his body and his head lolled to one side.

I'm not sure what I felt at that moment. Shock? Sadness? I also don't know if his confession was true or a result of his cancer-riddled brain. But as he said, there's not much anyone can do about it now.

BUSH STADIUM

Bush Stadium has been a significant part of the community. Nestled at West 16th Street in Indianapolis, the stadium was initially constructed for the Indianapolis Indians baseball team and christened Perry Stadium after the team's owner, Norm Perry. Its Art Deco style made Perry Stadium stand out as one of the most aesthetically pleasing minor league ballparks of its era.

During the 1930s and 1940s, Bush Stadium was a hub for minor league and Negro League teams such as Indianapolis ABCs, American Giants, Athletics, Crawfords, and the Indianapolis Clowns from 1944 to 1962, cementing the team's status as a key player in the city's baseball landscape.

In 1942, during World War II, the ballpark was renamed Victory Field as a gesture of patriotism. However, it was renamed Bush Stadium in 1967 after former player, manager, and president of the Indians, Donnie Bush. The stadium has many historic event highlights, such as serving as a venue for the 1987 Pan American Games baseball tournament, doubling as historic ballparks, such as Comiskey in Chicago and Crosley in Cincinnati in the 1988 film *Eight Men Out,* and the Indians' four consecutive American Association titles from 1986 to 1989. Due to its decline and eventual abandonment, Bush Stadium officially closed at the end of its 1996 season. At that time, the team moved to its new home, Victory Field, in downtown Indianapolis.

Undergoing a remarkable transformation in 2013, Bush Stadium has evolved into the Stadium Lofts at Bush Stadium, a vibrant residential apartment complex that symbolizes Bush Stadium's enduring impact on the city.

CAPITOL MURDER
BY JANET E. WILLIAMS

As the last of the legislators straggled out of the Statehouse, Fran dragged her trash bin and her sloshing bucket and mop into the office of the House Republican leadership. She sighed as she surveyed the mess before her—scattered pizza boxes, some empty and some with half-eaten dried-out slices; empty Coke and Pepsi bottles dropped onto the floor; used napkins strewn across the worn and dirty carpet.

Fran glanced at the clock on the wall above the doorway. Half-past midnight. There was no good reason for the session to have run so late but for the senator from Johnson County who dragged out the budget debate over funding for everything from banning trans students from school sports to removing controversial books from public school libraries. At this hour, it didn't matter to Fran how the debate turned out, it just meant she'd be working into the wee hours of the morning leaving no time to sleep before heading to her day job.

What happened under the copper-topped dome of the State-house did little to make Fran's life better. The so-called tort reform bill that passed a few years ago made it nearly impossible for her to sue the drunken driver who killed her husband two years ago as he drove home from his night shift at the Amazon warehouse outside of Indianapolis. When Jerry got that relatively high-paying job, she thought the family's money struggles would be over. But no. They got worse when he was killed just a couple of months into the job by that drunk who turned out to be the son of a state senator with a high-priced lawyer. Since her day job wasn't enough to support herself and her two teenagers, she got a position with the company that contracted to clean downtown buildings. That's how she ended up on the night cleaning crew at the Statehouse.

"Would it hurt you to clean up after yourselves?" Fran shoved the debris from the pizza boxes and soda bottles into her rolling trash bin and then dumped the overflowing wastebaskets on top.

Fran shook off the anger that rose up inside of her every time she thought about the accident and the drunk who derailed her family's dream of a better life. She really needed this job, even though it paid barely above Indiana's already low minimum wage to supplement the income from her day job as a receptionist in a medical office. Still, even with two jobs, she barely made enough to cover living expenses for her and her children, now teenagers.

She choked on the lingering scent of the cigarettes and cigars that permeated the outer room of the speaker's office and then dumped the overflowing ashtray into her bin.

"Pigs," she muttered as she wiped dust and ashes from the desk occupied by the speaker's receptionist. "I thought smoking was supposed to be banned here." She figured she'd clean up the cigarette butts ground into the carpet when she vacuumed.

Fran took a deep breath before she entered the speaker's office. This was the man whose reckless son killed, no murdered she corrected, her husband. She felt the anger rising again and was grateful it was late enough so she wouldn't have to face him.

As she wheeled her trash bin into the inner office, she saw a man's gray head slumped across the desk. Her heart skipped a beat when she realized it was Sen. Ralph Gardner and she might have to face him after all.

"Senator Gardner?" Fran called softly as she crossed the room. As she worked her way around the desk to tap him on the shoulder, she spotted a shattered photograph of who she thought was Gardner and his son on the floor. Beside it was the Sagamore of the Wabash plaque that usually hung on the wall behind his desk. She picked it up to place it on the desk when she spotted the red smear of what looked like blood on the corner. She screamed loudly enough to waken the senator, or so she thought. But when he didn't move, she leaned over to tap him on the shoulder. That's when she spotted the gaping and bloodied wound on the back of his head. The thinning gray hair was streaked with blood that had flowed down the side of his face and onto the desk.

As she backed away from the senator, a man in a capitol police officer's uniform charged into the office.

"Ma'am, you, ok?" the young officer asked from the doorway.

"T-this," Fran stammered as she pressed against the wall, the plaque still in her hands.

The officer, looking from her with the plaque in her hands to the bloodied body slumped across the desk, drew his gun and demanded, "What did you do?"

<hr>

Tracey stumbled in well past her 8 a.m. start time and went straight to the capitol snack bar next to her basement office for a cup of coffee.

"I heard it was a real late one," Ange said as she rang up Tracey's coffee.

Tracey nodded and then yawned. "I hardly got any sleep."

"No muffin today? I saved your favorite, blueberry," she said as she placed the muffin, wrapped in tissue paper, on the counter.

"You're too good to me." Tracey pulled out her wallet and placed a five-dollar bill and two ones on the counter. "Thanks. Keep the change."

Tracey fumbled for her keys while balancing the muffin on top of the coffee lid before finally pushing open the door to her shabby office. The detritus of past generations of statehouse reporters was ground into the torn brown carpet. Schedules of committee meetings and floor votes on key pieces of legislation were strewn across the table that stretched almost the length of the office. She made her way past the chairs and overflowing trash baskets to get to her desk where she dropped her computer bag and purse before carefully setting down the coffee and muffin.

"I can't keep doing this," she sighed, slumping into her chair.

As she popped the lid off the coffee and began to take a sip, she heard the buzz of some of her fellow reporters outside her office. Tracey tried to concentrate on logging into her computer but stopped when she overheard someone say, "Yeah, I hear he was whacked over the head with his Sagamore."

Tracey's morning fog lifted immediately, and she tore straight from her office to the hallway where the gaggle of reporters had gathered.

"Whacked? Who was whacked?"

"You didn't hear?" asked Dan, the reporter from the local public radio station.

"Hear what? I just got here."

"It's been all over the news this morning," Steph, the reporter from a newspaper in northwest Indiana, said as she turned toward Tracey in surprise.

Of course, she missed something big on the first morning in months that she hadn't turned on the morning news or listened to public radio on her way into work.

"What? I just got here because the copy desk kept me up half the night with a bunch of stupid questions."

Dan nodded sympathetically and as he was about to speak, Steph said, "It's Senator Gardner. Someone bashed his head in last night."

"What? Was it a robbery? Did someone get him in the parking lot?" Tracey asked, her mouth agape.

"In his office," Steph said. "I heard from the Capitol police that he was at his desk when someone bashed him in the head with his Sagamore of the Wabash."

"Wow. When?"

"Late last night a little after midnight. Everyone was gone except the cleaning crew," Dan said.

"They know who did it?"

"They called in IPD and I've heard they're questioning Fran, the night cleaning lady," Dan replied. "Andy, the capitol cop on the night shift found her in Gardner's office. Andy told me she was holding the plaque, and it was dripping blood."

"Fran? A killer? They can't possibly think she did it," Tracey said, shaking her head.

Dan shrugged as he said, "I don't know but it sure doesn't look good. Remember, it was Gardner's son who killed her husband."

Tracey was dumbfounded at the thought that the hardworking woman she chatted with on her late nights at the legislature could be capable of such a violent act. She snapped out of her reverie when her phone began buzzing. Pulling it from her pocket she looked at the screen and sighed before saying she had to go and darted back into her office. She closed the door.

It was her newspaper's main office downtown and the conversation didn't go well. Her editor demanded to know why she didn't have anything on the biggest story at the Statehouse since the governor collapsed and died while delivering his state of the state address three years ago.

Her explanation, which wasn't received well, was that pain-in-ass night copy editor kept her up with endless picky questions about her story. That particular editor was infamous for his endless late-night questions, but her dayside editor didn't care.

"I'm on it," Tracey firmly told her editor and then filled him in on what she had learned from her fellow reporters. "And give me another hour and I'll have the story ready for the website."

She caught up fast and by lunchtime she had her own scoop. Gardner wasn't the bloodied corpse. It was actually Brad Douglas, a Republican senator from Hamilton County, and he was face-down on the multi-page budget legislation. She confirmed that Gardner's Sagamore of the Wabash was the murder weapon and that Fran O'Connor, the night cleaning lady, was being questioned at Indianapolis Police Department headquarters.

LITTLE WORK WAS ACCOMPLISHED that day as reporters, lawmakers and staff chatted among themselves about what could have happened. Every reporter filed his or her own version of the Douglas murder but initially, without much of the new information Tracey had tracked down. Most had to print updates to correct the name of the actual victim.

The next day, police issued a brief news release with a few more details from the investigation and autopsy. "Douglas," police said, "had died of blunt force trauma to the back of his skull and likely died between 11:15 and midnight."

"So, while I was down here arguing with my editor about my story someone was upstairs pummeling Douglas with Gardner's Sagamore." Tracey was chatting with Brent Reeves, the spokesperson for House Republicans.

"Looks like it," Brent said, his hands jammed into his pants pockets. A long-time communications director for House Republicans, Brent Reeves was the guy every reporter turned to for insider information and tips about what issues might arise during the legislative session. He could always be counted on for solid updates and insider gossip and was always available to chat with Statehouse reporters. Everybody liked his easy charm and his athletic build, sandy blond hair and ingratiating smile didn't hurt.

Tracey nodded as she mentally ran through the previous evening's events.

"No. Wait. Something's not right," she said suddenly.

"What? What's not, right?"

"The timing," Tracey said. "Fran was here in the basement offices mopping the hallway. She stopped in when I was talking to Steve and that was about 11:30."

"She could have made it upstairs by midnight."

Tracey shook her head. "No. I heard her. She was mopping the floors here until after midnight. Most of you were all gone by then."

"Seriously? Police say she had a motive because of what Gardner and his son did to her family," Brent said.

"But it was Douglas," Tracey said.

"Well, you know Gardner and Douglas kind of look alike. Big guys, gray crewcut and always wearing the same blue suit. And he was at Gardner's desk."

"I know, but the timing doesn't add up. I know she was down here when someone killed Douglas," Tracey said. "I noted the time because of the way my editor was nitpicking my story."

"Interesting," Brent said, before checking his watch and telling her he had to take off for a meeting. As he headed down the hallway, he turned to her and added, "You'll keep me posted on what you hear, won't you?"

"Yes, and you'll let me know if you hear anything, too."

Brent nodded and after he hurried away, Tracey poked her head into the neighboring office.

"Hey, Dave," she said. Dave looked up from his computer as she continued. "You remember when Fran came around last night? You and I were about the last ones here finishing up."

"Yeah, so?"

"Check out the news release about the autopsy." As Dave looked it over, she said, "The time. It's the time. If Douglas was killed before midnight, then Fran couldn't possibly have done it. She was here. We chatted a few minutes after I got off the phone with my editor and it was definitely after midnight. I remember asking her about her daughter.”

“The one who was injured in the crash?” Dave asked.

Tracey nodded.

Dave studied the news release for a moment. “Whoa, you’re right. I heard you talking last night right after she stopped in here.”

“Then let’s go,” Tracey said. “The cops are still upstairs talking to House staff. They need to know Fran was down here until past midnight. And if Douglas was killed before then, she couldn’t have done it.”

THE MURDER of Brad Douglas was still the top story the next day as both Tracey and the paper’s police beat reporter were tracking down new information. That’s why Tracey arrived early that morning and as she approached her office, fumbling for her keys, she saw a figure in the shadows.

“Fran! What the...”

Before Tracey could finish, Fran rushed forward and embraced Tracey.

“If it wasn’t for you, I might be in jail right now,” Fran said, releasing Tracey and wiping a tear from her eyes. “But what you told the police, they realized I couldn’t have done it.”

“I knew you couldn’t do something like that,” Tracey said, reaching for a tissue in her purse and handing it to Fran.

“Not Senator Douglas, no,” Fran replied. “But that Gardner? I hated him for what his boy did to my Jerry and how they twisted everything in court. But I’d never...” Her voice, trembling, trailed off.

“I know, Fran, I know,” Tracey replied.

Fran wiped away another tear and then, added, “I just wanted to stop by and thank you. I have to get to my day job. See you tonight.” She scurried off.

“What’d Fran have to say?”

Tracey turned, startled by the voice behind her. It was Brent.

"She just wanted to thank me for talking to the police last night."

"Good thing you were here," Brent said and when Tracey didn't respond, he added, "You hear anything else about the investigation?"

"Not a thing. Our cops reporter is checking with investigators," Tracey replied. "You hear anything?"

"Nothing. Gardner seems pretty freaked out that Douglas was killed in his office. Maybe that's why they've called off today's session."

"Yeah, just what was Douglas doing in the speaker's office?"

Brent shrugged. "Who knows. The pages he was looking at were all covered with blood. Investigators took them away as part of the crime scene."

"He had no business there," Tracey said. "You know what he was looking at?"

"The budget bill. He said he wanted to check one of the appropriations but the pages were soaked in blood. Not sure that really matters anyhow," Brent replied. "Anyhow, leadership is meeting in one of the meeting rooms upstairs and I have to be there. Gardner's office is still a crime scene."

Brent dashed off and Tracey returned to her office and texted the cops reporter.

"*You have anything new on the Douglas murder?*" she typed into her phone to Sam Jenkins, the dayside police reporter. Her phone buzzed and Tracey answered.

"Sam? You got anything new?"

"Maybe. One of the crime scene techs told me there was blood spatter on some broken glass on the desk," Sam replied.

"Broken glass?"

"Yeah. Someone smashed a photo on the desk, and they think whoever did might have cut himself."

"They checking for DNA?"

"Yes, but they don't expect results back until tomorrow at the earliest," Sam replied.

"What was the photo?"

"I don't know. There was no photo. Just the broken frame."

Sam hung up and Tracey headed to Brent's office, which was next to Gardner's office and outside the crime scene tape.

"Brent. Got a minute?" Tracey asked as she poked her head into his office.

"For you, always," he replied, looking up from his computer. "You hear anything new?"

"I just heard that there was a shattered picture frame mixed up in the blood and mess on Gardner's desk."

"Oh yeah? I hadn't heard that," Brent said.

"Sam just told me. You were in Gardner's office a lot. Any idea what was in that frame?" Tracey asked.

Brent shook his head. "The only photo Gardner kept in his office was a family portrait of him, his wife and kids."

"Why would anyone smash that?"

"Who knows why anyone does anything."

"Mind if I peek in the office?" Tracey asked and before Brent could respond, she moved closer to the crime scene tape and leaned into the doorway to see the office.

"Wait, don't," Brent said, a moment too late.

"Couldn't have been the family photo. I see it over there on the table behind the desk," Tracey said, pointing.

"Then who knows?" Brent, who moved his hands from his keyboard to his lap, shrugged.

"Maybe the police have more information," Tracey said, adding, "By the way, any word on when lawmakers will be coming back?"

"Maybe not til next Monday. Everyone's pretty shaken up by Douglas' murder and the speaker said he wants to give police time to do their jobs."

"I don't think it's because they miss him. I don't think anyone here in the building liked Douglas much," Tracey said. "Especially after he settled with that intern who filed that complaint against him for sexually harassing her."

"Leadership investigated. They cleared him," Brent said, turning back to his computer screen. "I have this report to finish up before Gardner gets back. I'll send out a notice when they're back."

"Sure. Thanks."

Tracey returned to her office to check in with Sam to see if he had any new information. She especially wanted to know if police had checked out the intern, Megan Conley, because she had begun working in the governor's office after she filed her complaint and was in the Statehouse the day Douglas was killed. She texted Sam and they agreed to meet in a coffee shop halfway between the Statehouse and police headquarters.

Tracey was nearly finished with her coffee when Sam finally arrived.

"Only 20 minutes late," she said as she checked her watch and then swallowed her last gulp of coffee.

"Yeah, sorry," Sam replied as he slid into the booth across from her. "But you won't be so upset when you hear this."

"And?"

"Got a preliminary report on the blood spatters on the shards of glass. They didn't belong to Douglas, but they show a close relative match," Sam said.

"What? I don't think anybody saw any of his family at the Statehouse the day he was killed."

"I don't know what to tell you, but that's what the preliminary DNA test shows."

"Wow. What was in that photo?" Tracey asked.

"That's why I'm late. The lead detective told me that whatever was in the frame is missing," Sam said.

"Then what about the DNA? Douglas only has one son. Do they think he might have done it?"

"No, he couldn't have. Young Brad Douglas has an air-tight alibi for the time his dad was killed. He's doing graduate work in the UK and investigators confirmed he's been there since just after the holidays."

"Someone else in his family?"

"It looks that way but everyone in his immediate family has been accounted for."

Tracey slumped back in her seat. What possible explanation could there be for the DNA match?

"I suppose it could be wrong," she said after a long pause.

"True but unlikely. Things might change with the final report, but I doubt it. These guys at the crime lab know their stuff."

"Yeah, but there has to be an explanation."

Sam nodded. "Now, what were you going to tell me."

"Just wanted to know if you knew anything about the photo and the smashed frame. Like who's in the photo?"

"No, like I said, the photo was missing. I think everyone is assuming it was Gardner and his family," Sam replied.

"No. The family photo is still in the office. It has to be something else." Tracey shook her head as she spoke.

"Then let's check our sources before we tell the desk anything about this," Sam said.

"We don't have enough on this anyhow."

***

Tracey filed an update on the murder, describing the mood at the Statehouse and how lawmakers would return for business the next week. She included a few brief details about the investigation from Sam but left out information about the blood.

After lunch, she stopped in Brent's office to see whether he heard anything new.

"I would have thought you'd take a day or two off before the lawmakers return," Tracey said.

"No. The quiet gives me a chance to catch up on some work. The speaker wants to hold a press conference Monday."

"Really? Does he have some information about Douglas that no one else has?"

"No. He just wants to slow down the gossip mill and get back to business."

"I know I asked you about this before, but has anyone figured out what was in the broken picture frame? Who was it and why was it in Gardner's office?"

"No. The photo was gone. There was just the broken frame. Why? What are the police saying?"

"I don't know. Our cops reporter is checking," Tracey replied. "It might be nothing but I'm curious about who smashed the photo and why. And did it have anything to do with the murder?"

"Who knows why anyone kills?" Brent asked, rising from his chair.

"True," Tracey said as she turned to leave. That's when she noticed the bandage on his left hand. "What happened? Another home repair accident?"

"Yeah. Did this last night," he said as he held up his bandaged hand. "Fixing a hole in my fence. I slipped with my saw and cut the side of my hand."

"And you're left-handed, too," Tracey said.

"I'm used to it. I'm doing stupid stuff like this all the time. Remember last year when I broke my finger with a hammer? At least this time it's just a little cut." He walked around his desk and led Tracey from his office. "I've got a meeting in ten. I'll catch up with you later."

"You better be careful," Tracey said as she headed toward the steps to her basement office.

A few minutes later she was heading for the snack bar when she saw a familiar figure paying for his coffee.

"Hey Brent! How'd you get down here so fast?"

"What?" The figure at the counter turned around.

"Oh sorry," Tracey said when she realized the man wasn't Brent. "I thought you were someone else."

"I get that a lot around here," the man said. He was tall and lean with sandy blond hair, a lot like Brent's Tracey told herself.

He extended his hand and told her he was Brad Douglas and then added a junior when Tracey looked surprised.

"I thought you were Brent Reeves. From the back you look so much like him," she said.

"I have to meet this Brent guy. You're not the first person who mistook me for him," he said.

"I can see a resemblance but now that I look closer not so much."

"I hope I'm better looking." Brad flashed a smile and with that she could see how much he looked like his father, the late senator.

"I'm really sorry for your loss," Tracey said. "Have the police figured out who did it yet?"

"No. But I haven't talked to them yet. I just got in from London this morning and thought I'd come straight here and pick up Dad's personal stuff. Mom's pretty wrecked by all this," he said.

"The police remove the crime scene tape?" she asked.

"No, but police said I could go to his office and pick up some of his stuff. One of the detectives is meeting me there," Brad said.

"That's got to be tough, losing your dad like that."

"Yeah. My dad could be a son of a bitch, but he was my dad," he said, letting out a sigh. "I better get upstairs."

Tracey watched him walk away before approaching the snack bar counter for coffee.

"Poor guy," Ange said as Tracey paid for her coffee.

"Yeah, poor guy."

THE ONLY UPDATES on the murder of Senator Douglas came from the police beat where Sam reported that the blood spatter at the scene was a close DNA match to the victim. Investigators couldn't explain as the senator's only blood relative was nowhere near the capitol the night of the murder. That bit of new information was the source of much gossip when lawmakers returned for business at the beginning of the following week.

In the first session since the murder, lawmakers spent the morning offering tributes to Senator Douglas, extolling him as a dedicated legislator who never stopped working for the people. That dedication, they agreed, got him killed in the wee hours of the morning when he was pouring over the budget bill.

Reporters watching the spectacle from a row of tables in the back of the chamber had a hard time to keep from rolling their eyes. Tracey, like her fellow reporters, knew that Douglas' colleagues considered him a grandstanding buffoon who did nothing unless it benefitted him politically or personally. Douglas' son and wife were seated in the front of the chamber as one by one members paid tribute to their slain colleague. This was the kind of hypocrisy Tracey had difficulty swallowing. But unless the colleagues were willing to go on the record about their real feelings about Douglas, Tracey would have to write about the tributes. And then, it would be back to business in the Statehouse as the investigation dragged on.

Except it wasn't business as usual that same afternoon when Tracey learned the local prosecutor had empaneled a grand jury to further investigate the murder. Lawmakers, House staffers and other Statehouse employees were summoned to the courthouse to answer questions about the day of the murder. Sam covered the comings and goings of the witnesses, but all were sworn to secrecy so as a result, he could get no information about what was happening behind the closed doors of the grand jury room.

On what was supposed to be the last day, Tracey and the other Statehouse reporters were summoned to testify. What was frustrating, they were sworn to secrecy and threatened with contempt of court if they revealed anything that happened in the grand jury room before indictments were returned. But there wasn't much to say anyhow because all Tracey did was repeat what she told investigators that first day about where Fran was the night of the murder. Neither she nor any of the other reporters had much to share.

When Tracey left the grand jury room, she saw the lead investigator in a heated conversation with Senator Douglas' son, Brad. She stepped out of their line of sight so she could overhear the argument.

"Look, detective, all I'm asking for is the photo of my dad and me that was in that broken frame," Brad said, his voice rising in anger.

"And I'm telling you we don't have it. All we have is the broken frame," the investigator said.

"Somebody has it. That's the last photo I took with my dad and I'd like it back."

"Sorry. I don't know what to tell you. If anything turns up, I'll let you know." The investigator walked away.

So that's what was in the broken frame, Tracey said to herself. And what was it doing in Gardner's office?

Tracey's next stop was Brent's office to ask him what he knew or heard. When she reached his office she saw that the secretary was away from her desk so she entered Brent's office. He wasn't there, either. She approached his desk to leave a note saying she stopped by when she noticed the corner of a photograph sticking out from under a pile of papers. She took her pen and carefully pushed the papers out of the way so she could see the photo.

"What's this?" she mumbled as she looked closer. It was Senator Douglas with his son, Brad, standing with fishing poles in front of an old cabin.

"Hey, what are you doing?" Brent demanded as he entered his office.

"This photo? This is the one that was in the frame, wasn't it?" Tracey said as she picked it up.

"You have no business going through my desk." Brent grabbed the photo and taking her by the arm, removed her from his office.

"What are you doing with that photo?" Tracey asked as she shook herself free from Brent's grip.

"If it's any of your business, I found it in the speaker's office after the murder. Now get out." Brent had turned red with anger.

"Not until you tell me what's going on. I overheard Douglas' son tell investigators about the photo. It was him and his dad," Tracey said. "It sounds just like that photo."

"I told you I found it. I'll make sure Senator Douglas' precious boy gets this photo. Now would you please go."

Tracey left and returned to her basement office, shaken by the hostile encounter with Brent, with whom she normally had a good relationship. Her phone buzzed as she unlocked her office door. It was Sam.

"Sam, you hear anything new?"

"You sound upset," Sam said. "What's wrong?"

"I just had a run-in with Brent Reeves. Seems he had the missing photo from the broken frame," she said. "I found it on his desk and I know I shouldn't have done it but he walked in on me and was so angry he scared me a little."

"Brent Reeves you say?" Sam said. "I just heard from a source that they were able to match the DNA on that blood sample using a genealogical database. He told me it matches to Douglas' son."

"Young Brad?"

"No. They traced it to Brent Reeves. The DNA shows that Brent Reeves is the son of Brad Douglas," Sam said.

"That can't be. Brent Reeves can't possibly be the son of Senator Douglas. Brent told me his dad was a truck driver and died in an accident when he was five," Tracey said.

"No. They're planning to bring him in for questioning as soon as they can find him."

"Well, he isn't hiding anywhere. Brent's upstairs. I just saw him. That can't possibly be true," she said. "But then..." She stopped as she considered Brent's behavior that evening.

"But then what?"

Startled, Tracey turned to see Brent standing in her doorway.

"Brent!" she said loudly enough so that Sam could hear her. "Come on, have a seat. I owe you an apology."

Brent slowly crossed the length of the office to where Tracey sat behind her desk. With one swift move, he grabbed her phone and tossed it to the floor.

"Go on. But then what?"

"Nothing. But then nothing," Tracey said, sliding her chair away from the desk to get as far away from Brent as she could.

"What? You afraid of me? Your old friend Brent?" His voice was so low she could barely hear him.

"N-n-no."

"You should be. You know, you shouldn't go around snooping where you don't belong." He leaned over the desk and was so close she could smell his breath. Whiskey. He'd been drinking.

"Brent, you should know they matched your DNA to the blood on the broken glass."

"What? How?" Brent backed up and dropped into a chair across from her desk.

"Sam told me they matched it to you through one of those genealogical databases. He knows you're here, you know," she said quietly. "I told him there was no way you could have done this."

Brent said nothing for a long moment before, in a sudden motion, slamming his fist on the desk. "He raped her you know. The bastard raped my mother. And then he pretended like neither of us ever existed while he gave that boy of his everything while we had nothing."

"Wasn't your father a trucker driver?"

"That's the story my mother told me until I was old enough to hear the truth. It made me sick when she told me. That's why I got the job here. To see up close and personal the bastard who used my mother and abandoned us."

"You confronted him in Gardner's office, didn't you?"

Brent nodded, wiping tears away with the back of his injured hand. "He said it was ancient history, that my mom was a whore who seduced him. That he already had son and had no room for the likes of me."

"What about the photo?"

"I had that with me when I confronted him. I shoved it in his face and told him I'd tell everyone what he did and then what would his son and wife think of him then. He just laughed and that's when I slammed the photo on the desk and cut my hand."

"Why? Why did you hit him with the plaque?"

"He kept laughing. Told me I was a fool and would only hurt myself and my mother. So, I grabbed the closest thing I could find and hit him and hit him again."

"He was a bastard and hurt a lot of people," Tracey said quietly. "You have to know we would have believed you, especially after that latest incident with the intern."

"I wasn't thinking straight. I was so blind with rage." Brent quietly wept as he spoke.

Tracey rose and picked up her phone, which had landed in the corner of her office.

"The screen's a little scratched but it's still working," she said, dialing the phone. "Sam, it's me. I have Brent Reeves here with me and he has something to say to the investigators."

"You okay? I already told the police that he was with you. They should be there any minute," Sam said, relief in his voice.

"Thanks, Sam. We'll be waiting." She disconnected and then turned to Brent. "The police will be here any minute. It'll all be over soon."

Brent nodded, defeated, and said, "You're right. It's over." As he turned to leave, a police officer stepped behind him with handcuffs in his hand.

"Brent Reeves, you're under arrest for the murder of Brad Douglas," the officer said as the handcuffs clicked on Reeves' wrists. Tracey heard the officer advise Reeves of his rights as they turned to leave.

As they departed, Tracey sat down at her computer and called her office, her phone cradled on her shoulder against her ear as she began writing.

"Sam," she said as her colleague answered. "They just picked up Reeves. You'll have the story for first edition."

INDIANA STATEHOUSE

The Indiana Statehouse, at the corner of Capitol Avenue and Washington Street in downtown Indianapolis, has served as the seat of state government since its completion in 1888.

The original statehouse was located at the then state capital in Corydon, in southern Indiana, when the state joined the union in 1816. It served as the capital until 1825, when it was moved to the more centrally located Indianapolis.

The first statehouse was completed in 1835, but within three decades was considered outdated and unsafe. Plans were begun for a new building that now sits at the current site.

Construction of the neoclassical statehouse began in 1878 and took a decade to complete, at a cost of $2 million. Architect Edwin May based the design on a classical Renaissance Revival style and modeled it on the U.S. Capitol. Built with Indiana limestone, it has a central copper-topped dome and Corinthian columns.

Within the building are the chambers for the Indiana House of Representatives and the Senate, the state Supreme Court, and offices for state officials, including the governor and lieutenant governor.

THE GIRL IN THE AQUEDUCT
BY STEPHEN TERRELL

I was settling in on my couch, preparing to spend my afternoon watching an early-season Purdue football game on television, when my office cell phone rang. "Detective Lieutenant Hickman," I answered.

"Sorry to bother you on your day off, Joe," the familiar voice at the other end of the phone said. "But we've got a nasty one down in Metamora. We need someone with experience to get down there before the local sheriff's office messes things up."

I sighed. It was Deputy Superintendent Don Pettigrew. My boss. "What have you got, Don?"

"You familiar with Metamora?"

I scratched my head. "As familiar as most, I guess. It's down on the White River Canal. There's an old grist mill and a tourist train. Some old shops. My wife dragged me down there a few times, but not for a while."

"There's an old wooden aqueduct that takes the canal over Duck Creek. It's the only one like it left in the entire country. That's where they found a body this morning."

"In the aqueduct?"

"Yep. Tourist trains still run on weekends. A woman riding on the train this morning saw a body hanging out of one of the chutes on the side of the aqueduct. To be more accurate, she spotted a woman's hair and part of her scalp. The local sheriff's office showed up and marked off the scene. They've called us to take over the investigation. They don't have any experience or equipment to handle something like this. So far, they haven't disturbed anything. At least that's what they're telling me."

"Metamora is out Highway 52, isn't it?"

"That's it."

"I think I'm about 40 minutes away. I'll be on the road in five minutes."

"I'm calling the crime scene unit out of Indianapolis. It will probably take them 90 minutes—maybe more—to get everything together and get to the scene. I'm also sending Guy Rudd from the Versailles Post. He's a good young detective. He should be there before you."

It took me a few minutes to get out of my jeans and into a blue pattern sport coat and khaki pants. I slipped my badge into my interior jacket pocket and Glock 19 into its shoulder holster, and I was on my way, running lights and siren.

Metamora was built in the 1830s on the dreams of the Whitewater Canal as a commercial link from Indiana's farms and forests to the major markets in the east. But by 1839, only a few miles were finished, and the state was bankrupt. The town survived only as a quaint weekend tourist attraction, a low-key world of small shops housed in historic unpainted wooden structures selling tee-shirts, assorted knick-knacks, and items that straddled the line between used, antiques, and junk. Only a handful of residents actually lived in the town.

Forty minutes after leaving the house, I pulled off U.S. 52 onto the small county road leading into the town. On busy weekends, the narrow streets were reserved for pedestrians, but my flashing lights got me past the private security that blocked the roadway. I weaved through people toting shopping bags and eating elephant ears until I got to the still-functioning 180-year-old gristmill that straddled the canal. I could hear the giant wheel creak with the sound of wood on wood, making endless circles that turned dried corn into cornmeal and grits.

I turned right onto the main street parallel to the canal and the Whitewater Valley Railroad, which survived only to serve the tourist trade. It was from a car on one of these railroad excursions that someone had spotted the body in the aqueduct.

I tweaked the siren occasionally to move curious onlookers from the street as I made my way alongside the railroad and canal. Ahead, I could see a Franklin County Sheriff's car with lights flashing that blocked the road. The deputy leaning against his vehicle waved me past. Perhaps a quarter mile farther on, I could see the aqueduct looking much like a covered bridge. A state police car and two Franklin County Sheriff's SUVs, lights flashing, were parked alongside an ambulance and a white sedan with a single blue light flashing on top, likely belonging to the coroner.

Guy Rudd, the young detective from the State Police Versailles Post, greeted me as I stepped from my car. "So, what do we know?" I asked.

Rudd shook his head. "Not much. A tourist, a young woman, spotted a body hanging from one of the sluices that drain excess water from the aqueduct down into the creek below. The woman was riding one of those short train excursions and saw it as she looked out."

"Did you take a statement from her yet?"

"A brief one. She's pretty shook up. There's really not much she can add other than she saw the body and screamed. The conductor got the train to stop and called the police. No one else was around the body."

"How about the other people on the train? They see anything?"

"I've got a local deputy getting the names and contact information from all the passengers and crew," Rudd said, pointing.

I looked east and saw the back end of the train sitting motionless perhaps a quarter mile down the tracks.

"Are the passengers still on the train?"

"The crew didn't let anyone off. When I got here, I walked down to the train and chatted with the passengers. There are only ten of them. I got the impression that most didn't see anything."

I nodded. "We can follow up later. Do we know anything about the body?"

"Not really. You can see her hair and just a bit of her head from the railroad tracks, but not enough to tell much except that she's probably been there for a while, but you can't see much of her from here. From up on the aqueduct, the water is too murky to see through. We won't know anything for sure until the tech guys get here and pull her out."

"Any idea what age range we're looking at?"

"She's pretty bloated. From what little I could see from standing on the train tracks, she's probably young, but I couldn't even tell that for sure."

"Who was first on the scene?"

Rudd nodded toward a skinny, dark-haired deputy sheriff who looked to be in his late 20s. His face was sallow, and he seemed to be leaning against his SUV for support. "That's Ronnie Hargreaves," Rudd said. "He responded to the call. As you can see, he's not handling it too well. Probably the first time he's seen anything like this."

Standing beside Hargreaves in an ill-fitting uniform was a short, middle-aged man with a balding head and a large belly. I recognized him as Franklin County Sheriff Tyler Haskins. From my experience, he seemed more like a glad-handing politician than a policeman. However, protocol required that I talk to him before talking to his deputy. I walked over to where they were standing.

"Sheriff Haskins," I said, holding out my hand. "Joe Hickman."

We shook hands. "Sure, Joe. I remember you. We had you over in Brookville one time to talk to the Lions. Looks like we've got quite a mess here. To be honest with you, we've got a small department. We're not equipped for an investigation like this. I'm glad you guys are stepping in."

I nodded, happy to hear that I wasn't going to have a pissing contest over who was in charge of the investigation. "We'll do everything we can on this."

Haskins looked back toward Metamora where a crowd of tourists turned gawkers still stood watch. "Guess we're putting a pretty big dent in the shopkeepers' business today."

"It looks like your men are keeping everything under control," I said. Stroking the local sheriff's ego always helped smooth local cooperation in any investigation. "I understand your deputy here was the first on the scene."

Haskins lowered his voice so that the deputy couldn't overhear. "His name's Ronnie Hargreaves. He's only been with the department about a year. Mostly, he patrols the school zones and handles school security. He just happened to be on duty today. You might go easy on him. He's a bit shook up."

I nodded, then moved past Haskins to the young deputy. "First one is always the toughest," I said.

"I hope so," Hargreaves said, a slight quiver in his voice.

"I'm Joe Hickman. I'm going to be in charge of the investigation. I understand you were the first one here."

"Yeah. There's only three of us on duty on weekends for the entire county. I was the closest to Metamora when the call came in. I thought someone was just doing something stupid and got caught on the aqueduct. I didn't know it was someone dead until I got here."

"Did you do anything at the scene? Touch the body? Move anything?"

"No, sir. I didn't. I didn't even go over to the aqueduct. Once I saw her, I called it in and waited for the sheriff."

"Well, I'm going to take a look, Deputy Hargreaves. Would you mind coming along?"

"We'll both come along," Sheriff Haskins said, not allowing

Hargreaves to respond. Hargreaves hesitated, his face turning white. For a moment, I thought he was going to pass out.

Hargreaves stumbled several times as I led him and Sheriff Haskins up the embankment to the railroad tracks where Detective Rudd was already standing. "You can see her from here," Rudd said, pointing down the side of the wooden aqueduct where two spillways, each about one-third of the way across the structure, released a steady flow of water that fell perhaps twenty feet into Duck Creek, a small stream that ran under the aqueduct.

It took a few seconds for my eyes to focus, but then I saw her, or more accurately, what little I could see of her. Long strands of blonde hair hung like a wet mop in the water in the second spillway. You could see the shape of the back of a head, but little more.

"If you really want to see, you'll need these," Rudd said, offering a pair of binoculars. "You may have to move down the tracks to get a good look."

I took the binoculars and moved in the direction Rudd indicated. As I focused in, I could see a hint of what remained of the victim's face. The features were bloated; the skin was discolored and beginning to slough off. It would be challenging to make identification.

I heard a sound behind me. I turned to see Deputy Hargreaves vomiting into a nearby bush.

"Let's take a look from inside the aqueduct," I said.

Rudd and Sheriff Haskins followed me to the aqueduct entrance, Deputy Hargreaves lagging behind. It reminded me of the covered bridges I had explored in my youth. Giant half-wagon wheels braced each side. Above, a pitched roof formed a cathedral ceiling dotted with cobwebs and mud-packed wasp nests. A slow-moving current of dirt-colored water fifteen feet wide moved through the center of the structure. We walked down a narrow walkway along the inside of the aqueduct to the spillway where the body was located.

"How deep is it here?" I asked.

"Not very," Sheriff Haskins answered. "Four feet, maybe five.

When they ran the canal boat, it was just enough water to get it through."

I stared into the water. It took a minute before I could make out the faint outline of a body but nothing else.

"Something must be holding her down," Rudd said.

I stared into the water for a long minute. "Can we block this water off and empty the aqueduct? We'd get a much better look at her and any evidence."

"You have to call DNR," Sheriff Haskins said. "They control the canal. It'll be hell trying to get ahold of them on the weekend."

I turned to Rudd. "Get busy on that. I don't care if you have to pull the governor out of a football game. I want this section of the canal drained, and I want it done today."

As I started to walk back, I noticed Hargreaves had stopped at the entrance to the aqueduct, leaning against it, his face still drained of color. I walked past him without saying anything. The crime scene tech van had arrived, parking next to my car. I walked over to where the techs were exiting their van. I explained what little I knew of the situation, then added, "I don't want you doing anything to alter the scene or pulling her body out until we find out if we can drain the water out of the aqueduct."

They nodded, then one of them said, "Anything worth eating around here?"

"Plenty—if you like meat on a stick and elephant ears."

It took some firm persuasion, cajoling, and a bit of shouting, but by mid-afternoon, the DNR approved blocking the canal and temporarily rerouting the water into Duck Creek. The equipment wasn't on site until Sunday morning. By that afternoon, the water level was low enough to investigate the crime scene.

It was a grim process. From bloating, discoloration, and skin condition, it was evident that the girl had been in the water for some time—maybe weeks. She was fully clothed—a tee shirt, jeans, and sneakers. Her legs were wrapped in a heavy chain attached to a cement block. Nearing eight o'clock, with sunlight fading, the girl's body, still wrapped in chains, was removed from the aqueduct and sent to Indianapolis for examination.

As the body passed by, I heard Sheriff Haskins half-whisper. "Oh, God. I think that's must be Addi Whitaker."

"Who's that?"

Haskins hung his head. "Sixteen-year-old high school girl. Her parents reported her missing a couple of months ago. They hadn't been getting along, and well, we just thought she ran away. There wasn't anything pointing us in a different direction. I figured when she got tired or hungry, she'd come back home."

I looked directly into Haskins's eyes. "She's home now."

I WAS in my office Tuesday afternoon when medical examiner Sophia Garza called. "I've got some information on that girl in the aqueduct," she said. "I won't have the written report with all the test results for another week or more, but I can give you the basics."

"Go ahead."

"Using dental records, I confirmed the girl is Addisyn Whitaker, age 16."

"Got anything on cause of death?"

"Yes. Her skull was fractured. Severe blunt force trauma to the head."

"Before or after she went in the water."

"She was dead when she went in the water—no water in her lungs. But there were other injuries, too. She had a dislocated jaw fracture, a fractured orbital bone, two cracked ribs, and her shoulder was wrenched out of place."

"Sounds like someone beat the crap out of her."

"She took quite a beating. And there's one more thing."

"What's that?"

"She was two months pregnant."

LESS THAN AN HOUR LATER, I was on the road toward Brookville. In my nearly twenty years as an officer, too often I had to destroy the hopes of parents, wives, husbands, to confirm their worst nightmares. No matter how many times, it never got easier.

I called Sheriff Haskins and asked him to join me in notifying the family. We agreed to meet at his office and go in one car. I asked if the family had a pastor who could go with us. By the time I met him at the Sheriff's Department, the minister at the local United Methodist Church was waiting. He looked to be in his early 60s, with short gray hair and deep-set steel-blue eyes that bore the weight of having to console many families who faced death far too early.

I rode with the Sheriff while the pastor drove his own car. We pulled up to a well-kept two-story house in a neighborhood of older houses only two blocks off the main highway in Brookville. As often happened on these notification visits, the door opened before we were halfway up the walk. Both parents stepped onto the front porch to meet us. Their eyes were red and full of the knowledge of what was to come. I was confident that word spread that a body was found in the canal and that they knew their daughter wasn't coming home again—ever. But now it was being made certain.

Because he was local, Sheriff Haskins delivered the news. If the parents had any questions about the investigation, I would answer them. We didn't have the foresight to decide who would bear the brunt of the parents' verbal attack. But they decided that for us.

"You could have done something before this ever happened," Hank Whitaker said, his voice harsh like acid thrown in our faces. "You knew what was going on, and you didn't do a damn thing about it."

The venom was aimed at Sheriff Haskins. Lucille Whitaker tried to pull her husband back and soothe his rage, but she had little success.

"It was all over that social media shit. Instagram or TikTok. Whatever the hell it is. The kids all knew that teacher was not acting right with our daughter. But you didn't do a damn thing. Now she's dead, and you're still not going to do a damn thing."

Sheriff Haskins was taken aback. He took several steps away from Hank, stammering as he tried to get words out in his defense. "But... but Hank, we did. I had the deputy out at the school look at that stuff. It was all kids making stuff up and spreading it around. I can't do anything about that."

"Making stuff up! I've got a daughter I have to put in the ground. That's not making stuff up! You..."

I stepped between Hank and the sheriff, afraid that Hank was ready to throw a punch.

"Hold on, Mr. Whitaker," I said. "I'm in charge of the investigation. I don't know anything about what you're talking about. You want to fill me in?"

Hank stood frozen for a moment, then the rage drained from his face and was replaced by inconsolable grief. When he spoke again, there was a quiver in his voice. "It was that teacher up at the high school. Mr. Kolacki. That's his name. He's the one that done this. It was all over that social media stuff that he was having his way with my daughter."

"Now, look, Hank," Haskins said. "I sent out Ronnie Hargreaves to look into that. He's our security officer with the high school. He knows the people out there. The school looked into it. There was nothing to it. Those were just kids spreading rumors trying to get the teacher in trouble because he's strict on them."

Thinking of the victim's pregnancy, I thought about saying, "Maybe not." But I thought the parents needed to absorb one bit of bad news before facing more. I went in a different direction. "I'll look into it again, Mr. Whitaker. What did you say that teacher's name was?"

"Kolacki. Dylan Kolacki. He teaches social studies and is the girls' volleyball coach."

On the way back to the Sheriff's Department, Haskins let me know his displeasure. "Why'd you tell Whitaker you'd look into that? He's a hothead, and he's obsessed with this shit about that teacher. This Kolacki guy is pretty strict with his students, and they don't like him. The school principal looked into it and found there was nothing there."

At that instant, I decided to break protocol and keep the Sheriff's Department out of the investigation.

THE FOLLOWING DAY, I went into my office in downtown Indianapolis and reviewed the statements taken from the train passengers. As I expected, they did not add anything to the investigation. The medical examiner's written report came in by email. It confirmed the information Dr. Garza had provided me by phone the previous day. It added that Addisyn Whitaker did not have any alcohol or drugs in her system.

I had looked over Sheriff Haskins' file on Addisyn's disappearance, such as it was. There were a few sparse notes from Deputy Hargreaves reporting on his interviews with a couple of Addisyn's friends and his talk with Howard Blankenship, the school's principal. Noticeably missing was an interview with the teacher who Hank Whitaker thought was abusing his daughter. I decided that it was time to confront whatever relationship Addisyn may have had with her teacher.

I made the nearly ninety-minute drive to Addisyn's high school. There was a hollow silence in the school hallways that told me that news of the girl's death had spread to the school. I walked directly to the principal's office.

I knew immediately what kind of small-town school administrator he was. His office was decorated with framed degrees and certificates from every seminar he had ever attended, even thank you certificates from the local Kiwanis, Lions, and Chamber of Commerce, the type of trivial things most executives quickly relegate to a bottom drawer or a trash can. I introduced myself, and he greeted me with a salesman's smile and a limp handshake.

"Good to meet you, Officer Hickman, or can I call you Joe?"

I didn't bother responding or wasting time trying to build rapport. "When did you learn about the accusations that Dylan Kolacki was molesting your student, Addisyn Whitaker?"

The color drained from Blankenship's face. He stammered, trying to fill time until his brain caught up with his mouth. "I... I... Well, it was... There was nothing to it."

"How did you find out about it?"

"Someone overheard Addisyn talking. Sort of bragging, I guess, in the hallway."

"Who was that?"

Blankenship dismissively shook his head. "Oh, I can't remember. It was just some chatter."

"But you can't remember who it was?"

"Someone overheard it. Maybe mentioned it in the teacher's lounge. I don't really remember."

"You said bragging. Was that about having sex with a teacher?"

"I don't know exactly. One of the other teachers overheard it and mentioned it to me. She didn't think it was appropriate and was concerned that it was an effort to get Mr. Kolacki in trouble."

"So, you were concerned about the teacher?"

"Why yes. Of course. These students use social media as a way to get back at teachers. Get them in trouble. Mr. Kolacki is very strict and a difficult grader. That makes him a target of this type of stuff by students."

"So, what did you do?"

"I called Addisyn into the office. Her and Mr. Kolacki."

"At the same time?" My voice betrayed my outrage.

"Why, yes. He was the teacher mentioned. He had a right to know what he was being accused of."

"And when she was in a room with you and Mr. Kolacki–two men, both of whom were authority figures. She, of course, said no."

"She said she never said anything about Mr. Kolacki."

"So, for you, that was the end of it."

"Yes. I explained to Addisyn that spreading lies around school or on social media could result in her getting in serious trouble. But that was it."

"When did all this happen?"

"Oh, maybe in March. I know it was before spring break."

"Did you report this to the police?"

"There was nothing to report. I may have mentioned it to Ronnie, the deputy who serves as the school security officer. But that was just in passing. There really was nothing else to it."

I had been fuming since the sheriff had effectively brushed off Addisyn's disappearance as being a teenage runaway. Now, Blankenship's cavalier approach to reports of a teacher having sex with a student pushed me over the line. "You pompous ass! That girl was two months pregnant when we found her body." I stood. "You know the law requires you to report accusations of child sexual abuse. You'll be lucky if you don't end up in jail. Call Kolacki down here now, then get out of my sight. And don't you say a damn word to anyone about this."

The principal stammered, his face turning red. He then stomped out of his office, slamming the door.

Ten minutes later, Dylan Kolacki swaggered into the principal's office, where I was waiting, seated in the power position behind the principal's desk. Kolacki was a tall, skinny man with long sandy hair that hung onto his neck.

He held out his hand, but I didn't respond. "Sit down," I commanded. I pulled out my well-worn copy of the Miranda warnings from my inside jacket. I read them to Kolacki as his mouth began to drop open.

"Do you understand each of these rights I've read to you?"

"I, uh,..." Kolacki stopped, then shook his head. "What's this about?"

I slowly enunciated each word. "Do. You. Understand. Each. Of. These. Rights. That. I've. Read. To. You."

Kolacki's jaw tightened, and his hands formed into tight fists. After a long, silent moment, he finally answered. "Yes. I understand. But what's this about?"

"Tell me about your affair with Addisyn Whitaker."

Kolacki's recoiled in his chair. "I don't know what you're talking about. Principal Blankenship looked into those rumors and found nothing."

"Principal Blankenship has his own troubles to worry about. Addisyn was the girl found in the canal in Metamora."

Kolacki slumped, his head hanging. "I heard the rumors this morning. It was spreading all through the school."

"She was pregnant. And you're my number one suspect. So, it's time you come clean."

Kolacki's hands began shaking. His voice quivered as he spoke. "Pregnant? How far along? I mean, I didn't know. I didn't have... Look, I...Okay, I shouldn't have done it, but Addisyn...I did some things with her I shouldn't have done. But she wasn't some little innocent girl. She came on to me."

"You're a teacher. You're supposed to be the adult in the room."

There was a long pause. When Kolacki spoke, his voice was barely above a whisper. "She never told me she was pregnant. And I didn't kill her."

"When was the last time you saw her?"

"It was the last day of school. May 22, I think."

"When was the last day you had sex with her?"

Again, there was a long pause. Kolacki leaned forward, his arms crossed at the wrist, resting on the desk. "We only had sex two, maybe three times. The last was on spring break. That would have been in late March. After that, I told her we couldn't do it anymore. I told her we had to wait until after she graduated. Then she would be 18, and I wouldn't be her teacher anymore. We could maybe get together again and not have to hide it."

In the silence that engulfed the office, I stared at him, thinking. If he was telling the truth, the baby couldn't be his. And he knew that by admitting sex with a student, he had just ended his teaching career. Finally, I said. "My crime techs will be here in about an hour. Here's what you're going to do. First, you are not going back in that classroom. Ever. Not only here, but anyplace. Second, you will go into the teachers' lounge and stay there until my crime lab people come to get you. You are going to give them any DNA sample they request. Then you will take them to your car, let them search it, and take samples of anything they find. Do you understand?"

"Don't you need a warrant for that?"

"Not if you give us consent. But if you refuse, I'm going to put cuffs on you right now. Then I'm going to march you through this school at the next passing period so all the students get a look at who you really are."

Kolacki buried his head in his hands and gave a short nod.

I radioed for a crime scene van. While waiting for the techs to arrive, I called the principal back into his office. "I need to talk to a couple of girls, friends of Addisyn mentioned in the sheriff's file."

"I don't know," Blankenship said. "I think someone should be in the room with them."

"That's fine, but not you," I said. "Who else would you suggest?"

"Maybe Mrs. Carver. She's one of our English teachers in charge of the yearbook. She's pretty close with the students."

"Call her down."

A few minutes later, a tall, sharply dressed woman entered the principal's office. Her speech was as formal as her posture. After a brief discussion, she agreed to stay in the office while I questioned Addisyn's friends.

Anne Rutherford was the first girl summoned to the office. She was a tall, lanky girl with stringy dishwater-blonde hair that hung shapelessly past her shoulder, wearing jeans with small horizontal rips along her thigh and an oversized sports jersey. Mrs. Carver introduced me and emphasized that she wasn't in trouble. "You've heard about Addisyn?"

The girl looked down and nodded. "Everybody knows. It's all over the school."

Mrs. Carver continued. "The police need to ask you a few questions. I'll stay here while he's doing it. Is that okay?"

There was a short hesitation, then she nodded.

"I'm sorry about your friend," I said. "I just need to ask a handful of questions. First, when was the last time you saw Addisyn Whitaker?"

"I saw her over Memorial Day. A bunch of us went to the state park to swim and hang out. I'm not sure I saw her after that."

"Did she ever say anything to you about your teacher, Mr. Kolacki?"

Anne's demeanor immediately changed. There was a flash of anger in her eyes. "Yeah. She said he was a perve. The whole school knew about him." Angry tears filled her eyes. "Did he do this? Did Mr. Kolacki kill Addisyn?"

I shook my head. "We're looking into it, but I don't think so."

Anne pointed her finger at me. "You knew about it, though. You knew about what Mr. Kolacki was doing with Addi."

I tried to be understanding. "I'm new to this. I didn't know anything about your friend until her body was found on Saturday...I didn't know anything about Mr. Kolacki abusing her until today. But now that I'm involved, I'll investigate every possibility."

"But you cops knew," Anne insisted. "Addi told that creep deputy at the school."

"Do you mean Deputy Hargreaves?"

"Yeah, he's the one. Deputy Ronnie. That's what he told us to call him. But we all know he's a creep."

"So why do you call Deputy Hargreaves a creep?"

"He always tries to act cool. Gawking at all the girls.

Commenting on how sexy we look. Telling us he was going to have to take us for a ride in his cop car. Just sorta creepy."

"What did Addisyn tell Deputy Ronnie?"

"She told him about that perve, Mr. Kolacki. I know she did. I was standing right next to her when she did it. She told him about how Mr. Kolacki had, well, done stuff with her."

"Stuff?"

"Oh, God. Sex. Do I have to draw you a picture?"

I took a deep breath. "When was this?"

"Right when school was getting out for the summer. She waited until then because she didn't want to be around Mr. Kolacki anymore."

"So, what happened then? Did Deputy Hargreaves take a report?"

"I don't know. All I know is that I saw Addisyn getting into his police car a couple of days later. They were leaving the school."

"Did you talk to Addisyn about it later?"

Anne shook her head. "No. I didn't see much of Addisyn after that. I think she started seeing some guy, so she wasn't around much."

After Anne left, I sat in the principal's office, thinking through the information I had uncovered. No one had done right by Addisyn. I was determined I would not fail her.

Two techs arrived, and I directed them to the teachers' lounge with directions to take fingerprints and samples of hair and saliva from Kolacki. When they finished, I took them to the parking lot. Kolacki pointed out his battered Camry. I told the techs to go over it for hair, blood, and fibers and anything else that might connect the teacher to Addisyn.

I kept going over my conversation with Anne Rutherford when something clicked into place. I dashed to my car and called Sheriff Haskins on his cell phone. After we exchanged greetings, I got right to the point. "Sheriff, early last summer, did Ronnie Hargreaves ever file a report about Dylan Kolacki molesting or raping Addisyn Whitaker?"

"No. If he had, I'd have made sure it got investigated. If there was anything to it, I'd have sent it to the prosecutor."

"You're sure?"

"Absolutely certain."

I stood in the school parking lot, thoughts circling in my head.

"Joe? You still there?

"Yeah, Sheriff. I need your permission to search Hargreaves's patrol vehicle."

"What do you want to do that for?"

"Just following a lead. Do I have your okay?"

"Sure. Search all you like."

"One more thing. Do your patrol cars carry chains for pulling motorists out of ditches or snow drifts?"

"Sure. But we don't use them much, though. Usually, we just call a tow truck."

"Don't say anything to Hargreaves, but send him out to the high school with his vehicle. Tell him I'm arresting Dylan Kolacki."

"The teacher?"

"Yes, the teacher."

I called the two crime scene techs from where they were processing Kolacki's car. I explained what I wanted them to do as soon as Hargreaves arrived. We did not have to wait long.

Hargreaves pulled into the school parking lot, lights flashing and siren blaring. He stopped next to me and jumped out like a television cop. "What's going on?"

"Give me your keys and stay right there."

Hargreaves protested, but after talking with the sheriff on his radio, he handed his keys over. Thirty minutes later, my crime scene techs confirmed that they found blood in the back of Hargreaves's service vehicle. They quick checked and found that the blood matched Addisyn's blood type. It would take several days to verify the DNA, but I already knew the source of the blood.

I walked to where Hargreaves stood, fidgeting. I stared into his eyes. "Did you really have to kill Addisyn Whitaker?"

His eyes went wide, and then he shook his head and gave a feeble laugh. "What is this? A joke?"

"No joke. My crime techs have already found blood and hair in the back of your SUV. The blood type matches Addisyn. It will only take a few days for DNA to confirm it belongs to her. And when we check your DNA, I'm certain it will match Addisyn's baby."

Hargreaves stood stiff, every muscle tight. Then suddenly he lunged to get back in his SUV. I stuck out my leg and tripped him. He went sprawling across the parking lot. I planted my knee in his back then grabbed one arm and pulled it behind his back. I used my weight to keep him from moving while I grabbed the other arm and and put on the handcuffs, clicking them tight. As I read Hargreaves his Miranda warnings, he began shaking and burst into tears.

"I didn't mean to," he said between sobs.

"Don't give me that shit, Ronnie. I saw her." I resisted the urge to pound Ronnie's face into the asphalt. Instead, I hoisted him up by the handcuffs and threw him headlong into the backseat of my cruiser.

DUCK CREEK AQUEDUCT, WHITEWATER CANAL AND METAMORA

Nearly 180 years old, the historic Duck Creek Aqueduct is the nation's only remaining wooden aqueduct. Located on the eastern edge of Metamora in Franklin County in southeastern Indiana, it carries the historic Whitewater Canal over Duck Creek.

Metamora and the Whitewater Canal date back to the heyday of Indiana's canal dreams—canals intended to link Indiana's farms and forests to the major markets in the eastern United States. But by 1839, only 76 miles of the Whitewater Canal were finished, and the state was bankrupt.

The canal carried keel boats across the Duck Creek Aqueduct

from Lawrenceburg to Hagerstown until the end of the Civil War. But now Metamora, population 402, the canal, and the aqueduct only serve weekend tourists.

A horse-drawn canal boat operated on the canal from 1989 through 2019, taking passengers from Metamora across the Duck Creek Aqueduct and back. However, service stopped temporarily due to the pandemic, then permanently in 2022 when the front keel of the boat collapsed during a safety inspection. However, tourists can still take the Whitewater Canal Railroad past the Duck Creek Aqueduct or walk along the footpath from Metamora to get a close-up look.

SECRETS AT THE INDIANA WAR MEMORIAL

BY CAROL HALL

As Rex entered the Indiana War Memorial, he tried focusing his thoughts on the men lost on the USS Indianapolis and not the man in the black jogging suit he had just met outside. He had no real ties to the USS Indianapolis fatalities or the causalities but he wanted to feel connected to the tragedy. By focusing on the event he could feel good about himself and take his mind off his other role, his role on the street which paid the bills. He could sit in the communications room and talk to visitors. He would be part of history not a part of his seedy life style. No one but him knew, he hoped. He imagined what the public thought of him when they entered the cubby room of the USS Indianapolis. He wanted to playact like he was serving others and really doing something for his county and not committing a crime. As much as he wanted the public to admire him, he feared someone would accuse him of subterfuge and allege him of trying to look the part and play a law-abiding citizen instead who he really was. Those thoughts consumed his life with worry and anxiety. Today he felt especially fearful. Rex felt someone was following him. His real name was Rex but folks outside the Indiana War Memorial knew him by another name.

At the information desk, the security officer, known to everyone as Doug, was attempting to organize himself for the day. It had been a long problematic two days at home having to deal with his parents and other family members since the death of his brother. Inside the War Memorial he stepped into his professional role. He tried to make himself look as if he had authority from behind the desk. He wanted to be noticed by the general public and feel important. As he was trying to assume this role he heard: "One, two, three." *She's counting the tiles to the front desk.*

The counting stopped. Since Doug no longer heard her, he decided she must be inside the ladies room. At least that was her usual pattern. Then he looked up. "Uh?" She was now in front of him staring into his face but avoiding his eyes.

"Yes, I see you, Julie. I know what you want. Just one minute." Doug took one of the desk keys and unlocked a cabinet. He looked down to the bottom shelf and grabbed one of several plastic bags with something resembling terry cloth on top. As he picked up one of the bags, he felt the bottom of it. Since he was now familiar with what she needed he knew it was what Rose left for her.

"Here." He handed the bag over to Julie. "I hope this is enough for today. Rose isn't here yet. She won't be in until later. You could have waited." Julie grabbed the bag from him and sprinted away. Doug looked at her. *What else will that woman do today to make my job difficult? Rose needs to be here when we open. Why does Rose always get special privileges because she is a single woman with grandmother responsibilities? Both Julie and Rose think they are so entitled.*

Doug's thoughts moved to Henry, another fly in the ointment. *The one person who caters to everyone else but me. He's always checking on me instead of doing what he could be doing to make everything a smooth running operation here. How would the place run without him? It would be wonderful, less stress!*

Doug took a gas station coffee cup out of the bag next to a pastry. Everyone made fun of him for drinking his gas station coffee which they called poor man's Starbucks while showing off their gourmet coffees. *My coffee is still warm, not hot, but warm and it kept the pastry at the perfect temperature.* He took a sip. *Yes. That hits the spot. Okay. Sandwiches here, chips, and an apple.* Then he felt something inside his pocket. *Still there. Maybe today I can take care of this.* He smiled. How he wished he had the guts to follow through with that one special request from his family. Thinking about the room at the top of the building, Doug looked up at the ceiling. Then his eyes moved forward.

A woman with two small children stood in front of him. "Sir. There is a strange person. Well, I think it's a female, in the women's restroom."

"I know, I know. But I can't go in there. If you are afraid, you will just have to wait until she leaves."

"But I think she is bathing in the sink. My girls need to use the restroom." The mother glared at her two children. "I told you girls to go before we left the house. Didn't I say this place might be scary." Then she said to Doug. "This is one of those places recommended to parents to take field trips with their children. We live in a small town."

"Ma'am, I cannot go in there. A female employee should be here any minute. She's probably running late as usual. Life gets in the way sometimes. Oh, there she is now."

"Rose, this lady would like to use the restroom. It sounds like you know who is sink bathing. Rose, please see if Julie is almost finished? Sorry, Rose, this is in your jurisdiction. I can't go in there."

The Mom looked at both Rose and Doug. "It's not just me. My girls are afraid to go in the restroom."

Rose looked at Doug. "I'll take care of it. Don't I always?" She walked toward the women's restroom and a few minutes later returned carrying the same plastic bag Doug had handed to Julie. The contents looked dissimilar from before and rather nasty looking even through the plastic. He watched Rose walk away with it. He knew she was probably taking it to the trash receptacle. He didn't know or care where as long as it and its contents did not come behind the desk.

Doug just wanted to finish his usual morning activities, putting his lunch in the cabinet and having his morning coffee. He believed Rose had taken care of the problem since the Mom and two girls came out of the women's restroom later. Doug hoped a tranquil day could begin. His coffee was half gone. His stomach rumbled so he wished it would be close to lunch time. Then he saw Julie eyeing the front doors. She had on different clothes from before and looked clean and primped after looking so ragged, filthy and disheveled. She must be waiting for the mission food truck before taking her journey to neverland with her imaginary friends. Considering the huge homeless population, Doug knew he should appreciate Julie was still the only homeless person who had special in-house privileges as per Henry and Rose. What he worried over but kept to himself was Julie's connections with other folks from the streets who may try to find a way to gain the same special privileges.

"Oh, hell!" he yelled out loud realizing he spilled what was the rest of his coffee. *Hopefully no one heard that.* He got up leaving his post to grab some paper towels left on a shelf not seen by the public and didn't notice a person coming around the side of the desk. He thought he saw something or someone exit the area from the corner of his eye.

Doug's point of concentration ended when he heard, "Sir, do you know when the seminar starts?"

"What? Where? Seminar? Which one?" Doug turned his head.

"I was told there was a special history club meeting today."

"Sorry, you need to go over to those ladies over there. They can connect you with anything going on." Doug looked over and saw there was no table by the entrance to the meeting room. "Oh, they're not there today. I think Rose stepped out for a minute to check on someone in the women's restroom. I really can't help you. Just go over there and wait until I find someone to help you."

The man kept staring. Doug felt the man was staring a hole right through him and then walked away quickly. As the man turned away, Doug had a feeling of déjà vu. The man looked so familiar. He had seen him before here at the museum. *Maybe I am imagining something or someone. The blue parka he wore looked so familiar.*

The man left. Where did he go? Inside the auditorium? Maybe. Doug knew his eyes did not deceive. The man was there and then in a blink had gone. Doug was positive he had seen him in the building before. He saw Rose leaving the auditorium. "Rose, do you know anything about a history lecture? There was a gentleman here inquiring. I looked for you but you were not at your post."

Rose rolled her eyes around. "As usual I had to take care of a security problem. I believe security is your jurisdiction. I knew this was going to be a strange day when I got up this morning. Who is that person who just went into the auditorium?"

"Maybe that was the man who asked about the history lecture and then disappeared."

Rose rolled her eyes again. "No one disappears around here. You just are not paying attention. You are the security person."

"But do you know anything about a history lecture?"

"No." Rose looked at Doug as if he'd lost it. "I can check the schedule but I am positive there are no lectures, history or otherwise anytime this week." Rose started to walk away.

"Where did I put my lunch?" Doug felt he was losing it.

Rose responded, "You seem to have many problems today. Who misplaces his lunch?"

"Maybe I can join the homeless at the Mercy Center Mission food truck." Doug laughed his comment.

"They don't serve on Wednesdays. Just Tuesdays, Thursdays and Saturday." Rose explained. "That reminds me to ask you. I wonder what Julie does for food on Sundays and Mondays. Or today?"

Doug scratched his head. "You'll have to ask Henry. I think they have a special arrangement. Just like you and Julie with the grooming, I thought maybe the USS Indianapolis folks have a place for her to hibernate for a few days. She is always walking out of there with a bottle of water. And that is the only place around here that serves bottled water unless there is a reception which includes bottles of water. Oh, where is the American cheese sandwich? Now where is the rest of my food? I'm still missing a ham salad sandwich, an apple and a bag of chips." Doug felt for something inside his pocket. "Wait a minute, I'm missing...oh, no, not that too. Oh, wrong pocket."

Rose rolled her eyes and walked away.

WHENEVER JULIE WENT DOWN the long tunnel, she could feel her heart beating. But today was special. She felt extra nice and cleaned up. Rose gave her some really nice clothes and that soap smelled wonderful. It was great to feel dry fresh armpits and be wearing some clean underwear. If only she could get to a beauty salon. And she found herself a real picnic: a ham salad sandwich which she knew was really made from Kroger bologna, a bag of potato chips and a big juicy red apple. It worked for her knowing a security person was so careless. "Bad for him, good for me," she said out loud. It was easy for Julie to manage to beg a bottle of water from the USS Indianapolis guys. She wished they would keep soda in their cubby or maybe they have some but hid it too well. At least they were good for something. Cookies from the history event last Saturday were a big hit, she thought. She wished she had grabbed more.

As she entered the museum area, she started walking by the various display cabinets. She recognized each one, French and Indian war, American Revolution, another war with England, Civil War, World War I, World War II and Afghanistan. She verbally acknowledged each of them. Many of the earlier nurses seem to sit inside the displays waiting for her. They were her sisters in war.

"Every war has its ladies. I can say hello and smile when I stop by each of them. I think I will dine in a bunker today." Julie did not care if heads turned to look at her as she spoke out loud.

"As I will be dinning with Larry again in a bunker near the surgery tent, I can eat my lunch and enjoy my luncheon date with Larry. Oh. Wow! This does look good. Better than military food."

Then she laughed. "I passed on the waxy cheese. I did leave the nasty cheese sandwich for the security guy. Where are you, Larry? Lunch is ready."

"MOMMY, isn't that the lady we saw in the bathroom? She's talking out loud and no one is with her."

"Come here, Sara. Abby give me your hand. Let's go in this room."

"Mommy, you said we would see real Indians and we would see where Daddy used to live." Abby looked up at her mother.

"I thought Daddy lived across the street." Sara glared at her sister. "The Indians aren't real."

"I didn't see Daddy today, Abby. This is a museum. It's all pretend. I explained that to you."

Sara noticed Julie looking at them. Then she heard her say "Little angels."

"Mommy, the lady said we were angels."

"Let's go, girls."

"I'M GOING to follow the angels."

Julie watched with envy as the mother whisked her little girls away. Then she rose, leaving the rest of the picnic lunch and followed the mother and children on out of the area. "I left the rest of the lunch for you, Larry."

REX LOOKED around the USS Indianapolis communications room. "How do Dan and Mark go through so much water? There was an entire case here a week ago. They didn't even touch the soda. Maybe they don't know about the soda. I guess I do a good job of hiding it." He looked up and thought he saw someone out of the corner of his eye, coming out of the auditorium wearing a dark blue parka. *Oh, no. it couldn't be.*

Rose looked away. *Sirens. They're outside. Oh, my. Not today.*

To Henry, Wednesdays were his Mondays. He wished today could be a hump day with his schedule. Traffic was always bad. Then his cell phone rang. He hit the green icon on the dash. It had to be answered. He recognized the number. "Yeah, this is Henry Armstrong."

Henry heard from his phone. "We have another one. Looks almost like the one from last week. And there is a DEA agent inside your building."

"I'm on my way in, detective. I should be there in approximately fifteen minutes. Traffic was backed up. I believe there was a crash this morning."

Another dead body. Probably another stupid homeless person. At least this one was across the street. Hopefully it wasn't a murder. Maybe an overdose. Hopefully the staff would not need to be interrogated again.

Henry tried scrolling down the numbers on the dash for the one saying front desk. *No one is picking up. What the…No special events are scheduled today. Sure hope no school groups are coming through today or are parked across the street near where the body is. I wonder if Julie knows this one. Let me try Doug's cell.*

The desk telephone rang but Doug never heard it and never felt his cell phone vibrate. He realized a crowd had zipped to the door where they were congregating. *What was going on?* It had to be some type of security issue. He grabbed the walkie talkie and followed the mass of bodies.

"Hey folks, what is going on? Let me through. Security here. Please move. I need to get through."

Doug looked out between the mass of heads and shoulders. The problem seemed to be across the street. A crowd was surrounding a person on the ground. He pushed his way through the crowd and ran down the steps. As he was crossing Michigan Street he could see EMT's trying to maneuver a body onto a gurney. It wasn't in a body bag. There was nothing covering the face of the person.

Doug looked back and saw the woman with the two little girls crossing the street. She looked frantic. Right behind her was Julie. *It has to be someone Julie knows.* He watched for a reaction from Julie but she could be very stoic. He looked up. Henry had arrived.

"Where have you been, Doug? I've been trying to call you for a good twenty minutes."

"Busy morning. A lot going on. You know how it is. Julie back doing her thing. I think she stole my lunch. My food is missing. You weren't there with your usual handout and the lunch truck wasn't here. My food is gone."

"Disorganization on your part should not cause a major flaw in the security of the building which includes you answering the telephone. But you were busy thinking about lunch."

Doug kept his eyes on the crowd. His mind was elsewhere. He felt the small plastic sack inside his pocket. He was hoping today was the day. Maybe he could deliver it today.

A thick crowd surrounded the body while a tall robust detective tried to control the gathering: "Move away folks. Unless you know the victim or are a witness." One by one the crowd began to disperse.

"Gawkers," one of the first responders said.

The crowd thinned out. Rex, Doug, Rose, Julie, Henry, and a woman with two small children and a few remaining others stood around a tall heavy set detective. "Okay folks. I know just one of you must know something about this man and maybe what happened," the detective said.

"Can someone watch my girls while I look?"

Julie stepped forward. "I can."

"No," the mother responded as she clinched the tiny hands.

Rose stepped forward. "Go ahead. Ma'am. I can take them."

As the mother let go of each little hand Rose slid her hand into a hand of each child. Rose held hands with both little girls, one child either side of her.

Julie looked at Rose holding the little hands. Then her eyes drifted toward the sky. She needed to get back inside the building tonight to sleep. Where else would she go? She remembered she also needed to find food for her next meal. Her thoughts returned to Larry. She didn't notice the rest of the people surrounding the young woman.

The atmosphere surrounding the young mother was one of apprehension and nervousness punctuated with quiet. No one was breathing except for the woman. What no one noticed was the mysterious man from the auditorium standing behind the others.

The crowd watched as the young mother went forward. She stood there silently for a few minutes. She stared at the face of the man lying down. She shook her head negatively. "I do not know this person." Everyone in the crowd exhaled in relief. The mother retreated. Rose took the children to her. The mother grabbed their small hands and hurried away.

Several others went closer to the body and shook their heads. One man walked away and looked back as if maybe he was wrong. As Rex observed this, he knew he needed to get away. He knew he should have stayed at his post at the *USS Indianapolis*.

Rose saw Julie standing by a trash receptacle. She crossed to her. "Julie, I think they need you to look at the person. It could be someone you know."

Julie stared at the bark on one of the trees. Rose could tell by the expression on Julie's face, the deceased was someone with whom she was familiar. Rose looked up and received a nod from Henry. He studied Julie's reaction.

Rose recognized the man who had been sitting in the auditorium that morning. She watched him as he made a wide circle around the area, took a quick look at the body then walked away. She saw Henry slowly approaching Julie. Henry tried to take her arm but she pulled away with a sudden sulk and then faced the opposite direction. Henry said something to Julie. Rose looked for a response but there was none. Rose watched Doug and noticed he kept feeling something inside of his pocket.

What no one observed was Rex, who began walking the area while trying not to be seen. At one point he moved in between two of the remaining gawkers trying to mask his presence.

Rex wanted to get a good look at the man on the ground. He knew him. It was the man he had met earlier that day, the man in the black jogging suit. After recognizing his early morning customer, Rex turned to walk away. His head was down but could see a male figure coming toward him.

Doug, Rose and Henry all watched Rex as the man in the parka took something out of Rex's pocket. As Rex was being led away, they heard him exclaim: "I didn't intentionally kill him. It was an accident. I didn't know what was in that baggie. I am just a delivery man."

Doug's mind was a thousand feet away at the top of the building across the street, a beautiful room at the top of the War Memorial with a glass roof stained glass motifs surrounded by portraits of generals from World War I.

Today is the day. I can do this. Doug patted the little plastic sack in his pocket as he headed up to the top of the Indiana War Memorial to leave something of his brother for all of eternity.

After leaving the little plastic bag in a crevice, he saw Julie. She was crouched down in a place not noticeable to the hundreds of visitors coming in and out of the magnificent upper room. Doug knew this was the place she stayed during the night. It would be their secret. Henry had followed both of them and stood in the doorway as Rose stood behind him and watched all three.

INDIANA WAR MEMORIAL

The Indiana War Memorial, which faces Michigan Street, is bounded by Michigan, Pennsylvania, Meridian and Vermont streets. It has a square formation intended to resemble the Mausoleum of Halicarnassus in Turkey, one of The Seven Wonders of the Ancient World.

The building has three floors. On the first floor is the Pershing Auditorium, reception rooms, exhibit space, USS Indianapolis communications room replica, and a hallway full of flags and memorial plaques. Listed on the plaques are the names of all Hoosiers who participated in World War I in addition to all Hoosiers who are missing in action or were killed in World War II, the Korean War or the Viet Nam War.

The top floor is the shrine room. In the center stands an altar and above it a beautiful glass ceiling. On the walls hang portraits of generals, not just American, but others serving in World War I.

A long hallway leads to the bottom of the building which is a museum with displays and memorabilia from all the wars in which Americans fought, beginning with the French and Indian War, contested from 1754 to 1763. Some of the local military heroes have display cabinets with their uniforms, dog tags, canteens, medals and other memorabilia. One of the local heroes is Graham Martin, one of the first African-American officers in the U.S. Navy. He commanded a ship for four years during World War II.

MURDER ON THE AVENUE
BY JOHN F. ALLEN

*T*he Madame C.J. Walker Theatre
Indianapolis, Indiana
October 1959

SHE WAS PRETTY.

Almost as pretty as Billie Holiday, and just as dead.

All I knew was that the young woman was a lounge singer who worked with a jazz band. According to the marquee, her name was Delilah James and judging by the crowd of people who had come to see her, she could certainly draw a crowd.

My job was to investigate and find the murderer. As one of a handful of Negro homicide detectives with the Indianapolis Police Department, I was one of the only cops who cared when a Colored woman was found dead.

The dressing room where she was found was dark, with the only light from the row of vanities along the left wall. Shadows throughout the room added to the ominous setting. The scent of perfume and cosmetics lingered in the air. Nothing more than faint traces of a much less melancholy time.

A crime scene photographer snapped pictures of the young woman and the room, as he moved carefully to avoid disturbing any potential evidence. She worked with a local jazz band, one of the last ones scheduled to perform here for the year.

The Madame C.J. Walker Theatre was at one time, the mecca of entertainment for the Colored community in Indianapolis. Lately, Negroes had been displaced from the once thriving Colored neighborhood, to other places around the city. Some were able to afford houses in the suburbs. As a result, folks weren't coming out to the theatre much anymore.

"Detective Sea Ferguson."

I turned to see a young, Negro, uniformed officer. He was visibly nervous and nauseous.

"Yes, Officer?"

"We've cleared out the ballroom and formed a perimeter around the building," he said, as he stood with rigid aversion to the presence of the corpse.

"Good, when the coroner arrives send him in."

"Yes sir," the officer said, as he turned to leave the room, along with the crime scene photographer.

Alone, I scanned the dressing room again.

There were minimal, but obvious signs of a struggle, such as broken, displaced furniture, scuff marks on the floor, torn clothing on the victim, and she was wearing only one shoe. Not to mention the dark bruising around the girl's neck.

I knelt next to the body. It had already been outlined, and despite the obvious trauma, the expression on her face was almost serene. Her hair was splayed around her head, the limbs of her corpse akimbo. The sequined gown she wore sparkled in the ceiling lights, which gave her an ethereal glow.

I saw traces of lipstick smear that I hadn't seen before and leaned in closer. The aroma of perfume mingled with a faint, acrid odor I couldn't place, emanated from her body.

A hand tapped my left shoulder. "Purty, young thang ain't she?"

I stood and took the mug offered from my partner, Detective Russell Jackson. He was short and slightly rotund, with a bald head. His ebony skin glistened from the muted lighting.

"Yes, she *was*," I said, as I took a sip of coffee.

Jackson pulled a small notebook from the inner breast pocket of his jacket. "She was a local girl, lived a couple of blocks from here, over on Bright Street."

I pursed my lips. "Any next of kin?"

"From what one of the other singers told me, she lived with her momma, unmarried, and no children. She say she found her like this after rehearsals. I figure we'd notify her momma after the coroner arrives."

I took a sip of my coffee and nodded.

"She also told me Delilah had a boyfriend named Leroy Manning who's mean as a rattlesnake." Jackson referred to his notes. "They say he's a nickel and dime hustler and alley mechanic, and he was here earlier before the rehearsals. Manning and Delilah got into it bad before he stormed out."

"Where is the other singer now?" I asked.

Jackson flashed a toothy grin. "I got her stashed in the property manager's office. I figured you might wanna ask her some questions of your own."

I took a sip of coffee and nodded. "You know me so well."

Jackson tipped a gestural cap at me. "I aims to please."

I smirked. "So, it looks like we have a prime suspect," I said. "Does he have a record?"

Jackson grinned. "Is fat meat greasy? Street gamblin', petty theft, assault, and an illegal weapon charge. He got sent up for eight years at Pendleton."

I pursed my lips and rubbed my chin.

The sound of a person entering the room shook me from my reverie. It was Dr. Wendell "Bulldog" Sherman—*County Coroner*. He was a short, portly man, who wore rumpled clothing and smelled of black licorice and flatulence. His pate barely caught the vanity lights which cast dull shadows across the ruddy, pock marked skin of his face.

"How's it going *boys*," he barked, as he knelt down beside the body with a grunt.

Jackson and I looked at each other with a bitter frown. Bulldog was one of those crackers who liked to think he was a friend to the Negro. But the truth was, he was just as prejudiced in how he spoke and thought, as any other racist white person. In his mind, calling two grown Colored men, *boys*, was no big deal.

He had the reputation that he held a certain predilection for our food, our music, and our women. In fact, he was a frequent patron of the Walker Theatre, even when his wife wasn't accompanying him.

"Bulldog," we both chimed.

He checked for a pulse, as he was obliged to do. Truth was, you didn't require a medical degree to be named coroner in Marion County, but rumors had it that Bulldog was incompetent. It was his gullible assumption that his nickname was a reference to his college football prowess, and not his countenance.

Bulldog shook his plump head slowly as he stood. His fat, loose, jowls quivered, which gave him the resemblance of his nickname.

"She was a pretty little Colored gal," he said, with a lecherous grin.

"You got here fast," I said.

Bulldog harrumphed. "Well, luckily I just happened to be in the neighborhood."

Jackson and I glanced at each other.

"From the looks of things, looks like somebody with a mean streak came after her, and choked her to death."

I stifled a chuckle of amusement that this *educated* white man, who clearly believed he was superior, and would only state the obvious. If we had been white, veteran homicide detectives, things would've been said much differently.

"We won't know everything until the autopsy but looks pretty open and shut to me. What do you boys think?" Bulldog asked, his beady eyes glared at us like tiny blue marbles.

"It would appear so," I replied.

Bulldog looked at me quizzically, "Do you have another theory *detective?*"

I smirked. His emphasis on the word detective was another racial jibe, all too common from white men like him. Bulldog wasn't very bright, nor as clever as he thought himself to be.

"No, not at the moment. I've just learned in my ten years as a homicide detective that things aren't always as they appear. Present company excluded, of course. But, as you said, we won't know everything until after the autopsy. Good thing Doc Garrison will be handling that."

Bulldog frowned, his pug shaped nose flared, his face went beet red, and I could've sworn I saw smoke billowing from his large, floppy ears. I knew I'd hit a sore spot. He was such an incompetent pathologist, that his first and last autopsy resulted in the family of a heart attack victim having a closed casket funeral. The county hired Dr. David Garrison as the official Medical Examiner almost immediately.

"Are you being wise with me, Ferguson?" he growled.

"Why not at all Doctor. Why I'm just a poor Colored gumshoe trying to make something of himself," I said, with as much aplomb and covert sarcasm as I could manage.

Bulldog sneered, as he turned to leave in silence.

Once he had left, Jackson and I turned to each other and laughed.

BERNICE TROTTER WAS a mahogany-complexioned young woman, with large doe-shaped eyes and full lips. She was the other singer Jackson had spoken to earlier. Her body trembled despite my jacket draped across her slender shoulders. Bernice was obviously rattled, and for good reason. But, in spite of her current ordeals, she was being very cooperative.

"So, Miss Trotter, according to what you told my partner, you saw Delilah get into a heated exchange with Leroy Manning earlier this evening?"

She let out a sigh and silent tears streamed down her rounded cheeks. Her red eyes stared out at her interlaced hands, which rested on her lap.

"Yes, that's right," Bernice said.

I pursed my lips. "Do you have any idea what they were fighting about?"

She shook her head. "No, not really. All I heard was Leroy yell at her that, she better handle things, or else he would, once and for all."

"To your knowledge, was Leroy prone to violence toward Miss James?" I asked.

Bernice turned her head and closed her eyes before she turned back to speak. "Ain't no secret Leroy got a temper. Though he mostly just yell at Delilah, but this was different. Whatever he was pissed off about, it was bad. I ain't never seen him go off like that. He grabbed her round the throat and was about to wring her neck like a chicken."

"What stopped him?" Jackson asked.

She flashed a doleful grimace. "I suppose it was on account of me. I took after him with a mop handle and wailed on him good. The other girls and the musicians must have heard the commotion, cause they came running into the dressing room. Leroy tore off right after that. She said she wasn't feeling well, so I gave her a tonic. I told her to go lie down in the dressing room for a while."

I gave a grim grin. "That was very brave of you Miss Trotter."

She shrugged. "I don't know about all that."

"Was there anything else going on in Miss James' life, or that happened recently, that you can remember?" I asked.

Bernice sat in silence for several seconds, her large, dark brown eyes glazed over in thought.

"There was this creepy white man who always came to all of her shows. He would steal glances with her after we ended. One time, I think he even sent her flowers," she said.

"Can you describe him?" Jackson asked.

She pursed her lips. "He was heavyset, but he always wore a hat and sunglasses."

Jackson and I glanced at each other.

"Thank you, Miss Trotter. You've been very helpful," I said, as I took my jacket, and Jackson and I left the room.

JACKSON and I arrived at the morgue early the next morning. The Indianapolis Police Department is never in a hurry to investigate the death of a Colored person, even a murder. Luckily for us, Dr. Garrison was invested in his job regardless of what color the cadaver was. Garrison was at least sixty years old, if he were a day. He was a loner, no wife or kids. Being the Marion County Medical Examiner was his life, and according to him, he preferred it that way.

The distinctive odor of antiseptic cleanser and formaldehyde permeated the morgue and added to the gloomy atmosphere. Of course, the sheet-covered body on the slab in front of us definitely contributed in its own right.

"Detective Ferguson, Detective Jackson, too bad we always meet under these circumstances," Garrison said, with a hearty handshake.

The Medical Examiner was a friendly man. One of the very few white men who was eagerly willing to help find justice for Negroes, and work with Negro cops. He and I were both about six feet tall, but due to a back injury he sustained during the Great War, he walked with a stooped posture. His thin, gnarled frame, aquiline nose and his natural tonsure, gave him the appearance of a vulture.

Garrison pulled back the sheet from the corpse of Delilah James. Her complexion last night had been an even chestnut, but today the gray pallor of death gave her an eerie ashen appearance. Despite the numerous dead bodies I'd seen during the course of the recent World War and my time on the police force, the death of a young woman or child always hit hardest.

The 'Y' incision along the front of her upper torso extended to her abdomen and was a grotesque marring of what had once been the body of a beautiful, young woman. Jackson averted his eyes whenever possible. He always took issue with the nude bodies of female victims.

"Were you able to determine a specific cause of death?" I asked.

Garrison harrumphed. "It's funny you should ask that question so pointedly, Detective. I spoke to Dr. Sherman earlier this morning before you arrived. He seemed agitated and demanded to conduct the autopsy himself. When I refused, he told me how he surmised the victim died. I reminded him that I was the county medical examiner, and it was within my purview, after a complete postmortem examination, to come to my own conclusion."

I smirked. "I bet old Bulldog was none too pleased with your exertion of authority?"

Garrison grinned. "He most certainly was not. The asshole had the nerve to threaten to go to the mayor about it. I told him if he was so inclined to do so, then have at it. Then, I hung up and fast tracked the autopsy."

Jackson and I both snickered.

"Anyway, all appearances would indicate that the victim died as a result of bodily trauma and strangulation, given the finger shaped contusions on her neck, numerous ones on various areas of her torso, and a broken hyoid bone. But you'd be wrong."

The overhead light created an opaque glare on thick lens of Garrison's eyeglasses, as he picked up a clipboard and scanned it. Jackson recorded what the medical examiner said in his notebook. As it was our usual dynamic that my partner recorded everything about our cases, and I would later compose the submitted report.

"After interviewing one of the other singers, we learned that Miss

James' boyfriend...a thug named Leroy Manning...attacked her earlier that evening, allegedly strangling her," I said.

"That would explain the slight inconsistencies in the contusion patterns and minimal neck swelling. A broken hyoid bone is usually a clear indicator of strangulation. It's possible the suspect broke her hyoid bone, and she survived. However, those who do survive would most likely die shortly afterwards without immediate medical attention. Given the timeline between the initial attack and time of death, it's cutting it close," Garrison said.

Interesting, I thought.

"Besides that, the lack of petechial hemorrhaging was the first indicator that strangulation wasn't the *actual* cause of death. The second indicator was the liver mortis discoloration. Her general complexion was light enough for me to detect it upon a thorough inspection," Garrison said, as he held up Delilah James' left hand.

A dark, purpling of her fingertips which wasn't visible last night, was apparent hours later.

"Given the body temperature, rigor mortis and lividity, I'd say death occurred no less than twelve hours ago. However, what was most interesting was what actually killed her and her prenatal status," Garrison said, as he passed the clipboard to me.

"Prenatal status? You mean she was in a family way?" Jackson said.

Garrison nodded, "Yes, Detective. I'd say she was about three months pregnant."

I listened as I scanned the clipboard. My eyes zeroed in on the listed cause of death, "Cyanide poisoning."

Garrison pursed his lips. "Ahh, yes. I read your report, and it mentioned a faint, acrid odor from the victim's mouth. This is an indicator of cyanide poisoning, as are confusion, headaches and nausea."

Jackson shook his head. "Bernice Trotter said that Delilah wasn't feeling well earlier before the show and went to the dressing room to rest. One of the dancers, Lynnette, told me they put in a backup to replace her, and when she went to go check on her, was when she found her body. I reckon that was from that poisoning.”

“That’s correct,” Garrison chimed. “Also, according to your report, the body was discovered around 7 p.m. Cyanide is a fast-acting poison, which means she ingested it no more than thirty minutes prior to time of death. So, the timeline factoring in lividity, is pretty accurate.”

I nodded, “That would explain why there weren’t more signs of a struggle around the room. The poison incapacitated her, and the killer staged an attack while she was dying.”

“Why’d they do that?” Jackson asked. “It seems to me, that once she took in that poison, she was as good as dead anyway.”

“To throw off suspicion, I suppose, although I’m not sold on Leroy Manning being the mastermind behind this,” I said.

“It’s a pretty elaborate and well-timed ruse, I’d say,” Garrison said.

“I don’t believe the murderer expected a thorough investigation into the cause of death of a Colored woman. The dynamics of Miss James’ relationship with Manning and the timing of events, resulted in a serendipitous situation.”

Garrison and Jackson glared at me.

“Serendipitous situation?” Garrison mused.

Jackson shook his head with a grin, “Ferguson, you and your ten-dollar words.”

I smirked, “Either of you have change for a C-note?”

ACCORDING to one of Jackson’s informants, Moe Harris, Manning hung out at his establishment, Moe’s Pub. It was a seedy joint in Haughville, a predominately Colored neighborhood, about a mile west of the Avenue.

We’d spent the better part of the afternoon scouring Manning’s police record. He’d had multiple arrests for assault and battery, disorderly conduct, illegal gambling, and petty theft. His military records were delayed due to some sort of paperwork snafu. We were told they should arrive no later than tomorrow. All we knew was that Manning had served in Korea and received a dishonorable discharge.

It was after seven in the evening when we arrived. The bar was lined with a number of local residents, likely plant workers, taking in a drink before they headed home to their families.

A J.J. Johnson tune titled, *"Naptown USA,"* played on the jukebox in the far recesses of the pub, between the marked restrooms. A few men were gathered around the two pool tables along the left side of the room. They looked up as we entered and quickly resumed their attention on their games.

The air was hazy with cigarette smoke, which further muted the dim lighting. Co-mingling odors of liquor, smoke and fried chicken made a temporary home in my nostrils, as we surveyed the pub.

Moe stood at the far end of the bar, wiping it down and fixing us with a mean glare. He wasn't happy with helping the police, especially since most of his patrons were hoodlums and thugs. Being labeled a stool pigeon would definitely be bad for business.

Moe nodded stealthily to a large, dark-complexioned man nursing a beer, and holed up adjacent to him at the bar. The man was Leroy Manning. He was powerfully built, his forearms were like telephone poles in width, and his neck, what was visible, resembled a tree trunk. Manning's face was fixed with a sinister scowl.

We approached with caution. Manning's propensity for violence was well-documented in his police record. From talking with his arresting officers, he didn't have a problem with taking a swing at them either.

As we reached him, Jackson stood to his left and behind him, while I advanced from his right. I knew he could feel our presence, but he didn't react in any way.

"Leroy Manning," I said, as I held up my badge.

He continued to ignore us.

"I need you to come with me down to the station, regarding the murder of Miss Delilah James."

"Leave me alone cop. I got nothing to say," Manning snarled.

"We'll see about that. On your feet and don't make any trouble," I said.

I knew that he was going to make trouble. He couldn't help himself. I was prepared for that very scenario. Manning rose from the barstool and unfolded to a height of at least six inches taller than me. His records indicated he wore about two hundred and seventy pounds, but he looked as though it was closer to over three hundred.

Manning stared down at me with a sneer. "What you gonna do, little man?"

I was a proficient boxer in the Army during World War II, and out of serious practice. But some things are like riding a bicycle.

He swung on me; I ducked and connected a left roundhouse to his right kidney and followed with a right hook. Given my weight and the precision of the blows, this combination would've felled any average man. He shrugged off my punches with minimal reaction. An almost lecherous grin spread across his ebony face. Apparently, Leroy Manning was much more than average and got off on violence like an aphrodisiac.

He grabbed me by the collar and lifted me from the floor, only to shove me to the ground like a ragdoll. As he stood over me a bizarre gleam flashed in his eyes. The other patrons who were sitting at the bar scrambled for the exit, as I elbow walked towards the door, and tried to get to my feet.

A loud snap sounded and caught Manning in a stunned silence. I took the opportunity to scramble from the floor. Once standing, I saw him turn around and face a shocked Jackson, who held a splintered half of a pool cue.

Manning grabbed Jackson, tossed him onto the nearest pool table and proceeded to choke him. The players headed for the exit as fast as their feet could carry them. I grabbed a beer bottle from the bar and cracked it over Manning's head. As he turned away from

Jackson, I took a small truncheon from my coat pocket and jammed it into his left kidney.

He focused his full, enraged attention on me in that moment. I swiftly kicked him in his Johnson and cracked the truncheon across his already bleeding head. Manning stumbled towards me, as Jackson crashed a chair across his back, and he fell to the floor. Before he attempted to get back up, I kicked him with all my might across the head. He lulled against the hardwood, unconscious.

Winded, both Jackson and I leaned against the bar to catch our breath.

Moe placed two shots of bourbon on the bar near us. "On the house."

We each took one of the shot glasses, clanged them together, "Cheers," we said, in unison.

After we downed them in one gulp and exchanged a glance, we both erupted into guttural laughter.

LEROY MANNING SAT RESTRAINED in an interrogation room. Jackson and I stood across the table from him. With a bandaged head, and his face contorted in an angry glare, Manning sat in silence.

Jackson stared at Manning from across the table. "Where were you yesterday between 6 p.m. and 9 p.m.?"

"Mindin' my business, pig," Manning spat.

I smirked. "I wouldn't be such a jackass, if I were you, Mr. Manning. We have a witness who saw you attack Miss Delilah James at the Walker Theatre."

Manning sighed deeply. "I was meetin' with my parole officer. Check with him."

"We will. But in the meantime, why did you murder Delilah James?" I asked.

Manning sneered, "I ain't kill that bitch!"

Jackson reached out and slapped him with a sap. "Watch your mouth. Show some respect for the dead mother of your child."

He reeled from the blow and looked up with a sneer. "That bi...," he started, but thought better when he saw Jackson raise the sap again. "Her baby ain't mine neither."

"Yeah, that's a good a motive as any in my book. You found out she was pregnant, she decided to keep it, which you weren't happy about, and you got rid of them both. Does that sound about right?" I asked.

"Wrong," Manning said.

I opened the file we had just received.

"You're a violent man, Mr. Manning. You've got several charges for assault and battery in your record. And, it says here you were dishonorably discharged from the Army for attacking a superior officer. You spent eight years at Pendleton, where you were less than a model prisoner."

"And, so what? The pen ain't exactly a country club," Manning sneered. "If you cops were half as smart as you thought you were, you'd know I ain't the father of Delilah's baby."

"Oh really? How is that?"

Manning rolled his eyes. "If you dicks had bothered to read my service record, you'd know I had the mumps *real* bad when I was a kid. Docs say I can't have no kids."

I thumbed through his file and my eyes rested on the medical report that confirmed what Manning said.

"So, the baby wasn't yours. That doesn't change the fact that you attacked and threatened her before she was found murdered. You still have plenty of means, motive and opportunity."

"Me and Dee have our issues. And yeah, we got into it yesterday. But I ain't kill her," Manning said.

Jackson and I shared a glance.

"If you didn't kill her, who did?"

Manning shook his head. "I don't know."

I slammed my fist on the table. "That's not good enough! You have to tell us something, or this *all* falls in your lap."

Manning fumed. "You barkin' up the wrong tree. Y'all need to be lookin' at that white man, the one who always shows up to her shows and always sendin' her flowers."

Jackson grimaced. "What white man?"

"That doctor, hounddog... You know, he shows up when dead bodies are found."

"Bulldog, the coroner?" Jackson quizzed.

"Yeah, short, fat man. Always tryin' to be cool with Colored folks, knowin' he don't like us any more than any other cracker. He was there last night, dressed up in a hat and sunglasses, thinkin' ain't nobody gonna know who he is," Manning said.

I remembered that Bernice Trotter mentioned that a white man was a fan of Delilah James and attended her shows. She described him exactly as Manning had.

Jackson grunted, "You think Delilah was messin' around with Bulldog?"

Manning frowned. "Yeah, I know she was. If that baby belong to anybody, it's him."

Jackson and I exchanged another subtle glance.

"What do you know about Bernice Trotter?" I asked.

Manning snickered. "Friend? That bi...," He looked at Jackson, before he continued. "She ain't no friend of Dee's, she a back stabber and was always after the lead singer spot. Now that she dead, Bernice took over as lead. She knew Dee was about to sign a record deal and move outta Naptown. That's what we was gettin' into it about yesterday. Bernice was jealous of Dee and went out of her way to make trouble. She tried to get Dee locked up once before, by plantin' drugs in her purse, but police couldn't prove it. She know all about that workin' in the Apothecary part-time."

"Bernice Trotter is an apothecary assistant?" I asked.

Manning shook his head. "Yeah, don't you cops know nothin'?

Her daddy is the head of the joint. She always mixin' up tonics and concoctions for the singers' headaches and shit."

Jackson and I exchanged a glance. So now, Bernice Trotter had become the focus of our investigation and most viable suspect.

———

MANNING'S PAROLE officer verified his alibi. We sent him on his way and headed down to the Walker Theatre for another chat with Bernice Trotter.

We made our way through the throng of people, into the building, and to the stage.

Bernice Trotter stood at the side of the stage talking with the other singers. Now that she was the lead for the band, her energy was much more confident.

Jackson and I were within twenty feet of her when she saw us. Her eyes widened slightly. She abruptly pushed through the other singers and darted backstage.

"Miss Trotter, stop," I yelled.

She froze.

"We need a word with you," I said.

She nodded and darted into one of the dressing rooms. It was empty, so we locked the door behind us for privacy. Bernice sat at the vanity located near the back of the room and lit a cigarette.

"What can I do for you officers?" she asked, after blowing a plume of smoke into the air. "I'm kinda busy. We have a show tonight, in case you didn't realize it."

I smirked. "Oh we know. We saw your name on the marquee, and the line of people waiting to get in. Things are certainly looking up for you lately. I mean with Delilah James out of the way, you got the coveted lead singer spot and all."

Bernice took another drag on her cigarette.

"Exactly what does that mean, detective? I earned my spot with this band. I heard people talk. They knew I was a more talented singer than Dee. The band only kept her on as lead because her yellow ass was more appealing to the white audience. My solo last month drew in the crowd and received rave reviews."

I pursed my lips.

"I'm sure it did. But Miss James still had the record contract and was moving out of the city with the band right behind her. And where would that leave you, exactly?" I asked.

"Well, I guess we'll never know now. Because *now* I have the record contract, and the band."

"What about your job at your father's apothecary?"

She rolled her eyes and tsked, "I don't care about that. I got what I want."

"So, no more *homemade* tonics, like the one you gave Delilah?" I asked.

Bernice's eyes grew wide briefly before she flashed a coy grin.

"Certainly, you're not implying that I had anything to do with Delilah's death, are you?"

"Oh, we're doing more than implying it. You had means, motive, and opportunity. Miss James was poisoned by cyanide. Leroy Manning has an airtight alibi. And Bulldog Sherman is too incompetent to pull this off. Besides, he was in love with her. After all, she was pregnant with his child, wasn't she?"

"Yes, that's right. She told me that old white man knocked her up. She said she was going to keep the baby, but that she didn't need him, and planned to break things off when she left Indianapolis. He had every reason and opportunity to kill her. She was keeping his bastard child and moving away. You should be looking at him, not me," Bernice said.

"No, I don't think so. We asked around to the band members and they saw him leaving just before the time of death. You, on the other hand, were present the whole time, and you stood to gain the most from Delilah's murder. And, you had access to the poison used, which could have easily been added to one of your headache tinctures. After all, you said she wasn't feeling well before the show, and you gave her something to calm her nerves, right? A cyanide laced tonic would've done the trick."

Bernice Trotter stood. "No, it can't end this way."

As we closed in on her, she exited a backdoor of the dressing room. We chased her through a corridor, as she exited a door which led to a back alley. Seconds later, before we reached the door, screeching tires, a blaring horn, and a blood curdling scream prefaced the grisly scene we viewed once we stepped outside.

"Oh my God," Jackson exclaimed.

I stood in stunned silence, as Bernice Trotter's bloodied body lay immobile in the street. The driver of the vehicle which struck her, climbed out and blabbered hysterically. A crowd of onlookers screamed in terror.

In a short time, the sounds of sirens could be heard in the distance. This isn't how I'd have wanted it, but I suppose justice has been served.

THE NEXT DAY, the newspaper reported that Delilah James' murderer had died tragically in an automobile accident late last night. As far as the investigation was concerned, case closed.

Jackson and I knew that this Murder on the Avenue wasn't quite concluded. At least not to our satisfaction. We arrived at Dr. Wendell "Bulldog" Sherman's office shortly after 8 a.m.

"Well, looks like you boys closed the case. The murderer of that Colored girl received her just rewards, and all's well that ends well, huh?" Bulldog said, with a dismissive tone.

The morning newspaper was spread out on his desk, opened to the article about the case. He folded the paper and put it aside, before resting his interlaced hands atop his desk.

"It would appear. But there are a few things we needed to clear up with you, for our records," I said.

With a quizzical glance, Bulldog gestured to the chairs in front of his desk. "What exactly can I do you for?"

I pursed my lips before speaking.

"How long did you know that Delilah James was pregnant with your child?" I asked.

Bulldog's face flushed bright red, and his breaths became shallow. "Pregnant? Why would I know about that?"

Jackson chuckled, "Because you the daddy, man. We know about the affair, and we know she told you she was gonna keep the baby."

Perspiration ran down Bulldog's face as he loosened his tie and took a gulp of coffee. "I don't know what you're talking about."

I pulled a tape recorder from my briefcase and played the recording of Bernice Trotter. Once it finished, Bulldog's face fell and he slumped in his chair.

"Three things, *Bulldog*. First, you will no longer refer to grown, Colored men as boys. EVER!"

Bulldog's mouth flew open, so I pressed on before he could speak. "Second, you will resign as the Marion County Coroner, effective immediately."

"Now you see here. I'm not going to let two ni..."

I glared at Bulldog, "Choose your words carefully, Doctor. I'm speaking now, and you will hear me out! And third, you will provide anonymous donations towards funeral expense for Delilah James *and* Bernice Trotter."

"And why the hell would I do that?"

"Because if you don't, the fact that you were having an affair with Delilah James and fathered her unborn child will be leaked to the press. No, not the white papers, of course. But, even printed in the Indianapolis Recorder, word would spread. And, the resulting scandal would result in your forced resignation as coroner, a nasty divorce, and you being ostracized from your good ole boys friends. Especially the mayor."

"You wouldn't dare," Bulldog stammered.

"We most certainly would. See, these facts were legitimately uncovered during the course of our investigation. As a result, we are under no obligation to withhold this information from the public."

Bulldog was visibly shaken. Perspiration beaded on his brow and his body trembled. "Okay, I'll do it."

We nodded and stood. "You've got until end of day tomorrow, otherwise the next story printed on this case won't be to your liking," I said as we walked out of his office.

Once we were in the car, Jackson grinned. "Were you really planning on releasing that information to the Recorder?"

I shook my head. "No, but I would've hounded him until he did exactly what I demanded. That would've included a candid conversation with the mayor. If he knew what his brother-in-law had done, he'd have canned him for the hell of it."

"Man, you something else. Remind me not to ever get on your bad side," Jackson said, before we both broke into laughter.

MADAME C.J. WALKER BUILDING

The Madam C.J. Walker Building is a prominent historical structure located near downtown Indianapolis on the corner of Indiana Avenue and West Street. It was added to the National Register of Historic Places in 1980, was designated a National Historic Landmark in 1991, and is of especially great cultural significance to the local Black community.

The four-story, multi-purpose structure was erected in 1927 and named in honor of Madam C.J. Walker, the African-American hair care and beauty products entrepreneur who founded the Madam C. J. Walker Manufacturing Company. The site formerly served as its world headquarters.

It was designed by the Indianapolis architectural firm of Rubush & Hunter and is one of the most recognizable buildings in the state. The building is known for its African, Egyptian, and Moorish motifs, and holds the distinction of being one of the few remaining African-Art Deco buildings still in existence in the United States. The building currently is utilized as the headquarters for the Madam Walker Legacy Center.

During its heyday, it was renown as a preeminent entertainment, business, and commercial hub to the city's African American community from the 1920s to the 1950s, The Madam C.J. Walker Theater, located within the building, was arguably the most popular Black entertainment venue during that same time period. The theater is widely known for featuring jazz acts, such as local greats Wes Montgomery, Freddie Hubbard, J. J. Johnson, and many others.

NO GHOSTS
NEED APPLY
BY MARY BISCHOFF

ulie Lancaster, nurse and damn good knitter, blinked at the smartly uniformed employee behind the polished wooden facade of the front desk. "I'm sorry?" she managed to say. Tired and stiff after the nearly two-hour Friday afternoon drive down from Indianapolis, she had lugged her suitcase and knitting bag up the imposing stairs, across the broad veranda and into the lobby of the majestic West Baden Springs Hotel.

This National Historic Landmark in French Lick, Indiana had been in its day dubbed the "Eighth Wonder of the World" for the engineering marvel of its amazing six-story dome-topped atrium. When the hotel opened its doors in 1902, the unique circular resort boasted the world's largest unsupported dome until the Houston Astrodome opened in 1965. Beautifully restored and reopened in 2007, the neoclassical hotel with its distinctive Moorish-style towers was now hosting, among other things, the Wonders of Wool weekend knitting retreat that Julie was attending.

"What do you mean, I don't have my own room?"

The clerk, Nadine, looked genuinely regretful. "Knitting Escapes, who organized this retreat, only booked double occupancy rooms." She peered at her computer screen. "Your assigned roommate is

Sandy Sanders, and you'll be on the fourth floor. She hasn't checked in yet."

"What about moving to a different single room?" Julie tapped her credit card nervously on the counter. "I don't mind if it's a little higher in price. I'd rather not share a room if I can avoid it."

"I'm so sorry," Nadine consulted her computer again. "We have a large golf tournament here as well, so I'm afraid we are completely booked up."

"I guess it will have to do." Resigned, she handed over her credit card. Julie twisted to admire the circular lobby, with its beautiful tile floors and sparkling stained glass windows. She was determined to enjoy her first knitting retreat. The event brochure had promised multiple crafting workshops, plenty of opportunities to buy yarn and other knitting-related paraphernalia, plus fine dining and a spa experience.

Julie was looking forward to learning some new knitting techniques, exploring the historic resort area, and then topping off the long weekend with a relaxing lunch in the atrium restaurant before driving home. Maybe she'd even take the rail trolley over to French Lick Springs and visit the casino before she left.

"DEATH, there is death here!" A woman's heavily accented voice rang out over the background sounds of the lobby, rising in intensity. "So much DEATH in this place! Soon, it vill valk among us!"

Every head in the lobby turned towards the speaker, a tall, buxom woman in an exotic floor-length caftan posed dramatically in the entryway, arms lifted, allowing time for the man filming her on his phone to circle around in front and re-frame her.

"Oh, no." Eyes closed, a thin whisper escaped Nadine's lips. "Not her again."

"Can you FEEL it? So many spirits—they LINGER here! Trapped —TRAPPED—vith no vay to move forward to the next plane! Soon another vill join them!" The woman's ample chest heaved as she gestured theatrically, clasping her hands together and drew breath to continue her declamation, only to be interrupted by a hotel official who sidled up to her and spoke quietly. A flash of irritation quickly crossed her face before she composed herself and continued loudly. "Madame Zara must REST before the séance tomorrow! The spirits avait us!"

With a flourish of her caftan, she plucked a key card from the hotel staff's hand and swept towards the elevators. Her camera operator, a tired-looking older man, trailed her, handing out flyers to those waiting in the check-in line as he went.

The young man behind Julie accepted one. "Wow, I subscribe to her on YouTube! I'll definitely be there!"

Julie accepted a flyer and perused the lurid cover. "Madame Zara knows all and sees all? Talk to your dearly departed?" She turned back to Nadine. "Halloween come early this year?"

Nadine plastered a polite smile on her face. "She films her YouTube videos here. They are very—popular, I've heard." She handed Julie back her credit card, as well as room key card, map of the grounds and the Wi-Fi password. "Registration for Knitting Escapes is in the Caddy Sinclair Room, but I don't believe it opens until 5 pm."

Plenty of time to get upstairs and get unpacked, Julie thought. She thanked Nadine, picked up her bags and walked out into the hotel's huge circular atrium before heading up to her room. Stepping out into the vast Pompeian Court nearly took her breath away. Sunlight poured in from the skylights and clerestory windows a hundred feet overhead and glittered from the mullioned windows and delicate balconies of the six floors of hotel rooms, set between huge white columns, that ringed the enormous interior space.

Some two hundred feet across, Julie felt almost like she had stepped into a cathedral, with the beautifully tiled Rookwood Pottery fireplace and numerous potted plants adding a splash of color to the cream and gold interior. Clusters of comfortable sofas, chairs and tables dotted the mosaic terrazzo floor, appearing almost as doll furniture in the immense space. *So beautiful!*

Once upstairs, Julie was delighted to find her room had a balcony overlooking the massive atrium. Luxuriously appointed, the spacious room was impeccably decorated without being stuffy or pretentious. She laid claim to the twin bed nearest the bathroom by depositing her bags on it, then admired the view from the balcony. Sinking down in a plump armchair, she consulted the Wonders of Wool program.

Let's see, she thought. *Shall I go to "Socks: Toe Up or Toe Down?" Or maybe "Steeking: Dare to Cut Your Knitting?"* Deciding to unpack later, she grabbed her bag and headed downstairs to the conference area, looking forward to a fun weekend, meeting new people and learning new things.

JUST BEFORE MIDNIGHT in front of her hotel room door, Julie hitched her scarlet lace stole back onto her shoulders, then juggled her packages to dig in her bag for her key card. She had been self-conscious at first about wearing her own colorful knitted work out in public, but quite a few other retreat attendees had been showing off their beautiful handiwork as well, and she had received several compliments.

What a great first night of the retreat, she thought, humming contentedly. She'd attended several seminars, bought more yarn than she really needed, had an excellent meal at Sinclair's Restaurant, then met up with several new friends at Ballard's Bar to congenially debate if knitting was better than crocheting—*well, duh!*—discuss their favorite patterns of knitted items worn in movies and even some non-yarn-related topics.

Giggling to herself, Julie fumbled out her key card and managed to open the door. She may have had a few more cocktails than usual, but at least she didn't have to drive the long way home.

She stepped into the dark room, fumbling along the wall for the light switch. Someone had drawn the curtains and not enough light seeped in from the atrium windows for her to navigate the unfamiliar space. *Was her roommate here yet? Better to wake her up than to fall over on top of her! That wouldn't be a good start!* She couldn't hear a thing except the hum of the air conditioner. *Was there even anyone here?*

Dropping her bags, she ran both hands along the wall until she found the light switch and flipped it on. Blinking in the sudden light, she looked around the room.

One bed still held her undisturbed suitcase but her knitting bag was open and the contents—half-done projects, knitting needles, yarn, stitch markers, scissors—were all scattered haphazardly across the white bedspread.

Hey, exclaimed her inner voice outraged at the tangled mess, *that's my good yarn I got in Scotland! 80% wool, 20% silk!* She had brought it along in hopes of finding just the right pattern to make something wonderful with it.

The other bed closest to the window was indeed occupied, the inhabitant almost completely hidden beneath the bedspread. Tousled reddish-brown hair peeked out of the edge of the crumpled coverlet, and a limp hand dangled off the side of the bed. Julie's eyes narrowed as she tried to focus. *Did the skin kind of look—purple?* Alarm bells, somewhat muffled by the alcohol she had consumed earlier, began to ring in her mind.

"Hello?" Julie stepped closer, cocking her head to listen intently. The coverlet was preternaturally still, and she couldn't hear any respiration. She bumped the bed with her leg. "You okay?"

No response. No movement under the cover.

The bells clanged harder. *Something was definitely wrong here.* She took a deep breath, reached out, grabbed the edge of the white fabric and pulled it back for a look.

Underneath lay the body of a young woman in her mid-20s, fully clothed, even to her sandals, dressed in a frilly shirt and leggings. She appeared to be merely sleeping, except for the livor mortis on the dangling hand and the knitting needle that had been thrust through her left eye socket and well up into her brain.

Size 9, 10-inch straight stainless steel knitting needle, Julie's brain supplied helpfully. *I have a set just like—hey!*

Knowing it was hopeless from her nursing experience, she nonetheless checked the cool wrist for a pulse. Nothing. Rigor had not set in yet.

Dead! Not only dead but murdered, and with MY knitting needle! She moved numbly over to the phone and called the front desk to tell them there was a dead body in her room. Remembering the words of Madame Zara only a few hours before, she shivered. *If the hotel wasn't haunted before*, she thought to herself, *it probably was now.* After a startled pause, the front desk clerk assured her that help would soon be on the way.

Hoping not to contaminate the crime scene any more than she already had, Julie stepped out into the curved hallway to wait for the police. Nervously, she paced up and down the corridor, flinching at shadows and thinking furiously. *Was the killer still around? Who was that woman and why was she killed? And with my knitting needle! Obviously I didn't do it*, she thought, *but who did? Was someone trying to set her up? Why? She didn't even know anyone here in this town.*

As with most law-abiding citizens, she had a favorable impression of the police, but suddenly her future depended on how well the local constabulary did their job in finding the murderer. She bit her lip and thought of her favorite detective, Sherlock Holmes. *Where's Robert Downey Jr. or Benedict Cumberbatch when I need them most?*

The elevator pinged to herald the arrival of police and security personnel. Relieved by their presence, Julie identified herself to the French Lick police officer and explained what she had found. Eyeing her skeptically, Officer Barnes collected her information carefully in his small notebook.

Taking some black nitrile gloves from his pocket, he opened the door and led the way into the room. "Whew," Julie said, "she's still there." *Crap, did I say that out loud?* She was sure she'd seen a movie once where the murder victim had disappeared without a trace once the hero had stepped out of the room. *Okay, I've definitely had a bit too much to drink,* she thought a little hysterically.

"Tell me exactly what happened," the police officer instructed. She walked him through her actions and remained by the door, careful to touch nothing, as he inspected the body and the room. He questioned her about her activities both in the room and since her arrival at the hotel. "And did you notice anything unusual during your visit here?"

Julie hesitated. "Well, not really, no."

Officer Barnes looked up from his notes. "What does that mean? Did you see someone do something or someone made threats?"

"The only thing that struck me out of the ordinary was this, " Julie retrieved the crumpled flyer from her pocket and thrust it towards the officer. "This woman, this Madame Zara, made a big fuss when I arrived." She hesitated. "It's probably nothing but she said something about death being near."

As one, they turned to look at the body in the bed.

"And you say you don't know the woman you found here in your room?"

Julie shook her head. "No, she doesn't look at all familiar. I assume it's my roommate for the knitting retreat, Sandy—Sandy something."

"Well, no, that can't be," said a prim voice from the open doorway. A distinguished silver-haired man in a lovely cable-knit lavender sweater hesitated there, clutching a purple Hobbii knitting bag in one hand and a small leather overnight case in the other.

"Why is that, sir?" asked the officer politely but brusquely.

"Because—because *I'm* Sandy Sanders."

About ten o'clock the next morning, at a small table tucked into the rear of Café Sinclair's, Julie took a swallow of excellent coffee. She savored the last bite of her stuffed French toast and brushed the crumbs from her lips with her napkin. Sitting back in her chair, she regarded her tablemate with a bemused smile.

"That was wonderful." She paused. "Tell me something, Sandy. What made you decide to stay and share a room with me? For all you know, I could be the killer."

"My dear girl," Sandy said, slicing his waffles precisely along the lines after slathering the indentations with butter, "one doesn't reach my age without getting a certain feel for people. Anyone with any sense could see that if you were going to kill someone, you wouldn't be stupid enough to leave their body in your room."

Lacking any evidence that either of them had even known the dead woman, much less had a motive to kill her, the officer had released them with the caution to stay in the area until a detective had the chance to take their statement. Fortunately, there had been a cancellation so the hotel staff had been able to offer them a different double room. "We can still share if you want," she had hesitantly offered, exhausted but unwilling to leave the older gentleman in the lurch without a place to stay. While they were waiting for the police to give them leave to go, she had complimented his sweater and he had teared up, saying he had knit it for his late husband.

"Excellent," he had said. "I'm too exhausted to even think of finding another place to stay, even relatively close to here. I've been looking forward to this weekend for so long. You certainly are quite safe from me, you are definitely not my type. And besides," his gentle brown eyes twinkled behind his horn-rimmed glasses, "it's not like you're a crocheter!" They had both laughed—Julie would be the first to admit that hers might have been a little on the hysterical side— and they had gladly followed the bellboy to the new room.

They had been awakened a little after 9:00 am by the return of her bags once the forensic specialists were done with them—*albeit missing one of her needles, and she sure wouldn't be finishing the scarf that was half done on its twin*—and now, after a few hours of sleep, they were enjoying breakfast and comparing schedules, determined to make the best of the rest of the weekend. Sandy had been a most considerate roommate, except for his meticulous re-arranging her personal items in the bathroom according to size and color.

"I think I'll do *Movie Knits: From Sherlock to Outlander* and *Continental versus English Knitting* this morning and then the sweater workshop this afternoon. And, of course, the vendors' room. Again!" Julie said.

"Of course! I've signed up for the sweater workshop as well." Despite his old-fashioned appearance in a tweed suit, hand-knit pink vest and bow tie, Sandy had produced a state-of-the-art laptop from his bag and was expertly negotiating the internet. He tsk-tsked to himself. "That poor girl that died in our room is all over the news. That, and ads for this Madame Zara reading tonight. We should go to that. It's going to be streamed on YouTube Live."

"Is it a séance? I don't know if I'm up for that," Julie said.

"From what I see of Madame Zara's channel, she claims to be a psychic medium." He whistled. "You can book a private session with her for only $850! My, she has a lot of subscribers." Sandy glanced over the top of his laptop at Julie and chuckled. "Surely, she can reach the dearly departed and tell us who killed her. That would certainly eliminate us as suspects."

A tall athletic man in his 30s stopped at their table and discretely flashed his badge. "Julie Lancaster?" At her nod, he continued. "I'm Detective Sam Kozlowski of the Indiana State Police. May I join you? I have some questions."

"Of course," Julie murmured and scooted aside for him to pull up a chair.

"I'm Morgan Sanders, but everyone calls me Sandy. I was there also, last night. Would you like some tea, Detective?" A true crime aficionado, Sandy was practically beaming. How exciting! First a murder and now a real live detective. This retreat had certainly started off with a bang. He sobered quickly. "A tragedy, of course, under the circumstances. Have you found out who the poor girl was? The papers didn't say her name."

"Thanks on the tea but no," the detective said and pulled out his notebook. "The deceased was Vyvyan Smith, age 24, of Indianapolis. She had a record so her fingerprints were on file. Did either of you know her?"

Julie shook her head. "To my knowledge, I've never met the woman."

Sandy chimed in. "Me, neither."

"Can you both please tell me where you were last night between six and ten?"

Julie pushed her plate away with a sinking feeling. "I hope we aren't suspects," she said, digging in her bag to check her program.

"Just trying to get an idea of what all was going on and where everyone was. You first, ma'am," the detective said, pen poised.

"I had dinner here in the restaurant about 6:30, I think," Julie said. "I went to the *Fixing Dropped Stitches* at seven for a while, and then wandered around some. I was in the bar until about 11:45 or so, when I went up to my room and found her—the body."

Detective Kozlowski jotted down the names of the people she remembered talking with, then walked her through the whole experience yet again. He turned another page in his notebook and turned to Sandy to collect his information. "And you, sir?"

"I had dinner with friends who came in unexpectedly from out of town, that's why I was so late to the retreat. We finished around ten, and then I drove down from Indianapolis," said Sandy. "I arrived just before midnight. There was some confusion at the front desk when they tried to tell me that I had already checked in, but obviously that was not the case."

Julie could almost see the detective's ears perk up.

"Tell me about that," he said.

"Everyone was extremely nice about it, and they finally decided it was just a computer glitch," Sandy said. "So that took a few minutes to get straightened out. I got my key card and went straight up to the room because I was so tired. I hadn't realized until I checked in that we would be sharing rooms, and I was dreading it would be someone —-incompatible." He smiled at Julie. "But thankfully it wasn't."

"That would explain how the victim got into your room," Detective Kozlowski said thoughtfully. "According to hotel security, a key card swiped in at 9:27 last night. So that definitely wasn't either of you?"

"No," Julie said. "I left about six or so for dinner, then I didn't go back to the room until I was ready to call it a night."

"Unfortunately, for privacy reasons, there are no security cameras in the halls, so we don't have any footage of who entered the room. I'd like to have our fingerprint specialist get your prints for elimination, once you're done here."

"Mine will be on the needle," Julie said, sneaking an apprehensive look at the investigator. "I was knitting a scarf with that set."

The detective shook his head. "My expert said it was unlikely he'd get anything from the murder weapon, given its small diameter, but I'd like to rule your prints out from what we've found in the room. The hotel is letting us use one of their offices while we're here, just down the hall." He looked back to Sandy. "And if you don't mind me asking, sir, it's a bit unusual to find a man at a knitting retreat. What brought you to sign up for this and share a room with a stranger who would probably be a female?"

"There are actually quite a few male knitters," Sandy said a bit stiffly. "My grandmother taught me to knit and it's become quite the hobby for me, now that I'm retired. I didn't realize that I would be sharing a room until I checked in and they made me aware." He frowned. "The organizers really should have made that clear up front. I shall definitely be giving them some negative feedback about that. Although after meeting Julie under such trying circumstances last night, she feels like an old friend, so it might have been a blessing in disguise. Knitters are a generally accepting bunch, you know." He winked at Julie wickedly. "Now, crocheters, they might be another matter completely."

Detective Kozlowski looked puzzled. "Aren't knitting and crochet pretty much the same?"

They both stared at him, aghast.

"Oh, my goodness, no!" Julie said. "I suppose you could say they are similar in that we both make things with yarn but that's about it. Knitters use different types of needles, depending on what they are making. Socks, for example, you might use double-pointed needles, or a small circular needle. You can knit Continental or English." She recognized the glazed look coming over the detective's face as one common to non-crafters receiving way too much information and cut herself short. "Crocheters use a hook. I don't know much about that since I knit. Most crafters do just one or the other, and there's a friendly rivalry between the two sides."

The detective thanked them both and said he would be in touch if he had any more questions. He warned them not to disclose any details to anyone, especially about the murder weapon, as they were withholding that information from the press.

Silently, they watched him leave the café, and Julie heaved a sigh. "Why am I afraid that I'm still a suspect?"

"Buck up, my dear," Sandy said with a smile and patted her hand. "He seems an intelligent man, and I'm sure he will figure it out."

When Julie had her fingerprints taken, Sandy insisted on having his taken as well. "I could be lying about my alibi," he said cheerfully to the nonplussed technician. Delighted, he couldn't wait to post about this experience on his true-crime Facebook group. Once he got clearance from the police, of course. Just like them, he smiled to himself, he couldn't discuss an active case.

Troubled, Julie wiped the ink from her fingers. She knew perfectly well that she was innocent, but she worried that somehow the police might arrest her anyway. *I've heard some horrible tales of miscarriages of justice.* She knew from years of reading mysteries that sometimes the person who "discovered" a body really was the actual killer. Hopefully, Detective Kozlowski would find the real culprit before long, but just in case, she made a pact with Sandy to stay alert for any clues that might lead to a motive for the killing or that might point to the real murderer.

Vowing to stay on the lookout, they split up to attend their various panels. Over the course of the day, they met frequently to compare notes. The murder was the talk of the hotel, and Julie was either treated with blatant suspicion or pounced upon by those who wanted all the gory details. *I might as well throw away my 'I knit so I don't kill people' T-shirt right now*, she thought, striving to find humor in her situation but failing miserably.

After depositing the fruits of their day in their room (she had definitely attained SABLE—Stash Acquisition Beyond Life Expectancy), they took the rail trolley ride to the French Lick Resort for a change of scenery, dinner and a little gambling. After a lovely dinner and some unproductive rounds on the slot machines, Julie and Sandy headed back to the West Baden Springs Hotel in plenty of time to join the crowd waiting in line for the séance.

"Do you really think we'll find out anything at this séance?" Julie asked as they took their place in the queue.

"You never know, it's worth a try," said Sandy with a cheerful smile. "Maybe she will channel Sherlock Holmes and he will solve the case!"

"He's a fictional detective," Julie muttered at his back as he turned away to speak with the people ahead of them. "Fictional!"

Sandy nudged Julie when he noticed Detective Kozlowski coming down the hall towards them. He passed without a word, showed his ID to the person manning the door and disappeared inside the conference room.

Madame Zara's cameraman came along the line and handed out numbered tickets. Only those whose numbers were called would be able to enter for the actual reading, he announced to a general groan after handing them all out. Producing a black silk bag, he made a show of thoroughly mixing the contents and pulled out slips one at a time, reading the number aloud.

"5312! That's me!" Julie exclaimed, excited in spite of herself.

The very last number called was Sandy's number, 5313, and the disappointed crowd drifted away.

"I'm glad you're coming in too," Julie clutched Sandy's arm. "I hadn't thought we might not both get in."

The chosen twenty entered the darkened room and were directed to take seats at the large central table. Multiple cameras were positioned on tripods around the room, and special stand lighting focused on the empty chair at the head of the table. Small, scented candles flickered on the tabletop, casting dancing shadows on the walls, and New Age music played softly in the background. The rear of the room was curtained off by black drapes.

The cameraman disappeared behind the curtains. As they waited, despite the tranquil music, Julie began to feel uneasy. "I've got a bad feeling about this," she whispered to Sandy, who patted her hand reassuringly.

"It should start any minute now."

Part of the curtain was flung aside to reveal Madame Zara, framed against the backlight, holding her hand dramatically to her head.

"The spirits are vith us tonight!" she exclaimed. She stalked forward and settled herself at the head of the table, her long blood-red gown billowing around her, rubies sparkling at her ears and throat.

"You must hold hands vith the person you are next to. No matter vat happens, no matter how the spirits reveal themselves, do NOT let go! This is for YOUR protection!" She glared around the room. "If you have doubts, leave now! By staying, you accept the risks—the DANGERS—that the spirits may pose to you!"

Swallowing nervously, Julie extended her left hand to the woman next to her and clutched Sandy's hand tightly with her right.

The lights dimmed even further, leaving only Madame Zara in the pool of light. Gripping the hands of the persons on each side, she threw her head back, shut her eyes and intoned, "Spirits of the dead, I summon you! I feel the presence of so many here, trying to get a message through to this side of the grave. Come forth, spirits of the dead!"

Julie jolted and the room gasped as the table in front of them heaved itself slightly into the air, then settled to the floor with a heavy thud.

Madame Zara crowed triumphantly. "Yes! The spirits surround us! Come, spirits, speak to me!" She swayed back and forth, muttering under her breath. "I am getting a message. This message is for someone with the initials AM."

There was a soft gasp from the other side of the table, and a tremulous voice whispered, "That's me. Anne Marie!"

"The spirit is someone who recently left this plane, they were so sad to go, but they are in a better place now."

"It must be my father," the woman across the table sobbed. "He died two weeks ago!"

"Yes," Madame Zara continued. "He says he has something to tell you, something very important. There is something you must know!"

"Daddy? Daddy, please tell me what it is!" the woman said, urgently. "I miss you so much!"

There was a lengthy pause.

"No," Madame Zara said regretfully, "he is gone now. He must gather the strength to call across the void to me again. In time, all shall be revealed. I vill arrange a private session for you after we are done here."

Julie bent close to Sandy in the dark and whispered, "That's how she makes her money." Someone hissed for her to shush, and she fell silent as the medium spoke again.

Madame Zara paused theatrically. "There is a troubled spirit here —a spirit in anguish! She passed in violence and in grief, here, here in this very hotel." An eerie moan echoed around the room and the table shuddered again. "Why? Why did you do it?" she said in a much younger-sounding voice. "I loved you like a sister and you killed me!"

A man spoke from the foot of the table. "Who? Who did?"

"She is—J. L. She is—here—here in this very room!"

"What!" Julie cried in consternation amid the uproar from the audience. *Those were _her_ initials!*

"That's a lie!" shouted Sandy, beside her.

"Stay still!" Madame Zara shouted. "The spirit must..."

The candles on the table went out abruptly as a cold wind swirled through the room. Julie and Sandy clutched each other as they stared at the medium, who looked—surprised?

"Tom, you bastard!" A female voice hissed out of the shadows. "You rammed that knitting needle into my eye! YOU killed me!"

"What are you doing, Sarah?" The man leapt up from the foot of the table as all the lights came on and the background music stopped. Everyone turned to look at him.

Julie's brow creased. *Was that the man who had been in line behind her when she checked in?*

"Stop the feed!" he shouted. "What are you up to, you double-crossing bitch?"

The audience's gaze swung raptly back to the head of the table.

"I didn't say that!" Madame Zara had suddenly lost her heavy Eastern European accent, and what came out of her mouth now was pure Midwest. "You're the one who thought it would be a good idea to kill her and use the publicity!"

Detective Kozlowski appeared from behind the curtains, cuffs in hand, and grabbed Madame Zara as she leapt from her chair, shouting threats incoherently. He secured her and held his badge high for all to see. "Indiana State Police, everyone just stay put."

Uniformed officers streamed through the door and wrestled Tom to the ground as he tried to force his way past them to escape.

The detective said, "You two are under arrest for the murder of Vyvyan Smith, and other charges, including fraud and identity theft." He paused, becoming conscious of the enthralled eyes of the in-person spectators and the fact that he was live on camera to possibly many more viewers. "And someone turn off that recording!"

LATE THE NEXT MORNING, Julie sat, contented, in a rocking chair on the grand veranda looking over the hotel's beautiful grounds, the trees just starting to show the warm oranges and red of fall. Sandy, dapper in a soft heather-gray ribbed sweater, sank down into the chair next to her and toasted her with his glass of a particularly nice Italian white wine, enjoying the last little bit of their weekend before heading back home.

"Look, here's our favorite detective," Sandy said, lifting a hand to wave at Detective Kozlowski, who was walking out the door.

"Our favorite live one, you mean," Julie smiled. "Sherlock Holmes is pretty hard to beat!"

Detective Kozlowski walked over to join them and they exchanged greetings. "You folks heading back to Indy?"

"We are," said Julie. "We've already made arrangements to meet again at the next West Perry Yarn Crafters Guild meeting."

"Hopefully it won't be nearly as exciting," the detective said with a smile.

"I certainly never expected there to be a murder, a séance or an arrest on my first knitting retreat, and we got all three," Julie said. "It was like something out of one of my Sherlock Holmes books! And I still don't understand," she said, her curiosity burning. "Who was Vyvyan and why did they kill her?"

Detective Kozlowski replied, "Madame Zara—her real name is Sarah Tinsley, by the way—has been making money on YouTube with her videos pretending to contact the dead. Her brother Tom would lurk in the lobbies of the hotels they use for the séances and get the names of possible victims for the so-called psychic readings. Vyvyan gathered information from background checks and social media for Madame Zara to fabricate her 'messages from the dead.' Tom heard Julie check in so he then had Vyvyan use Sandy's name to get a room key and lured her upstairs. It was good luck for you, Sandy, that you checked in late. Otherwise, you might have walked in on the murder."

"I'm very thankful I missed that part," Sandy replied, fascinated, and really, only a tiny bit regretful.

The detective continued. "When Vyvyan wanted a bigger share of the loot, Tom and Sarah were afraid she would expose their racket and they couldn't have that. They decided to kill two birds with one stone, so to speak. They would silence Vyvyan and generate lots of views—and thus money—by holding a séance purporting to reveal her killer."

"How horrible," Julie sighed. "All for the sake of money,"

"It was sheer random chance they picked you to frame, Julie." Detective Kozlowski said. "Tom lured Vyvyan up to the room by claiming he had her final share of the money they'd gotten from previous victims, then he killed her. I guess he thought that using one of your knitting needles would be more evidence against you."

Julie shivered. "Well, I certainly don't want it back. But what about the séance? We were picked at random for that. We saw the camera guy draw the numbers!"

"He simply noted the number he gave you and then called it out, ignoring the number he'd actually drawn." Detective Kozlowski leaned against the balustrade and enjoyed the cool breeze. "The whole thing was rigged. The table was on a lever to make it appear to levitate, and they broadcast low-level infrasonic tones to make people feel nervous. The entire gang couldn't wait to give us all the details and blame each other once we started interrogating them."

"So, there wasn't a ghost at all?" Sandy said, disappointed.

"Of course not," said Detective Kozlowski. "You all have a good trip home."

Julie exchanged glances with Sandy, thinking of the way that last 'message from the dead' had seemed different from the rest and smiled. "Like Sherlock Holmes said, 'No ghosts need apply!'"

WEST BADEN SPRINGS HOTEL

The historic West Baden Springs Hotel is nestled in the hills of Southern Indiana next to the Hoosier National Forest, a region famous for its natural scenery.

The current hotel sprang from the ashes of an older wooden hotel that was destroyed by a fire in 1901. Amazingly, it took less than a year to build the replacement, a six-story circular hotel, topped by a 200-foot steel dome, the largest unsupported dome in the world until the mid-1960s.

Famous for its mineral springs and casinos, it was the place to go in the early 20th Century to relax and recuperate, for everyone from movie stars to gangsters. However, after the Great Depression in the early 1930s, the property changed hands several times and went through periods of neglect. Fortunately, it was restored and reopened in 2007. The hotel enjoyed a friendly rivalry with the nearby French Lick Springs Hotel in French Lick.

Now owned by the same company, Preferred Hotels & Resorts, the West Baden Springs Hotel provides luxurious accommodations with world-class golf courses, indoor and outdoor pools, gardens, riding stables, a casual cafe, a world-class spa, and gourmet dining.

DANGER IN DANA
BY S. ASHLEY COUTS

"Just leave me alone." Bobby told his dad. He locked the door to his new room, in their new house, in their new town, Dana, Indiana.

"Ok," his dad, Darren, replied. "I guess I can't tell you this secret then."

The door opened a few inches, and the top of Bobby's head appeared. "So, what's the big secret?"

"No fair Bob. This is a face-to-face discussion. Open the door, son. I promise I won't bite." His voice had that pleading friendly, almost joking tone. He had a good relationship with his troubled son. It was his wife, Ruth who found the journey difficult. She seemed burdened by this, another move, in a long line of moves. Darren didn't want to upset the apple cart but, as a military man, he liked structure.

Bobby opened the door and moved to sit on his unmade bed. "So, what's this big surprise."

"It's a little dark in here," Darren said as he picked at the silver tape Bobby used to hold up the cardboard he'd put up to block out the light from both windows. "I don't get all this tape business. The Army provided us with a beautiful garden space. I thought you and your mother would love watching things grow. Maybe take up horti-culture? We can see if they have a class at your school. But you need light in here, son. Sunshine is healthy."

"Here's an idea," Bobby said in a bland tone. "Get me a knife. Then I can cut a peep hole in the cardboard and still be safe."

Darren smiled, refusing to give the kid bait.

"That might work," he said. "Sounds to me that you're afraid of something."

Bobby had pride. He recognized that language and remembered the bribe.

"So, what's the secret?" he asked. "Did you get me a rifle? That one I've been dreaming about all my life? If you ever kept a promise to me, it might make a difference. Maybe get me a bicycle? I really, really want that chrome and silver Schwinn."

"Bob, I'd love to but that one's a little pricey. Why not check out the Sears catalogue, circle pictures."

"So, you're saying forget it?"

"No. I'm saying let's compare costs."

After a pause, Bobby said, "It doesn't matter anyway. I'll be blown to bits by that Dana Heavy Water Plant."

"What are you talking about?"

"I'm not stupid. You told Mom your job is dangerous?"

Stuck between honor and family, Darren crossed his fingers and said, "There's no need for this tape and cardboard nonsense. You can trust me."

Darren was fully aware that nuclear bombs were the centerpiece of defense work at the Dana Plant, which was set up primarily for the Savannah River reactors. Dana residents, however, had no idea the Dana Heavy Water Plant was really a nuclear power plant. He couldn't tell anyone, especially his nervous teen-age son.

"Let's get your old bike out of the shed and check the tires," Darren suggested once again. Ruth had a concerned look on her face as she stood by, holding the cushioned chin strap.

"I'm no baby," Bobby said, pushing away the helmet.

"Put it on. I don't want anything bad to happen. You haven't been on a bike in a long time, and this is a whole new town and new streets. You might get lost," Ruth said.

"He'll be fine. He needs this experience. It'll be good for him to meet some new people, for goodness sakes."

"I'm not wearing the helmet," Bobby said as he tried to wrangle the heavy bicycle into place.

"My intuition tells me something bad will happen in this place, and the helmet is to help."

Ruth believed in hexes and bad spirits. She followed a wacky television preacher who preached hellfire and brimstone. To complicate that, she was convinced that Bobby had behavioral, social and psychological disabilities for which he needed special aides and classes.

Caught between the structured military man and his mother, Bobby was often confused. More so now that his father, employed by the US Army, was forbidden to discuss his work.

"You know I need my things. I miss my posters, you know, Elvis, Bridgette, Marlon Brando. Maybe I'll feel better once they're on my walls."

"Your posters will be there when you get back, I promise," Darren said holding the back of Bobby's bike as he mounted it. "Be open to new adventure."

Bobby tossed the helmet and watched it wobble in the grass, then defiantly pushed forward on the pedals. There was no way he'd look like some bubble headed freak. It was bad enough he was stuck with this clunker of a bicycle with a rusty rattle signaling every pedal rotation.

Along the route, every house looked different. There were palatial homes, maybe belonging to lawyers or doctors, built beside small, brick or clapboard houses. One house at the intersection resembled a miniature castle.

When he reached the business section of town, the Dana Café had a flickering, blue light around a closed sign in the window. Feeling somewhat dejected, he went to the only open store with a sign reading: DRUGS, COMICS, SODAS, SUNDRIES. Just the place to make a friend.

NARROW WOODEN PLANK flooring stretched out in front of him. Bobby saw the clutter of boxes, piles of paper, bottles, and pills. He was overwhelmed by the smells of shoe polish, Vicks, cigar smoke, and stale air. Bobby stared at the abundance of rifles, hand guns, shotguns, and weapons of all sorts displayed near the front of the store.

He felt nothing good could happen in this place. In fact, it could harbor monsters or vampires. His mouth went dry, and he could not swallow as panic took hold. Dust particles followed a shaft of yellow light, but the place remained deathly quiet, without a soul in sight.

Bobby licked his lips ready to call out but managed only a tiny mouse squeak.

Then the walls closed in on him. All those odors and thoughts started to swirl around. He took a dizzy step forward, lost his footing and fell against a blurry, dark shadow that reached forward with his imagined claws and grabbed him.

JACK PRESLEY TOOK his time with his morning coffee, enjoying private time inside his store's bathroom. People in Dana understood his schedule. He would pick his teeth in the mirror, clip errant whiskers from his goatee, then take time reading the daily paper. Everyone in Dana knew this, so he sometimes unlocked the door before starting his routine. In case of a dire emergency local folks knew to pound on his bathroom door. But when Bobby Hacker surprised him by opening his bathroom door everything changed.

"Oh my gosh. Hey, kid? Are you okay? I should have activated the bell." Jack spoke in a rush, hoping the kid wasn't hurt. "You must be new in town, right? Your dad's an officer at the plant, right? What is he? What rank is he?"

"Yeah, we just moved here." Bobby shuddered, his head still hazy. "I'm really not supposed to talk about my dad's work."

"Oh, sure. I get it. No problem."

Guiding the boy back through the store he held out a palm and said, "I'm Jack Presley."

Bobby stopped dead in his tracks and asked, "Are you related to the King, Elvis?"

Jack cackled as he reached up and pulled an overhead chain. Suddenly, a bank of fluorescent lights flickered on, brightening the whole place. Jack said, "Nope. But we have our own Hollywood stars, Ronnie and Donnie Middlebrook, twins who play the electric guitars and sing. They come to town every summer. Those boys, just teenagers, you know, will take the stage at the Ernie Pyle Festival and the girls go wild. My daughter is crazy about them."

"You have a daughter?"

He looked at Bobby as if sizing him up, then said, "She's probably around your age. She's a handful. We lost her mother a few years back to cancer. You want a soda?"

Bobby shrugged his thin shoulders and watched Jack dig into his worn corduroy pants pocket for change.

"I bet you're a good kid."

"I try."

"That's good," he said holding forth a quarter. "What's your name?"

"Bobby."

"Girls just confuse me, Bobby, with their pony tails, and bobby socks, and now my daughter seems to like bad boys. I don't get it. Like that James Dean fella."

Bobby pursed his lips letting out a puff of air. He'd never run into anyone like this guy in his life and was both fascinated and weirded out.

Bobby watched the guy's Adam's apple move as he gulped his soda. "The bottles are worth two cents. I save the caps too." he turned to Bobby. "What are you, fourteen?"

He nodded.

Jack grinned. "All kids your age love comic books. I think destiny brought you here if you believe in such things because I stock the goriest, brain curdling, grizzliest gut-rot magazines anywhere around these parts. Blood should literally drip from some of those pages, they are so horrid." He grinned and said, "You just take your time Bobby. I'll be in the back. If you find something you want, just let me know."

BOBBY WAS TORN between his father's practical ideas and his mother's fears as he eyed Vampire magazine. He cautiously picked it up with two fingers. He checked behind for evil spirits, ghosts, or anything moving. His mother's warnings echoed in his head. But the pictures were enticing. The vampire pictures reminded him of the store owner, with the cut of his mustache and the shape of his mouth. His mother would say that was Satan's way of hooking him, but his father would tell him that was nonsense. He peeled back one corner of the magazine and experienced a thrilling chill tingling through his body. A noise from the backroom caused him to snap the magazine shut saving himself from sin, just in case. Tucking the magazine back on the rack, he decided to look at other options.

He discarded a Hollywood magazine after looking at a few busty pictures of stars, then he noticed big, black headlines of a story in a newspaper. *"Russia plans to launch nuclear weapons toward Europe and the United States"*

Another chill tingled through his body as he kept reading. *"The world is going to end. There will be bombing.*" Bobby made a rash decision to throw temptation out the window. We're all going to die soon. He picked up the forbidden Vampire magazine and read like a starved child devouring every salacious word.

By the time he was a few paragraphs into the magazine and so far, his hands had not turned to charcoal nor were his fingers crinkled and green.

———————

"Here comes trouble," Jack called out to Bobby.

Then heavy footsteps slapped the floor.

"You got grandma's drugs or what? She's about to kill herself if you don't get them soon."

"Simmer down Blackie. It's not time for her script to be filled."

"Damn it. She can't eat dust Jack; she nearly chewed up the rug last month. That woman is mean without them little pink pills."

Jack shuffled papers around on his counter. "I'll put in another call to see if I can put a rush on it. To tell the truth, son, it's a pain. These pills come all the way from Indianapolis."

Blackie slammed his fist on the counter causing things to bounce. "Dumb ass government regulations. Before we know it, everything we do will be controlled by spies."

"It's tough everywhere," Jack said. Then to get Blackie to move on he said, "Hey, I just got that Vampire issue in. The one you asked about the other day."

"Great. Now you think I got the bucks to buy a magazine that might as well cost a trillion bucks. You realize that, in case you forgot, I live in Dog Town across the railroad track. You're a fancy uptown drug guy living over here by the school and in the big house." His sly wink was supposed to mean something to Jack. "I ain't got money to buy a magazine today and tell you what, you keep putting rare magazines on the rack and some poor kid might just rob you one day. Just saying."

"Blackie, you know I'll help if your folks ever need anything."

He spat on the floor and said, "Shit, Jack. We ain't no beggars. Us Kractes take care of our own."

"Okay, but that's a sad way to look at life, Blackie," Jack said. "In a town this small, where everyone knows everyone else, we need to look out for our neighbor. People need to lean on each other sometimes." He chuckled then pointed toward Bobby, "That's Bobby Hacker, the new kid in town. Go talk to him and be nice. He needs a friend."

Bobby's fingers hadn't turned green or shriveled. The idea that his mother might be wrong was puzzling because she was so adamant about things she believed in. He wanted to keep the magazine, but he didn't have any money and there was no way he would steal it because he knew stealing was a sin. He was trying to think of a way to convince his mother that the magazine was pure bunk when Blackie reached across and snatched the magazine.

"Move over bozo. You're in my spot." Blackie elbowed his way into the small space between Bobby and the wall.

"I didn't mean to get in your way," Bobby said.

"It's all good, kid," Blackie said holding the open comic book in his beefy hands.

Jack went back to work happily assuming the two boys had made friends when suddenly he heard a disruptive clatter.

"It's okay Jack," Blackie called out. "I just dropped some magazines. It's all good here. The new kid is okay. Promise."

Jack poked his head around the pillar just to make sure. Blackie's head popped out, a Cheshire Cat smile pasted across his face.

Bobby wasn't sure what to think. He was used to being the underdog and had a powerful need for friendship. His dad told him to have an adventure and make a friend. This situation seemed to fulfill both of those directions.

Blackie, quick as a whip, pushed him out of the way; then in the melee he stole the magazine, stuffing it under his belt buckle right in front of Bobby who watched the theft with eyes wide.

"Everything, okay, boys?" Jack asked.

"If you tell Jack, I might have to kill you."

STEALING CAME NATURALLY TO BLACKIE. The little pickpocket was born to two young carnies. At age five, his parents, Geno and Angelina, traveling with the Hagenbeck Circus, died in a motor vehicle accident. Blackie grew up with his grandmother Ginny, a pill-popping former high school beauty queen, and grandpop Rippa, who'd retired from the water company, also known as the Dana Heavy Water Plant. His grandmother, Ginny, who felt put-upon having to take a toddler in, called him 'little blackie' because she couldn't call him little "bastard."

Blackie had a pin-prick tattoo on his bare arm. It was the type of crude home-made 'tat' that cell mates and high school kids made by inserting ball point ink and stick pins or needles into their skin to profess love or carve a secret message or name; like carving a heart in a tree stump but more dangerous because of the risk of blood poisoning.

"Is that your girl?" Bobby asked when he noticed Bridgette's name etched in blue ink into the flesh of Blackie's skin.

Blackie lifted his shoulder. "Yep. That's my girl, Bridgette Bardot."

Trying to appear worldly, Bobby answered, "Nice tat."

"Nice rack? Man. Not cool." Blackie's fast fist response was alarming.

Eyes wide, Bobby pulled away quick. "Tat...I said tat."

"You're a jumpy little animal aren't you. You take drugs or what? Drugs would be good 'cause I can train you to be my go-to fetch and pick-up kid. I can use that."

Later, in front of the drug store on main street Blackie arched his back to look toward the Ernie Pyle Theater, and told Bobby, as they both held the handles of their respective rides, "Someday I'm gonna take Bridgette Bardot to a show at that Ernie Pyle theater but now I've got plans for you, good buddy."

Then, he turned the handle of his motor bike, and it began to rumble. He stepped on and said, "You know you are in deep, right? Stick with me and I'll show you how to change your thieving ways."

Bobby looked at Blackie in disbelief. "But...but I didn't do anything."

Then Blackie leaned in close. "You're really a dumb fuck kid, aren't you?" Blackie taunted, revving his motor bike by twisting the handle and turning his front wheel to bump into Bobby's rusty bike.

Bobby gritted his teeth but said nothing. He just wanted to get home.

At the corner Blackie said, "A teacher lives here."

"Okay," Bobby's fingers were sweating now.

"Did anyone teach you not to steal? Like maybe the Bible or something? That comic book you stole from Jack was one of a kind. You belong to me now."

"What do you mean?"

Blackie stopped suddenly. He reached across and grabbed Bobby by the wrist. "Cool your jets man. It's all good, I won't squeal on you. Although, that book means a lot to Jack. He travels to Asia and Vietnam, and Tibet and God know where. Comic book conventions are hard to get to sometimes. It's a weird hobby. Personally, I don't get it."

"It might look like a piece of ink and paper but in the right hands it's worth a lot of money."

Bobby had no idea of the worth of a comic book. His narrow knowledge of reading material up to this point had been Bible stories, required school lessons, the encyclopedia, and the dictionary. He occasionally was given a library book, like *The Old Man and the Sea.* But he struggled through letter by letter trying to decipher the difference between d and p.

This older guy, Blackie, was a bully. No doubt about it. But he was paying attention to Bobby and if he played along, maybe Blackie would let him finish reading the Vampire comic.

"I think theft in this county might get you ten years," Blackie told Bobby. "My cousin got ten years for auto theft but that was a little different. Comic books, now that's a lesser charge but still if you factor in the rarity and all," he paused to think. "Maybe they'll let you off with hard labor in the county jail. But they've got some big ass gorillas in there, man."

RUTH's back strained as she bent to yank weeds in the vegetable plot. At least she was learning a new skill, but she hated this. Looking at the positive, a diet of fresh vegetables would be healthy, and she was counting on saving money this winter by putting up canned goods. The idea of money in her pocket almost made the drudgery of hoeing palatable. Stopping to attend to a blister on her finger, she raised her head and spotted the visitor to her yard.

"Hi there, Mrs. Hacker. I'm Blackie." The boy's approach was enthusiastic.

She'd been told that Dana folk were friendly and could be trusted, but she had a quick flash of *The Raggedy Man* from her favorite childhood poem. Right away the boy explained his presence. He had met her son Bobby and had come by hoping to catch him. And in minutes, he had convinced the exhausted Ruth a take a seat in a nearby lawn chair.

Then, after surveying the garden plot, Blackie took the hoe in hand and began to hack aimlessly at chunks of dirt and grass along one row.

"Where's your husband that he makes you do this hard work?" Blackie leaned on the hoe and met Ruth's eyes.

Ruth stifled a giggle, thinking Darren would be amused at this situation, a rag-tag gypsy kid flirting with his wife. But Blackie was so kind and polite she found herself listening to his sad family history.

"I bet you're thirsty," Ruth said. "I'll fix some tea in the sunroom." Ruth wiped her hands on a towel.

Blackie followed her like a lapdog watching every move. It amused her.

Over tea, he related stories about his grandparents, and told how his grandfather became ill working at the Dana Heavy Water Plant. How the workers wanted to sue but there was so much paperwork involved and so much money needed for lawyers that nobody had taken the first step. She listened with sympathy as Blackie rambled on, but there was nothing she could say without jeopardizing her husband's employment with the military. She was relieved when he finally asked if Bobby was around.

***

ONE WEEK LATER, Darren was standing in front of the big yellow house at the corner of Main Street and Washington in Dana. The major, his commanding officer, was on the porch with the front door open behind him. They had just finished an important meeting, and it was not good news. Darren's back slumped for a second, then he straightened his shoulders, said goodbye to the major, and walked resolutely toward his own house. The gravity of the mission slowed his gait. He had just received unwanted information. And orders he must obey because it was not only his duty but his life.

Just as Ruth gave her life to the Lord or whatever latest fad piqued her interest, Darren gave his to the United States Army. He, however, had been consistent in his loyalty since he was nineteen years old, just a kid barely out of high school. He followed orders and expected his family to understand.

"Call Bob, we need to talk," he directed Ruth. His tone and the fact that he'd called his son "Bob" indicated this would be a serious discussion

"But we just moved here. We haven't even finished unpacking," Ruth told him after hearing the news.

"You'll be fine while I am gone," he told her. "Tend the garden and watch it grow. Make new friends here in Dana. I'm a Mason you can join Eastern Star and join a church here. Every summer they have the Ernie Pyle Festival and parade. Bob, try harder to make friends before school begins." Darren attempted a reassuring smile, but he was rushed. "Do you remember where all my gear is?"

A lot changed once Darren went away.

Ruth went to work redecorating every room. She began to stockpile seed catalogs, canning jars and tiny rubber rings. After that it was new recipes to try and taste. With Ruth obsessing over food, Bobby turned to Blackie for attention. This was the worst choice possible.

— — —

BLACKIE SCRUNCHED up one eye to look through the peephole that Bobby put in his bedroom window covering. Blackie made a big show as he maneuvered his body against the cardboard and silver taped window. This was a ploy because he knew exactly what he was going to say. In truth, he figured this was a lot of trouble for nothing.

"You see it don't you?" Bobby pressed his body against Blackie's rear end.

"Back off, perve." Blackie threw his hand back to push Bobby away. "What am I supposed to see out here?"

"See those huge towers?"

"So?" Blackie made a big show of bending to looking toward the distance antenna towers and satellite dish of the Dana coast guard station. Everyone in Dana knew these structures were there. "Yup. Looks like they are spying on you. That's their tower," he said, backing away from the cardboard patched window.

Blackie rubbed the stubble on his chin. By now, he knew how to ramp up Bobby's panic. "Actually," he added, "they have spy satellites watching you from the sky. Nothing is private anymore. The Reds can map your every move."

"You mean someone out there might be watching while I eat and go to the bathroom? That's against the law, isn't it?" Bobby's eyes widened in alarm.

Blackie gave the top of Bobby's head a light snap. "The government is the law. They can do what they want."

Bobby had no good response. He settled on the bed and watched Blackie who was now strutting around the room in his smelly red tank top. The brown Fedora hat maybe worked in Blackie's favor.

"Is this your dad?" Blackie pushed a gold framed photo in front of Bobby's face. "The big, brave army guy?"

"It's an old picture." Bobby looked small and defeated on a bed surrounded by wall posters of his favorite heroes.

"Your dad's off saving the world for everyone, ain't he? Except that doesn't mean he gives a crap about his one and only son. But look who's here. I am the one holding all the cards here, the one who makes decisions, and I don't forget that I've got you by the, ahem, balls."

Bobby, sheepishly, looked down and said, "I thought we were friends now. I thought you'd forget that silly magazine business."

"I don't need no friend. Do we need to go back over the facts, bozo?"

"No, no, I remember now. You're the Master," Bobby said handing Blackie a wash rag and some soap and pointing him toward the small sink, like an obedient puppy.

"What do I need this shit for?"

"I just want to serve your needs, Master. You said you have a girlfriend. I thought you'd want to wash up before your date."

"Um, I'll do it later," Blackie said throwing both items on the bed.

"Ok with me," Bobby said. "Give me a few minutes and maybe I can come up with a better idea, Master."

"Cut that Master shit or I'll knock your block all the way to China."

Bobby nodded and gave Blackie a half smile. He figured if he could find a way to make himself valuable, things would even out.

After a few minutes he came up with another idea. "I just remembered, I have something." Bobby crossed to his closet and opened a box, poked inside and rustled through the mess. "Here it is," he said laying a folded paper on the bed. "If some enemy decides to blow up Indiana with an atom bomb, these plans show how to protect everything."

"This is what you're wasting your time on?" Blackie asked with a snort. "Stupid blueprints for a bomb shelter?" He reached across to smack Bobby, but his hand stopped mid-air. "Take this shit and tear it to bits. My plan is way better."

Bobby crumpled the plans and tossed it against the wall. "So far, you've given me nothing but talk."

"Okay, then. Listen to this." Then Blackie explained his dangerous plan which involved his girlfriend Bridgette, Bobby and Blackie driving up to the Heavy Water Plant, ignoring all red flags and caution.

"I like you good enough, but I've got morals. I'm not going to kill for you," Bobby said.

"Nobody knows what they'll do in a crunch, and that's a fact."

"What kind of girl is going to go along with that? She's not a blow-up doll."

Naive Bobby had no idea what that meant, so Blackie clocked him.

THE CRESCENT MOON matched the color of Bridgette's sparking sapphire eyes. Jack called her "Bree" because the nickname was easy to say, and it didn't matter that Blackie preferred some Hollywood name.

She was Jack's daughter in the long run, so that didn't count. There was no battle in her mind. But Blackie owned her heart. Bridgette touched her crescent necklace to her throat.

Loving a bad boy was not easy. But she loved to bury her face in the folds of his leather jacket, touch the strands of his oily hair, and even feel his sometimes sweet, sometimes sour kisses on her mouth.

Jack also called her stubborn and obstinate, but she knew since her sibling's death, she could get away with murder. Jack would do anything to fill that hole in his heart.

Perhaps it was selfish that she said Bobby was just a broken kid who'd said nothing about the comic book theft. She felt justified because she was just a broken kid who'd also suffered loss, her mother of cancer, her brother in that accident. And Jack was so absorbed with his fantasies and silly collections that he didn't know what to do with her.

Now, she picked up the dirty, crumpled Vampire comic book from Blackie's bedroom floor and laughed. It was such a tiny betrayal in her mind. Blackie was her baby, cute, adorable and hers. She could envision herself as the Vampire Queen, holding the keys to Jack's store. While her dad thought she was a silly girl, she was watching his every business move. Love might make you momentarily crazy, but it doesn't make you stupid.

Blackie reached out a warning hand and said, "Hold on," as his borrowed car bumped over a series of grates on the yellow painted section of road. "Those cheap mothers don't pay crap for these government roads." He looked over his shoulder toward the frightened passenger strapped into the back seat.

They were driving through a brushy open field, headed toward the Dana Heavy Water Plant, a place Blackie swore to have previously scouted out and determined to be safe because he was on a mission to impress his lady by driving her to the edge of danger. He was lying and Bobby knew it. Guards with M16 rifles and snipers with lenses were patrolling along the high fence that surrounded the entire area. This was a dangerous mission.

Bridgette was sitting beside Blackie, casually clipping a star barrette into her hair. Maybe she was unaware of the danger or perhaps she was along for the thrill. But as tree branches snapped at the windshield, Bridgette's long silver nails dug into Blackie's skin.

From the back seat, Bobby whispered, "Where are we?"

"Shush. See those yellow florescent stakes. That means guards. You want to get us shot?"

"No."

"Then, hold your tongue."

Blackie's grip on the wheel was tight and Bobby could hear him gnashed his teeth. That was the only sound other than the crunch of grass under the tires.

"We're here," Blackie whispered. He turned the key and the world went silent. Slowly, their eyes adjusted to the dark. Bobby imagined Blackie was really a vampire, bringing his victims out here for sacrifice.

Up front, yellow and red lights flashed. Danger Restricted Area. Caution. Do Not Enter.

Blackie reached over, pulled Bridgette into his arms, and whispered, "Kiss me baby."

Suddenly all hell broke loose. Bright lights surrounded them. Sirens were blaring so loud that Bobby had to put his fingers in both ears.

Out of the darkness an army of men wearing battle fatigues and holding weapons surrounded them. An ominous vehicle lumbered up the drive and parked at the bottom of the road with cannons pointed their way, blocking their exit.

Blackie did not look so tough trying to explain what stupidity led him to this point. In the brilliant glare, the three teens were silhouetted, bad children waiting to learn their punishment.

After some time, Bobby was taken to the side to have his identification scanned in a separate officer's light. Bobby dropped his father's name right off the bat. Darren Hacker's name carried a lot of weight. Bobby also told the guards that Blackie beat him up and planned to sabotage the Dana Heavy Water Plant. He lied easily because he'd learned from the Master.

Bridgette ended up fine because Blackie taught her how to scam in bad situations.

Blackie, the MPs discovered, was wanted for a prior burglary at an empty house in Dog Town. They booked him on that and held him for a later trial. He was seen scrubbing floors at the Vermillion County Juvenile Detention Center.

Word of the event went around town, and Bobby gained lots of new friends at Dana High School. Sometimes on the weekend he'd get together with Bridgette and go to Lake's Soda Fountain in Dana to share a cherry Coke and read the latest gruesome comic books.

He considered himself the new bad boy in town.

DANA, INDIANA

In 1957 we moved to Dana, Indiana, the birthplace of World War II journalist Ernie Pyle. My dad was a Methodist minister with two churches, Dana and Bono. Bono is a small country church three miles south of town and the church where the Pyle's family held memberships. Ernie's favorite aunt, Mary Bales, was in her 90s, and I affectionately knew her as "Aunt Mary."

While folks know about Dana because it is Ernie Pyle's place of birth, in the 1950s there was much more to the town. Because of its proximity to Peru, circus performers retired there and the U.S. Army stationed their families there. Folks would plant vegetable gardens and ignore the farm-like silos producing materials to make a bomb more powerful than the one dropped on Hiroshima, Japan, at the end of the Second World War.

THE OPERATORS
BY DIANA CATT

Nothing ever exists entirely alone. Everything is in relation to everything else.
  —Buddha

I turned their whole path and their whole course, and I caused the path of their course to be accelerated, so that they might be purified quickly, and they might go upwards quickly.
  —Jesus Christ, Pistis Sophia: Book One, Chapter 27

We affirm that the existence and personal identity of the individual continue after the change called death.
  —Declaration of Principles, Indiana Association of Spiritualists

Seeing is different than being told.
  —African proverb

Steve Dall and his sister, Dovie, buried their Gran last week. It was a natural passing, no drama. Steve had expected to hear something from Gran by now, but knew these things could take time. His sister, however, wasn't sure.

"Shouldn't it have happened by now?" Dovie asked as she seated herself next to Steve on the front porch swing. "If it was going to, that is. Probably just a lot of *woo woo*."

He knew what she meant. "Don't worry, Dove. Gran knows better than anyone how this works. She'll find us." He pushed a bit with his feet and the swing gently swayed back and forth.

"But, what if something's gone wrong? What if her Way's broken? That can happen, right? Maybe we shouldn't be planning to move yet."

Steve thought it was too early to suspect something that drastic. Time in the afterworld was unpredictable. Anyway, before her passing, Gran and Steve often discussed relocating from Chesterfield, Indiana, to California. Camp Chesterfield, the historic home for spiritualists, was a dream place to live and work for Operators like himself and Gran. But, they would be in greater demand in California, the land of lost and troubled souls, with LA especially in need of their talents.

"Now is perfect," he said. His hands rested, fingers unmoving, on his thighs. "You're done at Ball State. I'm ready for a change. Don't worry. Gran'll find the Way to us no matter where we happen to be living. We're interconnected, remember?"

Dovie nodded. "That's what Gran always said, but I don't know. Maybe she got this all wrong."

"Trust me on this, Sis. Besides, I've already got the realtor coming day after tomorrow."

Dovie shook her head. "I'm not a kid anymore, Steve. I need to understand. You can't leave me out of this mystery. I want to do what you do. What Gran did. If it's real, you've gotta teach me."

Gran had always said Dovie could become an Operator if she ever wanted to push herself. "Okay," Steve said. "Lessons begin tomorrow. We'll start in the morning at the Trail of Religion." They sat together in comfortable silence on the swing until late into the night.

THE TRAIL of Religion was one of Steve's favorite spots at the Camp. The limestone busts of the world's great religious leaders were displayed there. Each religion had their own technique for restoring spiritual balance or reconciliation in the fashion of operators like Gran and Steve: using drums, chants, prayers, prayer beads, song, dance, tapping, and even sand painting to create deliberate vibrations which adjusted the soul and restored balance and harmony.

Dovie had been there many times, of course, since their house was on the property of the Camp, where many Indiana spiritualists lived. However, because of Steve's natural talent, Gran spent more time explaining to him how their skills were universal among religions.

"Some of this you already know, but I'll start with the basics," Steve told Dovie. "We believe there is a physical interdimensional connection between our soul and the souls of all our loved ones in this life and loved ones and ancestors who have passed." He raised an eyebrow and Dovie looked skeptical. "It's an ancient idea," he continued. "Our language is sprinkled with terms related to this connection and to manipulating it; phrases like soothing the soul, creating balance, soulmates, kindred spirits, twin flame, karmic connection, even love at first sight."

He pulled up a picture on his phone and showed it to Dovie. "We can't visualize this structure entirely because it extends into the next dimension, but operators and other spiritualists are sometimes able to catch a glimpse of the energy coming out of the head of a person, like an aura or a halo. The art world is full of images showing a glow around or extending above the head. Gran called it the Way."

"You've actually seen the Way?" Dovie asked. "For real?"

"Yeah. But remember, I helped Gran for years before I mastered the technique. The Way is the coolest thing to see and it's even cooler to manipulate it to get a person back into harmony."

"Why didn't Gran teach me how to do this?"

"I can't say, Dovie, but now that you want to learn we can get started. Want to sit in on my group session this afternoon?"

"Love to, thanks."

THE REALTOR ARRIVED EARLY the following morning and toured their property. Steve and Dovie agreed to terms and the For Sale sign went up in their yard. The realtor advised them to sort through everything and get personal items out of the house ASAP.

"Wouldn't hurt to paint," the realtor said. "And don't forget to check the attic."

Steve shook his head. "I'm not painting and I don't think there's an attic."

The realtor shrugged and said, "There's always an attic. Access's probably in a closet."

Later in the day, Steve finished cleaning up his room, started on Gran's room, and found the attic access in her closet. He wondered how he'd lived there his whole life and not known it existed. The white rectangular recess in the ceiling mesmerized him. Goose bumps formed on his arms and he felt a strangling urge to run like a little kid. He backed out of the closet and took a big breath. The intensity of the moment slowly abated. Steve laughed at his reaction and went to the garage to locate a ladder.

A few minutes later, Steve reentered the closet and set the ladder under the access panel. Before he'd reached the second rung, Dovie appeared at the closet door.

"Need some help?" she asked. Her kinky black hair was covered by a rainbow bandana and she was pulling off pink latex rubber gloves.

"Done with the bathroom already?" Steve asked.

"Yep. Then I saw you go by with the ladder and thought you might need a hand."

"Thanks, but I don't think so."

"I've finished with my room, the living room, the kitchen, and the bathroom. It's time for a break. Could you give me a lesson now? You promised."

Steve eyed the ceiling panel, cognizant of the unexplained feeling of dread, then studied his sister. He *did* promise after all. "Okay, but it'll have to be a quick one. There's still a lot to do on this house." He led her out of Gran's room to the front porch swing.

"You already know Gran and I use different techniques," Steve began as he settled in beside Dovie on the swing. "I'm a tapper, Gran chanted. I don't know what'll work for you. Some operators sing, others play music. Some rap." He lifted his shoulders. "It's all about controlling vibration patterns."

"That's the part I don't get. How'd you learn?"

He shrugged again. "Honestly? I don't remember. It just came naturally, I guess." Dovie frowned so Steve added, "But Gran thought you'd be able to do it when you're ready. Here, give me your hand."

Dovie placed her hand in his, palm up. Steve gently tapped his fingertips on her palm.

"That tickles," she said. "Does it mean something?"

"Yeah. It's a specific pattern for the trail that connects you, me, and Gran to loved ones in the next dimension. I'm intensifying the vibration of the sub-atomic particles to make it visible." He lifted an eyebrow without pausing his fingertips. "At least I think that's how it works."

"Now? You can see it now?"

He nodded and continued tapping. "It's faint. Only gets intense if a soul's in trouble."

Dovie stared alternately from Steve's face to his rapidly moving fingertips. Steve's gaze was glued to a point over his sister's head. After a few minutes Steve stopped and abruptly stood up.

"Don't stop," Dovie said. "I'm sure there was a shimmer. Come on, Steve, just a little longer."

He didn't meet her eye. "Look, I need to check out the attic before the daylight's gone and we need to finish getting the house ready to show.

The realtor said we could have showings as soon as tomorrow." He tried to control his voice. "I'll give you another lesson later. Maybe we can go to the Camp, by the brook. That was one of Gran's favorite spots."

Dovie pushed her lips into a pout. "Slave driver. That wasn't much of a lesson or a break. How about a Starbucks? I'll go get it."

Steve nodded his answer, afraid his voice would give away what he'd seen. The quick glimpse he'd just had of the blocked ethereal trail that connected his immediate family convinced him that Gran's soul was in trouble, and he was on his own. Dovie's first image of the trail shouldn't be one of so much confusion.

He strained to appear normal, to refocus on the job at hand. He headed back into the house to the closet where the ladder waited. The thought of Dovie out of the house for a break filled him with unreasonable relief.

Steve forced himself to stand at the foot of the ladder and stare at the ceiling until he heard Dovie's car back out of the garage and she was safely on her way to get coffee. At the same time, a sense of dread descended on him; worse than the feeling he'd had during his earlier trip into the closet. Even worse than the feeling he'd had when the ambulance transported Gran's lifeless body to the funeral home.

Each aluminum step resounded like a hammer's ping as he moved upward. When the ceiling access panel was within reach, the goose bumps flared again on his arms. He swore under his breath. How could he panic at the thought of an attic? He pushed upward on the panel with both hands. It resisted at first, but after applying more pressure, it moved. There was a lip around the rim of the access and once the panel was lifted above that, he pushed it to the side.

Steve had never been afraid of the dark but the rectangular opening above his head threatened like a gaping black hole of doom. He desperately wanted Gran to appear and give him a pat on the back and a soothing, "there, there, Stevie, nothing to worry about now."

With trembling hands, Steve continued up the ladder until his head was even with the opening. Here, the air turned dense, and he struggled to breathe. Sweat popped on his forehead. Steve forced his head through the opening expecting a cloud of dust. Instead, flashes of a dark and terrifying memory exploded his brain into fragments of fright. His heart pounded in response to the surging adrenaline-induced urge to run.

To run like hell.

Steve squeezed his eyes shut and tried to add substance to that wisp of memory. It wouldn't take form, but the attempt to focus eased his panic. When he reopened his eyes, he spotted a light switch mounted on the nearest support beam. A flip later, a series of dust-caked bulbs glared into action.

Although dim, the light improved his mood, and he released a snort at his momentary panic attack. All that emotion for nothing but a few boring boxes stored on the platform around the opening. Three, to be exact. The only frightening thing would be to discover mold or water damage that would decrease the property value. In fact, he was bummed to see a few inches of black at the roof's peak. He piled up the three old boxes in stair step fashion and climbed them for a closer look at the potential damage.

The realtor hadn't mentioned the consequence of a sleeping bat but Steve didn't think it bode well for his LA plans. He wished he hadn't found the stupid attic access to begin with, then took a step down his makeshift tower and smashed his foot through the bottom box. Glass shattered. Steve winced and hoped he hadn't destroyed something valuable.

He removed his foot, peeked into the box, and plunged headlong into a time warp nightmare. A pair of dark, penetrating eyes stared up into his. The hundred or so fragments of broken glass reflected the dim light from the attic infusing a semblance of life into the portrait. Steve jumped back in terror at the sight of the old woman's face, stumbled over his own feet, and hit his head on a nearby truss. He dropped to the floor.

When he opened his eyes again, the roof peak was slightly out of focus and a lost squadron of pterodactyls were soaring. He blinked tightly several times and the pterodactyls became a small bat taking flight. Steve cursed the old biddy whose portrait had startled him. He lay unmoving and observed the erratic course of the creature overhead. Eventually, it departed into the darkening outside universe through a tiny opening by a vent under the eave. His head pounded to the near-silent dance of wings and he felt like crap. Literally. He was lying next to a pyramid of bat guano that had built up directly under the roosting bat.

Steve stood and shook the debris out of his hair and clothes. All he needed to do was get these three boxes down to the dumpster, seal up that hole by the vent, sweep up the bat crap, and never go into any attic ever again. The busted box with the old woman's picture would be the first to go. As he moved toward the box, flashes of memory haunted the edge of his mind with those dark, accusing eyes at the center. She'd been staring at him—a little boy quaking from fear mixed with guilt and shame compounded by those unrelenting coal black eyes.

He peered through the broken top flaps of the box. "Well, old hag, you gave me a scare." His voice echoed in the empty dimness and he looked over his shoulder. Did he see a hint of movement? He stared at a spot midway across the floor, tapped his fingertips against his thigh. Nothing materialized.

He turned back to the portrait. It depicted the life-sized head and shoulders of a seriously unfriendly looking woman in an oval carved wooden frame. Steve turned it over, shaking loose the remaining shards of glass, and looked at the feathery writing on the back. Mrs. Iris Dall, 1898. "Great-granny, I see," Steve said. "I'm sure glad Dovie and I didn't get your looks." He thought the frame might be worth some money down at Shapiro's Antiques, even with the glass front broken.

As he placed it back in the box, face down this time, a soft russet lump in the corner of the box caught his attention. He grabbed up the little bear he'd known as Jackie Bear, still wearing its bright red vest and shook it free of glass shards. Jackie Bear was missing one brown button eye. Then Steve noticed one of Jackie's legs was hanging by a thread.

And the screams started.

It wasn't Steve screaming. At least not the present-day Steve. These were memory screams. But the terror in them was as real today as whenever it had happened. Steve's heart pounded and his legs began to feel rubbery.

The memory took shape. He wanted to force it back into oblivion, but it avalanched. There'd been a man, there in the attic. Steve could remember him in his white T-shirt and jeans. He could remember the shimmery particle trail reaching from the man's head and stretching into the nether land. The image terrified him. He'd never seen a trail on anyone and didn't know what it meant.

And the man was yelling and hurting him. Little Stevie screamed over and over and struggled to free himself from the man's grip. Jackie Bear had been caught in the struggle and the knife sliced across the toy's leg at the seam before entering Stevie's leg. Stevie felt Jackie's pain intertwine with his own. His fingers began to quake and he tapped against his leg as a reflex to the pain and fear. He watched the shimmery trail coming out of the man's head change consistency to the rhythm of his tapping fingers and a barrier of vibrating particles formed that seemed to concentrate the man's force away from Stevie.

Then suddenly Gran was there. Yelling curses at the man, trying to pry loose her young grandson from the man's violent grip. Steve saw it as if it were happening today. He heard Gran's cold, snappy order, "Daray. Stop. Right now."

He'd seen a shimmery trail emerge from Gran's head, too. Little Stevie's fingers tapped a pattern on Gran's arm and he watched her trail molecules shift and rearrange into a more comforting pattern. Gran stared at him in surprise for a moment, then gently removed his fingers from her arm and folded them into a tiny fist. She whispered to Little Stevie to turn around and stand very still.

In the midst of the turmoil, pain, and confusion of the moment, Stevie obeyed Gran. He turned his back to the man and his attention was caught by that horrible old lady picture. The black eyes bore into him, watching the little boy's pain, accusing him. Terror clouded the details, but he distinctly heard Gran threaten the man. "You'll never hurt another child again." This was followed by the man's scream, then silence. Seconds later, Gran picked Little Stevie up and carried him down the ladder.

Present day Steve, desperate to escape the terror of the memory, fled the attic. When he reached the curb in front of the house he stopped and looked up and down the street, unsure of his next step. He sucked in gulps of night air and turned back to look at the house. Light leaked out of the attic vents. How could he have lived there his whole life and not known that chamber of horror existed? Now Gran was gone and there was no one to explain the horrific scene he remembered in such vivid detail.

He paced along the curb trying to sort through the images in his mind, searching for another conclusion, unconsciously rubbing the scar on his upper thigh. He was startled by a car turning into his driveway. Dovie's cheerful voice greeted him and announced coffee and more packing boxes. Her cheerfulness faded as she approached Steve with the Starbuck's offering.

"What's going on? You look like you've seen a ghost." Then a hopeful, "Did you see Gran?"

Steve shook his head and reached out for the coffee cup. That's when he realized he was still holding Jackie Bear.

"It wasn't her spirit," he said. "It was a memory about her. I think she's in trouble after all. Come on."

Steve ran back to the house, trying to explain his memory to Dovie, who followed. "Something bad happened that day, Dove. She called him Daray. That was our dad's name. He was hurting me and I think Gran hurt him. Maybe killed him."

"Killed him?" She leaped to her next question. "That would mean she's trapped? Oh no, not Gran. Are you sure?"

"No. Maybe. I don't know. But there might be enough force left up there that we can find out."

The terror of the long-ago memory overwhelmed Steve again as he passed through the attic access. He grabbed Dovie's hand and pulled her through the opening to stand next to him in the dimly lit area. "Can you feel it?" he asked in a hoarse whisper.

Her eyes were wide and alert. She gripped his hand like a lifeline. "Yes."

A wave of emotion poured across Steve with the force of a tsunami and he hung onto his sister to keep himself upright. He dropped Jackie Bear to the dusty attic floor and felt pain crash through him as the bear landed. His fingers trembled as they had in his memory. He was helpless with fear.

"Tap out Gran's pattern," Dovie said. "Like you did on the swing."

In his panic, he couldn't remember it. All he could do was stare at the malevolent shimmer materializing in the center of the room.

"Steve," Dovie shouted. She grabbed his hand and tried to remember the pattern he'd earlier tapped into her palm. Her rendition was crude but he recognized it. It broke through his fear and spurred him to action. He tapped furiously onto his thigh.

A shape began to materialize. He heard his sister gasp.

"I see it," she said under her breath. "It's vaguely like a person. Is it a ghost? No, wait. There's two shapes together. It's like they have elongated heads that go on forever."

Steve didn't have time to agree. "Focus," he said. "We've got to free her. Daray's path is here too, and they're intermingled or are on top of each other. She's trapped. We've got to do this, Dovie. Focus on Gran's pattern."

Steve was tapping rapidly on his thigh, studying the path, visualizing subtle changes in the particles. It wasn't enough. The blockade extended beyond the usual contour, stretching out to where the shared trail entered Dovie and himself. Steve was shocked to come upon a barrier with this strength. The particles spun wildly, reversed direction, fought his manipulations. He'd never encountered this directed opposition to his operator's ability. It must be coming from Daray. He struggled to make every tiny movement of his fingertips effective.

But to no avail. He wasn't going to free Gran and it scared him to the depths of his soul.

Then he heard Dovie. She'd started chanting and was varying her intonations and pitches to create a hypnotic serenade. It was like working with Gran again. Dovie's newfound ability allowed her to respond to changes in the particle pattern of the trails with increasing accuracy.

Little by little, the combination of the chant and the tap patterns was having an effect. Steve could see the patterns separate, particles align. The barricade in Gran's trail grew thinner. Daray's remained unchanged, blocked at an impenetrable depth. The individual sub-atomic pieces of Gran's trail slipped, one by one, into time-worn, comforting alignment.

Then, like a dam bursting, Gran's trail opened. Her spirit could flow above, below, and all through her trail. The release washed along the shared trail through Steve and Dovie in a rush. Gran was free. The battle ended. She was on her Way to the next dimension.

Then Steve noticed a new vibration appear in the trail and recognized Gran's handiwork. He watched in fascination as particles moved into a symmetry that he knew would repress once again his memory of Daray's long ago attack on him and Gran's defensive, fatal response.

It was Gran's gift to him, he realized, at the same moment it was forgotten forever.

Steve's spirit lightened. His tapping intermingled in the atmosphere with Dovie's chants. They felt the unification of the trail with Gran and a renewed sense of operator purpose. Dovie's laugh tickled the air. She hugged Steve and tried to twirl him around. "We did it. We contacted Gran. That was so awesome."

"And look at you. You're an operator. Now *that* was awesome."

Dovie's grin filled her face. "Hey, don't forget about your coffee. I picked up some pumpkin bread too. Come on, let's celebrate." She pounded down the rickety ladder.

As Steve reached out to flip off the lights he spotted a russet lump on the attic floor. "I don't believe it," he said. "Jackie Bear. Wow, I haven't seen you in ages."

He picked up the little toy with the red vest and dangling leg and wiped dust off its head. As he straightened up, he thought he saw movement in the center of the room. He stared in that direction and tapped a pattern on his leg but nothing materialized. It must have just been dust particles. Nothing more. He turned out the lights and climbed down the ladder. He'd head back up later with the duct tape and broom.

"Hey Sis. Know where Gran kept her sewing kit?" He studied the frayed stitching on his bear's leg. "I've got some repair work to do."

HISTORIC CAMP CHESTERFIELD, A SPIRITUAL CENTER OF LIGHT

Camp Chesterfield was founded in 1891, and is the home of the Indiana Association of Spiritualists and located in Chesterfield. In 2002, the camp was designated an historic district, the "Chesterfield Spiritualist Camp District," and listed on the National Register of Historic Places.

Camp Chesterfield offers weekly Spiritualist Church services; a college comprised of a Seminary, the School of Mediumship, the School of Healing, and the School of Metaphysics; as well as psychic readings for patrons.

The Camp features the Hett Art Gallery and Museum, the Western Hotel, the Sunflower Hotel, the Chapel in the Woods, the Cathedral of the Woods, the American Indian Memorial, the Totem Pole, the Garden of Prayer and Sentinel Angel, the Labyrinth, the

Toadstools, the Trail of Religions, the Chesterfield Lighthouse, the Fountain and Memory Gardens, the Buddha Garden, and about fifty residential homes on the property for spiritualists.

Visitors can also find reference books, crystals, sing bowls, totems, jewelry, stones, statuary, incense, candles, essential oils, tarot cards, and much more at the Tree of Life Books and Gifts store.

The grounds offer a quiet place for meditation, reflection, comfort, and transformation. This space is far from ordinary... it is considered sacred.

THE MOVING BLUES
BY CULLEN COLE

Burt had been off the clock for fifteen minutes when he turned his police cruiser onto Logan Street. The old neighborhood, the Conner Street Historic District, was a national landmark now, but it was still just home to him. With preservation statutes and gentrification, it looked like a quaint bit of Americana—something straight out of a 1950s fantasy. Duty had called him here too often for him to pretend it was anything more than an illusion, though. No matter how much you dolled it up, this was still a workingman's neighborhood. It had been a good place to grow up and was still a good place to live.

Scanning his neighbor's homes with his high-powered spotlight, careful as always to avoid the windows, he never ended his patrol until he pulled into his driveway. He kept watch over the people that lived here and noticed all the little things as he drove home.

Three bikes and a big tree branch downed in the late season thunderstorm last week were left out in the yard at single mother Brittany's house. Sour, old Mrs. Potter had missed her trash can again when throwing out her latest mega vodka bottle from Costco. Anthony, Democratic Party coordinator for the county, had plastered his yard with political signs–everything from Harris/Walz 2024 to Lopez for School Board.

Burt made a mental note to check in on Brittany this weekend. It looked like she could use some help. Maybe if her ex had the kids, she would even offer to make his Saturday night a little more cozy and a lot less lonely.

Passing Emma and Lyle's house, he noticed the lights in the front room were still on after midnight. Emma must have insomnia again. He drove another block, turned onto 12th Street, into the alley, and parked in the garage behind his red, clapboard bungalow.

Burt hung his hat on the hook inside the door and unbuttoned the top two buttons of his blue uniform. He locked his gun and holster in the safe in the laundry room, then set about feeding his fish, Goldie and Kurt. He looked in the frig, but found nothing appealing to eat. Out of Budweiser, too. Damn. It had been a long day, but he was still too revved up to go to bed.

Although a chill had crept in after sunset, Burt thought it was probably still a pretty nice night for a walk, and maybe a little company, too, if Emma was still awake. He grabbed a windbreaker from the hook near the door and headed out. One block south, he could see the light inside Emma's house still illuminating half her front yard.

As he neared her porch, he could see her shadow moving across the curtains of the front room. He smiled as she stood, her very pregnant belly projected grotesquely huge against the drapes, like a funhouse mirror. She stretched and put her hands to the small of her back. He contemplated the misery of carrying something so heavy in such a precarious place and decided for the ten millionth time—he was glad to be a man.

He paused on the stoop where he could hear Emma inside singing, "Hush, little baby, don't say a word. Momma's gonna buy you a mockingbird. If that mockingbird won't sing... "

Burt had always loved her voice. She sounded every bit as good as she had in high school choir and the musicals she'd performed in then. When they'd dated senior year, he'd listened to her for hours while helping her rehearse. Smiling at the memory, he stood in front of the peephole so he wouldn't scare her when he rang the bell. A moment later, the door swung open and Emma welcomed him in.

"Hey, Stranger! What are you doing out so late?"

"Just got home from work." Burt surveyed the moving boxes stacked in huge heaps around the perimeter of the living room. "Saw your lights on my way home and thought I'd check in and make sure you're okay."

Emma gave him a quick hug and ushered him inside. "I'm glad you did. It's always nice to see you. And I'll miss these unexpected visits when we move."

"So will I." Burt nodded toward the boxes. "Looks like you're just about ready. When do the movers come?"

"Ugh! Tuesday. I don't know if I'll be ready by then. Everything's packed, but I was hoping to sort through everything first so we don't end up paying to move boxes of garbage and things we'll never use." Emma laughed and ushered Burt to the couch. "Lyle has been so wonderful. He's already got the nursery painted and set up in our new place. It almost looks like a home before we even get the furniture moved."

"I'm not surprised. He is the most organized person I've ever met. Unlike you!" Burt laughed, waving an arm toward the chaos of the room. "I don't know how you two ever got together. I guess opposites really do attract." Burt looked shyly at Emma from beneath dark lashes. "So, how are you two doing? It must be hard living apart these last few months?"

Emma gave a heavy sigh. "Yeah. I've been missing him." She stood and walked toward the kitchen, talking over her shoulder. "But only a few more days. I can't wait!" Emma returned with a bottle of beer, which she handed to Burt. She sipped from a glass of water before sitting next to him on the couch.

Burt nodded his thanks. "I will certainly miss you when you go, but I'll be very happy to know you're not alone at night anymore."

He took a deep swig from the bottle, wiped his mouth on his sleeve, and settled back into the couch. "This serial killer that's been running loose the last six years has certainly amped up his game in the last couple of months. We've recently found three more bodies."

Emma sat forward, startled. "Are you kidding?! A serial killer here in Noblesville? I hadn't heard. I guess I've been so busy with…" She indicated the mess in the room. "I haven't been listening to the news. How long has this been going on?"

"Around six years, give or take."

"Wow! I think I remember hearing something about that a couple of years ago, but I thought you caught the guy."

"No. You're thinking of the guy outside Chicago. He's locked up now."

Emma settled back next to Burt. "Glad to hear it. So, there's still one out there? I mean here?" She shivered.

"Yeah. We've been keeping the details quiet. He was pretty prolific at first, but there hasn't been much to go on for a while. We've been reporting the deaths, of course, but withheld relating them to the serial killer, so as not to create a panic or tip him off to what we know. He hasn't been too active the last year or so. We even thought he may have moved on. Until now." Burt turned to Emma, looking directly into her eyes. "But between you and me, I've been keeping an eye out for *you*. The victims all bear a small resemblance to you."

He recalled the last few victims.

The pretty, young waitress whose nose had the same slope as Emma's. The unidentified woman who had the same spacing of the eyes and the same high cheekbones, Burt recalled as he straightened his shoulders. "Not pregnant, but still a lot like you. He seems to have a type."

Emma gasped, looking dismayed. "Now you're scaring me."

"Good. I mean to. I want you to be extra careful." Burt glanced around as if someone might overhear him. "And I probably shouldn't tell you this either, but there was another woman found last week in Fort Wayne. We haven't tied her to our cases yet, but..."

Emma gulped, her eyes now large and round. "That's where we're moving to."

"I know. That's why I'm telling you this. I want you to be aware and alert." Burt took one of her hands in his. "I want you to be safe."

"You've succeeded! I'm so aware and alert, I may never sleep again!" Emma laughed half-heartedly, before removing her hand from Burt's grasp. "Well, now maybe I *will* get all this sorted before Tuesday."

"Can I help? I'd feel better if I could stay awhile and make sure you're okay."

Emma looked at him doubtfully. "Are you sure? I mean, I would definitely feel better having you here, but you don't have to work."

"Yes. It'll be a good way to pass the time. Now that I've planted that seed of caution, we can talk about something more pleasant while we get you ready for your new life."

"If you're sure?" Emma accepted a hand up from Burt before leading him to the chaotic stacks across the room. "These still need to be sorted and repacked."

They each tackled a pile of boxes, opening them and sorting through the contents while they made small talk. Burt held up a baseball mitt, a questioning look to Emma.

She nodded and reached for the mitt. "See? This is my problem. Every time I come across something I haven't seen for a long time, it brings up old memories." After studying it a moment, she put it in a box marked sports equipment.

"Like that old mitt. Reminds me of playing softball with your sister, Jenna." Emma's focus softened as she gazed into the past. "Which, of course, reminds me of the day she brought me home with her after practice." She looked at Burt. "And I met you."

Emma diverted her gaze and stared into the box. "Those were some good days, weren't they?" Tears threatened as she gazed wistfully at Burt.

Burt held her eyes for a moment, shook his head, and looked off into the distance. "Yeah. We had a lot of good days together."

"Why did we break up, anyway?"

Burt turned toward her and looked at her extended belly. "Well, you obviously found a better man!"

"That's not the way I remember it. You broke up with me," Emma said, just above a whisper.

Burt looked puzzled. "Really? I thought you broke up with me."

Emma spoke more forcefully. "*No*. Remember? We were at Luigi's having pizza, when we suddenly got into a big argument over something stupid and then..."

Burt faced her. "Yes! Then you broke up with me and walked out."

Emma grew serious. "No. *You* broke up with *me*. Then, I walked out."

Burt laughed. "No. I *never* would have broken up with you."

Emma's cheeks flushed with anger. "Well, you did."

Burt finally realized the serious tone their conversation had taken. "I can't believe that. But if I did, then I was a total schmuck. I was *crazy* about you."

Emma turned back to her box, concentrating on sealing it with packing tape. "Well, you sure didn't waste any time hooking up with Chelsea the Cheerleader after that." She tossed the box on a finished stack a bit more forcefully than necessary.

"Chelsea?" Burt scratched the stubble on his chin. "Oh yeah, Chelsea. I forgot about that." He chuckled. "I was only trying to make you jealous, so you'd come back to me. Guess that backfired, huh?" Burt stopped what he was working on and turned to Emma. "You know there's never been...I mean, I always hoped..."

Emma stopped him with a hard shake of her head. Discouraged, Burt taped the box he was working on, then turned to a pile of boxes under a huge plastic sheet. He pulled the tarp onto the floor and lifted a chest off the top of the pile.

Emma pointed at the heap he'd just uncovered. "Oh, you can

leave those alone. Those belong to Lyle and I think he's already gone through it."

Burt set the chest on top of another box to get it out of the way, but the box was unsteady and the chest toppled off, falling open. A small black duffle bag fell out. He picked it up by one of the handles, intending to put it back in the chest, but the bag gaped open. Burt froze when he saw what it held.

"Umm, Emma? I think you need to see this." Burt stepped over to the couch and sat, placing the bag in front of him on the coffee table.

Emma stood stiffly, holding her back, and walked over to join him on the couch. "I was ready for a break, anyway. What is it?" She sat and took a long drink of water.

Burt pulled out an item from the duffle, held it up, named it, then laid it on the table. "Rope." Emma looked uninterested. He continued pulling items out. "Latex gloves. Duct tape." Emma leaned back and examined a torn fingernail. "Old blanket. Foldable shovel. Hunting knife."

Duffel emptied, Burt looked expectantly at Emma.

Emma wrinkled her brow, confused. "So? What's this?"

"It looks like a serial killer starter kit."

Emma laughed nervously. "What are you talking about?"

Burt leaned forward, inviting her to look more closely at the objects on display. "It looks like a serial killer starter kit."

"Don't be ridiculous! What would something like that be doing here?"

"That's what I'd like to know."

"What are you saying?" Emma shook her head no. She turned to Burt. "You think?" Her eyes grew wide with fear. Burt nodded grimly.

"You can't think Lyle...?" Emma stood and started putting the items back in the duffle. "No. That's impossible! Lyle is a good man! A wonderful man! He would never." She clutched her belly. "No! No! No!"

Burt rose and put his arms around Emma. "It's okay. It's okay." Emma relaxed into his embrace, and he stroked her hair. "It will all be okay. I won't let anything happen to you." Emma stiffened in his arms. "But we need to look at this logically. Let's sit down and talk about this."

Emma distanced herself from Burt as they sat. "This is ridiculous! You can't really believe that Lyle could…" She waved her hand at the items still on the table. "I'm sure there's an explanation for all this."

"I'm sure there is," Burt said, his voice gentle. "What could it be?"

"I don't know," Emma said defiantly. "But I know there is one. I mean, this is Lyle we're talking about."

"Well, I may be biased, but the only explanation I can think of is the obvious one." Burt tried to keep his tone soothing. It was obvious how much this was upsetting her. "How long have you been married? Six years? Well, how long do you think this killing spree has lasted? Six years." Emma glared at him, but he continued. "And isn't that about how long you and Lyle have lived here? How well do you know Lyle? Where is he from? Maybe I should check for murders in that area, too, wherever he was before he moved here."

"Stop it. You've got it all wrong!" Emma leaned forward, trying to convince Burt. "Lyle is *not* a murderer! He is the gentlest, kindest man I've ever met. He's so…so boring!" She picked up the rope, set it back down again. "This could be camping gear, or maybe he was going to dig up a few trees for our new yard or something. I don't know what it means, but I *do* know it does *not* mean what you're saying."

"I hope you're right, Emma. Truly, I do." Burt reached a hand to her, which she rebuffed. "But we have to be smart about this. It looks all wrong. The evidence…" Emma glared at him. Burt changed his tack. "The *possible* evidence is pointing to the *possibility* that Lyle has been up to something *potentially* very bad. For your sake and peace of mind, and for the baby's sake, we need to check this out."

Emma shook her head violently. She grabbed her phone. "I'm going to call him right now. You'll see."

Burt tried to stop her, but she held the phone out of his reach.

"No! That's not a good idea!" Emma speed dialed her husband and put it on speaker. "We don't want to tip him off!" Burt reached for her phone again as it rang. Emma slapped his hand away and put a finger to her lips as Lyle answered.

"Hi, Honey. I hope I didn't wake you." Emma waved a hand at Burt and he slumped back on the couch, defeated. "I was up late packing and started missing you. I just wanted to hear your voice."

Lyle answered groggily, the sound of voices and canned laughter in the background. "Hi, Babe, yeah. I miss you too." They could hear a click and the television was muted. "Guess I nodded off watching the Late Show. Are you OK?"

"Oh yeah. Don't worry about me. We're fine, baby and me. Just missing you."

Burt rolled his eyes as Lyle answered. "Me, too. Less than a week now. I can't wait to see you. Put my arms around you and..."

"Me, too," Emma interjected. "Hey! Before I forget, I was going through a few things and I wanted to ask you about a couple of them." Burt frantically shook his head no. Emma waved him off. "Remember your old hockey jerseys? I think the moths got to them. Do you still want those?"

"Yes!" Lyle sounded a bit more alert, but his voice was still tinny over the speaker. "Don't throw those out. I'll see if I can get them fixed up later, but definitely keep those."

"Okay. I thought so, but figured I'd better check. Also, there was the weed whacker thingy. We have two of them in the garage. Do you want both of them?"

Lyle did not hesitate. "No. Just the green one. Be sure to keep the battery and charger with it. You can set the orange one by the curb. Maybe someone else will want it before the trashman comes."

Burt gestured for her to wrap up the call before bringing up the duffel. Emma ignored him.

"Mmm, hmm. I'll do that. Just one more thing." Emma hovered over the phone. Burt leaned in intently. "There was a black duffel bag inside a chest. Do you still want that?"

Burt huffed angrily. Emma frowned and put a finger to her lips to shush him.

There was a long pause before Lyle answered. The silence was so heavy you could cut it with the hunting knife glinting dangerously in the phone's reflection. "I don't know what you're talking about. A black duffel? Doesn't sound familiar."

"No? You sure?" Emma and Burt sat on the edge of their seats awaiting his answer.

There was a muffled sound, then "Nope. Drawing a blank here."

Emma sighed in relief while Burt looked as if he'd choked on a chicken bone. There was another long pause.

Lyle broke the silence. "Why don't you just throw it in with the rest of the stuff and I'll look at it later."

"Okay, Honey. Will do. Sorry I woke you. I'll let you get back to sleep. I love you."

"Love you too, sweetheart. Sweet dreams." Lyle made a loud smooch sound.

Emma returned a louder one before hanging up. She looked nervously at Burt, who put his head in his hands.

"Damn. I wish you hadn't done that. Now I need to put a rush on getting this stuff to forensics."

Emma wrung her hands. "So, you really think...?" Burt nodded, still not looking at her. Emma eyed the contents of the bag now strewn across the table. "Well, in that case, there's something else you might want to have checked out. I found it yesterday and I didn't think anything of it at the time." Burt looked at her expectantly. "It's in the box on top of that stack in the corner." Emma pointed to the stack of boxes where he'd found the duffel.

Burt strode to the pile, stood on the tarp, and reached for the top box. "Here?" He looked over his shoulder at Emma, who stood awkwardly and nodded, rubbing her belly. Burt turned back to his task. He set the box on the floor and struggled with the packing tape. The heavy duty tape refused to break despite Burt's efforts.

Emma picked up the hunting knife from the table and crossed

over to him. She stood silently behind him for a moment before plunging the knife deep into his neck. Burt grabbed at the knife, but there was no strength left in his fingers. Emma took him in her arms and eased him onto the floor.

Burt looked into her deep brown eyes, thought how much he had loved this woman and thought he saw his love reflected there. He tried to touch her face, but his arm would not respond. Darkness overcame him before he could comprehend what had happened.

"I'm so sorry, love." Emma stroked the hair back out of Burt's face as he gurgled his last breath. "I really wish you hadn't dropped in tonight and dropped my bag. I *told* you to leave that pile alone." She cradled him there on the floor. "You never did listen. It's actually all your fault. I've never been the same since you broke up with me."

She confessed her hurt and anger, the cruel things she'd done to relieve her pain. It was her duty to rid the world of those evil women. She knew just by looking at them, the horrible thoughts that dwelt inside them. The world was a much safer place for everyone - Burt, Lyle, her baby - without those awful women.

When she was through, Emma struggled to her feet and wiped her bloody hands on her sweatpants. She folded the tarp over Burt's body, expertly wrapping it the same way she'd done many others - without spilling a single drop of blood. Turning the chest on its side so that the opening faced the body, she rolled the heavy package inside. She heaved the chest onto a furniture dolly and carted it to the garage and her waiting SUV. As she pondered the best way to lever the chest inside, Emma rubbed her swollen belly and sang, "Hush little baby, don't say a word. Mama's gonna buy you a mockingbird..."

CONNER STREET HISTORIC DISTRICT

Beneath the quiet charm of the Conner Street Historic District lies a deeper, older Noblesville—one forged in gaslight and grit.

Between 1840 and 1947, this neighborhood grew alongside the railroad and the natural gas boom, its prosperity etched in ornate facades and imposing gables. Today, 146 historic buildings line its streets, their styles ranging from Queen Anne and Italianate to Colonial and Craftsman, each one like a character in a well-worn mystery novel, eager to spill a few secrets.

Passersby will find turrets and wrap-around porches, stained glass and gingerbread trim. Notable landmarks like the whimsical Craig and Craycraft Houses make it easy to imagine whispering neighbors, unsolved puzzles, or the occasional ghost with good manners.

Today, Conner Street feels more like a glimpse into small town, middle class America. The streets are lined with trees that seem to lean in for a better listen. Shadowy movement caught behind curtains makes one curious about the people living within. And every mailbox, every garden gate feels like the first clue in a charming whodunit.

For mystery lovers, it's the kind of place where stories practically write themselves in their imagination.

JOHNNY NEVER CAME MARCHING HOME
BY RAMONA G. HENDERSON

I stood on the Isle of Crete, looking out at the bay as the sun began to set, giving a purple hue to the massive gray structure floating in the water. Twenty-five years since the end of the Second World War and she was still at sea. The Hellenic Navy named the ship Syros, L-144, but I knew her as LST-325. The ship's presence reminded me of who I really was. And who was I? A shipbuilder, an Army veteran, an auto plant foreman, a family man. And an imposter? Lorraine focused on my eyes. "You look sad."

"It brings back so many memories," I said. "That ship took me across the English Channel when I was wounded."

"Are you sure, my love? It's a Greek ship."

"It used to belong to the United States Navy. It's a ship like the ones I used to help build before I went into the Army."

"It brings back memories of your home in Evansville. Do you wish to go back there?"

I smiled at her. "No, that was so long ago, and I have no desire to go back. You and France have given me a better home than I ever had there."

Neither of us wanted those memories but they were always there, on some days more vivid than others.

"We should go, Charles. The restaurant will be full."

"Go ahead and get us a table. I'll join you in a little while."

Lorraine kissed me. "What is it with you Americans and the sunset?"

My eyes followed her until she disappeared into the restaurant. Then I turned toward the ship and the memories it was stirring in me. After all these years I still wondered if my past would catch up to me some day. If so, would those I cherish the most still accept me?

MY PARENTS and sister were killed in an auto accident when I was nine and I was taken in by an uncle, Woodrow Watters. He was my only living relative. At the time, I didn't realize what a horrible man he was. Uncle Woody was twice divorced and shifted from one job to the next. It appeared to be lousy luck until I learned the truth. He was an alcoholic and mean as hell when he was drunk. I lost count of the number of beatings I'd endured. I locked myself in my room or stayed at my friend Nick Jackson's as long and as often as I could. His parents seemed to recognize my situation and were very good to me.

Uncle Woody was supposed to manage the money my parents left. I never knew how he squandered it, but after three years, we had to sell the house where I grew up and move to a small apartment a few blocks away.

When I was thirteen, I got a job at a neighborhood grocery stocking shelves and cleaning. The job was another way of escaping Uncle Woody.

WORLD WAR II created a tremendous need for ships, boats, planes, and ammunition. Local manufacturers with defense contracts transitioned to building military equipment and it changed Evansville practically overnight. A massive shipyard was built next to the Ohio

River. Thousands of people swarmed into the city looking for work. Most people with extra rooms rented them. Federal prefabricated houses and mobile homes sprung up like mushrooms in a damp forest, and our city would never be the same.

My friend Nick and I graduated from high school in the spring of 1942. A week later, we applied for jobs at the shipyard. We worked nights, making more money than an eighteen-year-old could imagine.

The work was grueling, and the constant sounds of metal clanging and warning bells from cranes were, sometimes, overwhelming. To me, the noise was the worst part of the job, along with the threat of injury. An accident occurred every day, and many were debilitating.

Four months into the job, Nick and I decided we wanted to contribute more to the war effort and would join the military. Nick passed his physical with flying colors. I was shocked to learn I was 4F. The doctor who examined me told me I had flat feet.

When I told Nick, he was more surprised than I was. "You played basketball and ran track in school and never noticed a problem. You can outrun me. That doctor must be some quack."

Uncle Woody was happy I was 4F. He said it was better for me to stay at the yard and keep making good money. By then, his alcoholic liver had finally caught up to him, and he was too ill to take on the occasional odd job. I was the only one keeping a roof over our heads. Three days after I was declared 4F, I took him to the hospital, where he died the following week.

THE DAY after Uncle Woody's funeral Nick and I stopped at our favorite restaurant with a bar. I was on my way to work, and it was Nick's night off. Buster Jones, the barkeeper, knew us well because we had been there many times to take Uncle Woody home when he became too rowdy. He knew we liked to listen to the juke box, so he would let us sit at the bar. He also knew we weren't old enough to drink and would only sell us Cokes and root beer.

As we sat at the bar talking about my experience with the doctor at the recruitment center, a guy next to us started talking. "Don't worry about it. If this war lasts much longer, the Army will gladly take you."

I recognized him as a swing shift worker but didn't know his name.

"I'm Johnny Watters, and this is Nick Jackson," I said. We work the night shift at the shipyard."

He reached out his hand and shook both our hands. "Charlie Keegan. I worked the swing shift but gave my notice last week. Yesterday was my last day. I'm catching a train for Fort Benning at six in the morning."

"Where's that?" asked Nick.

"Georgia," said Charlie.

"Lucky you," I said. "Nick here is going, too, but hasn't received his notice yet."

"Figured I'd stay at the yard until they notify me," said Nick. "My family can use the money."

"It doesn't seem right to leave your family behind. I don't have anybody. I should be the one going," I said.

"You're like me," said Charlie. "Everybody kept asking me why I didn't take a few days off before I left for the Army, but I didn't have anyone to spend them with. I'm an orphan. Never knew who my parents were. Guess the Army's going to be my family now."

"My parents died when I was nine. I had an uncle who took me in, but he was a drunk, so things weren't so great," I said. "He recently died."

"At least you had a roof over your head that wasn't an orphanage," said Charlie.

"Believe me, you wouldn't have wanted to deal with my uncle."

Charlie talked to us for a good hour while frequently glancing at his watch.

Finally, Nick asked him if he was expecting somebody.

"A girl I know was supposed to meet me here to tell me goodbye. Looks like she's not going to show," said Charlie.

"Your girlfriend?" asked Nick.

"No, not really. Just someone I hang out with occasionally."

A few minutes later, Charlie left the bar. "Nice talking to you guys. I gotta get home and finish packing."

I wished him good luck. I had another hour and a half before the night shift started. As we sat on bar stools sipping our last Coke of the evening, someone grabbed my left shoulder and spun me around. "What the hell," I said, looking at a fist directed toward my face. It was attached to a muscle-bound guy who was probably six four.

"Keegan, I told you to stay away from my Sally," the guy said.

"He's not Keegan," yelled Nick.

The guy leaned in closer to my face. "Sorry, bud. Thought you were the guy who's been messing with my girlfriend."

"No problem," I said as I centered myself on the bar stool.

Buster saw what happened. "Don't need any trouble tonight. If you're looking for Keegan, he left a good ten minutes ago. Now, get out of here." He motioned toward the door with his hand.

"Buster, who was that?" I asked.

"Jerry Sledge. Works swing shift at the yard. He's a bully and mean when he drinks. It's just a matter of time until he gets into real trouble. Good thing for you Keegan's leaving town tomorrow since you look so much like him."

I'd seen Sledge leaving the plant many times while I waited in line to clock in for my shift. His large size made him stand out. Until that night at the bar, I never knew his name.

Nick and I finished our Cokes and left, heading for a concrete wall along the riverfront to sit until it was time for me to go to work. Then we walked toward the shipyard, talking loudly to be heard over the sound of machinery. We saw someone running fast as we passed the area where the cranes were working. He disappeared into the darkness.

"What do you suppose that was about?" I asked.

"Don't know," said Nick as he scanned the blackout area of the shoreline. "Someone's lying down there."

"Oh, God, do you think he got knocked down there by one of the cranes?" I asked.

"The cranes in this area aren't operated during blackout," said Nick.

"There's stuff on top of him." I said.

"If he fell, he could have hit those pipes on the way down causing them to roll on top of him," said Nick, who started to make his way closer to the man.

"What are you doing?" I asked.

"We need to get help for him if he's still alive. Either way, we'll need to tell somebody."

I followed Nick down. He bent over the man and felt for a pulse. "I can't feel anything. Help me move this stuff and roll him over. Get him off his face so he can breathe."

We were shocked at the sight of the guy's face. It looked like raw hamburger meat.

Nick felt for a pulse again. "He's dead. What the hell happened to this guy? I'm not sure this was an accident."

"You think someone threw these pipes on him to make it look like one?" I asked.

"They didn't do a very good job of it," said Nick.

The man was dressed in the same kind of khaki-colored work shirt and pants that I was wearing. "He's dressed like a worker," I said.

"Good Lord, I think this is that guy we talked to at the bar," said Nick.

"Charlie Keegan?" I asked.

"Yeah." Nick started rifling through his pockets. "I'm going to see if he has any identification on him."

"Let the police do that," I said.

Nick opened the guy's wallet. "It's Keegan. His work ID is here, along with his draft card and everything."

We looked at each other, and I could tell we were thinking the same thing. "Do you think Sledge caught up to him, beat him and killed him?"

"It could be he used brass knuckles on him or maybe a piece of iron pipe. Plenty of that around here," said Nick. "You can't even recognize him. I bet he stopped here to get one last look at the shipyard before going home and Sledge jumped him."

"I wonder why none of the security guards noticed?" I asked.

"They'd be changing shifts now. Maybe none around." Nick scanned the area as he talked. "It's so low and dark here, I doubt the guards on the hill could have seen it."

"I'm going to find a phone and call the police."

Nick grabbed my arm. "Wait, don't you see this is perfect?"

"Perfect that the guy's face was smashed to the point it killed him?"

"No, that you could be him," said Nick.

"What?"

"Sledge mistook you for him. You have the same dark wavy hair, the same size, dressed in work khakis. Don't you see, Johnny, this is your way into the Army."

"Oh, no. Absolutely not."

"Hear me out. All we need to do is put your work ID and billfold on him. You can get on that train in the morning. His face is so messed up, no one will ever know."

"I'll know. And if the Army finds out they'll throw me in jail for who knows how long. Are you crazy? No way I'm doing that."

Nick continued to go through Keegan's pockets. "That's everything. Now, give me your billfold and work ID."

"No," I said. "I'm not doing that."

"Maybe you don't really want to go fight for your country."

Nick had been daring me to do things since grade school, usually because I lacked confidence. He opened the billfold. "His address is in here. You can spend the night and get what you need to take in the morning. If you're quiet and leave when it's still dark, none of his neighbors will see you."

"What if Sledge didn't do this? What if it was an accident? He might show up at Keegan's place."

"I'm sure that big guy we saw running was Sledge. How many guys that size have you seen around here? He'll be the only one who knows. He sure as hell can't go to the police and explain that this is not the man he murdered."

I swiped at the sweat on my brow. "What about Sledge's girl-friend? She could show up."

"If the girl wanted to say goodbye to Keegan, she'd have come to the bar. She's probably with Sledge now, and he won't let her leave. Come on, Johnny. Guards will make their rounds any minute."

I don't know why I let Nick talk me into it. I was eighteen and foolish and thought going to fight the enemy would make me heroic. But it also meant I could never come home again, hero or not.

"All right, I'll do it." I handed Nick my billfold and ID.

"You ever been fingerprinted?" asked Nick.

"No. Have you?" I asked.

"No. Keegan probably was when he was inducted."

"Whoa, the Army has Keegan's prints," I said. "This isn't going to work. What if they print me when I get to the camp?"

"Why would they?"

"I don't know."

"Stop worrying and give me your work gloves." He put on my gloves and wiped my wallet on his jacket. Then he pressed Keegan's fingers on it, shoved it into his back pocket, clipped my work ID onto his shirt, and stuffed my work gloves into his pants pocket. Then he handed me Keegan's belongings.

We left the shipyard about when I should have been clocking in for the night shift and made it down the first dark alley we came to and headed for Keegan's apartment. It was two rooms on the third story of an old Victorian house. An outdoor staircase led to his place. We walked up quietly and entered. One room had a couch, a small stove, and a refrigerator. The other was his bedroom. It was obvious Keegan was telling the truth about not having a family. There were no pictures, scrapbooks, or letters to indicate otherwise. We found seven photographs of Keegan with different women but no love letters.

"Looks like Charlie played the field," said Nick. "I'll get rid of these." He hung around for an hour and helped me search the place for anything I needed to pack in the bag Keegan left on his bed.

Before Nick left, he promised he and his family would see I had a proper funeral and would dispose of my things. I told him about a few photographs of my family and other sentimental stuff I didn't want to give up. He promised to keep them and see I got them back after the war.

"Write to me at Fort Benning."

"I will." Nick gave me a goodbye hug. "Good luck, Johnny. See you when the big one's over."

I COULDN'T SLEEP all night. I always thought when I died, I wouldn't know it. Everything would just turn black. It was a weird experience to realize I didn't exist anymore. I thought about the Jacksons and the sorrow this would bring them, especially Nick's younger sister, Doris. She was fifteen, and I was very fond of her. She was like my own little sister.

I started to worry. What I was doing was a crime. Someone might recognize me and question my identity. What if Keegan was lying about his family? It appeared he had no family, but what if he did? What if he had people as close to him as the Jacksons had been all my life? I found his high school diploma. That seemed to indicate someone had looked out for him. They could come looking for him someday. Are orphans encouraged to complete their education?

What if he was lying about growing up in an orphanage? I chastised myself for letting Nick talk me into this.

I got out of bed before four and bathed. I was hungry and ate some stale bread and two apples, the only food left in Keegan's apartment. Then I grabbed my bag and headed for the L & N Depot. The cool morning breeze felt good against my face as I walked along Fulton Avenue. The depot was quiet at first. Then, around five-thirty, the place began swarming with young men.

At about six o'clock, a man instructed us to line up when he called out our name in alphabetical order. When Keegan was called, I didn't initially move.

Damn, my first mistake.

I then quickly stepped forward and got in line. The man with the list gave me an odd look but said nothing. When roll call was finished, we began boarding the train. When I stepped onto that train car, it hit me that it was likely the last step I would ever take in Evansville. I took a seat in the rear of the car and began to relax. The train stopped in Owensboro to pick up more men. By that time, I was exhausted, so I pulled my cap down over my eyes and fell asleep.

The jolt of the train stopping awakened me. I rubbed my eyes and looked out the window. The guy across from me said "Better get going, buddy. We'll only have a twenty-minute stop."

"Where are we?" I asked.

"Somewhere around Nashville."

"Already?"

"You've been sleeping a long time, buddy."

I stood and followed the others out the door. It felt good to stretch my legs. I headed for the john and then looked for something to eat. I bought a Coke, a Hershey bar, and two sandwiches to take with me. When we settled back into our seats, the guy across from me started a conversation. He said his name was Ben Culley from Vincennes. He and his sister worked at Servel making wing panels for Republic P-47 Thunderbolts until he got drafted. He was worried about leaving his sister behind and hoped she could find another young woman to share the apartment with her.

I told him I understood his concern with all the strange people and droves of soldiers from Camp Breckenridge wandering around Evansville. Wanting to avoid conversation, I finally told Ben I was still tired and needed to sleep more.

The doctor at Fort Benning noticed my flat feet. "Guys with feet like yours don't pass their physical, soldier."

I shrugged. "No one mentioned anything about them, sir."

"They must have been in a hurry that day. Do they cause you any problems?"

"No, sir. I ran track and played basketball in high school. Never had any trouble with them."

"All right. I suppose as this war goes on, we'll no longer consider feet like yours an issue."

He sent me to get inoculations, and it was the last time anybody would mention my feet. I sighed with relief as I walked out of the room.

Boot camp at Fort Benning was no picnic. The rigorous combat training left me with aching muscles at the end of each day. I would often lie in bed at night, thinking I had given up my freedom to fight for everyone else's freedom. The sergeant assigned to our platoon was relentless. I'd seen him bring more than one guy to tears. One of them was Ben Culley, the guy I met on the train. I gave him tips on how to handle the bully without ending up in trouble.

It was the first time in my life I appreciated Uncle Woody. The fear and terror I endured from him was the best preparation for Sergeant Edsel Burgoon that a guy could ever have. I was also grateful for the strenuous work I had done at the shipyard. Because of it, I was a lot stronger than some of the guys in my platoon.

Two weeks after I arrived, I received a letter from Nick. He told me about going to Johnny Watters' funeral and that he had been buried next to his parents. He and Doris had saved some of their friend's things to remember him by. The Jacksons were devastated about what happened. He said there were many rumors about whether it was an accident at first. In the end, the police decided it was murder. Nick had been questioned by the police and told them he had walked part way with Johnny that night and separated from him about two blocks from the shipyard to head home. Sledge had been the main suspect, but his girlfriend gave him an alibi, and they couldn't find any proof.

Nick's request for the Marine Corps had been granted, and he had received his notice. He was being sent to Parris Island in South Carolina and would leave in a week. A few days later, I received another letter from Nick with local news. Sledge had volunteered for the Army. I wondered if it was his way of escaping further questioning by the police. That letter was the last time I would ever hear from Nick.

AFTER THIRTEEN WEEKS of basic training, I was comfortable with my new identity. I no longer hesitated when someone called me Charlie.

Our training cycle was supposed to last forty-four weeks, but our unit got orders to ship out in the forty-first week, the end of June 1943. I was glad to leave Fort Benning, Sergeant Burgoon, and Georgia's giant mosquitoes, but a little afraid of what might lie ahead. The scuttlebutt was we were headed for Europe. I had only traveled to southern Illinois and Kentucky. My mind couldn't imagine what Europe would be like.

On the ninth of July, the waters off the coast of Sicily were alive with an Allied armada, a vision that would stay in my mind forever. It made me proud of the people at home working day and night building those ships and boats and proud to have been a part of it.

The temperature must have been a hundred degrees, and the terrain was rugged and mountainous. Most of the shoreline was narrow, making it difficult for amphibious operations. The wider beaches lie to the southeast and west of the island. Seven divisions were ordered to wade ashore to the southeast beach. I was in one of those divisions. The water was deep, and we held our rifles and ammo above our heads to keep them dry. Despite forty-mile-per-hour winds threatening small craft at sea, many aircraft pilots becoming disoriented in the darkness and shifting sandbars, the Army established a beachhead fifty miles wide by the end of the first day.

The Seventh Army suffered more than two thousand casualties the next day but kept advancing. A few days later, Mussolini was stripped of his power, but Italians continued to fight with the backing of the Germans. Sicily was the Allies' gateway to invading Italy the following September.

Before boot camp, I had never fired a gun, but I was a quick learner and became good at it. Throughout the whole experience on Sicily, I kept hearing Sergeant Burgoon's voice 'It's either you or them, kid, and if it's not them, you're dead.' I found it wasn't so hard to shoot a man when he was trying to kill you. I didn't know it then, but the battle to take Sicily prepared me for the invasion of Normandy.

When I worked building landing ship tanks I never imagined being on one sailing towards battle. But that's where I found myself on June 6, 1944. None of us wanted to think about what lie ahead. Some of the guys prayed and others cleaned their guns to pass the time.

Omaha Beach was hell. The whole war was like hell, but this was the worst I'd seen. I was with the fourth wave. The slaughter I was fighting my way into made my stomach turn. I was fortunate to make it to the beach, only to be pinned down by German snipers. Smoke from burning vehicles created camouflage allowing me to advance to the sea wall where a group of us fired at the snipers on the cliffs. As I readied to fire, the butt of my Garand burst into splinters. I felt the sting of a bullet in my right side, and I fell to the ground. The grime on my uniform was turning red with blood oozing from my body. The soldier next to me yelled 'medic'. The soldier and a medic took hold of me and dragged me to a seized German pill box where our wounded were being held temporarily. When my bleeding was under control, two stretcher bearers lifted me onto a stretcher and carried me to an area of the beach designated safe. They laid me on the sand next to other wounded awaiting evacuation. A landing craft carried us to a LST anchored farther out in the channel.

On board, I was given morphine and could barely stay awake. The soldier to my left wasn't going to make it. A priest was giving him last rites. *What's a priest doing in an unholy place like this?* That was the last thing I remembered of being on board LST-325.

MY EYES WERE crusty from sleep. I opened them slowly and saw a man was adjusting tubing connected to a transfusion bag.

I tugged at the oxygen mask on my face. "Where am I?"

The man adjusted the mask. "You mustn't remove that. You're in a military hospital in England. I'm Dr. Mayfield. I removed the bullet from you. You're one lucky bastard. From the splinters I found, it appears the bullet hit your arm and rifle butt as you were firing. It prevented the bullet from reaching your heart. There's slight damage to your right lung, but you'll live to fight another day, soldier. I need to get back to surgery. One of the sisters will take good care of you."

A nurse approached my bed. "I'm Sister Gleda. I'm going to clean your face with a warm cloth. Then I'll moisten your lips and mouth with a swab."

She smiled, and it reminded me of the way my mother smiled at me when I was small.

ONE DAY, Sister Gleda introduced me to a young woman with a French accent. "This is Lorraine. She is working with the Red Cross. She is happy to write a letter to your family and let them know you're safe."

"I don't have any family," I said.

Sister Gleda looked puzzled. "When you were awakening from the anesthesia, you kept talking about Johnny and Nick. I thought they might be your brothers."

"No, just boys I knew when I was growing up." I hoped I hadn't said anything to make her more curious about my past. "My parents and sister died in an automobile crash. I mean, that's what I tell people. I grew up in an orphanage. I was left there when I was an infant and never knew who my parents were."

"Perhaps a friend you wish to write to?" asked, Lorraine, the Red Cross worker. "Someone you knew from the orphanage."

Lorraine was so sweet and pretty. It made me wish I had someone to write to. "No, there's no one. I don't know their where-abouts anymore."

Sister Gleda looked as if she wanted to say something else but didn't. She took my vital signs and left.

It could have been because of my conversation with Sister Gleda or just being able to dwell on something besides the next artillery firing. But that night, I was restless, thinking of my past. I wondered if Sister Gleda had heard me say something while I was under the effects of morphine. I worried she would bring it to the attention of my superiors. As time went on, I became more suspicious that she knew my secret.

WILLIAM HAWLEY, a British soldier in the bed to my left had taken shrapnel in the face. His eyes were covered with bandages. Every afternoon Lorraine would come to read to him. I listened to the stories she read. One day when she finished reading, I got up the nerve to ask her where she was from.

"My home is in Lyon, France," she said. "I came to England to study the language. I hope to teach English and Spanish someday. When the war broke out, it became too dangerous for me to travel home. I had to remain here."

"Your family must be worried about you," I said.

"Yes, but they know I am safe. At least they did until these past few days." She looked as if she was about to cry.

I reached out and touched her hand. "I'm sorry. I didn't mean to upset you. This war can't last much longer. You hear the news. The Allies are advancing every day."

"He's right, Miss Lorraine," said William. "You'll be back with your family soon."

"I appreciate that you try to cheer me," she said. She looked at her watch. "It's time for us to serve tea. I must go."

ABOUT THIRTY MINUTES LATER, Lorraine returned with another volunteer and a cart with pots of tea, coffee, and plates of biscuits. As I finished my biscuits, a man pushed someone in a wheelchair next to my bed. I couldn't believe it. The guy in the chair was Ben Culley.

"Ben, how long have you been here?" I asked.

"A couple of months."

His leg was propped up and covered from top to bottom with a plaster cast. "I wish I had known. I would have come to see you."

"My leg is messed up. The doctors don't think I'll be able to return to active duty. They're going to have me do therapy to get me well enough to ship me home."

"Sorry to hear that. But I sure as hell am glad to see you're alive. Does your sister know you're coming home?"

"Yes, we've been writing to each other. She and the rest of my family can't wait to see me," he said.

"That's great. I'm happy for you."

"How about you, Charlie? Will you be discharged?"

"No, the doctor says I'm not healing as fast as he'd hoped but I'll still be returned to active duty."

"Maybe most of it will be over by then," said Ben. "Will you go back to Evansville?"

"Probably not. I don't have any family there. I think I'd like to see more of the world."

"That sounds nice," said Ben.

The man pushing Ben's wheelchair returned. "Time to go back, soldier. Don't want to overdo it the first day out of bed."

"All right. Come see me tomorrow, Charlie."

"I'll do that. Bye, Ben."

THE NURSES PUT me through a routine of passive exercises twice a day so my muscles wouldn't get too weak. As I became stronger, I was able to do the exercises by myself. After five and a half months the surgeon decided I was well enough to return to active duty.

As the time grew nearer for me to leave, I found myself dreading it. I knew it was mainly because I would never see Lorraine again. I couldn't bring myself to tell her how I felt. Even if she had feelings for me, too, it wasn't fair to get involved with this young woman when I was going back to the fighting and may not survive. So, I said nothing.

It was November when I was released from the hospital. As I waited on the dock with a couple of hundred soldiers, I heard someone yell Charles. I turned to see Lorraine standing there.

She handed me an envelope. "Please come back to me, Charles." she said. "Come back to me."

I wrapped my arms around her and kissed her. I was now twenty-one years old. Twenty-three in Keegan years. The time I should have been dating girls, going to movies, and dancing at parties had been spent in training, in trenches, on ships and on the battlefield trying to survive. Lorraine was fond of me, and I hadn't even recognized it.

"I promise, I'll do my best to come back to you."

VICTORY IN EUROPE finally came on the eighth of May 1945. The joy on the faces of the French citizens warmed my heart as they waved and shook our hands. Still cautious, I avoided reporters and turned away from cameras. The war was not over, and my platoon was sent to Germany to deal with prisoners of war.

On September 2, the Japanese signed the official documents of surrender and the whole damn thing was finally over. I thanked God I had survived. I received an honorable discharge and made my way to Lyon where Lorraine and her family lived. We were married the following summer. We have a wonderful life together and three amazing children.

Ben Culley was my only contact in the Evansville area. He sent me clippings from the newspapers. One had the list of Indiana residents killed and missing in the war. Sadly, my friend Nick died at Okinawa. The list was in alphabetical order. I scrolled down to find Jerry Sledge went missing in the Philippines.

I have lived with guilt for taking Charles Keegan's identity but what good would it do to tell anyone? I asked God to forgive me for being an impostor and for the killing I did during the war.

LORRAINE APPROACHED and took my hand. I was still staring into the bay.

"Charles, it's dark. They're holding our table. Please stop looking at that old ship and come to dinner."

"There's something I need to tell you."

"About Johnny?"

"You know?"

"When Sister Gleda could see I was falling in love with you, she told me you were an imposter. She was going to report you to the officer in charge of your platoon. I convinced her not to."

"I was young and foolish. I did it so I could get into the Army. Lorraine, I am so sorry I lied to you all these years. I was afraid of losing you."

"I never considered it a lie because I already knew the truth. Charles, I fell in love with you, not your name. I only regret I didn't tell you long ago that I knew why you never wanted to go home."

A HERO MADE OF STEEL

The USS LST Ship Memorial purchased LST-325 in 2000. The ship is docked on the Ohio River in Evansville, where it serves as a memorial to all the sailors who served on landing ship tanks. Tours of the ship are available and in late summer the ship sails to other cities along the Ohio River.

LST-325 was launched at the Philadelphia Navy Yard on Oct. 27, 1942, and remarkably has been sailing ever since. Landing ship tanks were invaluable Naval vessels during World War II and often referred to as the workhorses of the Navy. They transported soldiers, military vehicles, and all sorts of military equipment. They were also used to transport the wounded. The fact that they could be maneuvered in shallow waters allowed the Allies to get close to shore. LST-325 saw action during the invasions of Sicily and Salerno in Italy, and of the Normandy beaches in France.

After being decommissioned by the United States Navy, LST-325 was transferred to the Hellenic Navy in 1964 under the Military Assistance Program. The ship was renamed RHS Syros L-144 and served the Greek Navy until spring of 1999. In the fall of the same year the ship became the property of the non-profit corporation the USS LST Ship Memorial, Inc. through an act of the United States Congress.

A group of brave veterans made the LST-325 seaworthy and sailed her from the Isle of Crete to the United States, where she has a permanent home to share her history.

DUNES DAY
BY ELIZABETH A. SAN MIGUEL

"Jake, money is tight. You either need to get a job or stop drinking."

Jake looked at his Dad and considered. Since the job in question he would be forced to get was most likely at a fast-food restaurant, and his newly, well maybe not that new, joy in alcohol now that he had turned 21 was in jeopardy, this was quite the blow.

"Well, that's quite the Sophie's choice you're giving me." Jake deadpanned.

The left side of Jake's Dad's mouth curved up ever so slightly. Jake wondered momentarily if that was in mirth or disapproval. "Yes, Jake, deciding on drinking or working is just like having to choose which child must die. Let me know what you decide by the time you are ready to head back to school." He looked back down at the paper he was reading.

Disapproval. Duh, of course it wasn't equivalent. Why were old people so literal? Well, why was his dad always so literal with him. Jake was sure if his sister made a similar, wildly exaggerated comparison he would have just laughed. Totally bogus. And his dad was no stranger to the concept of hyperbole. He used it often.

And school. Jake thought of his university with longing. It was a three-hour drive away, but that was far enough from home for Jake to feel as if he was his own person. All he had to do was get A's in all his classes, which while not easy, was so much less responsibility and pressure than he felt when he came home.

Jake wondered again why he had decided to take his housemate Ellie, his best friend since they were in first grade, up on her offer to give him a lift home for Thanksgiving break. Ellie's parents had provided her a car. A brand new 1994 Volkswagen Jetta. Jake knew that if he ever wanted a car, he would have to buy it himself and it would definitely be used. Still, cars were a responsibility Jake didn't want either. It was good to have friends with things. But now he was pretty much stuck here until Ellie decided to head back to Bloomington.

He nodded at his father and headed to the door of the small house where he had grown up.

"Where you headed?" Jake's dad was still reading the paper and clenched his fists a bit causing the paper to make that crinkle sound. Jake wondered what might have upset his Dad.

"Dunes, probably. Something wrong?" Jake looked down. He was looking at a write-up about Mrs. Allen who had died recently at the nursing home where his sister Susie sometimes volunteered. Mrs. Allen had been friends with their Gran.

"No. Kinda cold right now." Jake's father frowned.

"Yeah, but that means no one else will be there."

Jake thought he could ponder his super stupid choice.

"Hmm. Maybe take your sister with you."

"Dad, she doesn't need me to watch her."

"Jake, let me rephrase. Take your sister with you."

Jake realized there was something his Dad was trying to say without saying it. He also realized it was pointless to argue.

"SUSIE! Get your coat on, we're going for a walk."

"I don't wanna go out. It's cold," she yelled from her bedroom.

Jake looked at his Dad and shrugged his shoulders.

"Susie, GO WITH YOUR BROTHER."

Jake noticed the vein on his father's right temple that throbbed a bit. Weird. Susie had always been her Daddy's little princess.

Susie, who had put on her pink coat and gloves headed towards the door, said nothing. Her frown and the huffily crossed arms spoke volumes. It's not as if he wanted her to go with him. But she would likely miss the cues because Jake was sure the girl had no empathy. Well not for her long-suffering brother.

Once outside Jake was glad to see that while it was cold there was no snow or ice. "Bikes?"

Susie nodded. They went into the garage, got their bikes and headed to the Indiana dunes. The house was just over a mile away to the beach located just east of the southern tip of Lake Michigan. In the spring and summer, the place was inundated with people. Jake still loved it there then but in late November, it was a cold, windswept place he loved for the solitude.

"What's up with Dad?" Jake sped up a bit. Susie peddled faster to keep up.

"How should I know." There was the tinge of brat in her tone.

He was sure she knew why their Dad was grumpy but since the reason would likely make her look bad she would never say.

Jake just rolled his eyes and they biked in silence. His mind wandered back to the drinking problem. He needed money for alcohol. Too bad there weren't more psychology tests he could sign up for to get extra money. Of course, most of them provided little money. Five bucks per test was normal for a few questions about how they thought or felt about something. Some of the tests provided a larger amount but usually you had to win at something to get the money. No win. No money, not even $5. The last one he had taken, he had won $50 by drinking and then taking a test. Jake figured they had offered up the prize and so no one would goof up on purpose because they were "so" drunk. As a psych major he was often required to take part in studies as part of the curriculum. Everyone gravitated to the ones where you could get paid.

Ellie, who worked at Kinko's, had made him some calling cards on red card stock with a little devil face and text of Jake Palmer, Smartest Drunk on the IU Campus and Not Nearly As Saintly as He Used to Be. Jake loved those cards but he frowned a bit at the Not Saintly. His grandmother had said that to him when he came home from work at the Burger Blast tired, grubby, and hot last summer. He had always tried to be solicitous of his grandmother, but after she asked how his day went, he had snapped at her. He laughed when she responded with his rescinded sainthood status. He had apologized and laughed. Gran, who had been the center of all their lives since Jake had been a child, had passed away about a month ago and was why he had come home for Thanksgiving. He hoped only having one gaping hole at the dinner table instead of two might help.

There were not enough psych tests to provide a supplemental income required to purchase beer or vodka. Maybe he could get a grant or scholarship. Dear person with money, please give ME some so I can buy vodka. Okay, don't mention vodka.

As expected, the Dunes were deserted. The wind and fog gave the place an eerie feel. Both he and Susie parked their bike and then walked to the water's edge. On clear days it was possible to see the Chicago skyline in the distance. Today was not one of those days. The gray skies and ominous clouds gave the beach a desolate feel. Jake savored the peace he felt looking out in the distance at what he thought was likely to be snow later in the day.

He looked at his sister, arms wrapped around herself, shivering and...he realized she was sad.

"You have no idea why Dad is grumpy, really?" Jake pressed.

Susie's shoulders dropped and she shrank further into her jacket and frowned. Looking up at him he realized she was tearing up and shaking her head no at the same time. Jake sighed inwardly. It was such a pain being the responsible one. Still if he ever wanted to be a psychologist he may as well get used to figuring out what was wrong with all and sundry around him.

"Susie, you can talk to me if you want. What's going on with you?" Jake was pleased with how he sounded. Sincere-ish. And yet, was that Susie's infamous side eye?

"You...are so full of crap." She walked back to her bike, got on, and peddled away. Jake let her. She was 13 after all. She didn't actually need a chaperone.

And now he could be alone in one of his favorite places on earth. Lake Michigan and all of the Great Lakes had formed as the ice age ended and the glaciers had melted about 14,000 years ago. People had been living around here for about as long. But Jake liked the feeling of possession and solitude.

He knew the area wasn't his and he wasn't actually alone, but on those rare occasions he couldn't see nor hear anyone, he found the illusion was enough.

A grant or scholarship. He would have to find out if there were any he could apply for and then write a letter. He would need to tailor the letter to the needs of the grant but some things would remain the same. His parents didn't have a lot of money and were the main financial support for their Gran or had been anyway. He walked up and down the beach front for about a half hour and then realized he was freezing. It was time to head home. After retrieving his bike, and leaving the general area of the beach his pedaling became more difficult. He looked at his front tire which was now noticeably flat. Jake cursed inwardly, got off his bike, and started pushing it, hoping to get home before his fingers, toes, or other appendages succumbed to frost bite.

Jake was about halfway home next to a wooded area when he saw flashing lights. There were police cars blocking off the area. Jake thought a car accident was most likely but didn't see anything mangled. A police officer waved him down.

"Where you headed?" the uniformed officer asked.

"Home. What's going on?" Jake looked around trying to see what might have happened.

"Which way is home?" The officer responded to Jake's question with a question.

Jake pointed in the direction he was heading. "Any info on what's going on?"

"We're looking for someone," the officer said. "Make sure you stay on the road and don't head into the woods. Okay."

Jake was about to ask more questions when another officer yelled but Jake could only hear parts, "...in our sights...angel...death."

"Move along," the officer in front of him said.

Jake moved along, slowly. When he finally got back to the house, he put his bike in the garage and added "patch bike tire" to his mental to-do list. When he headed into the house, his mother was in the kitchen doing prep work for tomorrow's big meal. She looked up at him and smiled. Then she looked beyond him. "Where's your sister?"

"Uh, she left me a while ago. I figured she would be back before me."

"She's on her own? Why didn't you stay with her?" Jake's dad said.

"She doesn't need a babysitter."

"She's only 12 years old. She needs someone," his dad said.

"She's 13 and what do you do when I'm away? She's been going out on her own since she was like nine or 10."

Jake's parents looked at one another and shook their heads. His mother went so far as to bring her hands to her mouth.

"What? It's true. Why does she all of a sudden need someone around her all the time?" Jake asked. His parents stood there mute. "Whatever."

"She's been kind of delicate lately. She was there when your gran passed. And you know she volunteers at the nursing home, right? She was there when Mrs. Allen passed as well. And then just yesterday Mrs. Blaise passed too right after Susie spoke to her," his mother said. "She has such a big heart and she cared for all of them. It's been hard on her."

"Jake, I didn't want to spell things out for you earlier. You two used to be close and I thought maybe she might open up to you. It's why I wanted her to go with you. But she left you? How long ago?"

"Uh, about an hour ago. She yelled at me and left. Uh, do you two know what's up with the police in the woods?"

"Police? What?" The slight lift in his dad's tone made Jake's gut clench.

"My tire went flat riding back and I was walking along the back road because it's quicker. There were a bunch of police cars. The officer asked where I was headed and that they were searching for someone."

His parents stared at Jake. "That is literally all I know, well on that topic."

"We need to get out there and look for her." His dad grabbed his coat and keys and headed to the door. "Greta, maybe you can call around and see if she's with a friend, or something."

She nodded her head and headed to the kitchen phone. "Jake, you come with me and show me where the police are."

"Don't you think you're overreacting? She's been out of sight for only about an hour. There was once I ran away from home and was gone for over 24 hours and you didn't even mention it when I walked back through the door."

"Jake, you're in college. Being away from home doesn't count as running away. Susie's much younger," his dad said standing just outside the door.

"I was eight!"

"Jake, move it."

Jake, who had not even taken his coat off, made a huffing sound reminiscent of his sister, and headed to the door.

"By the way, it doesn't count as running away if you just go to your aunt's house one block over. She called us to tell us you were with her and had run away because we were paying too much attention to Susie."

"Oh, well, glad that problem got all cleared up."

"Jake, she's been extremely sad and depressed lately. This behavior is NOT like her. Okay."

Jake's dad got in the truck, leaned over to unlock the passenger door so that Jake could get in. He had started up the car and put it in gear almost before Jake could get the door closed.

The police cars and the same officer were on the road. Jake's dad pulled over and got out of the truck and headed towards the officer.

"Sir, can you tell me what's going on here? I think my daughter may be missing."

The officer straightened a bit. "How long has she been gone?"

Jake's dad was quiet for a moment. "About an hour, but she came this way with her brother and he said something was going on here." Jake got out of the truck, walked slowly over to them, and when the officer saw him, Jake shrugged, embarrassed.

"How old?"

"Twelve."

"She's 13," Jake huffed.

"Yes, she just turned 13."

"Well, not just. She turned 13 a month ago." Jake wrapped his arms around himself and stomped a bit, trying to deal with the cold.

"Well, we are in pursuit of someone, but I'll call it in."

"Her name is Susie Palmer. She's about five feet tall, thin, long brown hair, brown eyes. She was wearing a pink coat, gloves, and boots."

The officer walked over to his car, lifted the radio handset and let everyone else on it know that if they found her, she was to head home because her family was worried about her.

Jake then thought about the other radio call he had half heard earlier. Did he hear angel of death? Isn't that what they called people in hospitals and nursing homes who bump off people because they can? Jake stopped breathing for a moment as he thought back to his latest abnormal psychology class. Were angels psychopaths? Could his sister have been knocking off all those old people? Jake thought back to the section on psychopaths. They had no empathy towards animals or people...like long suffering brothers.

Jake remembered one of Susie's little friends mentioning that she had no issues pithing the frog in biology class and then opening it up while it was still alive and looking at its organs. Okay, yes, that was the assignment and Jake had done the same when he was in that class. But he hadn't liked it. And how many people had died around Susie lately? Oh, man, had she killed their Gran? He needed to talk to her before this came out.

"I would like to get out there and search. What if she was abducted by whoever it is you're chasing,?" Jake's dad said to the officer.

The officer was shaking his head. "Sir, we can't let you out there. We are looking out for her and will get her home if we find her."

"Dad, I think I'm going to walk back to the house." His dad looked at him and realized that Jake meant to go look for her by taking a different path. His dad nodded and Jake took off the way they came, but once out of sight, he walked into the woods. He knew the area better than most since the woods backed up to his neighborhood. He had probably spent years there, treating it as his own backyard.

Oh God. Susie was an angel of death. What was he going to do? This would kill his parents. But maybe he could have Susie let his parents know and they could get her some help. Was psychopathy curable? Maybe she wasn't so far gone and could be helped.

Jake spent a good hour walking around the woods and wondering if he would ever find her. He thought he would need to give up soon or he would probably freeze to death. And then Jake remembered one place he hadn't searched.

Big Hill was a towering hill of sand, foliage, and rocks where the beach and the woods met. There was a bit of an overhang that would protect from rain and wind. Both he and Susie had spent a lot of time there as kids watching the waves and feeling like they were the only people in the world. It was hard to see unless you were right up on it. At the bottom of the bank was Susie's bike. Jake looked up. Was that a flash of pink? Yep, he saw her now. She was seated on their rock seat. Jake snorted a bit. These things were all named when he was eight or maybe younger. Creative writing wasn't what he was into so may as well call a rock seat a rock seat or a big hill a big hill.

Jake bounded up the hill, none too quietly, and poked Susie in the shoulder. She jumped a bit and looked up at him in, was that fear on her face.

She shook her head, "You are such an idiot."

"I'm an idiot? I've been looking for you over an hour. Dad actually went and told the police you were missing." Jake looked at where Susie was looking. A tall thin man stood there looking stern. "Oh, hi. I didn't see you there. I'm Jake and you are?"

"That's Mr. Blenheim. He's a nurse at the home where I volunteer. I think he, uh, Mrs. Allen and Mrs. Blaise," she said sotto voce. Jake's heart started beating fast realizing he had empathy since he could feel her fear. Jake wondered if Mr. Blenheim had figured out that Susie was the angel of death.

Jake turned to him and nodded. "Hey, we have to go. My parents are freaking out that she has been gone so long."

"The police? He called the police?" Mr. Blenheim asked.

"Well, he didn't call them. They are all over the place looking for, uh, someone," Jake said, trying not to look at his obviously guilty sister.

"Someone? Who? Who're they looking for?" Mr. Blenheim looked back and forth between Jake and Susie.

Jake looked up and then down and wondered why he was so bad at lying, "No idea." In his head he kept thinking not her. They aren't looking for her.

"You are the worst," Susie said under her breath.

Okay, no empathy but was she telepathic?

"We need to go. Thanks for watching out for her," Jake said.

"No," he said.

Crap he was going to make a citizen's arrest of Susie. "Look, she's super young. Can't you just let us go?"

Susie nodded her head. "Super young. A bright future," she said.

She stood up and grabbed Jake's hand.

"Sit. Back. Down," he yelled.

Jake thought he seemed more unbalanced than Susie. And then the other shoe dropped. "Suse, were Mrs. Allen and Mrs. Blaise patients of Mr. Blenheim?"

"Yep," she said quietly. Jake decided if they both got out of this he would never, ever let Susie know that he thought she was the psychopath. Jake wasn't sure if Blenheim was armed but didn't want to test that theory.

"Uh, look, why don't you take Susie's bike. You might be able to get away with some wheels," Jake said.

Mr. Blenheim looked at the bike. Her bright pink bike that she had begged for last year.

"It's pink," he said.

"Yes, but it's sturdy. It should get you out of here," Jake said. After what seemed like an hour of silence, Jake couldn't take it anymore. "We are young and healthy. You would not be putting us out of our misery."

Mr. Blenheim paced a bit on the ledge. Jake pondered if he could push him. It wasn't high enough to kill him, but it might slow him down long enough for the two of them to get away.

"You get it. I was just trying to help." Mr. Blenheim's arm jerked. Was that a gun he was holding? Jake stepped in front of his sister. A bullet would have to go through him to get to her.

"I totally get it. They were like super old and probably in pain." Jake nodded his head. "What you did was a mercy."

"Yeah, it was as if the sandman came and took them away," said Susie.

Sandman? Yes, sandman. Jake put his hands behind his back and felt Susie fill them with sand.

Jake took a couple of steps closer to him. "Mr. Blenheim, can I say, I think what you are doing is a service and brave. Risking what you are to euthanize people."

Mr. Blenheim stopped and considered for a second. "You have got to be the worst liar I have ever come across."

"Oh, well in that case." Jake threw the sand in his face and then pushed him off the ledge.

"Go! Go! Go!" Jake yelled to Susie's backside as she scrambled down the ledge, hopped on her bike, and pedaled away as fast as she could. He tried not to feel abandoned and hoped she was going to go get help. Jake started running toward home. If he could just get far enough away, he doubted Mr. Blenheim would be able to find him.

And that had been Jake's plan until he did a face plant after tripping on a tree root. Jake tried to scrabble up only to realize his ankle wasn't working the way he thought it should.

"Crap. Crap. Crap," Jake whispered in a rage.

"My sentiments exactly," said Mr. Blenheim. "That was not cool." He walked to Jake and looked at him.

What the hell did he have in his hand? Please don't be a gun, please don't be a gun, but it was, a small one to be sure. Jake suspected it would get the job done.

"Sorry?" Jake sat up against a tree.

Mr. Blenheim paced in front of Jake.

"They were already looking for you," Jake said.

"I know. They came looking for me at the nursing home. I high-tailed it outta there."

He ran from the home. Did that mean he always had a gun with him. This dude was nuts.

"Well, you might be able to argue insanity. Kill me and you probably won't be able to say the same."

Mr. Blenheim stopped. "You think you're some kinda lawyer?"

"No. I'm studying to be a psychologist."

"Throwing sand in people's face and pushing them over a ledge makes you a massive jerk."

"And killing old people makes you such a hero?" Jake regretted those words as soon as they were out of his mouth.

Blenheim approached Jake and stepped down hard on his ankle. The crunching sound, which Jake hoped was from the dead leaves rather than his bones, was in some ways worse than the pain. "If it wasn't broken before, it probably is now. I hope you die out here," Blenheim said.

Jake screamed in pain. The scream was embarrassing but it ended up saving his life. Blenheim lifted the gun and pointed at him but before he could fire, Blenheim tilted his head. Were those dogs?

"A gun shot will probably just lead them here faster," Jake said.

Blenheim held the gun, kicked Jake, and then turned and ran. The fear and pain caused Jake to disassociate for he didn't know how long.

Jake came back into his own. He would die if he didn't get back into the warmth and get help for his ankle. "Well, at least he didn't shoot me."

Jake looked for a stick that was sturdy enough to help him walk. He managed to lever himself up and slowly head towards the road calling out for help every ten feet or so.

He was never as happy as when he saw his sister and a several police officers heading towards him. At their head was Susie. She ran to him and almost knocked him over. Tears ran down her face. She hugged him harder than she ever had. Jake pointed the police officers in the direction Blenheim had run. And they did have two dogs. Working dogs who were not overly interested in Jake. Susie walked with Jake, acting as his support, the entire way to the road. Their father was there, next to his truck. Relief shone from his face and he hugged both of his kids tight.

Eventually, they took him to an ER where his ankle was X-rayed. The results showed he had a bad sprain, lots of bruising, and no break.

"Jake, thanks so much for finding your little sister," Jake's mom said as she came in the recovery room where Jake sat after having his ankle wrapped.

Susie and his father followed behind her.

"And saving her from that guy Blenheim," Jake said.

Susie rolled her eyes.

"And she turned around and saved you by finding you," his father hugged Susie and kissed her on the head.

"True. And Susie, we're sorry. We'll try to make up for missing your birthday."

Susie straightened up and smiled. "It's ok. I totally understand."

"What would you like for your belated day," his dad asked.

Crap. Of course. Jake's Mom and Dad realized they had missed her birthday when he had reminded them she was thirteen and not twelve.

"Really. You were upset because we forgot your birthday? Why didn't you just say anything?" Jake crossed his arms. He was lying in a hospital bed and she was the one who was being treated like a forgotten hero.

"Let me think about it Mom and Dad. I'm sure I can come up with something. I just didn't want to say anything since we were all so sad Gran had passed." Susie turned away from her parents and stuck her tongue out at Jake.

Jake's mom hugged her. "You are just the best daughter ever. How did we get so lucky?"

Jake gnashed his teeth and attempted to change the subject. "Did you know that Blenheim guy was killing people?"

Susie shook her head. "No. Not until I found him on Big Hill holding the gun. Things started to fall into place. I tried to leave and well, you saw what he was like. It was scary."

"I'm sorry you had to go through such an ordeal." Now her dad was hugging her.

"Dad, I haven't eaten all day. Could you get me something from the vending machine?" She said.

"Of course, sweetie. We'll get you something."

"I haven't eaten either. Can I get something?"

"I'll ask if it's allowed," his mom said. Both parents left the room.

After a few beats, Susie smiled. "Hey, thanks for helping me out."

"Would it kill you to say something in front of Mom and Dad."

She sat down on the edge of his bed. "Probably not, but why risk it."

"You were upset because everyone forgot your birthday?"

"If I had said anything I would just look like a jerk. Plus, I was, actually, am sad about losing Gran and Mrs. Allen and Mrs. Blaise." She shrugged. "Okay. What do you want out of this. I can arrange for you to get it."

"Suse, don't go overboard. I think they're hurting for cash."

"Yeah, I know. Gran's burial was expensive and it's not like they inherited anything. If you're reasonable in your request, I can probably arrange for you to get it."

Jake only wanted a drinking budget, but he would never ask for it. "At Thanksgiving dinner tomorrow, I will take the turkey leg."

Susie smiled. Thinking back to Thanksgivings past, they each had their favorite parts of the bird. Susie hated the leg and had no issue forking it over to Jake who would have probably gotten it anyway.

"I guess you are a pretty good brother."

And you are probably just a teenager and not a psychopath, he thought. Probably.

A few minutes later his parents returned with various goodies from the vending machine of which Jake could choose one or two. Since they were going to release him soon his mom didn't want him to spoil their dinner.

"Oh," his Mom said. "I almost forgot. You got some mail today. One is from your university."

She handed him a couple of letters from the depths of her purse. He opened the letter she mentioned.

Dear Mr. Palmer,

Due to your exceptional grade point average, you were put on a short list for the Alexander Memorial Grant for Exceptional Students. You are receiving this letter to inform you that you have been chosen to receive the $2,200 grant. See details below.

Jake noticed his father was looking at the letter and laughing. "Jake, you are the only person I know who can turn good grades into a drinking scholarship."

INDIANA DUNES

Roughly 14,000 years ago, the northern glaciers receded, leaving the Great Lakes and the Indiana Dunes in their place. Though in Indiana, the Dunes are at the southernmost tip of Lake Michigan.

The Dunes is an area of diverse ecology and stunning natural beauty. Butterflies, numerous species of birds, and an array of plant life can be found there. In fact, the Dunes has more types of orchids than Hawaii.

Ecology became a science around the turn of the 20th century when Professor Henry Chandler Cowles of the University of Chicago studied the ecological succession in the Dunes. This led to efforts for preservation of its habitats. And finally in 2019, the lakeshore was officially designated the Indiana Dunes National Park.

SOLDIERS AND SAILORS
BY ROBERTA BARMORE

The man came up too close as I was leaving the Birch Bayh building, home to the Federal Courts in downtown Indianapolis. He was dressed in an Army coat too heavy for the bright June weather, open over a red flannel shirt faded to pink and slacks that were too dusty to have a recognizable color. He had a dark blue knit cap and a grin that showed gaps in his front teeth. His posture was good. I couldn't remember his name.

"Detective Leigh," he said. His voice was hoarse, careful and familiar. He turned away to cough, covering his mouth with his left hand. It only had the first two fingers and a thumb.

The cough and the hand did it. Bill, no, Will. Army Will. He smelled like dust and soap, an improvement over what I remembered. His nickname brought the memory of his former aroma: sweat, alcohol and cheap cough syrup. He was a useful contact eighteen months ago.

I smiled at him. Might as well. "Army Will. This can't be your patch." The Federal Courthouse is notoriously unfriendly to the unhoused.

"Not hardly. I got a place. Do computer network stuff for the Bromeliad Center, half a year now." He looked both ways, squinting.

"Catching up what I missed? Yeah. A guy said you was spending time here, and," he paused to shrug. "I got a problem."

My name is Leigh Reid Moxon. I'm a licensed PI firm, all by myself, and it very nearly pays my bills. Oh, yeah, I'm non-binary. Not everybody likes that. Sometimes it's useful. "So ask. Asking's free."

He looked away and back at me. "Bad guys messing with people. Hurting some."

"Street people?" Will hadn't been too adrift from reality in his cough-syrup-drinking days.

He nodded. "Hardly nobody believes me."

Back when, he'd nod off and miss things, sure, but what he did see was real. "Walk with me to the Red Line stop." Hanging around outside the Birch Bayh building was only going to attract attention. I wanted to get on the bus for home. The walk to the bus stop in front of the Statehouse would give me an excuse to end the conversation. I set off. He could keep up or not.

Will fell into step beside me. He wasn't much taller than my 5' 8" and he leaned closer than I liked. "We got a real problem." He stopped to cough again and I kept walking. We were going to have to wait on traffic at Meridian and Ohio Street anyway. He broke off the cough to say, "Hey, wait," and caught up.

At the light, a steady stream of traffic was turning left in front of us to head north. City buses lined up in front of the Salesforce tower across the street, the traffic busy but not yet solid. Sunny, windy afternoon, pigeons swooping and people risking their necks on rental scooters. A phone company truck with one of those memorably forgettable names was parked in front of the bank across Meridian from the courthouse, a traffic ticket already flapping under the windshield wiper on the driver's side.

Will took hold of my arm just above the elbow and glanced north, up the sidewalk. "We shouldn't talk here."

I ignored his hand, watching the traffic. "Go to the police." IMPD isn't great with the unhoused, but these days they try harder than they used to.

To the south of us, the stone needle of the Soldiers and Sailors monument stood in the Circle, Victory on top with her back turned to us, staring south. Yeah, that was about right.

Will gripped my arm harder. "I told the cops. They look at me like I don't make sense."

Police are skeptical, especially with the unhoused. I said, "Mmm," to let him know I heard. My cop friends don't talk about compassion fatigue. They talk around it, living with it the same unseeing way you live with bad wallpaper in a cheap apartment.

The light changed and I started across, forcing Will to let go or keep up. He chose both.

"I got some money. Just help me get proof." He sighed, making it loud enough to be heard over the traffic. "They beat up Little Tony last night."

Little Tony's one of the hustlers who works near the Circle, which I shouldn't know, but my neighbors down the hall keep getting me involved in their good works.

Once we were across Meridian Street, I turned to him. "What do you care? That's not your thing."

He winced. "God no. But that kid served. Like me. Even if he was a crayon-eater."

I had to think about that. "You mean a Marine."

"He ain't the only one. I mean people getting hurt. The cops don't care."

Army Will wanted to set watch on a tent Little Tony had been sharing with an older woman, Anne. It sounded iffy, but he talked me into it. When I gave him my card, he surprised me by pulling out a phone, the screen splintered, to add me to his contacts.

I climbed aboard the quiet electric bus and rode home, wondering what kind of mess I'd volunteered for. Maybe my apartment neighbors are right about helping people. Probably not. It wasn't even noon yet.

Lt. Shirley is the only Public Information Officer at IMPD I know. She used to work community liaison downtown and if there was something unusual happening, she'd know. She might even tell me. I called from the bus and it went straight to voicemail.

Start thinking about something and you'll see it everywhere. The Red Line jogs from Capitol Avenue to Meridian Street at 18th. A panhandler had staked out the center-island bus stop, opposite the restored Art Deco Mercantile Bank. He had a new-looking backpack, dusty orange with hot pink trim lying on the concrete.

I got off the bus at 54th Street, not far from home, and stopped for lunch.

IT'S A UNIVERSAL RULE: you take a bite of food and your phone goes off. Lieutenant Shirley. I managed to mumble a greeting.

"Leigh? I've got a couple minutes."

I could hear a siren in the background. "Isn't there a law about...?"

She snorted.

Police are exempt anyway. "So, homeless people? You hearing anything about somebody harassing them, beating them up, worse?" I was outside Big Dan's Deli, where they've got tables and an awning. I waved a fly off my lunch while the siren sang into my phone ear like a demented cricket. They've got TV sets hanging inside the deli and the one in my line of sight switched to a screen with "special report" on it behind a news anchor at a desk, talking excitedly.

Shirley sounded impatient. "Like Tony the muscle-boy yesterday? Other than that, just what they always do to each other."

"So no increase?"

She didn't reply right away and that was an answer. "I just reached where I need to be." I heard the siren cut off. "Always so nice to talk to you." And she ended the call.

The TV image changed to a field reporter, with a blurry podium behind her, a scrubby-looking lot past it. Captioning scrolled across the screen, "...Two bodies found along railroad tracks on the South side..." The reporter said the same, called them telephone technicians, and interrupted herself with, "IMPD's news conference is starting now."

A fuzzy shape walked up to the podium and the camera zoomed in and focused on it. Lt. Shirley, uniform immaculate, hair immovable, expression grim. I left my lunch to the flies and moved closer to the TV.

<hr>

TOO MUCH WARMTH radiated from the concrete retaining wall behind me. The weatherman called it a heat dome. Even at three a.m., I could feel it. Army Will was next to me, a vague shape in the dim light. The smell of unwashed bodies wafted by as the breeze shifted, with a hint of something worse. Behind me, occasional tractor-trailer rigs screamed by on the freeway, above the retaining wall and behind a chain-link fence. In a fancier neighborhood, it would have been a tall concrete sound baffle. Here, nothing on my side of the fence but a steep hillside down to a vacant lot with a ditch through it.

The lot was dotted with tents and improvised shelters. The longer I watched, the more I could see among the weeds and junk. On the far side, a gravel alley emerged between a blank brick building and high board fence. Will was right; this was a good spot to watch from. Anne's tent was on the far side from us, a lopsided dome that had been green once.

He'd sworn something was going to happen here, tonight. "Those knapsack guys told her to shut up about Tony or they'd shut her up."

Will was relaxed against the warm concrete, his clothes blending into the shadows. Every time I looked over at him, his eyes were in motion. It was the only part of him that was.

Sweat was trickling down my back when Will spoke in a prison-yard whisper, lips barely moving. "If it stays so hot, the Q-tips will start dying off."

I tried to match it. "Q-tips?"

"Weather like this, the old ones cook. Find 'em in a day or two."

The heat felt more threatening.

A person on an undersized child's bicycle with a basket on the handlebars wobbled out from the alley and circled among the tents. Will tensed up. "Uh-oh."

I kept watching the encampment. A semi thrummed by behind us. In front of us, the bike rider parked, not too close to Anne's tent.

The person fumbled the basket, pulled out something the size of a big flashlight and worked a lighter with their other hand. In its light I could see the person was a young man. He applied the flame to the object, which caught fire rapidly. A bottle with a rag in it, a toy for idiots. He pitched it at the tent and it left a trail of fire. Flames spread across the tent and climbed before I looked away.

The bicycle rider had left while I watched the fire.

Beside me, Will hadn't moved. Now he exhaled like he'd been holding his breath. "Son of—" he said, standing up.

I stood up too. "What about Anne?"

Will was already in motion down the hill. "Moved out. Tent's empty, too."

I followed him, not as fast, mindful of the risks. Wreck a knee and you'll be careful, too.

Will stopped well back from the burning tent and waited for me to reach him. "Yeah. Figured they'd try that, or just whang it down." He looked up at me. "You get enough guys with pipes and ball bats and stuff..." He shook his head. "Fire is scarier."

It wasn't getting much attention. There were a couple people around, three or four more looking out from their tents, shapes visible in the light spilling over from the freeway. The fire died out quickly. The watchers turned away or ducked back inside, satisfied the ruckus was over.

I nodded. "If you've got it all figured out, what do you need me for?"

Will coughed and spat off to one side. "Who listens to me?"

WILL WENT from tent to tent, passing the word quietly, in short phrases: Anne was okay. Her stuff was okay. He circled back to the remains of the tent, curls of smoke rising from it. Will kept glancing up the alley. "I got people out watching. See where those knapsack guys go."

Knapsack guys again. "You're sure the guy who set the fire was one of them?"

"Who else?"

I could have made a list, from high school boys with too much free time and too little compassion, right through to a handful of alt-right militias that enjoyed preying on people who can't fight back. I let Will talk instead.

"They mean it. Stay out of their way or else."

"You heard that from them?"

"Not getting that close. Them guys is mean."

It was just the two of us by then, passing traffic whizzing by on the freeway up the hill every so often. A man walked out of the shadows in the alley and waved at Will to come to him. He headed that way and I started to follow.

It wasn't the right thing to do. The new man looked around, started to say something, stopped. I stopped, too, like I was meeting a feral cat.

Will went over and the two had a whispered conversation. He came back and said, "Our guy met a van a couple blocks away. Left the bike."

"So we've lost him."

"Might." Will frowned. "Lots of eyes. I put the word out. Got the plates for you. Says there was writing on the van." He handed me a scrap of paper.

The writing on the paper was surprisingly neat. "'07 Dodge van, gray" followed by the license plate number.

The Red Line bus had stopped running hours ago and the rest of the IndyGo system shuts down even earlier. I said goodbye to Will. He said he'd call me tomorrow and walked away.

I was a couple of blocks away, looking for somewhere I could wait after calling a rideshare that I couldn't afford unless I gave up lunch this month, when I heard a vehicle slow and stop in the distance, and a man's voice said, something, loudly. The shout rang down the empty street. I turned to see a gray Dodge van nearly two blocks away, with men beside it. They tumbled in, the door slammed and it drove away, the engine loud. It was too far to read the plates.

I got lucky with the rideshare app; a driver was ten minutes away.

Something was going on but I was too sleepy to see how it fit together. When there's nothing you can do, you might as well rest up.

WILL DIDN'T CALL, so I called Lt. Shirley. She set me up with a poker-faced IMPD detective at the neighborhood station just down College Avenue from my apartment building. I was enjoying a paper cup of their miserable coffee before my hair was dry. It went as I expected except for the very end. He closed his notebook and gave me a long look. "You might get an invite from the Feds," he said. "It'd be a real good idea to take it. And, kid? Get yourself some better clients."

I asked him what that was about and he just shook his head. "The department's best PIO is worried about you. I want to keep her happy."

It wasn't an answer.

I took the Red Line bus downtown, watching for Army Will or his knapsack guys, and spotted the one along Meridian Street a little north of where the bus route jogs. I got off at the next stop, walked back to Meridian and took my time walking down to the circle. There were four more, including the one on the sidewalk outside University Park, just north of the Federal building.

I kept moving and made a note of their locations. Then I jaywalked in front of the Salesforce skyscraper—fifty whole stories of naming rights—and continued down Meridian, finding one more sidewalk lurker with a garish backpack, looking like a panhandler but not doing any panhandling.

I nearly overlooked the one at the Soldier and Sailors Monument in the center of the Circle. Young, bearded, wearing a gray uniform, sitting at the top of the steps with a laptop open on his knees. Sitting on an orange knapsack with hot-pink trim. I watched from the side as he looked down at the screen and then up at the street. He raised himself up, moved the knapsack slightly and sat down, looking at the screen again. It was late enough that the construction crew had left. He was the security guard.

Maybe the knapsacks were on sale and I'd picked up Army Will's paranoia. The sandwich place on the Circle was open. I got bag of chips and a complimentary cup of water, and took out my phone. I checked block by block with an online map. Business names pop up, handy advertising for them and a real time saver.

By the time I was done, I was convinced Will wasn't paranoid. Every knapsack guy except the one the on the Monument steps was across the street from a bank. No bank, no knapsack guy.

I left heading east, away from the guy on the steps, and caught a bus home.

My phone woke me shortly after 2:00 a.m. The caller was breathing heavily. I need paying work, so I said "Hello?" anyway.

The voice that replied was slurred. "Leee. It's Will?"

Oh boy. I don't take in strays and I've got no time for drunks. "What happened?" He was going to lie. They always do.

There was a long pause. "I'm. Not. Sober." He spoke with the care of an apprentice mason trusted to set a row of bricks for the first time, placing each word with great seriousness. "They made. Me drink. A lot."

"Where are you?"

"A. Phone booth? Yeah. Like a phone booth!"

That was unhelpful. There are a few pay phones left in Indianapolis, though the odds are good that any you find will have been vandalized into uselessness.

Army Will snickered. "They, um, grabbed me. Kept asking questions. What I knew. Thought I passed out and left me. All alone." He sounded more sober, or at least less drunk. "I saw me some stuff. And I fixed those guys. I did." His voice turned sad. "They took my phone. Think they was going, going to kill me."

Someone with a well-developed habit can function at levels of intoxication that would leave a social drinker unable to navigate a doorway. They'll pass as sober, almost. My father had spent most of the last two decades of his life in that condition. Will was trying. His problem was that he'd been sober for the past six months.

Caller ID is a great gift in my line of work. My airweight laptop boots up fast and I kept the conversation going while I typed the number he was calling from into a search engine. "What's around you? Any businesses with a sign?"

He thought about it, coughed and said. "Lots a lights. Big rigs."

Tractor-trailers. "Are you inside or outside?" Any more, searches bring up lousy results at the top, sleazy people finder services, ads and rip-offs. I scrolled down to a full match for the number my phone was showing, a truck stop on the southeast side.

"One of them, a drive-up phone, you know?" The sound went muffled and Will said something I couldn't make out.

The line went dead.

I DIDN'T HAVE ENOUGH to go to the police. I got a rideshare to the truck stop instead.

There was no sign of Will at the phone booths. I gave the driver a twenty-dollar bill to wait and had to add another one before he agreed. He had an accent I couldn't place. This job was going to take me to whole new level of broke.

A truck stop at night is a collection of trouble, most of it barely asleep. The drivers mind their business, but there's a lot of working talent lurking, selling what you can't buy in the brightly-lit building. I started around the edges of the lot and someone hissed a catcall at me from the shadow of a trailer, "Ssst! Bitch, bitch, my corner, git." They stepped forward, into the light spilling from around the truck stop building. I could make out a shape, barely, skinny arms and legs and a dress like an oversized T-shirt. "You just get."

I held up both hands, palms out, a little above waist level. "I'm not working. Not looking, either." Try to get along and most people will do the same.

"Hngh." The silhouette gave me a sideways look. "Dunno even what you are."

"I think a friend of mine is lost here."

That got a laugh, a short bark without humor.

"He was on the phone."

She took a step closer and I hoped she wasn't going to pull out a knife. "The old bum?" She snickered. "He run off. Where he shouldn't." She gestured towards a row of trucks on the far side of my waiting rideshare.

"Thanks." I turned around, keeping to the shadows and trying to look like I knew where I was going. At the first group of parked trucks, I heard a familiar cough.

"Leigh. Keep walking." He didn't quite sound sober.

The shadows between the trucks were like old carbon paper, black with no depth at all.

"I think they're here. Like a phone company van. Don't know if they left." There was a thump. "Damn."

He was breathing heavily.

I tried to match his loud whisper. "I got a car." I looked towards the waiting rideshare and waved the driver to us.

Will sighed.

The driver was closer now, and he flashed a grin that showed a silvery front tooth. The car stopped right in front of me and the driver popped open the passenger-side door. "Get in!" he said, eyes wide.

"Will?" I spoke over my shoulder. "Move." I opened the back door and got in. Will stumbled though the lit patch to the open front door and slumped down in the seat, slamming the door.

The driver turned to me. "This is your friend?"

I thought a light-colored van had just turned into the lot. I didn't want to wait until it was close enough to read the writing on the side. "Yes. Go."

He sped up smoothly and got us out on the frontage road before speaking. "Like back home, this is. Who you piss off?"

I leaned until I could see his face in the rearview mirror. "You don't want to know."

He grinned. "Okay, but costs more."

Great. "I'll put it on your tip."

He shook his head. "Cash."

Will took hold of my arm. "Gotta tell you. This is important."

I spoke to the driver. "Another forty?"

He nodded and turned his full attention to the road.

Will didn't wait for me to lean back. "They're robbin' banks," he said, in a hoarse whisper the driver couldn't possibly miss. "Only not robbing 'em, exactly."

The driver moved a little. I looked up and caught his eye in the rearview mirror. He raised an eyebrow. I mimed drinking from a bottle at him, and then spun a forefinger next to my temple, and he looked back at the street.

Will snorted, but he spoke more quietly. "Money comes in, it goes out, late every night. Looks like they take some of it, buy that crypto stuff, sell it the next night and pay everybody. It don't make sense."

It made a little sense to me. I had forced myself to stay awake through an entire semester on financial crimes. One thing that stuck was banks have several different electronic systems to clear checks and reconcile accounts. One of them uses the federal reserve; the rest are privately run. There's "float" built in, an extra two days to process transactions. If a clever operator could intercept it, a "man in the middle" attack—but it's not vulnerable. The banks have too much at stake.

Will was still whispering. "I fixed 'em. Left me all alone and didn't even bother to log out." He snickered. "You'll see." He shook his head. "They got some fancy stuff. I seen one of those backpacks open. It's data-comms stuff. Like short-range microwave radio. You know what I did in the service?" He waved his three-finger left hand at me. "Until this. I was a data tech. 'Lectronic intel. Go out where we could intercept, right? They blew us up, everybody but me. But I know that stuff." He snuffled and spoke louder. "I know!" He turned away and looked out the window. "Blood all over me. Sent me home." I looked over at his reflection in the window. He closed his eyes.

If I were a better person, I would have been thinking about Will's trauma. I was wondering about dead telephone technicians, orange backpacks and what happens if a crook gets between a bunch of banks and their electronic clearinghouse. Wouldn't somebody notice? How long could they keep it going? They'd need someone familiar with the system. Physical access alone wasn't enough.

Army Will started to snore, slumped against the window.

At my apartment building, Will roused enough to not be a dead weight. I steered him into the elevator and onto my living room couch. It was just after 4:30 in the morning. I used the rideshare app on my phone to leave the driver five stars, went to my tiny bedroom, laid down on top of the covers and fell asleep fully clothed.

That was convenient when shortly after 7:00, someone started pounding on my door.

———

I MADE it to the living-dining room. There was no sign of Army Will except for a crumpled pillow on the couch.

"Federal agents, FBI. Open up." They kept knocking.

I got to the door muzzy enough to open it without speaking and backed up as they moved in.

There were two of them, looking like small-time lawyers. The door knocker was wearing a dark gray suit, a pale yellow shirt and a tie with a tiny pattern in two shades of gray. I knew that because the knot of his tie was at the same height as my eyes. He had dark brown hair, going gray at the temples. I didn't get as good a look at his partner, a blur in navy blue. Gray suit's aftershave smelled nice, an understated, clean scent that I didn't trust.

He looked down at me, held up an FBI ID and said, "LaFong."

I was in no mood. "'Lafong' yourself."

The agent in navy blue patted me down impolitely, found my Glock in its appendix-carry holster, took it and sat me on the couch. "I'm Special Agent Grossniklaus."

"You want my ID?"

He shook his head. "You are Leigh Reid Moxon. You are sole proprietor of a licensed private investigation firm and you are interfering with an ongoing Bureau investigation."

His partner was prowling around my living room and the kitchenette nook. "Nick," he said, "This...person...is the smallest-time PI I have ever seen."

True, and insulting. I thought FBI agents were supposed to be polite. "You're looking in the wrong place," I said, "My office is the card table, over there."

I keep my laptop computer there, a couple of notebooks. Cheap file boxes stacked under the table hold the rest of my paper files.

Agent Grossniklaus gave me a look that was almost affectionate. "Very helpful. What do you know about U. S. Army Technical Specialist William K. Jardine?"

"Who?"

"Ha. Amalgamated Telecommunications? Lyman Thomson? Richard Hinemann?" He leaned in. "How about Railroadmen's Commercial Bank? Mercantile Trust? P R & G?"

The last three were all banks along Meridian Street. Banks with Army Will's "backpack guys" nearby. Last night I wondered how long a tricky financial crime could go unnoticed. Maybe not very long.

Agent LaFong had drifted over to my card table and was looking it over. He held up the files from the tray. "You mind?"

"Knock yourself out."

Army Will had stumbled me in over my head.

The two feds didn't like my answers to their questions. They took me downtown, to an office in the top-heavy Minton-Capeheart Federal Building, looming like a giant concrete metaphor, and asked again. I told them I knew the bank names. They showed me a picture of Army Will on a computer monitor, younger, happier-looking and in uniform. I said he looked like someone I knew, and that got around to the subject of orange backpacks.

They had pictures of one on the computer. It was filled with gizmos that didn't mean anything at all to me, and I said so. They wanted to know what I knew about a destructive device in it.

"You mean like a bomb?"

They most certainly did.

The interview fizzled out after that. Agent Grossniklaus gave me his card in case I remembered anything else. It was edging into rush hour when I got out. I admired the gaudy murals on the outside of the ground floor for about two eyeblinks and headed towards

Meridian Street, hoping to find a familiar face panhandling around University Park and ask some questions of my own.

The park, by the time I reached it, was occupied only by retirees, a couple of mothers with children, and a middle-aged businessman with an expensively-bad haircut, holding a cellphone conversation while pacing back and forth.

No Anne, no Tony. No Army Will. Just an orange backpack guy, carefully not staring across Meridian Street at a bank. I decided to loop around the federal courthouse and head towards Monument Circle before he saw me. I didn't have to.

FBI cars are mostly big SUVs in muted colors. The one that veered to the curb in front of the guy I was watching lit up flashing red and blue lights behind the grille as it lurched to a stop.

The feds were rolling up the orange knapsack guys and I still hadn't found Army Will. I turned and looked towards the Circle. The FBI wouldn't move unless they were landing on the whole gang at once

Nothing. The Soldiers and Sailors Monument stood tall and quiet. On the steps in front of it, stone slabs and big orange tool chests behind a temporary construction barrier

The construction crew had knocked off promptly at four. Traffic was picking up and there was a scattering of pedestrians on the sidewalks. While I watched, the security guard picked up his orange backpack and ducked inside.

I hadn't told the feds about him.

It was a block away. I started walking, took out my phone and called the number Agent Grossniklaus had given me. It went to voicemail.

I walked faster. "This is Leigh Moxon. You missed one of your bank robbers. He's inside the Soldiers and Sailors Monument. White male, about 5' 10", medium build, brown hair, beard, wearing a gray uniform from a security company. I'm headed for the scene." I closed with my number, feeling only a little foolish about dropping into cop-speak.

I was tired of being jerked around by a bunch of high-tech crooks playing with more money every night than I'd ever see. I was angry at the way they were treating the unhoused, from the grimy saps they had watching their microwave data links to the people they'd abused to ensure they could operate freely. And I was annoyed that Army Will had vanished—or had been vanished.

They weren't good reasons, but they were enough. I got through traffic to the circle. The construction barrier wasn't much, a short fence like metal bike racks, with gaps in it. Up close, the monument is overwhelming. The statues are over twice life size, looming over the large doorway at the base. The plate glass door stood slightly ajar, the interior dimly lit.

Inside, it's a room within a room, the gift shop extending off to the left and wrapping around the base. To the right, the outer portion dead-ends in wall, leaving a shadowy alcove. The light was coming from the smaller interior room, where the tiny elevator and stairway begin.

I stopped just inside the door, listening. Traffic noise from outside. A distant metallic ticking. The large fountains at the east and west sides had been turned off for the construction project. The falling water usually hushes other sounds. Not now.

The gift shop area was worryingly unlit. There was another ticking sound from ahead of me, followed by a louder clunk and a rising hum. I stepped closer to the inner room.

The elevator was in motion. The narrow stairway wraps around the open shaft, over 300 steps to the top. Looking up, I could see the cables swaying, over the stone arch that frames the elevator doors.

There's dense wire mesh along the stairway. I couldn't see if he was heading down the stairs. I expected the elevator was a distraction. Listening at the bottom of the last flight, I wasn't sure if I was hearing footsteps or not.

The base of the elevator came into view. Light bloomed around it, bright and changing. I took a step back, trying for a better look.

The elevator car dropped behind the entrance structure, chimed, and the doors opened, spilling light, heat and black smoke: there was a backpack burning on the center of the floor.

Fire alarms went off and a man ran out of the stairway. I pivoted into him. He tried to sidestep, but there wasn't enough room and we both fell.

I expected it. He didn't. I tried for a bear hug but he twisted away.

He was out of breath, trying to stand. The light from the burning backpack in the elevator got brighter. "Better. Run," he said. The smoke smelled pretty bad. He twisted out of my grip and took a step towards the door, keeping low. I grabbed an ankle and tripped him.

He went down and I stood up, with a stab of pain from my right knee. I drew breath to tell him to stay down and started coughing instead.

The fire was starting to die out but getting outside felt like a good idea. I let him stand and we both stumbled out, just as a big SUV with government plates and police lights flashing behind the grille came to a stop on the Circle in front of us.

THE CASE LEFT ME BROKE. Army Will never returned. A week after the FBI had arrested the orange backpack gang, I received a postcard with a Nebraska postmark and a panoramic photograph of Lansing, Michigan on the front. It just said "Thank you. Check your PayPal. W."

The newspaper and TV stations ran stories about the gang. Three ringleaders had been arrested: Chief Technology Officer at one of the smaller banks, the only surviving employee of the phone-service company and the security guard I'd tangled with. They had stashed their ill-gotten gains in offshore accounts, and were facing murder charges in addition to bank fraud. The money might not ever be recovered.

The strangest part was they didn't steal it for keeps. They were diverting funds, buying fast-increasing cryptocurrencies, selling the crypto, pocketing the profit and seamlessly returning the original amount. As long as they kept the money moving, they pulled in a staggering amount, free and clear.

I was high and dry until the end of the month, when $400 arrived in my PayPal account from an overseas bank. I let it sit. If it was a mistake they'd take it back and if it was a scam, I wasn't taking the bait. Another $400 arrived the next month and I tracked the bank down in the Bahamas. They politely refused to offer any information.

On a hunch, I checked with the Bromeliad Center. They had received a much larger amount from the same bank for the last two months. Half-drunk leaving the truck stop, Will had laughed how he'd "fixed 'em." I was pretty sure this was the result. I'm not sure how to explain it when I file my taxes.

THE SOLDIERS AND SAILORS MONUMENT

A dramatic obelisk of Indiana limestone 284 feet tall at the center of Monument Circle in the heart of downtown Indianapolis, the Soldiers and Sailors Monument was commissioned in 1888 to commemorate Indiana's Civil War veterans. The monument was constructed over the next 13 years at a cost of $594,318, more than $22 million in 2025 dollars.

Designed by architect Bruno Schmitz, the monument includes fountains and massive sculptural groupings representing and named *War* and *Peace* at the base. It is topped by the 30-foot tall bronze figure of *Victory*, crowned by an eagle and holding both a torch and a sword, designed by American sculptor George Brewster. It was the first monument in the United States to be dedicated to the ordinary soldier, and now honors Hoosiers who served in the American Revolution, the War of 1812, the Mexican-American War and the Civil War.

Z IS FOR
(FUNCTIONAL) ZERO
BY B.K. HART

I was peeved the alphabet mysteries ended with the letter Y. I'm no Kinsey Millhone. The name Jane Longshot isn't mine either, but that's what I'm using for this report. Which is my attempt to exonerate a homeless man, one Anthony "Fingers" Morales, for the charges of murder. Obstruction, destruction of evidence, tampering with a crime scene and the lesser charges under Indiana Code Title 35, article 45 Offenses Against Public Health, Order, and Decency, Chapter 19. Failure to report a Dead Body 35-45-19-3. *Discovery or Handling of Human Remains*, were lower on my list but I figured they would resolve themselves if the murder portion was resolved.

One obvious difference between Kinsey and I is that I have electronic equipment practically IV-fed into my reality. She had to run down the hall to use a fax machine. I also don't think Kinsey was diagnosed with OCD. The biggest problem with obsessive compulsive disorder for an investigator is the tendency to find an endless array of interconnected strings. I learned to push forward if I notice I am rattling on, a bit like now.

My qualifications and investigative history:

As soon as I graduated high school, I joined the Army. I only puked twice getting through basic training. I learned to shoot rifles and other military grade equipment with some proficiency. Handguns, not so much, apparently there isn't a high degree of need for handguns in military maneuvers. I made it through three years of service before I realized the same level of assholery causing my flight from home, was pervasive in the military as well. Sexual harassment, power plays, and jerks ordering me to do activities which had no point. When I complained and was ignored, the situation escalated until I was provided with a *general discharge under honorable conditions*. This landed me in job training with an insurance company.

I started in claims, found I had an eye for noticing small idiosyncrasies between our "statement of facts" from customers, and say, official police reports. Frankly, this isn't uncommon. Seven out of ten reports will be off in small ways. Officers are in a hurry, the insured may be shaken or injured, either party involved could be having a bad day and didn't give details the proper attention. Then there are the other types of discrepancies: information the insured wished to remain private, details forgotten or not believed relevant at the time, or specifically omitted and outright lies to paint the insured in a more positive light. I had a nose for these.

Then I got a new boss...

See: *left home and army above—rinse, and repeat.*

Because I personally investigated my claims, often voluntarily in the field, I'd met and become friends with several law enforcement officers, some who later became private investigators. Private investigation seemed romantic and fun, a way to get out from the bureaucracy I found in the public sector. You know, be my own boss. Live the dream. That was four years ago, and the glasses are a bit less rosy these days.

I knew Anthony "Fingers" Morales from my time in the service. He was in special services with EOD, Explosive Ordnance Disposal. It's why he got the nickname "Fingers". Tony could fit into areas where other members of his team might be too fat fingered, technically it was *little fingers* but that was too long for a nickname, so Tony was just left with fingers. Sounds like job security except the obvious result was that Tony would end up in precarious situations more frequently than the average military grunt. Most EOD were tagged or safely detonated, not typically defused, Tony was continually called up instead of other personnel who were clearly available, much to his chagrin.

I only served for 90 days overseas before being granted a discharge and shipped back. When Tony and I found out we were both from Indiana, we struck up an unlikely friendship and kept in touch over the years. I hadn't seen him in person for close to five years and hadn't received so much as an email in at least two years, so I was a little surprised to receive a message that he needed help.

Pertinent details of the case, a deceased male found inside the grounds of the Crown Hill Cemetery. Yes, I know this is what the cemetery is for however this male was not interred. He was found leaning with his head tilted back against a fountained memorial with two quarters placed over his eyes. Autopsy reported death due to blunt force trauma to head, and body, with acute kidney failure. Additional crisscross patterned indentations across back, arms, legs indicating the body had at one point been against a grate of some type leaving the marks. The approximate age of deceased estimated between seventy-five and ninety years old.

The quarters had one very defined fingerprint, and more forensic evidence retrieved with confirming matches, all of which belonged to Anthony Morales. Provided courtesy of the U.S. Military. Pretty circumstantial evidence, and there were questions. I really wanted to have those questions answered. Tony refused counsel. He wanted to speak to me instead. I could think of a hundred reasons why this was a bad idea.

WE DISPENSED with the pleasantries - how you are doing, what are you doing here, when did you get out - and I got down to business.

"First, if you have the money, hire a lawyer. If you don't, take the public defender, it's better than nothing," I said.

"That would be a waste of time and money," he said.

Tony wasn't an ignorant man, so his attitude surprised me.

"Why is that?" I asked.

"I didn't kill him, so I'm not concerned about doing time for that."

I didn't point out that technically, he was already "doing time" for it since his butt was currently sitting in jail. I raised my eyebrows.

He smiled at me as if anticipating my thoughts, "I live on the streets, this is like vacation, reminiscent of the army. Three hots and a cot."

I nodded. Three meals and a bed. Wouldn't be my choice but Tony was strong and could likely hold his own in jail. I felt the authorities were mostly holding him not because they had hard evidence to charge him but because they were afraid they'd lose track of him on the streets.

"So, why did you ask for help if you aren't looking for exoneration from the murder?"

"I was hoping you could help me find Charlie's people," he said.

Who the hell was Charlie?

In a different tone, I asked. "Charlie who?"

"If I knew that, I probably wouldn't need you," he pointed out. "All I know for sure is that his name was Charlie, and I think he served in Viet Nam. He had a tat. Check with the coroner but I think it might have been his unit. I never could get a good enough look to tell what it was from but it looked like the kind most of us guys would get if we spent any time with the same unit. You know the type."

I nodded again; I did. I realized he was talking about the dead body so now I had even more questions. I'd have to talk to the coroner. I hadn't noticed a tattoo mentioned in the autopsy report and it should have been if there had been one.

"Okay, I can do this or try," I agreed. "Can you at least tell me how your DNA ended up all over the deceased as well as your finger-prints on the coins. And, why? I realize it's mostly circumstantial, but I've seen cases made on less."

"I moved him in a grocery cart to Crown Hill and placed him in a peaceful area, where he belonged. He was a veteran. He deserved to be buried in a place of honor, I don't care what his circumstances were the last few years of his life."

"And the coins?" I asked.

"You still have to pay the ferryman, Rat."

Rat. Nobody'd called me Rat since I'd left the Army. I'd forgotten the nickname. Rat terrier because I'd get ahold of something and wouldn't let go. I don't remember how I'd earned the name, but it stayed with me the entire time I was overseas.

I took copious amounts of notes. Where "Charlie" hung out, where Tony typically saw him, who was in the area, where he found the body. Everything Tony could remember about what he'd been told over the last few months living on the streets. Anybody who might want to cause harm, who might have been hassling anyone on the street. Ideas, because I was short on them, and I needed to start somewhere.

I dug as deep as I could and wrapped up the conversation. I was getting pissed off as I sat there jotting down notes. I noticed my emotions, but I wasn't sure why I was getting bent out of shape. That was annoying on top of the present obvious circumstances.

Tony noticed. Of course he did.

"You mad at me, Rat?"

"Yeah," I blurted, then pulled back a moment, "Yeah, I think I am. Why didn't you reach out to me when you got to town? I could have helped you get set up. At least give you a foundation to get started. I'm a bit peeved about that. You obviously knew I was here and how to reach me. Why didn't you call?"

He wouldn't meet my eyes. His thumbnail dug into the edge of the table and scraped the gunk from the groove. He shrugged.

He was quiet for so long; I didn't think he was going to give me any answer at all. I started gathering up my papers. It didn't matter. I'd still help him. He was like the brother I never had, and he hadn't reached out to me. I wasn't sure I could explain it.

"Sometimes, what you imagine in your head doesn't match reality," he said softly. "I *needed* to be on my own when I got back. I saw some things over there I didn't feel able to cope with when I returned. We all did, I guess. I found a sort of family on the streets, not unlike over there. I thought I could help protect people like Charlie. I was wrong."

His jaw clenched and he bunched up his fist, "I was wrong. I think maybe I could help more now. I needed to do what I did, be where I was, to get to this point of understanding. You get me?"

Then he looked at me and I saw the sheen of unshed tears.

"I get you. When you get out of here though, I have a couch. That's my conditional support on this. I find what I can for you and when you get out, you take the help. Whether you want it or not."

I didn't allow any tears to fall. He nodded agreement. I left.

I didn't state that I was going to get him out of jail. Maybe he knew me well enough to know that I wouldn't just investigate his friend. I'd dig up everything I could on what happened that night.

I SAT in my car for a minute and pulled myself together. I wasn't sure why this was hitting me so hard. I spent my life keeping my feelings close. I never wanted anyone to know how I felt about anything because emotions could be used against me. The bonds formed in the military were a different kind of thing, like I said, a bit like family. Only, better in my opinion.

I was mad at Tony. I was scared for him. I was hurt he hadn't thought he could call me. At the same time, I understood what he meant by needing that time. I didn't have people to come home to either, but I had job training and Indianapolis was the only home I'd known. Living on the street would never be an option for me.

I started making a mental list of things I wanted to get done today. It was late Friday, and I was going to run out of time to hit some businesses while they were still open.

I pulled the autopsy report back up on my cell phone and enlarged it, looking for the tat details, which I didn't find. I also noted the scribble signed off on the report didn't look like Marco Dunbar, the lead coroner. He would not have missed a tat and if a body with no id had come into the morgue, he would have at minimum pulled fingerprints which should have crossed to military records. I called Dunbar, got voicemail, told him I was on my way and asked him to please not leave.

Marco was waiting for me, and he didn't appear happy. I didn't feel it was because I asked him to wait, even though it was a Friday afternoon. He'd waited before, I mean, sure maybe not often and maybe not on a Friday night.

"You got my message?"

"Oh, I got it. I had to pull the body and look after reviewing the report. You said a tat and that should have been noted," he said, then turned as a tall, freckled-faced man approached. "You do the report on the DB in drawer twelve?"

Marco handed the report over, Howdy Doody took it, and shrugged. "Yeah, why?"

"You didn't notate the tattoo on the upper left arm?" Marco asked.

"Homeless guy, probably going to Potters Field," he stated.

"Carmichael, you're still on probation here, you know that, right?" Marco said.

I looked between them, then turned and looked at the wall pretending I wasn't witnessing this dressing down. I have great peripheral vision, and I saw Carmichael's face flush red. He looked at me, then back to Marco.

"Is there a problem?" he asked.

"Did you pull his prints?"

"I didn't get a local hit on his prints," Carmichael answered.

Marco took a deep breath and rubbed an exhausted hand across his forehead. "Is it because he was homeless, because he was black or because he was poor that you decided doing the barest minimum was ok for this man?"

I half turned and said, "I think his name is Charlie."

They both turned and looked at me. I moved a little further down the hallway and pretended to study a bulletin board.

I couldn't hear so much about the rest of the conversation. There wasn't anything of interest on the bulletin board either. I'd heard enough to know why there were discrepancies in the report. Now that Marco had Charlie's body, I expected more information.

Marco touched my elbow, "I'm sorry about that. I shouldn't have called him out in front of you. There's no place for discrimination down here. I don't have time for anyone doing a half ass job that I have to go back and re-do. You'll have to wait for me to get Charlie scheduled back on the table."

He looked at his watch. "I can pull his prints again and push those through the military database for you today though. I'm not going to be able to get the full report done."

"I can tell you where the crisscross marks came from, if that helps," I said. I told him about how the body had been transported via grocery cart to Crown Hill Cemetery.

"I took a preliminary look at the tattoo, it has numbers, probably his unit. Very hard to read but we can use some tech and get better detail. Wasn't a high-quality job," Marco scratched the five o'clock shadow starting to emerge along his jawline. "I don't think he was in Vietnam though. If I had to guess, he's too old. I'm thinking possibly Korea."

I made sure Marco had my contact information handy then I headed to where Tony said he'd found Charlie. I forgot Capitol was one-way southbound and had to drive around the neighborhood a few times to figure out the most likely hang outs. There were a couple of churches on Boulevard and the old post office on 34th Street. Both of which had large parking lots with plenty of places where someone could tuck up and sleep for the night. There were a few churches up Graceland as well. What I was looking for though was any sign of cameras in the area. The gas station on 34th was likely to have some external cameras but right off I wasn't spotting anything else that might be helpful. I jumped out of my car at the gas station and went inside to look around. The store was busy considering there'd only been one vehicle in the parking lot, and one beat up pick-up truck at the pump.

I spotted a couple of fellas that looked like they might be living on the streets themselves and decided to try my luck.

I walked up to them. The older man with a bandana tied around his head and baggy T-Shirt and sweats addressed me. "How you doin', pretty lady?"

I smiled and took out a picture of Tony. "I was wondering if you knew my friend."

"Wha'd he do?" asked a younger man who leaned around my aged target. I'd have placed him around my age with stringy brown hair pulled into a ponytail and what looked like a two week growth of beard on his face. He reeked of cigarette smoke and possibly something more recreational.

"He had a friend named Charlie and I'm trying to find some people who might know either one of them," I started to explain.

"I think Charlie was in Afghanistan or something," the young one started to say. The old guy popped him in the back of the head, not hard, but enough to cause him to jerk back and put his fists up.

"You ding-a-ling, Charlie was way too old for Afghanistan." The old guy turned his wise eyes to me. "I heard tell Charlie died. Everya' body saying Tony did it but I don't see that at all. They was kinda friends."

"Yeah, they were friends," I said softly, "I was hoping to find some information about Charlie. Who his friends were, where he hung out, if he had any family nearby. Was anybody hassling him lately?"

The younger man kind of shrugged and gave me a look that indicated he didn't want to get involved. I figured that out being an investigator and all when he quietly slunk away from the conversation. The old man seemed inclined to continue his conversation though so I offered to buy him a cup of coffee, or water, or anything else he might like of the meager offerings available. I bought a scratch off lottery ticket too, because, why not. Hoosier Dreams was a dollar, and I had a few dreams. The movie, Jaws, was a $2 scratch-off ticket and reminded me of my childhood, I bought one of those as well.

"I don't know if this means a thing or not, but we be having trouble ever since that new gang started up in this area. Young punks from over the Michigan road area started runnin' around here."

"You got names?"

"Oh no, they don't talk," he shook his head, "but they cause trouble. Breaking into cars and stuff, and then the cops come around and hassle us because we out here, ya know. We don't cause no problems. That's what the cops get wrong. It's like they think all we do is sit around and think how we might mess in our own neighborhood, but we live here too."

"What do you know about these new kids then?"

"Not so much, they's four or five of em. Ride in this jacked up chevy with the bump, bump, bump on the stereo. You know when they's around unless they tryin' to be sneaky. Then you might see their car sitting quiet three streets over from where they causin' mischief."

He said everyone just called him Alvie. He told me about a parking lot for the homeless, if you had a car, where you could get a shower and "shitter" as he expressed it. Then lamented that most homeless people didn't have a car and there was a waitlist, if I could believe that. I could believe it. I slipped him ten dollars because I didn't normally carry a lot of cash on me.

"I'm real sorry to hear about ole Charlie. He been out here a few years. We all watch out for the old ones," he said sucking on his front teeth. I wonder what he was considered since he looked on the old side to me. "The funny thing is, I think he had people here. In fact, I think they tried more than once to get him off the street and to come home but he liked the freedom."

I thanked Alvie again and then drove around some more looking specifically for businesses that might have cameras rolling. I thought the Shell station and the McDonalds on 38th Street was probably too far from where Tony said he'd found Charlie but I made a note. Then I found the breach in the fence near Byram Street where Tony said he had gotten into Crown Hill.

Crown Hill Cemetery was the final resting place of several notable persons, including President Benjamin Harrison and gangster John Dillinger. It's the highest elevation point in Indianapolis and includes more than 500 acres of beautifully landscaped grounds filled with memorials, fountains, graves, and 150 species of trees and plants.

Ironically, there always seemed to be a place on 38th Street where a vehicle had gone out of control and ended up barreling through the stone fence that surrounded the cemetery. In a revitalization attempt, the city had put medians down the center of 38th Street to plant maple trees, what the road was formerly named. I counted twelve trees still standing, most of them closer to the Michigan Road crossing than the Graceland Road intersection. I wondered if the trees had met their demise in the same manner as the stone wall surrounding the cemetery.

I was running out of daylight so I tried one of my detective buddies to see if he could help with running down footage. Let the police do their job while I tried to narrow in on any information I could get about Charlie. I was skeptical I could find more today, but I could at least start working on Tony's problem.

Detective Ron Ballard wasn't working today but he was willing to meet me for breakfast tomorrow morning after he had a chance to look at the case. I arranged to meet him at Patachou on Pennsylvania early in the morning. Then, I went home and began some therapeutic cleaning of my apartment. I had a decorative privacy screen I thought might work to separate my living area so Tony wouldn't feel like he was out in the middle of the floor. We'd both slept in worse places so I was sure he could adapt.

I ARRIVED at Café Patachou before 8AM and they were already busy. I was happy to get a table and start on a latte while I waited. It had been a while since I'd last visited this location on Pennsylvania Street. I used to work through cases here when I first went out on my own, until they got too congested for it to be comfortable location. I nursed my latte and sniffed the air appreciating the savory scents drifting out of the kitchen. I was leaning toward the Cuban breakfast, a fried egg over black beans, and rice, with avocado, sour cream and a kickass spinach-jalapeno pesto, and a little sprinkling of white cheddar.

When Ron arrived, I stood and gave him a hug. He wrapped his arms around me and gave me a big squeeze, lifting me off my feet, and forcing a laugh out of me. He was built like a bear, kind of brawny, very grey, arms and legs hard as logs. I always thought a real dad would feel just like Ron. I think the fact that he and Celia never had children made him treat me like I was one of his by default.

"How you doing, short stuff?"

This was a joke since my very average five feet five inches was precisely the same height as Ron's.

"I am good, how's Celia?"

We ordered and dispensed with the small talk amid the rising noise of the café. The clatter of silverware, the froth of the espresso machine, and the chatter from nearby tables slowly fading to the background as I leaned in to hear Ron and look over the police report he'd copied for me.

"So basically, you're right. We're mostly holding him for the weekend, so he doesn't disappear. All the DNA evidence is fairly circumstantial. It's enough to possibly convince a jury if we could establish motive, means, and all the above but the fingerprints could have been from coins your buddy gave to Charlie. The DNA on the clothes is logical since he moved the body. Technically, he could be charged with disturbing the body and tampering with the crime scene. We really aren't that interested in hassling the homeless, we just want to find who did this to him."

I told Ron where the body had been found and explained my driving around the neighborhood and what I had learned about possible cameras in the area. I knew the police department could get those things much easier than a private investigator.

"Alvie said they'd been having some issues with gangbangers in the area lately."

Ron grimaced and reached for some jam to spread onto his English muffin. He chewed around his words as he responded, "Yeah, we have been getting reports. It's been harmless harassment up to this point. I can get someone to roust a few of these boys and see if we can get any information from them."

"I cleared a space at my apartment for Tony. I can vouch for him and make sure he stays in one place until everything is sorted out on this. He was trying to do something nice for Charlie. He shouldn't be punished for that. I know you don't know Tony, but you do know me. Trust my judgment. Anything you can add to the case to help get him released on his own recognizance, I'd appreciate."

"That's up to the judge but I think I can talk to the detectives on the case and put in a word with the prosecutor. See if we can get some special dispensation, especially if it leads to answers about what happened. We won't be able to get anything done until Monday though so tell him to just buckle in for a few days."

There was a brief tussle over the check, but as I pointed out to Ron, I expected him and Celia to invite me over for a barbeque soon and I wouldn't be contributing to that meal. The fact that I could write this off on my taxes as a business expense seemed to convince him.

From the café, I went shopping for clothes for Tony, then food for the house. This was good because I wasn't hungry, so I wasn't buying a bunch of crap I didn't need. It was bad because I couldn't make up my mind on what I needed, or what Tony might like, and it was a Saturday, so everybody's mother was out shopping.

I'd spent way too long roaming the aisle when I got a text from Marco Dunbar.

James Isaiah Charles...

DOB 8/22/1930...

US Army 2/22/1949 until 8/30/1953...

Korea...last name Charles not first name

EXCITED that I had something to work on, I texted back my thanks and rushed home.

I did the obvious searches first, google. It's amazing what you can find with a google search. Right away I was able to find some generic service records. Unfortunately, our Mr. Charles was apparently too old to have the usual social media footprints so I found nothing useful on Facebook, Twitter(now X), or Instagram. And, gosh darn it, his name was too generic to even yield much that I could definitely say he was my guy. I couldn't think of a way to trickle down to offspring, siblings or spouses.

I checked for police records. None.

Voter registration. None.

In a stroke of genius, I tried public records for property taxes and to my surprise found a house located just north of 38th street. *On Graceland.* Practically around the frigging corner from where he would generally hang out with Tony.

Now why would a man who held property decide to live on the street instead of in his own home? The name might have been a coincidence. Maybe this property owner wasn't the same person who was tucked into a drawer at the morgue, but the name was an exact match. The home had been purchased by James Isaiah and Becca Sue

Charles in 1979. I had to believe, if this was not the same man, that they were at least related.

When one faucet turns off, turn on another...so I jumped down the Becca Sue Charles rabbit hole for a couple of hours. She was a little easier to follow. Church organizations, community meeting minutes, offspring, siblings and local activist groups, right up to the obituary showing she had passed away in 2021.

Well, shoot.

I poked at a couple of the offspring names but the boy names were pretty generic again, and the girl names were unique enough but too easy to change with marriages and I wasn't sure I was onto anyone who was an actual blood relative.

I had enough to do a drive by on Graceland tomorrow and see if I could find anyone home.

Just before I was signing off for bed Ron Ballard called me to let me know they had picked up a couple of the gangbangers and were questioning them Sunday, after letting them spend the night in a jail cell. Kids barely over the age of 18. His theory being an overnight might free their memory up a bit about the night "Charlie" was killed.

I told him the DB's real name, but the nickname was already imprinted on both of us. So, James Isaiah remained Charlie.

Sunday, I went to church. Drove by Graceland. Finished cleaning my apartment so it was respectable for guests. And, received an update from Ron letting me know that they were releasing Tony in the morning based on the gangbanger statements. He couldn't give me more details since it was an ongoing investigation, but Tony was clear.

I picked up Tony on Monday morning. I gave him the one-minute tour of the apartment, more like 45 seconds. It's small. I let him take a shower and dress in his new clothes. After breakfast, I handed him the Jaws lottery ticket.

"What's this for?"

"Luck," I said. "You never know. You can help me with the rest of running down Charlie's relatives. Help me knock on some doors."

He slipped the ticket into his breast shirt pocket with a shake of his head. I guess he didn't believe in luck.

We arrived at the Graceland address and tried knocking again with no luck. And, while I was joking about knocking on doors, it couldn't hurt since some of the neighbors might have lived here awhile. We went north, then crossed over and were heading back south when we noticed a car pulling into our Graceland address. We'd been striking out with neighbors anyway as few seemed to be home on a Monday morning. We hightailed it back to Charlie's house prepared to pounce on the new arrival which turned out to be unnecessary since the tall slender man was coming down the drive in our direction.

"Can I help you folks?" he asked as he approached, hands on hips, more confrontational than inviting. "Mrs. Lyons from across the street said you were knocking on doors, but you started at my house. This your car?"

I'd parked my red Toyota on the street in front of the property.

"We were trying to find some information on James Isaiah Charles," I said, taking the lead.

"He in trouble?"

I introduced myself and Tony and gave a brief description of the man I was trying to find but didn't explain why. I wanted to make sure he was related before passing more information.

He looked off down south Graceland, then he sighed deeply and dug his cell phone out of his pocket and typed something in. "You better step inside. I just texted my sister. She only lives a few blocks away so if we can give her a minute."

Tony and I exchanged a glance and followed him inside.

His name was Michael James, his sister was introduced as Millie

Thomas, married name. The home was clean, fully furnished with print fabric sofa and matching chairs, looking more museum preserved than lived in. We sat awkwardly on a couch. The home looked like it hadn't had visitors for years.

"Is dad alright?" He reached for his sister's hand and clasped it for reassurance. "We tried to get him off the street, but he'd come home and settle in for a few weeks, take his meds, seem okay and the next time we came by, he'd be gone again."

Tony nudged me and chin pointed to a photo on the mantel.

"I've been trying to find this man's family for a couple of days." I explained the tattoo, and my process that got me to Graceland. It was always best to rip the band aid off fast. "I'm sorry to say but I believe your father is in the morgue."

Millie began to softly weep.

Tony explained how "Charlie" had been a friend to him on the streets. Odd as it sounds, I think this gave his children some comfort.

We left them with the detective contact names on the case and I gave them Marco Dunbar's contact information so they could make arrangements for their father.

Successfully completing a quest, or case, can sometimes be more sobering than celebratory. I was feeling very somber. Tony was scratching his lottery ticket.

"How much is the jackpot on this Jaws ticket?"

"I don't know ten grand or something," I said and slid him a sideways glance.

"I won," he deadpanned.

"You're shitting me," I almost drove off the road and took my foot off the gas to pull to the side.

I held my chest, heart thumping. He grinned.

"Yeah, I'm shitting you."

I stared.

"You're a Turd."

I put the car into drive, and we drove home.

I finished writing my report for James Isaiah Charles and

submitted it to Anthony "Fingers" Morales. I never got a contract from Tony. There was no fee. It still counts as a closed case. Respectfully submitted, Jane Longshot.

IN THIS HOMAGE to Sue Grafton, "Functional Zero" is a term used to measure whether a community has ended homelessness for a population. In this case, veterans returning from active service. It's supposed to mean that homelessness is rare and brief for a specific population, and that the homeless population doesn't exceed a community's capacity to provide permanent housing. However, we continue to have an excessive number of veterans experiencing homelessness across our nation. Indianapolis estimates that 10 percent of its homeless population consists of veterans.

CROWN HILL CEMETERY

Crown Hill Cemetery in Indianapolis is the third largest non-government cemetery in the country. Established as a non-profit in 1863 during the Civil War, Crown Hill now spans 555 acres and is noted for several famous and infamous people who are interred there. One of the most notorious is John Dillinger, but other famous people include poet James Whitcomb Riley, former President Benjamin Harrison, Eli Lilly, Richard Jordon Gatling, U.S. Rep. Julia Carson, and Robert Irsay, the original owner of the Indianapolis Colt. His son, Jim, who owned the football team until his death in 2025, is also buried there.

Additionally in 2025, one of our fellow Speed City Sisters in Crime members, Hawthorn Fire Mineart, was laid to rest in Crown Hill.

The first person to be interred at this location was Lucy Ann Seaton, wife of Captain John Seaton, who was buried June 2, 1864.

She was 33 years old and died of tuberculosis. Her daughter, also named Lucy, was buried beside her mother a few months later.

More than 195,000 people are interred in Crown Hill, which is located on West 38th Street between Boulevard Place and Michigan Road. Another major entrance commonly used is through a Gothic Revival gateway on 34th Street and Boulevard.

Crown Hill offers public tours that include the locations of historical famous persons, the dead from the Civil War, the Underground Railroad and its connections, an Arboretum Bike Tour, and Skeletons in the Closet Tour that happens each October.

More information can be found at https://crownhillhf.org/visit/

SEND IN THE CLOWNS
BY SHARI HELD

Clowns are the pegs on which the circus is hung. — P.T. Barnum

Yancey Einhaus scurried up the stairs to the Miami County Sheriff's Office as fast as his eighty-three-year-old legs allowed.

"Sheriff Brewster, someone's trying to break into the circus museum." Yancey's sprint was interrupted when he crashed, gasping for breath, into the sheriff's sturdy oak desk. "You can catch him if you head out now."

The sheriff surveyed his late-night visitor. He arched his thick gray eyebrows and steepled his hands in front of him. Other than that, not another body part moved so much as a millimeter until he spoke. "You're in charge of maintenance for the circus museum, Yancey. Not security."

Patches of pink appeared on Yancey's jowls.

"Last year I damn near arrested the museum's hired photographer when you cried wolf," the sheriff said. "You one hundred percent sure this isn't another false alarm?"

Yancey looked down at his boots. "No. But someone's skulking around the grounds. Someone I never seen before. And museum season ended last week. Thought you ought to know."

"Trowbridge is on patrol tonight. I'll have him check it out. Probably some kid looking for something to do." The sheriff returned his attention to the newspaper on his desk.

Yancey was dismissed.

He shuffled out of the sheriff's office, but he hadn't given up. Far from it. He was sure something was up. His inner radar buzzed loud as a bumblebee in a bed of lavender.

Yancey recognized circus folk when he saw them. After all, until he'd retired, he'd been with one circus or another since he was a kid. He knew tons of troupers—trapeze artists, jugglers, magicians, dwarves, and sideshow freaks. Lots of former carnies traveled to Peru, Indiana, Circus Capital of the World, to pay their respects to the International Circus Hall of Fame. They gathered and spent time cuttin' up jackpots—telling grossly exaggerated stories about their escapades—and reminiscing about the good old days. Museum visitors were mesmerized by their tall tales. Not one of those circus folks had slunk around at night, keeping to the shadow, looking for all the world as if they were casing the place. Until now.

As the museum's sole paid off-season maintenance man and self-proclaimed guardian of the museum, Yancey felt an obligation to protect the glorious past of his beloved circus. From 1891 to 1944, Peru had served as the winter quarters for a succession of circus companies. The sheriff was a towner. He didn't understand what the circus meant to Yancey and others. The circus was a way of life that was gone forever. As far as Yancey was concerned, the real circus ended in 2017 when the Ringling Bros. and Barnum & Bailey Circus closed. Oh sure, it made a comeback in 2023, but it wasn't the same. No animals. No clowns. No sideshows.

"Brewster gonna investigate, or what?" asked Yancey's pal, Clarence, who had waited outside on a bench.

Yancey coughed up some phlegm and spit it on the side of the street. "He said he'd have Trowbridge drive by. The sheriff's retiring the end of the year. Don't want to upset the apple cart, I 'spect. We're on our own for this one. You stay put. I'll go see if that guy is still lurking around."

Yancey returned within fifteen minutes. "No sign of him. Everything looks intact. Let's visit Lottie's for a cup of coffee and a slice of rhubarb pie. Make a plan in case he comes back."

As they headed to Lottie's, Yancey, who was spry for his age, slowed his pace to accommodate Clarence's achy hip. Some thirty years ago, a circus horse had panicked, knocking Clarence to the ground during his clown act. His hip never had worked the same since.

When they arrived, they claimed "their booth," tucked in a back corner, away from the hustle and bustle of the other patrons. Especially crying babies. Yellowed stuffing escaped from the seats and random burn marks scarred the table's Formica surface. Their long-standing joke was that the broken-down booth fit the contours of their generous butts just fine. Plus, the picture window gave them a great view of the parking lot, so they could see everyone's comings and goings.

After they received their orders, Yancey and Clarence got down to business.

"You sure the guy was circus folk?" Clarence asked.

"That, or he was trained to be. He was light on his feet. Graceful as a big cat. Every movement slow and deliberate as he sneaked around the five museum buildings."

"How'd you see him? Your eyesight isn't getting any better."

"It ain't getting any worse, neither." Yancey tugged his bushy beard. "Besides, he was smoking. I followed his lit tip as he went from one building to another."

"If we're going to watch for him tomorrow night, I'll borrow some night binoculars from some hunters I know."

"Good. We can set up surveillance in the museum office."

"Wonder what he's up to?"

Yancey slammed his palm on the table so hard his fork flew off his plate. "That's exactly what we're gonna find out."

THE NEXT EVENING the two pals settled into the museum office, which also housed the International Circus Hall of Fame, and waited.

Clarence eased into an office chair in front of the window, covered his legs with the blanket his granddaughter had crocheted for him last Christmas, and surveyed his surroundings. "You spend much time here?" he asked.

"Whenever I can't sleep. Which is much of the time now. Calms me down. When I'm on the grounds, I can almost smell the circus—the burnt sugar from the cotton candy machine, the sawdust, the popcorn and peanuts, and the reek of fresh animal droppings. It all mixed together to create that distinct circus aroma. If I close my eyes, I can almost hear the stakes being pounded into the ground and the notes of the calliope. Can almost feel the electricity in the air when we opened a new show. There was nothing like it."

"I ain't no romantic like you, but this here sure beats sitting alone in my room at the senior's home working a crossword puzzle and drinking spiked Ovaltine," Clarence said. "Why, I…"

Yancey put his finger on his lips to silence Clarence and pointed toward the edge of one of the original buildings from the old circus winter quarters. "That's him."

They grabbed their night binoculars and watched as the stranger palmed a flashlight and peered into the North Wagon Barn. He ran the flashlight beam under the eaves, around the windows and doors.

"I knew the museum should have replaced the security over the winter months instead of waiting until spring," Yancey muttered. "I told them."

"Couldn't afford it. Would have had to dip into the money for restoring the research building. You know that. Hey, you think this guy could be writing a book on the circus? Need some info? We could help with that. Maybe he'd even give us a mention in it."

Yancey snorted. "Not likely. He's searching for something. And it's got nothing to do with a book."

They followed the stranger's movement with their binoculars until the darkness swallowed him.

"He must be staying at the camping grounds by the Mississinewa," Yancey said.

"So whadda we do now?" Clarence asked.

"Go to Lottie's." The scrunch of crisp October leaves accompanied them as they trudged down the street.

They'd been at the diner no longer than half an hour when a dusky-skinned, slender man with curly black hair slid into the booth across the aisle. He removed his battered baseball cap and buffalo plaid scarf, perused the menu, and gave the waitress his order.

"That him?" Clarence whispered.

Yancey stared the stranger up and down. "Yep."

As if their glances seared his skin, the stranger turned his head to face them and nodded.

They returned his nod. "You new in town?" Yancey asked. "Or just passing through?"

"Passing through. Attended a funeral in Texas for my stepfather. Thought I'd make my way to Indiana to pay my respects to the circus museum."

"You're a bit late," Clarence said. "Museum's closed until July."

"You circus folk," Yancey said. It wasn't a question.

"Yes. My granddaddy came to the USA from Tanzania back in the 60s. He was a lion tamer. My mother was a magician's assistant." He shrugged. "My father? Not sure even my mother knew."

"Ah, the dangerous arts," Yancey said, politely avoiding the father issue. "We were joeys. The only thing we had to worry about is tripping over our own feet in those ridiculous clown shoes. Sure made the kids smile, though. And that's what it was all about. What's your specialty?"

"I was into impalement acts. A knife thrower. Wheel of Death, and all that. I stayed with Ringling until it shut down."

"I see. I'm Yancey Einhaus, by the way. And that's Clarence Hope."

"Folks call me Jack. Last name's Majid."

"Both Clarence and I were born and bred right here in Peru, Indiana...Circus Capital of the World." Yancey stopped to slurp his coffee. "We can tell you anything you need to know about the museum."

Yancey could swear he saw a gleam in Jack's eye at that bit of information.

"Good to know. I do have a question. Is it true that *everything* from the Sarasota Circus Hall of Fame came to Peru?"

Clarence spoke up. "Yessiree. Peru bought the whole shebang, lock, stock, and barrel. Round here, we cherish our circus heritage."

"I can see that," Jack said. The waitress brought his order, poured more coffee, and faded away.

Yancey knew the conversation was coming to an end, so he eased in a few quick questions. "Anything in particular, you're interested in?"

"No, just curious is all," Jack said.

"Hmm. Hey, still carry your knife?"

Jack pulled back one side of his jean jacket to reveal a leather sheath traditional belt carry. "Never without it. Now, if you'll excuse me, I'm hungry as a bear. I'll be here for a few days, though. Maybe we can talk again?"

Clarence and Yancey nodded and rose to leave.

When they got outside, Yancey said, "That guy's looking for something. Something that came from the Sarasota Hall of Fame and he thinks it's hidden in our museum. The question is, what?"

THE NEXT MORNING the two cronies met at Lottie's for sausage gravy over biscuits, hash browns, and a pot of fully leaded coffee.

"You up for doing some research at the museum?" Yancey asked.

"Sure thing," Clarence said. "And I can use the computer at the retirement home to follow up on what I find." He picked up the *Indiana Plain Dealer* newspaper and fanned himself. "This is the most excitement I've had in years."

"See what you can find out about Jack's granddaddy from Tanzania. His name. The circus he was with. How he got here. Anything newsworthy. A scandal or something that seems off. Even general gossip. The same for his mother and for Jack. I'll connect with some circus folk. See if anyone remembers anything."

As they stood to leave, they saw two men arguing in the parking lot.

"That's Jack," Clarence said. "I never seen that other one."

As one, they scooted their butts back into the booth. Yancey motioned for the waitress to bring them more coffee. "Me, either. Let's wait a bit. See what happens."

A muscular man wearing a cowboy hat and a red quilted vest over a plaid flannel shirt shouted at Jack, ran at him, and shoved him.

Jack defended himself while appearing to try to appease the younger man. Everything escalated from there. Without warning, in a move smooth as a panther, Jack lunged forward and grabbed his adversary's hand, angrily jabbing at a large ring on the man's finger. Their words were harsh and loud enough to be heard inside, although unintelligible. The younger guy jerked his hand back, catching Jack off-balance. He lowered his chin, clenched his fist, and charged at Jack, nearly knocking him to the ground.

When the sheriff's car rolled into the parking lot, the other guy did a runner.

"Whatcha make of that?" Clarence asked.

Yancey tugged his beard. "It's clear they have history. Looked like a spat over that ring. Could be Jack owes the other one money. Could be anything. What I'd like to know is whether they're after the same thing. And if that thing is in our museum. If so, I'd reckon our boy Jack has some competition.

"Or maybe, that new guy knows what Jack's planning and is here to stop him," Clarence said.

"Yep, could be."

"If that younger guy was ever with the circus, I'm the spirit of P.T. Barnum," Clarence said.

"Definitely not circus," Yancey said. He opened his mouth to say more, but clamped it shut when Jack slid into a nearby booth.

Yancey nursed his coffee until Jack ordered. "Saw you and your buddy in the parking lot," Yancey said.

"My stepbrother, Ed Wiggins." Jack spat out the words as though he'd bitten into a burning ember. "No buddy of mine."

"I gathered," Yancey said. "He's pretty quick with his temper and his fists."

"He's always been that way. Got him in trouble with the law a while back. Did some time in prison. If I were you, I'd stay away from him."

"Must need to see you pretty bad if he followed you all the way from Texas."

Jack snorted. "He's not here to see me, he's here to. . . No offense, but it's none of your business, Old Man."

"Well, hope you two get it straightened out. We'll leave you to it." He and Clarence rose to leave.

"Maybe it's a fight over a woman," Clarence said when they were outside. "Remember when everyone had the hots for that blonde dame on the trapeze with the fabulous knockers? Angeline, I think it was. She sure was some looker. Made my heart pitter-patter when she was near."

Yancey snorted. "That wasn't your heart. Your pitter-patterin' was coming from further south. Nah, I think whatever they're fighting over is here in the museum. Why else would they both be here?"

Yancey slapped Clarence on the back. "Whatever's going on,

we'll get to the bottom of it. Ain't nobody gonna mess with our museum."

CLARENCE WENT to the museum to conduct his research while Yancey questioned a few local people about Ed and Jack. "Find anything?" Yancey asked Clarence when they met up later.

Clarence barely raised his head to acknowledge Yancey. "Plenty. There's a lion tamer from Tanzania name of Danso Majid who joined Ringling Brothers in sixty-nine. Jack looks late thirties, early forties. So, Majid's 'bout the right age for Jack's grandpappy. He had quite the reputation as the next Clyde Beatty when it came to cat training, but he wasn't much of a showman. You believe that? Why, if I could make the big cats jump through hoops without eating me for a snack, I'd strut my stuff. Lion tamers never lacked for female attention."

"Stay on track," Yancey said. "That doesn't give us much to go on. Anything else?"

Clarence puffed out his chest like the sole banty rooster in a henhouse. "I poked around for any news about Tanzania around that time. This could be nothing. But a few years prior to sixty-nine, an emerald-colored tsavorite garnet was found in Tanzania. It's two hundred times rarer than emeralds. Back then, it was priced at $10,000 per carat, and the article said the price per carat increases every year. We're talkin' a huge chunk o' change."

"So, take it home, Clarence. What's the significance to our museum?"

Clarence's grin stretched clear across his face. "Well, it was rumored that someone smuggled a tsavorite out of Tanzania 'bout that time. And get this, it disappeared once it got to the States."

"Hmm. Interesting tidbit, but I think we can assume that stone was cut and is residing in several women's jewelry boxes now."

"Maybe," Clarence said. "But get this. In his act, Danso Majid wore a turban with a brilliant emerald smack dab in the middle of it. And guess where his circus wintered over during his time?"

"Sarasota. Well, I'll be damned. And Jack seemed unusually interested in whether we bought everything from the Sarasota Circus Hall of Fame."

"Here's another mystery," Clarence said. "According to the rumor mill, Majid's death had all the earmarks of a homicide, but nothin' was proved. He was circus folk. The towners didn't put any teeth into the investigation. They wanted the circus gone."

Yancey whistled. "What if Majid realized someone was after him and hid that stone inside something that ended up at the Sarasota museum? Then he was murdered before he could retrieve it. Far-fetched. But makes as much sense as anything else."

"Would explain why Jack's here."

"And Ed, too, I reckon," Yancey said. "I say we do our own search for this stone. If it's here, we'll find it."

Clarence stood and stretched his legs. "Where do we start?"

"We know Majid was with Ringling Brothers, so we'll start with artifacts that came from there. Didn't Jack say his mother was part of a magician's act? I think I remember seeing some magician props somewhere. And tons of costumes."

The task was daunting for the two octogenarians. Almost everything, except for sixteen circus wagons, had come from Sarasota. Clarence stubbed his gouty big toe and crashed on his bad hip, cursing like a roustabout. Yancey, who inspected the circus wagons, encountered more than one splinter, and he twisted his right ankle when he missed a step while backing out of the ringmaster's wagon.

"One more place to look," Yancey said. "The storage area. I hoped we wouldn't have to go there. Everything's jumbled together in a gigantic junk pile. No order to it at all."

Clarence grimaced. "Think we could rest for a bit? Not sure I can tackle that job now."

"Sure. Let's lock up and head to Lottie's for tonight's chicken n' noodles and mashed potato special. My treat."

Angry shouting greeted them as they stepped outside. They ducked into the shadows and listened.

"Give me that ring before I saw your finger off to get it," Jack said. "It was my granddaddy's. You've no right to it."

"But I do," Ed said. "Your mom died without a will. My dad got everything. Now he's dead, everything's mine. And legally, there's not a damn thing you can do about it."

Ed pulled the ring off his finger and held it under Jack's nose. "You want this so bad?" He jerked it back as Jack reached for it. "Help me find the stone…the real prize. Then I'll give you your granddaddy's ring. At least you'll keep part of your stupid circus heritage."

Jack's laugh was hollow as a rotted tree stump. "The stone? You believe that old tale?"

"Old tale, my ass," Ed said. "My dad never put any credence into it. But you do. Else you wouldn't be here. When you came back to pay your respects to dear old dad, I saw you sneak into his office and rifle through his desk. I figured you were looking for the ring, which I'd already claimed. But when you found your mother's old diary and took off the next day, I followed you on a hunch. Guess it paid off."

"You think so? Well, you're on your own for this one. I'd rather give up the ring than help you." Jack turned on his heels and walked away, the full moon illuminating his path.

Ed kicked the side of the barn. "You self-righteous hypocrite! Think you're better than me. I may have done time, but you're a damn circus freak. You'll regret this. I'll make sure of it."

Yancey and Clarence waited fifteen minutes after Ed stomped off toward town before heading for Lottie's. For once they didn't engage in light-hearted banter. Each was deep in thought.

Once they were settled in their booth, Yancey broke the silence. "You called it right. It's all about the stone. Soon as we eat, we need to get back to the museum and find it before that Ed does. I didn't get a chance to tell you, but Ed's been rude to just about everyone in town. Didn't tip Ruby. Rushed by Mary Carmichael and nearly pushed her down the steps. I stopped by the sheriff's office and asked if anyone had complained about him. Told him he was a bad egg."

"He's a mean-hearted, spiteful prick, if I ever saw one," Clarence said. "We need to stay clear of him."

"That's the idea."

They ate their specials and trudged back to the museum. The leaves, iced with frost, sparkled and twinkled like jewels. But their thoughts were focused on a much larger gem.

THE STORAGE AREA was every bit the jumble of circus memorabilia that Yancey had described—posters, whips, costumes, props, trunks. "I'll take this side," Yancey said. "You start on the other."

They turned on the lights, but also had flashlights for close-up illumination.

For the next hour, they worked in silence, absorbed in the search.

"I could do with a break right about now," Clarence said. "How about you?"

"I could do with a whiskey. The good stuff. Not Old Grand Dad. We're gonna celebrate." Yancey held a vivid green stone up to the light, then danced his version of a jig between the stacks of circus paraphernalia.

"Well, I'll be," Clarence said. "I'd jump up and down if my hip would let me." He waved both hands in the air. "Wowzah! We found it. And to believe it's been here all this time."

The pair walked out of the storage area and Yancey locked up. Their pace picked up as they trod past the museum buildings on their mission for a quality nightcap.

"Yancey, now that we've found it, what are we gonna do with it?"

Yancey stopped. "Good question. I hadn't gotten that far."

"Technically, it belongs to Jack," Clarence said.

"But think of what selling the stone could mean for our museum. We could make movies to show to museum visitors. Purchase new costumes and hire people to serve as clowns. Hire a magician. Maybe even start a school for joeys." He stopped to catch his breath.

"But what about Jack?"

A man stepped from the shadows, a gun in his hand. Ed.

"You old guys have what's called a moral dilemma. Well count your lucky stars 'cause I'm here to help you out. I don't have any morals, or so I've been told. The answer's perfectly clear to me." Ed took a step toward them. "Give me that stone."

Clarence and Yancey exchanged glances.

"Come on, now," Ed said. "I don't have all night."

Like a choreographed circus act under the Big Top, Clarence hobbled off in one direction and Yancey, the other. Ed ran after Clarence, slammed him into the side of a building, and poked him in the chest with his gun. "Come on, Old Timer. Hand it over."

"You picked the wrong one to follow, Shit for Brains," Clarence said. "I don't have it."

"Why you smart ass." Ed raised his gun to smash it into Clarence's skull. A high-pitched swishing sound cut through the silence and Jack's knife sliced into Ed's hand, knocking his gun to the ground. "Dammit," Ed yelled as he knelt down, grabbing his wrist.

Both Jack and Yancey ran toward Clarence and Ed. Jack stooped and grabbed his knife, then kicked Ed's gun away and slammed him to the ground.

"Clarence, you okay?" Yancey asked.

"I'm fine, but I'm gonna need a dry pair of pants. And I'd like to punch that asshole. Who does he think he is coming to our law-abidin' town and treating us this way?"

Jack used his scarf to secure Ed's hands, taking his granddaddy's ring off Ed's finger and placing it on his own. The sound of a siren signaled the approach of the sheriff's car. Jack turned to leave.

"Here," Yancey said, handing Jack the tsavorite. "This is yours. You take care, now."

"Thank you." Jack tipped his cap to the two and disappeared.

The sheriff eased out of his car. "What the holy hell? How'd you two find out Wiggins is wanted?"

"We didn't," Yancey said. "He tried to rob us. Pulled a gun on us. We showed him not to mess with a pair of circus clowns."

The sheriff shook his head. "Ed Wiggins, I have a federal warrant for your arrest. Read him his rights, Trowbridge." The sheriff turned to Yancey. "After you came into the office and asked me about Ed Wiggins, I did some digging. Turns out he's wanted for federal gun law violations. Plus, after what you told me, local charges of attempted robbery and assault."

"You need anything from us, sheriff?"

"I'll need statements from you eventually, but for now, I'll be spending some time with Mr. Wiggins."

Within minutes, everyone was gone. "You give Jack the stone?" Clarence asked Yancey.

"Yep. You were right. It was his birthright."

Clarence smiled. "I figured you would. So, we gonna have that whiskey now?"

"You bet. But we'd better stick to Old Grand Dad."

Six weeks later

Yancey picked up the museum's mail from the post office. An envelope was addressed to the museum in care of "Yancey Einhaus." He opened it and a note fell out.

"Promise me you and Clarence will use this money for your-selves. I have contributed fifty thousand dollars to the museum in your names. Thanks for everything. Jack."

Yancey shook the money order from the envelope. It was for twenty thousand dollars.

"Well, I'll be damned." He hightailed it to Lottie's where Clarence was waiting for him.

Yancey slid into his side of the booth and placed the check on the tabletop in front of Clarence. "I think we can afford that top shelf whiskey now!

THE INTERNATIONAL CIRCUS HALL OF FAME

The Golden Age of the American circus, late 19th Century to the mid-20th Century, was a glorious time. People would come from miles around when the circus came to town. The big cats, elephants, the Midway, and the aroma of cotton candy and roasted peanuts—there was nothing else like the circus. The International Circus Hall of Fame in Peru, Indiana, known as the "Circus Capital of the World," preserves the history of the circus's heyday.

In 1892, circus owner Ben Wallace purchased more than two-hundred acres of farmland from the Miami Indian Nation. From 1892 to 1941, several circuses, including the Ringling Bros., used the land as their winter headquarters. By 1929, Peru was home to the largest circus winter headquarters in America, boasting 42 buildings.

In 1944, the headquarters closed, and the land returned to farmland. Sarasota, Florida became the largest circus winter headquarter and opened a Circus Hall of Fame. When the Sarasota Circus Hall of Fame closed in 1980, the City of Peru purchased its entire collection and brought them to the former Wallace property.

Today, only five original buildings and the Ring, where the big cats were trained, remain. The International Circus Hall of Fame houses circus posters, costumes, props, exhibits, and elaborate colorful circus wagons. Highlights include a bandwagon from the Barnum and Bailey Circus, considered the best ever made; the only clamshell bandwagon in existence; and a miniature of the Hagenbeck-Wallace Circus.

The International Circus Hall of Fame became a National Historic Landmark in 1982.

DEATH—IN 9 INNINGS
BY MB DABNEY

"Dana! Come on, honey. We're gonna be late," Drake shouted from the kitchen near the door to the garage.

The seven-year-old girl entered the kitchen with her mother in tow. The child wore shorts, a pink T-shirt with large white letters that proudly announced "Girl Power", and a baseball cap for the Indianapolis Hoppers.

Drake looked at his watch and grimaced.

"Oh, calm down. You've got enough time," said his wife, Shelley. "Besides, she had to feed Bryce first."

"She had to feed him *now*?"

Dana tugged on her father's arm

"Daddy, you told me I have to do all my chores before I can go outside," the little girl said with truthful, child-like innocence.

Drake's wife chimed in. "And aren't you the one who says we need to be stricter regarding her getting her chores done?" Shelley's eyes twinkled as she displayed a "Gotcha" smile.

His shoulders slumped slightly as he accepted defeat. "Bryce is a well-fed hamster. He wouldn't've starved to death before we got back."

"Dana, go sit in the car. Daddy'll be there in a second," said Shelley, adding, "Have a good time at the game."

"Okay, Mommy," Dana said as she exited.

Shelley wrapped her arms around Drake's 6-foot-2 body and pulled him close.

"I'm so happy my big, strong police detective is taking his favorite girl to a baseball game," she said. "Father/daughter bonding time."

Now the twinkle was in his brown eyes. "It's *you*...who is my *Favorite Girl*." he said, and they warmly kissed.

Separating, Shelley said, "Have a good time." But then her smile ran away as she admonished him. "Don't let that girl eat too much junk food and spoil her dinner."

THE MIDDAY JUNE sun beat down as father and daughter, hand-in-hand, walked through the front gates at Victory Field and headed in the general direction of their box seats along the third baseline. It looked like a sellout day.

"Good afternoon, sports fans, and welcome to Victory Field to see your Indianapolis Hoppers," a rich baritone voice blared over the public address system, reaching every corner of the 12,000-seat stadium. *"I'm T.K. Cameron, your announcer for this afternoon's exciting contest between your division-leading Hoppers and their arch-rivals, the Columbus Clippers, who are only a half-game behind Indianapolis in the standings. This is a critical game for both teams."*

Father and daughter carefully negotiated their way to their seats. Drake's police partner, Barrie Morgan, was already there in seats next to them, along with her teenage nephew Mason, who repeatedly pounded the pocket of his baseball glove as if he expected a fly ball at any second.

"Hello, Dana," Barrie said politely to the girl. To Drake, who was on the aisle, Barrie said, "These are great seats."

Drake loved baseball. Always had. Played right field in Little League, but pitched in high school and briefly in college, where his dreams of a pro career were dashed by his lack of control and power. Despite his size, he couldn't throw the ball from the outfield to the pitcher's mound without it bouncing a couple of times.

"Shelley operated on the owner's grandson at Children's Hospital last year," Drake said. "The owner likes her and sometimes he hooks her up."

He had already bought some popcorn for Dana and a bag of peanuts for himself, so they were ready to settle in.

"The Hoppers are taking the field with Dre Camry on the mound. A lefty, he's been strong this year, especially against right-handed batters. Camry's four and one, and has a one-point-five-four ERA," the announcer said. *"Bruce Owensby steps to the plate for the Clippers. He's a good lead-off hitter with a strong bat."*

Drake eyed the beer vendor who was one section over. He raised his arm to get the vendor's attention.

"Slider, inside. Strike one."

"There were a lot of patrol cars out there today. Near the entrance. You notice that?" Drake said as he reached into his pocket for his wallet.

"A swing and a miss. Strike two."

"Yeah. Probably extra help with traffic control," Barrie said through bites of a hotdog.

"I wouldn't think so, not from where they were stationed," Drake commented as he pulled out a 20-dollar bill. "Dana, sweetie, be careful. You're gonna spill all your popcorn."

Then all at once, a thought struck Drake just as a loud *Crack* echoed through the stadium.

"It's a solid hit. Going back, back, way back...in center field," the announcer said. *"It's a homerun for the Clippers."*

When the action begins in baseball, there are two games occurring simultaneously—one with the athletes and one with the officials. Fans focus on what the athletes are doing, nearly oblivious to the umps until a call is made. But periodically Drake watches the umps as a play unfolds.

He hadn't done that, until now.

Drake worked some security inside the stadium two nights ago. It was an easy gig, just walking around. And he caught most of the game, which the Hoppers won. That night the officiating crew included a woman, who was being especially heckled by fans. But in today's game, there were only male umps, which left Drake disappointed because part of the reason for bringing Dana was so she could see a woman officiating.

"What happened to the female umpire? There was a woman in this crew," Drake said, more to himself than to anyone else.

The crowd groaned as the runner rounded the bases, his arms raised in triumph. Drake, his attention still on the field, didn't see the beer vendor approach.

"Whatja gonna have?" the vendor asked.

The detective's cellphone vibrated just as Drake was about to say, "A lite beer, please." Phone in hand, he eyed the number and showed it to Barrie. They both recognized the caller.

"Hey, Chief. What's up?"

DRAKE SHOWED his badge several times to police officers during the walk into the depths of the stadium, down a long corridor and into the area that housed the locker rooms for umpires. Since roughly 95 percent of all professional umps are men, most locker rooms were designed for them. However, most professional parks had separate locker rooms for female umps.

And that is where Drake was directed.

Though somewhat muted, the game still came through speakers on the walls or could be seen on mounted television screens in certain locations.

"Three up and three down for the Hoppers. So, at the end of one full inning of play, it's one to zero for Columbus."

Before he headed to the crime scene Drake explained to Chief Wood that it was his day off and he was at a baseball game with his daughter, which Wood already knew. She said it is partially why she called Drake. He was already near the scene of the crime.

"I understand but you are one of my best detectives and I need to get a handle on this quickly and quietly," Chief Wood said.

Drake contemplated the situation but reluctantly said, "I'll ask Barrie to look after Dana while I go check on things. She's much too young to leave in the stands alone."

"Thank you, detective," said Chief Wood. "I'll assign patrol Officer Taylor to assist you. He's already there and he's been wantin' a transfer to homicide. He'll be eager to help."

After getting off the phone, Drake assured Dana he'd return quickly.

"Okay, Daddy. I'll stay with Miss Morgan," she said before adding, "Can I have some cotton candy?"

Feeling a tinge of guilt, he handed his beer money to Barrie, and left.

"Wellington grounds to short, a quick pitch to second and a throw to first. Gets there in time for a double play. Well done! But at the end of the first half of the second inning, it's still Columbus on top, one to nothing."

Once Drake reached the locker room, he sought out the officer in charge—Jonathan Taylor. They knew each other well. Taylor was standing next to a photographer taking pictures of a woman lying on the floor near the showers. Though obviously dead, there were few clear signs of injury, except puffiness around the eyes.

"What we got, Jon?"

"White female, age 29. Name's Monica Newman. We confirmed all that from her purse found in that locker there," Taylor said, pointing to a roll of lockers along an adjacent wall. "She's one of the umpires for today's game. Everything seems in order in the locker, although we haven't found a cell phone."

Drake patted his sides as if to search for something, then gave a sigh when he couldn't find it.

"Do you have a spare notebook and pencil? I wasn't expecting to need one today," he said.

Taylor complied.

"The cell phone could be important. Follow up on that. Have officers look around, in the locker room, hallway, trash cans. Who found her and how long has she been here?" Drake asked.

"Hard to tell how long exactly. Coroner's just getting here. But our victim was supposed to have a meeting with the other officials before the game. When she didn't show up, they called for someone with the team to check on her," Taylor said. "The other umps are all men, and they couldn't come in here. This locker room is locked. They got a woman from the Hoppers staff."

"Where is she now?" Drake said, looking down at the body and taking some notes.

"I have someone interviewing her."

"I'll want to talk to her, too," Drake said. "Why wasn't the game cancelled or at least delayed after she was found?"

A man, 60-ish, wearing tan slacks, an unbuttoned blue Oxford-cloth shirt and a blue blazer with a team insignia on the breast pocket, came over. A smartly dressed younger woman, 30-ish, followed him, a step behind.

He had the look of a person in charge. She had the air of a person brought up in privilege but with little other substance. Drake walked away from the body to greet them.

"Mr. Hightower, I didn't see you when I came in," Drake said to the owner of the team.

Before Hightower spoke, the woman stepped forward to address Drake.

"We wanted to keep things quiet for the time being," said the woman.

Drake's attention shifted, as did his weight from his right foot to his left, and then back again. "And who might you be?"

Hightower spoke first. "This is my daughter, Cindy. Cindy Hightower. She's our vice president for marketing and communications."

Cindy Hightower displayed more than a subtle hint of self-importance.

"Nice to meet you," he said politely, "but this is a murder investigation. I'm not concerned about PR. My concern is getting to the bottom of this crime."

Hightower silenced Cindy with a glance and spoke to Drake. "Yes. We understand. Detective Curtis, isn't it? I remember your wife, Michelle. Wonderful person and a great surgeon. She saved my grandson. Cindy and Tommy's baby. We will help you in any way we can."

Drake mustered his most stern expression as he looked at Cindy. "I will have your complete cooperation. Is that clear?"

The pair nodded.

A grounder to second and a throw to first, and Jason Scott is out to end the second inning with Columbus still ahead one to nothing," blared from the sound system.

"Now then, when did our victim arrive at work? At the ballpark? Any idea?"

Another man, more casually dressed, with the appearance of someone who worked outside with his ruddy hands, walked over to join them. "Walter Clayton, superintendent of the grounds," he said. "I overheard your question."

Drake acknowledged him without saying a word.

"I was here with Norman Winters, our manager, when the umps met with us before the start of the game," Clayton said. "Normally, the umpires arrive at the ballpark 30 minutes to an hour beforehand. After they arrive and have their own meeting, they inspect the grounds. She wasn't with the other officials then."

"What time was that?" Drake asked.

"12:30," he said.

"She must have gotten here between noon and 12:30," Officer Taylor opined.

"Who found the body?"

"A girl from my crew," Clayton said. "I was informed and then I informed Mr. Hightower."

"Was anything touched before police arrived?" asked Drake.

"No, sir. I secured the room personally," Clayton answered.

Drake looked at Hightower. "Why wasn't the game postponed or canceled?"

Hightower shifted uncomfortably.

"Three up and three down to end the first half of the third inning and the Hops are coming to bat. Next up at the plate—catcher Ramone Perez, a solid hitter with a two-ninety-nine batting average and five homers this year. He's hoping to get something goin."

"After the body was found and we called the police, we also called the league," Hightower said. "We had a discussion with the league and with the police department on the line."

The public address system and the announcer suddenly got their attention.

Crack.

"That's a solid hit into deep right field. Derek Header is back at the warning track and he leaps for it but it's GONE. Perez gets his sixth homerun of the year to tie the game at one-one."

"You were saying..." Drake said, drawing their attention back to the subject at hand.

It was Cindy Hightower who spoke up.

"After talking to the police and the league, it was decided we could continue with the game as long as it didn't interfere with your work," she said. "We didn't make a public announcement that someone died, which might have complicated your job."

"It's a three-member officiating crew, with a fourth alternate in case one of the others gets sick or injured or for some reason can't complete the game," Hightower said. "It's not unusual that one of them, especially the home plate ump, gets hit hard by a ball. Happens more than you think."

The PA system seemed to cut through some of the locker room tension.

"Hackett pops a foul ball up behind home plate. Josh Benson is there to make the catch to end the inning. Going into the fourth, the game is all tied up at one-one."

Drake noticed the coroner looking in his direction. He gave Taylor a quick nod, and the officer excused himself.

Cindy Hightower seemed to fidget as if she had more important things to do.

"Are you finished? Can we go now?"

"No," Drake said with more indignation in his voice than he intended. "Just a few more questions. Did the victim have any enemies to your knowledge?"

Hightower let out a dry laugh.

"Are you kiddin' me?" Cindy Hightower said. "She's an ump. Listen to that crowd."

Drake was again conscious of the PA. The crowd was loud and agitated and booing some call against Indianapolis.

"Everyone hates her. Umps in general," Cindy Hightower said. "Go out into the park and you won't find a single fan of umpires."

It was true and Drake knew it.

Everyone hates baseball umpires. It's easy to see why. The hatred isn't dependent on how well they do their jobs. In fact, the vitriol is in direct proportion to them doing a good job.

On every pitch of balls and strikes, on every call, half the people in the stands will be happy and half will think the umps need glasses. It's been the nature of the game since the beginning and umps know that.

Taylor walked back over.

Drake addressed the Hightower's. "Okay, you guys can go now. Where will you be?"

"I'll be in my office. I've got work to do and I can watch the game on my monitor," Hightower said.

"I'll be in our suite," she said pointedly.

"That'll be fine," Drake said, but added, "No talking to the press and neither of you leaves the premises. I may have additional questions." The pair walked away. But to Officer Taylor, he said, "I don't trust them. Put a uniform on them to make sure they don't leave. Now, what have you got?"

"The coroner says she appears to have been strangled. By hand. An autopsy will confirm that. Didn't appear to be much of a struggle. Someone strong."

"Time of death?"

"In our timeframe. Around noon, more or less, he thinks," Taylor said.

"They find a phone yet?" Drake asked and Taylor shook his head. "Keep on it. And see if Miss Newman had any enemies or any threats directed at her."

Drake turned to leave.

"Where are you going, detective," Taylor asked politely.

"Heading out to check on my daughter for a while," he said over his shoulder. "But I'll be back. Call me right away if you have any developments."

DRAKE HEADED out of the locker room, through the lower corridors and finally up toward the seats. He walked along the ground level, watching fans and feeling the energy of Victory Field, named for the Allied victory in WWII. Fans rushed back and forth to the concession stands for hotdogs, Cracker Jacks, French fries and lots of beer.

Drake wished he had one.

Others headed to the restrooms. Drake felt a sense of community with everyone in the ballpark. Even when people couldn't see the field, the announcer kept them informed.

There were collective groans as Columbus scored three runs in the fifth and cheers when the Hoppers responded with a run in the bottom of the inning. Drake took it all in but this job and the murder case was never far from his conscious mind.

It was 4-2 in favor of the visiting team when Drake got to his seat, only to find his partner's nephew sitting alone, pounding a baseball into his glove.

"Hey, Mr. Curtis. See. I caught a foul ball," the teenager said excitedly.

"That's great, Mason. Congratulations. Where'd everybody go. Where's Dana?"

Barely taking his eyes or his attention off the field, Mason replied, "She had to go to the restroom. Aunt Barrie took her. They just left."

Drake settled down into his seat.

The ebb and flow of baseball can be as fast as a 95-mile per hour fastball or as slow as a player trotting back to the dugout after being thrown out at first. There's time to think between plays, which is what Drake did, fondly remembering the times he went to the ballpark as a kid with his dad.

"I'm back, Daddy," said Dana. Drake hadn't noticed her coming but he stood up to let her inside to her seat, noticing what appeared to be pieces of cotton candy on the front of her t-shirt.

"How's it going, sweetie," father asked daughter.

"Good," she said cheerfully. "I think we're winning."

Drake looked up at the scoreboard way out in center field. The top of the sixth inning just ended with one runner on base and Columbus still ahead 4-2. The Hoppers were coming up to bat.

When they were seated again, Drake leaned over to Barrie. "How's she doing?"

"Seems like she's having a good day," Barrie said. "How's the case? I heard some whispers in the restroom. Some people saying someone died. But no specifics. Only whispers."

Drake detailed the developments and said nothing had changed since he last talked to Taylor five minutes ago. "No cell phone yet."

Suddenly, their attention was back on the field as Perez hit a solid double but the third base coach was waving him on to third. He ran like the wind as the cut-off player threw the ball to third. Perez slid and…

"Got him. He's out," said announcer T.K. Cameron. *"Should have never tried for third. But being down by two, I guess they had to try."*

"Daddy, why is that man so mad," Dana asked her father as they looked one section over and a few rows above the dugout. A large man wearing a t-shirt that didn't fully cover his potbelly was spewing venom at the third base umpire.

"You filthy moron. Can't you see. He was safe, you stupid, ignorant, blind bastard. I hope you burn in hell where you belong, you idiot," the man gesticulated as he screamed at the top of his lungs.

At that moment, two uniformed officers were walking up the aisle to position themselves on the far end of the man's row, while an additional two officers walked down an aisle to position themselves at the other end of his row. One officer on either end of his row moved toward him, beckoning him to one end. An officer reached for his arm and the man pulled it away but, seeing he had no way to escape, finally complied.

Drake's cell phone rang. "Yeah, Detective Curtis here," he said, never taking his eyes off the officers and the screaming fan.

"We have identified a person of interest," Officer Taylor said.

"I think I see them now," said Drake.

"He's being escorted up to a conference room in the executive offices for questioning."

"I'll be right there," Drake said.

"Oh, also detective, we also just found the victim's mobile phone. It was in a trash can not far from the women's locker room. I've got someone trying to unlock it," said Taylor.

Drake found his way up to the executive suites and the conference room just as the crowd started singing "Take me out to the ball game" during the seventh inning stretch. Two uniformed officers stood just outside the door, which was across the hall from Hightower's office. Taylor was still briefing Drake, who was taking notes, when Hightower approached, but Drake waved him off.

Once done, Drake and Taylor entered the conference room, where another uniformed officer stood keeping watch. Taylor remained standing at the door. The room was the first place Drake had been all day where he couldn't really hear the game.

The sweaty fat man stood at the far end of the table, fuming.

"Who the hell are you? And why am I being held here," the man said, barely containing his anger.

"I am homicide Detective Drake Curtis of the IMPD, Mr. Kinsella, and I have a few questions to ask you. Please take a seat."

Kinsella looked defiant but then took a seat. "Homicide, huh? What's that got to do with me? I want a lawyer. I know my rights. I watch cop shows on TV."

Drake sat down at the other end of the table and flipped through his notebook, checking his notes. Taylor stayed at the door.

"Pascal Kinsella," said Drake, looking down at his notes, then back up. He spoke calmly. "Where do you live, Mr. Kinsella?"

The man huffed, then sat back in his chair, folded his arms, and rested them on the top of his massive belly. "In Irvington. Off of Washington and Ritter."

"What do you do for a living? Where do you work?"

Kinsella scratched the day-old whiskers on his cheek and responded with a certain irritated resignation. "I'm a welder at a machine shop out in Speedway. Henderson's."

"And you like baseball. The Hoppers."

"I have season tickets, sure, if that's what you mean."

"But you don't like umpires," Drake said.

"Nothing but a bunch of cheating bloodsuckers. They'll call a game for whoever lines their pockets. Bunch of cockroaches who should be crushed."

Drake let that statement settle in the room. "I see," he said, staring hard at Kinsella. "Do you know Monica Newman? A cockroach to be crushed?"

"Who?" Kinsella was playing innocent.

"Monica Newman. One of the umpires for today's game."

"Women don't have no business callin' a game, being out on the field," Kinsella said. "Everybody knows they caint see worth a damn and ain't got the smarts to understand the nuances of the game. They should stay home where they belong."

"We've seen reports that you've threatened her," Drake said. "More than once."

Kinsella finally began to understand the reality of the situation. "That was just a small misunderstanding. I didn't touch her or nothin'."

"She didn't think it was just a misunderstanding. Neither did the Cincinnati police. That's more than a hundred miles from here in another state. That's a long way to travel for a misunderstanding."

Drake leaned onto his elbows on the conference room table. "She filed papers against you. Said you kept harassing her, threatening her, standing outside her apartment building. A Hamilton County court in Ohio issued a restraining order against you. You can't get within one hundred feet of her."

The door opened behind Drake but he didn't stop to turn around to see who entered. However, he did hear that the Hoppers had scored another run and now trailed 4-3.

"Mr. Kinsella, where were you this afternoon around noon before the game? Did you confront a cockroach that needed to be crushed?"

Drake never stopped looking down the table at Kinsella when Officer Taylor approached him from behind and whispered something into his ear. "You stay put," Drake said to Kinsella as he got up and left the room with Taylor.

"They're down in another empty office with it," Taylor said, leading the way.

"Columbus stranded two runners on base as Indianapolis held the Clippers scoreless in the top of the ninth. The Hoppers are coming to bat in the bottom of the inning down one run. A win in this battle is within reach as Hoppers second baseman Antonio Caruso comes to the plate."

"Good job," said Drake, and they entered a small office where one of the police department's tech guys was seated at a table with the victim's cell phone.

"You're sure it's hers?" Drake asked.

"Absolutely," Taylor said. "Once we were in."

"How'd you gain access?"

"People are incredibly lazy with these things," the tech guy said. "After I tried one-two-three-four, I tried her birthday and Bingo! I was in."

"Officer Taylor here said you found some specific text messages. Show me."

Drake pulled up a chair next to the tech guy on the right, while Taylor took up position on his left. They could all see the screen as the tech guy flipped through pages on the phone.

"She's been exchanging a number of calls...for more than a year... with one particular number that we can trace back to this area. And then there are the text messages. Here they are. This is back during the winter. February."

> **THOMAS**
>
> GOOD TIME LAST NITE LUV GETTING U OUT OF THAT UMP UNIFORM

> **MONICA**
>
> UR SO BAD!! I LOVE IT!

> **THOMAS**
>
> GOTTA KEEP IT ON THE DL

> **MONICA**
>
> I KNO I COULD LOSE MY JOB

"Apparently, that was back during spring training for umpires down in Florida," the tech guy said.

"Spring training for umps?" Taylor said.

Drake gave him a sideway glance but it was the tech guy who answered him.

"Of course. They have training to weed out the poor umps just like with spring training for players," the tech guy said as he flipped through more messages. "Now this gets interesting. It's from early April when things are heating up."

MONICA

HOW'D U GET IN THE LOCKER RM?

THOMAS

TOLD YOU I HV ACCESS. I GOTTA KEY

MONICA

GLAD U DO

MONICA

I CAME SOOO GOOD WHEN U HAD ME UP
AGAINST THE LOCKER LOL

MONICA

WHEN U COMIN TO CINCY?

THOMAS

COUPLE OF WEEKS. I WANT YOU DESPERATELY.
HV TO HV YOU U R MINE

"This is from May first," the tech guy said. "I'm pretty sure she was at home at the time."

MONICA

OMG THAT GUY NEARLY SAW U LEAVING MY
PLACE LAST NITE

THOMAS

WHAT GUY? WHO?

MONICA

CREEP FROM INDY HES BEEN FOLLOWING ME
HARASSING ME

MONICA

SOME GUY NAMED KINSELLA

THOMAS

I'LL HANDLE IT

MONICA

HE SCARES ME

THOMAS

U R MINE. NOBODY'S GONNA GET NEAR U OR
HURT U ILL BREAK HIS NECK

MONICA

?

"Right after that, she got a restraining order against Kinsella, the guy you are holding in the conference room. But she apparently was also getting increasingly concerned about this Thomas fella. He was getting both aggressive and increasingly possessive," the tech guy said. "I saw a couple of texts this month... I can show you... she sent to Gary Newman. Her ex-husband. She said she was going to break it off with Thomas and get back with him," the tech guy said, and continued, "But first let me show you her last texts exchange with this Thomas fella. It's from two nights ago and then early today."

MONICA

ITS OVER TOM I CANT SEE YOU ANY MORE

THOMAS

NO PLEASE. I HV 2 C U U CANT GO BACK
TO HIM

> **MONICA**
>
> DONT COME N 2 LOCKER. ITS OVER. I'LL CALL
> SECURITY

"That was back then. I guess he didn't go see her. But this is early today," the tech guy said.

> **MONICA**
>
> DONT COME. I'LL SCREAM I MEAN IT.
>
> **THOMAS**
>
> I DARE U. U WONT HV A CHANCE. IF I CANT HV
> U NO ONE CAN.

"Do we know who this guy is, who has access to the locker rooms and presumably to other areas of the stadium?" Drake asked.

"No, but he's clearly with the Hoppers organization. We traced the cell phone number back to the organization. Just don't know yet who it's assigned to," the tech guy said. "But it's someone high up who'd have access to the women's locker rooms."

He stood up, asked the tech guy to write down the number to the cell phone Thomas was using, and then thanked him. To Taylor, he said, "Have officers take Kinsella downtown. The Cincinnati authorities will be interested if he violated a court order. We'll check with them."

As he reached the door, Drake turned back. "Is Hightower still in his office?"

"I think so," Taylor said. "Officers are outside."

Drake headed down the hallway and stopped at Hightower's door. It was partially open but he quietly knocked before entering.

"Mind if I come in?"

"Oh, of course. Come on in," Hightower answered, rising from behind his desk and indicating chairs and a table where they could sit and look out a window at the ballfield. They could also hear the broadcast booth from speakers. "How's the investigation going?"

"How's the game going?" asked Drake.

"Bottom of the ninth and we're still down four to three. Caruso struck out to open the inning and Hackett fouled out behind home plate again. But Perez, one of our best hitters, doubled and they held him at second, which was a good call this time. If he was thrown out at third, it would have ended the game right then. Now he's in scoring position and Perez is perhaps our fastest base runner."

Hightower smiled and relaxed. "It's a close game. That's nerve-wracking for me but fans love it. Win or lose, it's good entertainment... and that's what we want, good entertainment... though it's better to win," he said and pointed out to the field. "The Clippers' manager is going out to talk to their pitcher. If he's smart... and I know he is because I tried to hire him to manage my team... he'll put in a reliever for the last out."

One more pause from Hightower. "You never answered my question. How's the investigation going?"

Drake studied Hightower hard. The next few moments would be telling.

"I think the killer is someone in the Hopper organization. Someone high up. They were having an affair with Monica Newman, probably since last year and certainly by early this year," he said. "They sometimes had sex here at the stadium, in the women's umpire locker room. The killer had access. They had a key."

Drake leaned forward, placed his elbows on the table and clasped his hands, leaving his fingers to form a steeple. His steely brown eyes bore into Hightower. "Who has access to the umpires' locker rooms, especially the women's locker room?"

"I keep that close. The groundskeeper, of course. You met him, Walter Clayton. Then, only me, my daughter... and... "

"And? Who?"

Hightower eased back in his seat and his eyes stared at a point in the middle of the table as if an unimaginable thought had just reached his brain. He didn't look up at Drake when he answered.

"Tommy." The name fell so heavily on the table it could have broken it. Hightower looked up with an anguish on his face that spoke of the hardship that would soon weigh like an anchor on his personal and professional life. "Thomas, my son-in-law. My grand-baby's father."

"Is this his cellphone number?" Drake showed him a piece of paper with the phone number written on it.

Unable to verbalize the answer, Hightower merely nodded.

Pushing his chair back from the table, Drake demanded, "Where is he now? Right now."

DRAKE WALKED down the hallway with two uniformed officers bringing up the rear. The cadence of their steps accompanied the broadcast of the last of the game as it filtered through speakers in the ceiling. Everyone in the hallway gave them space.

"*Big Richard Caldwell, 19-years of age out of Florida State. On the mound in relief, taking a couple of practice throws to loosen up his right arm. First round draft pick with a lethal fastball. I wouldn't be surprised if he's called up to the majors any day now,*" the announcer said.

Drake opened the door to the broadcast booth unannounced.

"*It doesn't get more dramatic than this. Bottom of the ninth, two-two count with two outs. The tying run in scoring position on second and the winning run at the plate. Doesn't get better than this,*" the announcer said.

"Thomas Cameron," Drake said quietly, looking down at his man.

Cameron turned around to see who had entered, irritation showing on his face for the interruption. But seeing Drake, another expression—resignation—replaced it. He locked eyes with Drake's before he turned back to the mike.

"*Like I said, a lethal fastball.*"

Drake looked out of the booth and onto the field. He could see the entire stadium. And in that moment, he remembered his childhood dreams of playing baseball. He didn't, however, feel sadness or remorse over a life he hadn't lived. Because he was living a better life, a life with more joy, satisfaction, and fulfillment than he could have imagined in his youth.

He was about to bring justice.

Drake focused on the mound as Caldwell studied the batter, glanced over at first base, and then settled into his pitch—a fastball.

Crack.

STANDING at the kitchen counter chopping vegetables for dinner, Shelley looked up as Dana and Drake entered from the garage. Dana, who was holding her stomach, let out a small moan and her mother rushed over to her.

"You okay, baby? What's wrong?" she asked, searching the little girl's face.

"My tummy hurts, Mommy."

Shelley looked at Drake. The motherly expression of concern she had for Dana was replaced with a look of agitation for her husband. "What did you do, Drake? Let her eat too much junk food?"

Mother took daughter's hand and led her out of the kitchen. "Come on, baby. Mommy'll take care of it." Glancing back at Drake, she didn't look happy.

Drake picked up a piece of a chopped carrot and popped it into his mouth. He hoped his upcoming execution at the hands of the woman he loved would be less painful than being hit by a line-drive.

But he doubted it would be.

VICTORY FIELD

Victory Field is a nationally recognized minor league baseball park on the west end of downtown Indianapolis at the intersection of West and Maryland streets. The natural grass field opened on July 11, 1996, and is the home of the Indianapolis Indians of the Triple-A International League.

The baseball field, which was named to reflect the U.S. military victory in World War II, was a replacement for Bush Stadium on West 16th Street, which itself had also been called Victory Field until the 1940s to 1967. The current park was a key element in the revitalization of downtown Indy at the end of the 20th Century.

The park has 12,230 permanent seats and room for 2,000 additional fans on the outfield lawn. Seated directly behind home plate, fans enjoy a magnificent view of the Indianapolis skyline to the northeast of the stadium.

HIGH MARKS
BY MARY BISCHOFF

The first day of July 1927 looked to be the hottest day of the year so far and it was a scorcher, with the temperature already approaching the 90s at 9 o'clock in the morning. Annie Mae Smith leaned against the railing on the top deck of the steamer *America* and dully watched the forested shore drift past in the blazing sunshine.

The steam-powered side-wheeled paddleboat was making its slow way up the Ohio River from Louisville, Kentucky, carrying hundreds of holiday passengers to the amusement park at Rose Island, Indiana. Her husband, the wealthy Mr. Edwin Smith of Smith Cooperage Industries, had celebrated a very profitable year of barrel-making by treating his workers and their families to a holiday outing for the Fourth of July at the amusement park, promising a grand picnic, baseball games, dancing, swimming and fireworks before returning to work.

Weary to her bones, Annie closed her eyes and turned her face into the humid breeze. Despite the noisy merriment of the other passengers, the sounds of the steam engine, and the band playing "Hello! Swanee, Hello!" inside on the dance floor, she felt oddly detached, the sounds muffled and distant. Gripping the rail a little tighter, she wondered if anyone would even notice if she slipped over the banister and fell down, down into the cool welcoming depths of the river.

How long would it take to drown? Would it hurt much? At least death by drowning would be over relatively quickly. Her mouth quirked bitterly. Even if it weren't for her darling two-year-old Ruthie waiting for her at home, she doubted that she would be brave enough to swing herself over the railing and just let go. Suicide was a sin, ensuring eternal torment, and she already was going through hell on earth as it was. When she had left her parents and their small Indiana farm to marry Edwin three years ago, she had no idea the man of her dreams would soon reveal himself to be the very devil.

The first time he hit her was when he accused her of making eyes at some strange man on their honeymoon in New Orleans. Later, he had apologized over and over, claiming it was her fault she was so pretty, every man wanted her. After that, he beat her for any number of reasons, from not having supper ready on time to her inability to please him in bed. Bewildered, she had tried her best but nothing she did seemed to be good enough.

"Mrs. Smith?" A hesitant voice intruded, and she opened her eyes, forcing her social smile into place. "Are you under the weather?" Ruby Davis, the stout wife of her husband's right-hand man, frowned at her with concern. Looking hot and uncomfortable in her old-fashioned tunic and ankle-length skirt, Mrs. Davis extended a hand to her. "Come sit down a bit. I fear the heat is too much for you."

Annie murmured her thanks and allowed the older woman to guide her to a seat deep in the shade of the roof. She glanced down as she sank into the chair, adjusting her skirt decorously over her knees, and was reassured. The thin lace jacket she wore over her peach silk dress, despite the sweltering heat, did cover the ugly dark bruises on her upper arms completely.

"There you are, Annie." Edwin came bounding across the deck towards them. "I was looking for you downstairs and couldn't find you. Thank you, Mrs. Davis, for looking after my silly little wife. You're all right, aren't you, darling?" His smooth good looks and flamboyant personality had always drawn attention wherever they went and now was no different.

Annie felt the curious gazes of the surrounding travelers and straightened in her chair. "I'm fine, really. It's just the heat, that's all."

Dr. Wilkins, an old family friend, made his way through the crowd. "Let me have a look at you, Annie." He felt her brow and took her pulse. "Yes, the heat can be overwhelming to ladies with delicate constitutions. I prescribe plenty of liquids and to stay out of the sun. You'll be right as rain in no time." He squeezed her hand in an affectionate manner and took the seat opposite hers.

Edwin looked around and called out sharply. "You there, boy!" A gray-bearded Negro in a steward's uniform hastened his way through the chairs to his side. "Get the missus some iced tea and be snappy now."

"Yes, sir, right away, sir," said the steward and went to get the refreshment, darting a sympathetic look at Annie.

Annie couldn't help shrinking back as Edwin bent down towards her. In what appeared to the onlookers as a loving embrace, he squeezed her upper arms tight as he kissed her cheek and enjoyed the flinch she couldn't suppress.

"Don't you dare embarrass me, you little bitch," he hissed into her ear. Straightening, he adjusted his stylish bamboo hat and said, "You can have a rest when we get to the island. I got us a summer cottage for the week. You deserve some time away from all your duties at home."

"But Ruthie..." Annie said, dismayed at this unexpected announcement. She had thought they would be returning to Louisville after the Fourth of July celebration Monday night.

"She's fine with my mother. I had the maid pack you some extra clothes." He smiled a shark's smile and leaned closer. "I want to enjoy your company without the girl hanging on your apron strings.

It will give us some time to be together, to try and grow our little family."

Annie knew that Edwin had been disappointed when their first child proved to be a girl instead of the son he was hoping for. He had made his displeasure quite clear after she and the baby had come home from the hospital to the three-story Queen Anne house on Chestnut Street. Annie adored the little blonde girl but her husband dismissed the child as unimportant due to her sex.

As soon as the doctor had said it was safe to resume marital activities, Edwin had been relentless about trying to produce an heir. When she had lost a second baby in a bloody rush a year later, he had made his displeasure clear with beatings and verbal abuse. He often came home drunk and some nights he never came home at all. Even though Prohibition banned the production and consumption of alcohol nationwide, he had found a way to procure the Kentucky bourbon he was so fond of. Indeed, one of the reasons his barrel-making business was so profitable was the high demand for containers in which to ship the illegal liquor.

Edwin turned to his business partner standing behind Ruby. "Come on, Bob. I want to play some euchre with that fellow that used to run the Tight Barrel Stave Manufacturers. You, too, Doctor, you can be our fourth. Annie will be fine." Without a second glance, he led the way down the stairs. Dr. Wilkins followed, with a reluctant glance back at Annie. She managed a slight nod of reassurance.

The steward hurried up to Annie with a tall glass of iced sweet tea. Thankful for the cold drink, she sipped the liquid and fanned herself gently with a wooden-handled paper fan. Closing her eyes, she prayed for guidance. She certainly wasn't happy with Edwin, but what could she do but stay with him? He would never countenance a divorce; men of his social standing would not allow such a thing. Her parents were poor. Even if they let her stay, they barely got by and she wouldn't be able to roam the hills barefoot hunting greens and rabbits to help provide food like she had when she was a girl. Not now that she had Ruthie to look after.

The Good Book said her duty as a wife, as Edwin so often reminded her, was to submit to him, and her parents believed that as well, being good Methodists. She was his until death did them part. Her eyes again went to the cool, beckoning water streaming past the side of the boat and she sighed. That was not the answer, tempting though it was.

Heaving a sigh, she opened her book, *Annie Oakley, Woman At Arms.* Her parents had named Annie after the famous sharpshooter from neighboring Ohio, who had amazed the world with her skills in Buffalo Bill's Wild West show.

Unable to concentrate, she put her book aside and picked up the pamphlet detailing the various entertainment that Rose Island, "The Beauty Spot of the Ohio Valley," offered. The 118-acre park, located on the Indiana side of the river, boasted a small zoo, pony rides, merry-go-round, Ferris wheel, roller coaster, shooting gallery, cafeteria, swimming pool, and more. There would be plenty to keep Edwin busy while they were there.

An hour and a half later, a series of loud blasts from the steam whistle announced their arrival at Rose Island. Once the boat tied up to the dock, an excited rush of travelers streamed off up the hill and between the three imposing pillars that supported the arched Rose Island sign that welcomed guests arriving by steamboat. Annie gathered her courage and her belongings and went ashore.

***

THE DAY PASSED by in a weary blur. She had pled the heat as an excuse to sit out the lawn games at the picnic, instead retreating with the older women to the shade of the trees, picking at a plate of deviled eggs, old-fashioned Kentucky barbecue and pineapple upside down cake.

Edwin was in his element, circulating through his workers, slapping backs, shaking hands and making sure everyone was having an enjoyable time. His athletic figure drew plenty of admiring glances in his well-cut tropical worsted suit.

One willowy blonde lady, daringly garbed in tailored white knickers and long strands of pearls, seemed to require quite a bit of his assistance on the croquet lawn. Annie couldn't help but notice how well-matched they looked as Edwin bent over the woman from behind, his strong arms around her, his hands on her hands on the mallet to help her aim and swing.

"That's Miss Porter," Mrs. Davis said from beside Annie, surveying the couple with disapproval.

"Oh?" Annie murmured faintly. "She seems very—athletic."

Her husband whispered something into the woman's ear, and Annie saw her white teeth flash, vivid between red-painted lips, as they both looked her way and laughed.

"My dear, don't you know? She's his secretary," Mrs. Davis said. "Mr. Davis says they are thick as thieves at the office." Seeing the wounded expression flicker over Annie's face, she hastily added. "She types and takes shorthand, you know. I'm sure it's a very professional relationship." Eager to tell the other wives that Mrs. Smith had been completely clueless about what her husband got up to at work, she gathered her belongings and retreated to the punch table.

Annie dropped her eyes to her plate and sighed. She felt such a ninny. Now she knew who Edwin was spending his time with. No wonder he worked such long hours and stayed away from home.

In the afternoon, she sat in the stands with the other wives and observed the baseball game pitting the Smith Cooperage workers against the Louisville Varnish Company employees. Edwin's gay mood was somewhat eclipsed when their team lost the game. Sweaty and disheveled, they went back to the cottage and changed for dinner. Annie wore a shirred-waisted frock of floral-patterned purple silk crepe and accompanied the sulky Edwin to dinner in the dining hall. Suitable for dancing, the dress was light and cool, and the silky material swished pleasantly against her stockinged legs as she moved.

After dinner, Edwin led her over to the dance hall. Miss Porter was there as well, radiant in a sleeveless emerald beaded flapper dress. Annie felt quite the mouse in comparison as Edwin guided her around the floor in a foxtrot as the band played "The Doll Dance," his neck craning to keep an eye on his secretary. At least he had given Annie the courtesy of the first dance. Soon, though, he abandoned her to a chair with the wall-flowers, to dance with several of the other wives, as well as Miss Porter.

After a sedate waltz with Dr. Wilkins, a man old enough to be her father, who had taken pity on her in her solitude, Edwin reclaimed her elbow with a grim smile, made their excuses and steered her out of the crowded pavilion, hurrying her through the alternating patches of thick darkness and the bright halos of light cast by the electric lampposts. Clouds stretched across the sky, and the promise of rain hung sweet in the air.

"You want him, don't you?" He growled in her ear as he propelled her ruthlessly along the deserted path towards the cottages. "Do you do for him what you won't do for me?"

"No, no, please!" She pleaded, bewildered. Surely Edwin couldn't be serious to think she had designs on the elderly Dr. Wilkins? The smell of liquor hung heavy about her husband, and she suspected that his iced tea at dinner had contained somewhat more alcohol than tea.

"I didn't realize I married a brazen hussy. You should be ashamed! Why must you make me punish you so?" Edwin forced her off the gravel path and up against a tree. The rough bark bit into the tender skin of her back and shoulders.

He held her firmly in place with one big hand and ran the other one up under her dress, cruelly pinching and fondling her. She felt so exposed. They were only half in darkness, and she prayed no one would come along the path and see them, sure she would die of shame if they did.

After her initial instinctive struggle, she lay passive against him, blind eyes staring over his shoulder into the darkness, and let him do what he wanted. She knew he liked it when she resisted him. Her lack of response infuriated Edwin. With a muffled curse, he shoved himself away from her and raked his hand through his pomaded hair.

"Worthless bitch! You don't even know how to excite a man, much less satisfy him," he said in a savage tone. "Go back to the cottage and wait for me. When I get back, you better be ready to spread your legs and do your wifely duty!"

Silent and despairing, Annie twisted away from him and fled back to the cottage, feeling that her shame must surely be visible for all to see. Fortunately, she only passed one strolling couple, and they were more interested in each other than her.

Flinging her dress and undergarments into the corner, vowing to burn them when she had the chance, she ran a cool shower and scrubbed herself from head to toe with castile soap until she felt more normal.

Donning the satin nightgown Edwin had bought her for their honeymoon and desperate to distract herself from what promised to be an ordeal once he returned, Annie looked around the cottage, trying to see it with the eyes of a vacationer. The one-bedroom cottage was spacious and included everything one might need to be comfortable, no matter how long the stay. There was a kitchen, complete with icebox and stove. The bathroom had all the latest modern amenities of a shower, lavatory and toilet; the sitting room included a table for four, daybed and lounging chair. The screened front porch had an Old Hickory settee, rocker and straight back chair. All the rooms had electric lamps for lighting. Such modern luxury! She had friends back home that still used coal-oil lamps and even candles in their homes.

Another new-fashioned amenity was the oscillating electric fan, which was priceless in these broiling days of summer. In an attempt to distract herself, she sat in the rocking chair in front of the whirring machine and paged through the day's copy of the Louisville Courier-Journal: Commander Richard Byrd, flying the first transatlantic airmail from New York to France, had run out of gas and ditched his plane in the English Channel; President Coolidge was fishing in South Dakota; and the Indianapolis Indians were to play the Louisville Colonels on Sunday. A new William Fairbanks film, *The Down Grade*, would be released at the end of the month.

At midnight, Annie switched off the lights as the cottage rules required. In the dark, she paced nervously up and down the screened porch, the flicker of lightning in the distance and thunder rumbling overhead. God, she hoped it would rain soon and wash the stifling heat out of the air.

The minutes ticked past on the mantel clock. Where was Edwin? He wouldn't be so blatant as to spend the night with that woman Miss Porter, could he?

Along about two in the morning, the storm finally broke. Lightning cracked overhead, thunder boomed and the rain began to pound down, bringing a refreshing coolness to the air. Annie pressed close to the screen and let the sound and fury of the storm wash over her.

Suddenly, the porch door crashed open. Startled, she turned to see her husband stagger in, drenched and disheveled, bright red lipstick stains on his neck and open collar.

"Bed!" Edwin roared. "I told you to be in bed!" Springing forward, he grabbed her by her short brown bob, wrenching her neck sorely, and dragged her flailing body into the bedroom. The dank smell of sweat and the faint scent of Shalimar clung to him, a perfume she didn't own. Had he come to her directly from Miss Porter? Flinging her down on the double iron bed, he stripped off his clothes, dragged her nightgown up to cover her head, and plunged into her without any preparation. What followed was both painful and humiliating.

After an eternity, he grunted his satisfaction and rolled off her, freeing her arms. She clawed the spit-sodden fabric of her gown out of her mouth and drew in deep, shuddering breaths. She had almost suffocated, the material pinned tight to her face under the substantial weight of his body laboring atop hers. His hand slapped heavily down on her belly, and she jolted, unable to stifle a cry.

"Worthless female," he mumbled, already half asleep. "If you don't give me a son, by God, I'll choke the life out of you and that little chit too."

Frozen, she lay there for a time, listening to his heavy snores. Once she was sure he was truly asleep, she painfully eased off the bed and tiptoed into the bathroom. She didn't dare run the shower less it wake Edwin up, but she washed herself as thoroughly as possible.

Leaning her aching head against the cool tiles, a phrase from her high school Latin class swam through her head. *In vino veritas*, or "In wine there is truth." The beast who had raped her tonight was Edwin's true self, not the charming facade he showed in public. There was no reason to doubt that if she didn't deliver him a son and soon, he might well kill her and marry again. If he did that, there would be no one to protect her darling Ruthie. She thought of her namesake, Annie Oakley, and how brave and bold she was. Closing her eyes, she prayed to God to show her a way forward. There was no way she was going to let that monster hurt her precious little girl.

Annie slept late and woke to the sounds of Edwin using the shower. She gulped down some Bayer aspirin with some lukewarm water, then dressed herself slowly. It would likely be another infernally hot day. The plentiful overnight rain had cooled the air only briefly and had turned the ground to a thick, soggy quagmire.

Edwin came up behind her as she was smoothing her loose cotton dress down over her hips. She froze as he bent forward to kiss her cheek. "Sorry 'bout last night, Annie," he said in a gruff tone.

"Didn't mean to hurt you. Too much to drink, eh? You forgive me, don't you, girl?"

She managed to smile at him, catching a momentary glimpse of the charming man who had wooed her so thoroughly in the days before their marriage.

The smile fell away as he continued. "When was your last monthlies?"

"The second week of June." Annie blushed to discuss so intimate a topic with a man, even if he was her husband.

"We'll try again tonight. In a few weeks, we'll know if my seed takes root in your womb or not. I need a fine strapping son to take over the cooperage business. An heir and a spare, even!" he said jocularly, shrugging into his clothes. "After we eat, I'm in the mood to hike up the Devil's Backbone. There's a good view of the river from there, I hear. I want to stretch my legs and see all the sights. How does that sound?" He didn't wait for her to speak. "When we come back, we'll get into our swim togs and try out that fancy new pool. Filtered water to swim in, can you believe that? Then we'll try our hand at the shooting range."

She wondered if he even realized that by wearing her swimsuit, she would be displaying all the bruises that he had given her. Well, not all of them.

Obediently, she followed him to the dining hall where she tried to do justice to the delicious lunch. Rose Island raised its own food so they had the freshest eggs, butter and vegetables. Fish fresh from the river were fried to perfection, and Annie managed to choke down half her plate.

After their meal, they hiked up the hill, where she dutifully admired the view, then they walked around through the famous rose gardens and observed the wild animals in the zoo. Annie felt rather sorry for the captive wolves, monkeys and the bear named Teddy Roosevelt. They all looked as miserable as she felt.

In the heat of the afternoon, she and Edwin donned their wool swimsuits and walked down to the pool. It was the largest artificial pool Annie had ever seen, one hundred feet by forty-two feet, with perfect, straight sides. The water danced and sparkled as the throng of happy bathers splashed and paddled about. Edwin sprinted past her and leapt into the deep end of the pool.

It took all of Annie's courage to doff her robe to enter the water. A group of women sitting on the benches openly stared at her bruises and whispered to each other. She quickly descended the steps at the shallow end and waded out to where all of her but her neck and head were underwater. One of the women commented in a loud voice that she must like it rough and the rest laughed. Annie sank further down, hiding her burning checks in the cool water.

Edwin greeted some of his friends with a shout and they soon began a boisterous game of tag in the deeper end of the pool. Wolf whistles rang out to greet the entrance of Miss Porter, who dropped her robe poolside to reveal a daring backless swimsuit in red and white stripes clinging tightly to her curves.

Securing her blond hair under a matching bandanna, she laughed and waved to the men, who called to her to join their game. "Look out, boys, here I come!" She ran to that end of the pool and expertly dived in, to their cheers and applause.

Feeling invisible, Annie watched their antics as they played in the water. Edwin would toss Miss Porter through the air into the arms of another man, who would pass her on, with shrieks of laughter, always being returned to Edwin. She watched as Miss Porter leaned into Edwin and he bent his head toward her. Was he going to kiss her? In front of everyone, including his own wife? Miss Porter laughed and splashed water in his face, then self-consciously moved away.

Annie was conscious of a fierce emotion growing deep inside, one she hadn't felt in a long, long time. It wasn't just humiliation or shame, although she did feel both of those emotions. Anger. No, not just anger. Rage. What right did her husband have to treat her this way? She had done her best to be a good wife to him, she kept a tidy house, cooked his favorite meals, mended his clothes. A terrible resolve came over her, and she wondered at her own cold determination. Something had to be done, and she had an idea of what to do. She just needed to figure out when and how to do it.

After dinner, Edwin insisted on going to the shooting gallery, despite the rain that had rolled in around sunset, keeping most folks indoors. Passing the brightly lit dance hall, crowded with noisy merrymakers, Annie trailed after him, feeling like a ghost. At least the rain made it cooler.

Dr. Wilkins came up from behind her and took her arm. "We'll be your cheering section, Edwin," he said. "A little rain never hurt anyone. Except wicked witches!" He guffawed heartily at his own joke. "That Baum fellow! What an imagination!"

Edwin splashed up to the counter, slapped down some pennies to the Colored attendant and picked up the .22 Winchester rifle. Whooping with glee every time he made a shot, he knocked down multiple moving cast-iron ducks, rabbits and bells. Sipping from his flask between shots, he soon began to miss more than he hit.

"I really think that's enough, Edwin," Annie said, wet and miserable in the mud.

"And I don't think it is!" he shouted at her. "Come on, Doctor! Take a shot!"

Dr. Wilkins frowned with disapproval. "No, Edwin. Let's go inside and get your poor wife out of the rain."

"Ah, yes, my darling wife. We wouldn't want you to catch your death, would we?" Edwin said nastily. "Tell you what, Annie, you shoot that little duck." He gestured at a small target near the top of the gallery. "Shoot that little duck and we'll go in. We'll see how like your namesake you are."

"Please don't, Edwin. I can't."

Edwin snickered. "You will if you want to get out of the rain."

Dr. Wilkins exclaimed, "Now, see here, Edwin!"

"Come on, Annie, be a sport! Just shoot the damn thing!" Edwin pumped the rifle to chamber another round and shoved it into her hands. As he did, she slipped on the muddy ground and grabbed at him to keep her balance. The gun cracked loudly in her ears, and she cried out in shock as something warm and coppery smelling splashed onto her face and hands.

Dimly aware of other voices around her raised in alarm and horror, she raised her eyes to Edwin's blue ones. Their gaze locked briefly, his eyes wide in disbelief, clutching his ruined throat, scarlet blood pumping through his fingers as he vainly tried to stop the bleeding. Horrified, holding her blood-soaked hands out in front of her as he fell backwards, Annie screamed and kept screaming until the whole world went dark.

***

ANNIE WOKE UP, propped against the pillows in the bed in her cottage. Her head pounded something fierce and her throat felt as if she had swallowed live coals. The electric light was on, and it was dark outside the windows. What had happened? Had it all been a terrible dream? Bewildered, she raised her hands. No sign of the blood that had covered them, and she was dressed in a pristine cotton nightgown.

As she stirred, Dr. Wilkins rose from the chair at the side of the bed. "How are you feeling, my dear?" he said kindly.

"I don't...How did I..." Her voice trailed off as she remembered.

"Mrs. Davis bathed you and put you to bed. She's getting you some broth. Do you remember what happened?"

"Edwin?" Annie whispered faintly.

The doctor shook his head. "I'm so sorry. What a senseless accident!" His lips firmed disapprovingly. "So careless of him, handling the gun like that. It's lucky no one else was hurt. I explained it all to the police."

"The police?" Annie's voice quavered.

"Yes, they came over from Louisville in their speedboat. I expect you'll have to speak to them later, but I've assured them that Edwin caused this dreadful mishap himself with his foolish deviltry. A grown man should have known better than to drink and cut up with a loaded rifle. Ah, here we are." He turned to the door as Mrs. Davis entered, carrying a covered tray.

Dr. Wilkins rose. "Now, you eat up, my dear. You must keep your strength up." He sat a small glass vial on the table. "I'm leaving you some laudanum in case you have trouble sleeping tonight. Mrs. Davis has offered to help you get packed up. In the morning, we will catch the first steamer and get you home to your daughter. I know this is a terrible tragedy, but you must be strong for her."

Annie thanked him, dutifully sipped the chicken soup with small painful swallows and watched as Mrs. Davis, the old busybody, emptied the drawers and packed the hand trunks, leaving only a change of clothes for the next day.

Afterwards, alone in the dark, she climbed out of bed and knelt to say her prayers, thanking God for her many blessings. Clearly, God had made Edwin offer her the gun, and God had surely put the plan, fully formed, into her mind at that very instant. Her earlier vague decision to do away with him burned away, and she knew precisely what to do.

She remembered the surprise in Edwin's eyes as she deliberately staggered in the mud, swung the rifle up, pressed it against his throat and pulled the trigger, almost simultaneously. All those years in her youth shooting small game had paid off. Like her namesake Annie Oakley, she had hit exactly what she was aiming at.

"Aim at a high mark and you'll hit it. No, not the first time, nor the second time. Maybe not the third. But keep on aiming and keep on shooting for only practice will make you perfect. Finally you'll hit the bull's-eye of success." - Annie Oakley

ROSE ISLAND

Located on the Indiana side of the Ohio River just upstream from Louisville, the Rose Island amusement park had its heyday in the 1920s and 1930s. The "island" is really a peninsula, enjoying scenic views from the top over the rugged hills and valleys of Southern Indiana and the Ohio River.

The 118-acre park featured a zoo, Ferris wheel, swimming pool, roller coaster, baseball diamond, tennis courts, golf course, and dining and dance halls. Visitors could come for the day or stay in the hotel or cottages. At its peak, the park enjoyed 135,000 visitors a year. Steamboats made frequent trips to the park from Madison, Indiana and Louisville. They included the steamer *Idlewild*, which is still operating today as the *Belle of Louisville*.

Rose Island was a popular attraction for years until the 1937 flood, which caused such sweeping damage that the site was abandoned. Now part of Charlestown State Park, very little remains of the amusement park itself.

The park offers a two-hour guided tour, though hikers are urged to be aware—the hill is pretty steep.

AUTHOR BIOGRAPHIES

John F. Allen is a speculative fiction and mystery author who was born and resides in Indianapolis. He is a founding and active member of the Speculative Fiction Guild, a faculty member of the Indiana Writers Center, and serves on the board of the Speed City chapter of Sisters in Crime.

John studied liberal arts at IUPUI with a focus in Creative Writing, and is an Air Force veteran, and a member of the American Legion.

John's debut novel, *The God Killers,* was published in 2013, and he followed it with a spin-off novella series titled, *Codename: Knight Ranger.*

He also penned a short story collection titled, *The Best is Yet to Come - Vol I,* the novelization of respected screenwriter, Demetrius Witherspoon's short film, *Submerge: Echo 51,* and has a featured story in the anthology titled, *SpyFunk,* published by MVMedia.

Roberta Barmore has been writing fiction since 1971 and has collected rejection slips off and on since 1980. She has been published a few times. Along the way, she has worked as a cemetery landscaper, paint store clerk, disc jockey, factory test equipment technician and television transmitter engineer.

She shares her 1924 home in the SoBro neighborhood of Indianapolis with one lodger, two large tomcats, a dozen antique typewriters and over seven thousand books. In her spare time not spent writing, she builds bookshelves (obviously), cooks, collects antique hand tools and operates an amateur radio station mostly consisting of 1930s equipment.

A native Hoosier, **Mary Bischoff** spent her childhood romping through cemeteries and reading 1930s comics in courthouse basements while her parents did genealogical research. Among her past jobs, she has been a licensed claims representative, a reservations agent for a major airline, owned her own medical legal transcription/proofreading business, and worked in an Indianapolis hospital during the COVID pandemic.

Now happily retired, she loves spending more time with her family, reading, writing, traveling, knitting and playing Pokemon Go, not necessarily in that order. Her first published short story, *A Not-So-Quiet Resting Place,* appears in the Sisters In Crime Speed City 2023 anthology *Amber Waves of Graves.* Her poems have been included in Gal's Guide Anthologies *Nourish* and *Female Friendship.* Her short story "Into the Fire" leads off *Beyond the Stars,* the Starbase Indy 2025 science fiction and fantasy anthology.

Diana Catt (www.dianacatt.com) has 20-plus short stories appearing in anthologies published by Blue River Press, Red Coyote Press, Pill Hill Press, Wolfmont Press, The Four Horseman Press, Speed City Press, and Level Best Books. She has co-edited four anthologies. Her collection, *Below the Line,* is available on Amazon. Her debut thriller novel, *Death Map* (Per Bastet Publications, LLC, 2022), is also available on Amazon. The sequel, *Route of Entry,* will be published in the spring of 2026. She is currently working on a horror novel, tentatively called *Ghost Walk.* Diana is the mother of three and grandmother of four. Since her retirement, she spends her weekdays active in the morning with Silver Sneakers and sedentary in the afternoon while writing and recovering from Silver Sneakers. Life is good.

Author, activist, and agent of travel, **Cullen Cole** doesn't sit still for long. When she does, it's on the back porch with her partner sipping fair trade coffee and enjoying the wildlife inhabiting their organic garden. She is a member of International Thriller Writers, Sisters in Crime, and the Indiana Writers Center.

S. Ashley Couts is a Greenwood native and an award-winning writer and exhibiting artist. She was a three-year teaching fellow for the Indiana Writing Project at Ball State University in Muncie, and has 20 years of experience in teaching and creating educational writing programs in public and private schools. She has short fiction in anthologies by Blue River Press, Rain Drop Press, and Speed City Press. Ashley is currently working on a collection of her short stories.

MB Dabney is a retired award-winning journalist whose writing has appeared in numerous local and national publications, including Indianapolis Monthly, the Indianapolis Business Journal, Ebony magazine, and Black Enterprise.com. He has co-edited two previous anthologies for the Speed City chapter of Sisters in Crime—*Decades of Dirt: Murder, Mystery and Mayhem from the Crossroads of Crime*; and *MURDER 20/20*—and has published numerous short mystery stories. He was a co-writer and co-producer of *Deadbeat*, a one-act play produced by the chapter that debuted at the Indianapolis Fringe Festival in 2018.

Michael has two novels to his name. *A Deadly Game, A David Blaise Mystery* (2023), and its 2021 prequel, *An Untidy Affair.* His third novel in the David Blaise series, *Pursuit of the Jade Empress*, is scheduled for publication in 2026.

The father of two adult daughters, Michael lives in Indianapolis with his wife, Angela.

Lillie Evans is a versatile storyteller, playwright, author, and film producer who writes under the pen name L. Barnett Evans. She's the co-author of four engaging cozy mysteries: *Grandmothers Incorporated, Saving Sin City, There's Something Wrong with Miss Zelda,* and *Whose Knife Is It Anyway?*

Evans and her co-writer, Crystal Rhodes, have written and produced three plays based on the characters in their cozy book series, including the latest play, *The Funeral.* This play has garnered several national and international awards. In 2025, Evans and Rhodes produced a short film of the same name.

Evans published a thriller, *Retribution,* the first book in a new series written by Evans and her writing partner. The dynamic team writes the Retribution series under the pen name Evan Rhodes.

Evans is a member of the Speed City Indiana chapter of Sisters in Crime, and is a co-editor of *Murder 2020,* and *Amber Waves of Graves,* two of the chapter's short story anthologies. In addition, Evans has appeared as a commentator on TV One's "For My Man" crime series.

Evans is an Indiana native and holds a Bachelor of Science degree from the Indiana Institute of Technology. Visit her at www.lilliebarnettevans.com or www.grandmothersincorporated.com. Her email address is: Lbarnettevans@gmail.com

Carol Hall, a retired teacher and probation officer, writes a column, *Candor From Carol,* for the Communique, a newsletter for the Central Indiana Writers' Association. She is also a member of Speed City Sisters in Crime, Southwest Writers, Fortnightly Literary Club, and multiple book groups. One of these book groups focuses on reading mysteries. She has a master's degree in criminology from Indiana State University. Carol and her husband, Charlie, have three children and seven grandchildren.

B.K. Hart is a writer of mystery, humor and horror, with several stories published in anthologies by Speed City Sisters In Crime. She has also been self-published as Brigitte Kephart and has been included in several horror anthologies with James Ward Kirk Publishing. She currently resides in Indiana.

Shari Held is an award-winning fiction author and journalist who spins tales of mystery/crime, humor, romance, and fantasy. More than 50 of her short stories have been published in magazines and anthologies, including *Hoosier Noir, White Cat Publications, Tough, Yellow Mama, Asinine Assassins,* and *Murder 20/20,* for which she served as co-editor. She is a member of Speed City Sisters in Crime and the Short Mystery Fiction Society. When not writing, she cares for feral cats and other wildlife, attends movies, reads avidly, and enjoys watching tennis. Visit her website, www.shariheld.com, for more information about her and her stories.

Ramona G. Henderson is a former assistant professor of nursing who has always had a passion for writing. Her stories are fiction and historical fiction that are mostly mysteries. She is also a playwright, and her comedy, *Operation Farley*, was performed at the 2018 Divafest. Her dark comedy, *The Malicious Birdfeeder,* was performed at the Indiana Ten Minute Play Festival in 2022. Her mystery stories were published in three previous Speed City Sisters in Crime anthologies. She gets inspiration for her stories from her native southwestern Indiana and places where she has traveled. She is a member of the Indiana Writers Center, the Indiana Playwrights Circle, and Sisters in Crime. She is a former board member of Speed City Sisters in Crime.

Elizabeth A. San Miguel is a new, if not young, writer who lives in Indianapolis. She graduated a from Indiana University, Bloomington with degrees in Journalism, History, and Fine Arts and a minor in Art History. She also received a Certificate of Applied Computer Science from Indiana University-Purdue University at Indianapolis. She spends her days coding in the statistical database language SAS and her evenings and weekends amusing herself by thinking up fun ways to kill people, literarily and not literally.

Stephen Terrell is a retired Indianapolis lawyer with a passion for writing. He now lives in Muncie.

Stephen's latest project is a historical true crime book about his great uncle's murder of his son-in-law in 1903 that made headlines across the nation. *The Madness of John Terrell: Revenge and Insanity on Trial in the Heartland* was published by Kent State University Press in 2024.

He has written three novels, including two legal thrillers, *Stars Fall* and *The First Rule*, and *Last Train to Stratton*, which follows an emotionally detached Chicago crime beat reporter who seeks to lose himself in the dullness of small-town America after his life is shattered.

Stephen writes the eclectic column, *On Second Thought*, for the American Bar Association's Experience Magazine. His short stories regularly appear in Speed City Indiana Sisters in Crime anthologies. His story, *"In Deepest Darkness,"* about the aftermath of a school shooting, was one of 10 stories selected to the Honor Roll in Best Mystery Stories of the Year in 2021. Another short story, *"Visiting Hours,"* won the Manny Award for short fiction at the Midwest Writers Workshop.

Stephen was selected to the Indiana State Bar Association's General Practice Hall of Fame and received the Indiana Lawyers' Barrister Award, the first solo practitioner to receive that honor.

Janet E. Williams has been writing her entire life, first as a child making her own books and later as an award-winning journalist for newspapers in Pittsburgh and Indianapolis as well as a nonprofit news site, *Indiana Citizen*. She has always believed that journalism is, at its heart, strong storytelling. Today, she uses her experiences covering courts, crime, and politics to create her fiction. Before retiring in late 2020, Janet worked with Franklin College journalism students at *The StatehouseFile.com*, and now is developing her fiction-writing skills with short stories as she works on her novel. She has had short stories published in Speed City Sisters in Crime anthologies, *Murder 20/20*, *Circle City Crime*, and *Trick or Treats*.

9 781737 525714